gift of
friends

THE KALEIDOSCOPE GIRLS

gift of friends

THE KALEIDOSCOPE GIRLS

BOOK FOUR

Kimberly Diede

ENDLESS RIPPLE PRESS

For my readers

The gift of your time
makes all of this possible

CHAPTER ONE

LYNETTE PAUSED AT THE top of her back stairs, unfazed by the damp grit and pitted concrete below her callused feet. A year ago, she'd have flinched away from the rough surface under the baby-soft skin of her pampered soles. She let the ornate wooden screen door slap shut behind her. If she'd still been in the city, she'd have jumped at that sound—so like the pop of a gun.

She pulled the moist air of a rain-soaked morning deep into her lungs. The crisp scent of pine sparked her taste buds, and she allowed her eyes to drift shut. It was easy to imagine the familiar zing of her favorite gin and tonic against her tongue following a slow, delicious nip. Once upon a time, that trigger would have exploded an uncontrollable longing for an actual cocktail, and then another. More would have followed until the jagged edges of her pain could be obscured beneath a pleasant haze of alcohol.

She opened her eyes on the exhale, grateful that, now, in this place, those cravings were less and less frequent.

After she'd fled New York City amid a worldwide pandemic for the quieter streets of Ruby Shores, the small town of her youth, she could feel her polished layers slowly dissolve. New sides of her personality, which she was finally allowing herself to explore, were slowly revealing themselves. This metamorphosis was one of the catalysts behind her early morning jaunt into a far corner of her backyard.

Normally, she would still be snuggled under the age-worn quilt that covered her bed upstairs. The quilt had replaced a black silk duvet she'd left behind in the city. The silk would have been out of place here—garish, even.

During those first few months after relocating, Lynette had felt like *she* didn't belong here either. Sometimes she still felt like an outsider.

She skipped down the worn surface of the stairs, one hand resting on the front pocket of her overalls so the heavy ring of house keys wouldn't bounce against her ample chest. She didn't need a wayward skeleton key to accidentally damage the implants she was finally coming to appreciate.

The end result of work performed by the world-renowned plastic surgeon who'd taken her from a B cup to a DD cup had always felt oddly foreign to her. She'd resented the change to her natural shape the minute the bandages came off. But gravity wasn't causing as much droop to her "girls" as her like-aged friends complained about experiencing. Maybe her enhanced breasts weren't so bad after all. If she still lived in the Big Apple, she likely would have gotten a few nips and tucks, too. But she lived in Ruby Shores now and never planned to move back to the city, so she would simply take care of what she had naturally.

Even before coming here, things like mani-pedis and appointments with her stylist had become impossible thanks to the city's lockdown. After wasting too many hours breathing in the toxic fumes of hair dyes and polish removers, she'd finally learned to accept her bare nails and untamed locks.

And then the virus got her. Her COVID experience made her grateful for the simple act of drawing deep breaths, but falling ill to the virus had done more than that. It was the conduit that finally galvanized her into action.

Selling her company and the apartment to move back to Ruby Shores had felt like the right move at the perfect time. Even her mother, Donna, who had been reluctant to leave her beloved city life, recently admitted that this was starting to feel like home for her again, too.

But Donna didn't understand Lynette's obsession with carving out a tiny place of her own in their backyard. The roomy, century-old home they'd moved into already had more bedrooms and living space than the two city-dwellers knew what to do with.

For Lynette, all that space felt overwhelming.

When Lynette was young, Donna had worked hard to provide for them, but there were months when she'd barely scraped enough money together to keep a roof over their heads and food on the table. Later, their neighboring New York apartment units had been considered spacious for city living. But those high-rise apartments had been compact compared to their current home.

It wasn't until Lynette realized she was spending entirely too much time in her walk-in closet, supposedly organizing a wardrobe that she'd drastically pared down with their move, that she finally realized why she was feeling so unmoored. She needed somewhere small and cozy to enjoy a cup of tea. Maybe get lost in the pages of one of the dusty old books the prior owners had left behind on the many shelves in their fully stocked library. Too much space, after a lifetime of smaller living quarters, made her jittery.

And she was pretty sure she'd figured out the perfect spot to rectify the situation—the old potting shed in a back corner of her property.

She'd only entered the shed one time, back during her first week as this majestic home's new owner. She'd shivered in disgust over the cluttered, shadowed interior and closed it back up again almost immediately. The jiggly old lock's effectiveness was questionable, so she'd added a padlock, then promptly forgot about the rundown little building.

But now, a year later, a new purpose for the old shed had potentially revealed itself. Today was the day she'd earmarked to revisit the small building, and she hoped to finally clear away the clutter and debris. Then she'd be able to decide if it was feasible to transform the space into the decadent, private oasis she envisioned.

Yesterday she'd trimmed away the lowest branches of the massive pine tree that towered over the shed, dwarfing it. The limbs had blocked the moss-covered brick pathway that meandered from the house and around a small rose garden before leading back to the shed.

The mound of cut branches had grown waist-high by the time she'd called it a day. Pine-scented cuttings perfumed the air nicely, but she worried that they would dry out quickly and become a fire hazard.

Last night, after twenty minutes of attempting and failing to scrub the tree sap from her hands, she'd called her friend Annie and asked to speak to her son, Relic. The young man agreed to swing by today with his pickup truck to haul away the cuttings. He'd sounded happy to earn a little money. Lynette knew many places around town were still struggling after long closures, and Relic had admitted to not having a summer job.

Pine needles poked at her bare feet as she approached the shed's locked door. "I probably should have worn shoes today," she said, stopping to pull a sharp barb out of the toughened skin on the ball of her left foot. She'd run back to the house for her tennis shoes if the shed floor turned out to be treacherous for bare feet. Ever since leaving the city, she'd sworn off high heels and, at least in the non-winter months, rarely wore shoes of any kind while at home.

She pulled the heavy ring from her front pocket and eyed its extensive assortment of keys. It was easy to locate the shiny new padlock key and pop open the extra lock. Corrosion around the original keyhole on the underside of the shed's ornate door handle looked problematic.

Living in an old house had taught her the value of WD-40. She'd even stashed a small can of it in the left side pocket of her overalls as she'd passed through the kitchen that morning. After injecting a quick squirt, hoping to loosen the locking mechanism, she turned her attention back to the ring of keys. She'd found the correct one for the door's original lock once before, so it had to be here.

The incessant squawk of a crow pulled her attention up to the antique weathervane atop the shed. She squinted at her obnoxious morning visitor, perched on the vane's bullet-hole-ridden metal horse. Streaks of rust, like blood, made it all look like a snippet out of a horror movie set.

"Oh, zip it, bird!" she hissed as she shook the heavy ring in the bird's direction. "I'm trying, okay?"

Eventually, she located the slightly twisted iron key and worked it into the keyhole, then held her breath until she was rewarded with a satisfying *click*. Air, heavy with the unmistakable scent of old oil and mothballs, wafted out at her.

The possibility of encountering any crawling, slithering, or flying creatures had terrified her when she first poked into the shadowed corners of this home—new to her but older than most—but her aversion had faded with time. Spiders barely made her pulse jump these days. The infrequent capture of a wayward mouse in a trap under the kitchen sink or in the musty basement didn't faze her much anymore, either.

Despite rusty hinges, the door wouldn't stay open of its own accord, so she shoved a cantaloupe-sized rock in place to keep it from swinging shut on her. Donna wouldn't be back until early evening, and if she foolishly got herself locked inside this old shed, she'd be stuck there until Relic showed up to haul away her clippings or she could call someone for help. A dead mouse no longer bothered her, but that didn't mean she wanted to be trapped inside with a live one.

She entered the shed and promptly stepped on the threaded shank of a long screw. Her breath escaped her in a hiss. Bare feet weren't going to cut it. She almost turned to go collect her tennis shoes when she spotted a pair of green rubber gardening clogs next to the door.

"Perfect!"

She gave each clog a quick shake to dislodge anything unsavory that might have taken up residence there before shoving her bare feet inside, then straightened and gazed around the interior.

What a mess.

Dust tickled her nose. Her eyes watered, and the long shadows made it difficult to see, but her vision quickly adjusted to the gloom.

With hands on hips, she studied an indistinguishable, sheet-covered lump that was as tall as she was. Floor-to-ceiling metal shelving units sporting equal parts rust and spider webs flanked the shrouded item. Individual shelves bowed under the weight of an assortment of old junk.

"Not exactly the welcoming, serene space I'm imagining. *Yet.*"

To help with her perusal, she pulled her phone out of yet another pocket—thanks to the practicality of her denim jumper. Using the flashlight, Lynette could better make out more hulking shapes that stood next to and behind the utilitarian shelving units. She remembered how Sybil, the grandmother of the woman she'd bought this house from, had fondly referred to this as the "potting shed." But to Lynette's untrained eye, it didn't look like there was even one spare inch of room in here to perform any actual work with plants.

More dust erupted when she pulled a sheet down, revealing a curious-looking metal statue of a girl standing in a narrow bowl and wearing a crown of flowers atop her wavy hair. Its greenish-blue hue was probably a warm copper before oxidation took hold. The statue was lovely, even with the patina.

A water fountain, perhaps? Regardless, it belonged outside and would look nice in the middle of the rose bushes her mother had tamed into some semblance of order. But she'd need help to get it out of the shed.

She groaned, realizing one allotted day to clear out the junk wasn't going to be enough. She'd have to go through the items on each shelf, open every cardboard box, and decide what to toss, donate, or keep.

The shelving units blocking the building's two windows would be the logical place to start. Once those were empty and the windows washed, the light should stream in, making this gritty task easier.

That decided, she retreated from the shed and retrieved three metal garbage cans from the side of the garage, knowing she'd likely need more.

Her stomach rumbled, and she patted the multiple pockets in her overalls, searching for the granola bar she'd stashed in one of them. She hadn't taken the time to eat breakfast or go on her morning walk, but the special treat should give her enough energy to carry her through to lunch.

Val—the sister of her old friend Renee—made the bars herself, and Lynette always tried to keep a supply on hand. The woman was attempting to get her bars into grocery chains around the state of Minnesota. Lynette suspected that if Val's business acumen was half as good as her baking abilities, she stood a good chance of success.

Maybe she should reach out and offer Renee's sister some help. She'd sold plenty of products in her own business over the years, and now that she didn't have her company anymore, there were days when she missed the work. She was even toying with the idea of testing her skills in the world of consulting.

But not today. Today, she'd get most of the junk cleared out of this shed. Which meant she'd have to do her best to keep distractions at bay.

She finished her granola bar and started with the top shelf of the unit that was blocking the morning light from flowing in through the east window. A hard tug on the handle of a white leather bag brought a heavy bowling ball crashing to the littered wood of the shed floor. Two inches to the left and she could have lost a few toes, despite the rubber garden clogs.

Taking it slower to avoid injury, she established a variety of piles in the circle of gravel outside the shed door. She struggled to decipher which items warranted donation versus what was just old junk to be tossed.

She'd never been much of a saver, herself.

Growing up, she and her mother kept their belongings to a minimum. This was partially to make their frequent moves easier, but also because there was seldom any money left over each month after rent, gas, and food to buy much else. There wasn't always enough for food.

Later, when she and Donna found success in New York, they surrounded themselves with shiny new objects—things they could never afford before. They'd left much of those items behind when they moved back to Ruby Shores to start this new life.

"Just do your best," she muttered, half expecting the crow from earlier to mock her, but there was no answering squawk this time. "No one has touched this junk in years. I just need to get through it all."

Lynette talked to herself often these days. Following months of isolation, and none of the work-related meetings that used to eat up a significant portion of her time, she needed to keep using her voice. Otherwise, it might get as rusty and ineffective as the hinges on the shed door. It didn't matter if she was the only one there to listen.

She worked her way down the shelves. Filtered sunlight streamed in through the cleared area in front of the window. The sunbeams highlighted floating dust motes in the air.

"Almost done with this section." She knelt down and rubbed her hands on her denim-clad thighs, surveying the assortment on the bottom two shelves. Dark patches of grime clung to her fingers where the stubborn pine sap from yesterday remained. Once she got these cleared off, she'd take a well-deserved coffee break before moving on to another shelving unit.

A battered, rectangular wooden box, coated with a thick layer of dust, filled most of the bottom shelf. Curious, Lynette reached for it, wondering what the long-forgotten vessel might contain.

"A stash of gold coins would be nice. Maybe some pirate's booty!" she joked, grunting when the top of the box caught on the shelf above it. It took some jiggling, but she pulled it clear.

Her knees protested as she struggled to her feet, holding the box against her hip. She took it outside, where she shook out her cramped legs and coughed yet again over the dusty conditions.

Bright sunlight revealed heavy carvings on the top and sides of the box. The lid stuck, but something tumbled around inside when she shook it, though there wasn't much weight to it.

"So much for finding gold."

Still, she had to know.

The rest of the junk on the bottom shelves could wait. She'd grab a rag—along with that cup of coffee—and wipe away some of the dust so she could better examine her discovery.

At the back steps, she set the box down, not wanting to drag the dust into the house. Her curiosity was growing by the minute over what might be inside.

She returned with a dampened rag and fresh coffee. She'd also grabbed a face mask from her purse, hoping it would help her inhale less of the irritating dust.

It didn't take long to accept that it would take more than an old rag to dislodge the dirt and dust wedged deep into the decorative carvings. But all she cared about at the moment was getting the box open. It turned out to be in better shape than she'd initially thought, once she'd removed the first coating of dust. Aside from one heavy scratch across the top right corner of the lid, there was no other apparent damage.

Still, the lid wouldn't budge. It was locked.

Remembering the reading glasses perched atop her head, she settled them on her nose to inspect the box. Finally, she spied what looked like two small keyholes nestled in the heavy carving on top. They were equidistant from the sides of the box, in its exact center.

Now what?

There was an old letter opener inside a rolltop desk in the house's library. That might work to pry the locks open, but she'd hate to damage the box.

Then she thought of the ring of keys she'd left in the shed. Could she be that lucky to find a key to the box amongst the assortment?

She set the box to the side, swigged more coffee, and hurried back toward the shed, noting the increasing heat of the morning sun on her neck and shoulders. It might get too hot to work out here all day. It would take her a week to clean out her future she-shed at this rate, but something told her the effort would be worth it. Starting with the box.

She'd always loved a good mystery.

Chapter Two

As she walked back to the shed to retrieve the keyring, the slam of a vehicle door caught Lynette's attention. Someone was in her driveway. She hoped it was Relic, arriving early to beat the heat. The keys and locked box would have to wait. She veered to the left and had nearly reached the back of their four-stall garage when she recognized voices. Relic had come early, and he wasn't alone.

"Annie!" Lynette hollered.

She broke into a jog, arms extended, as she rushed to the driveway and her friend. But fifteen months of social distancing had changed things, and she skidded to a halt near the front of a beat-up old pickup.

Annie was struggling to pull her arms free of a gray sweatshirt. A wide grin replaced her frown when she spied Lynette at the edge of the driveway, frozen in her awkward position. "You look like you could use a hug, but you also might still be battling a little pandemic-inspired social anxiety, my friend," Annie said, laughing. "I'm sorry, but it isn't a good look on you. Why are you wearing a mask outside?"

Lynette had forgotten about the mask. She yanked it off and shoved it into a pocket. Wearing one didn't feel as strange as it had at first, earlier in the pandemic. She let her arms fall to her sides. "I'm cleaning out a filthy old shed, and the dust was hurting my lungs," she explained. "It's so good to see you! Hey, Relic. Thanks for coming over to give me a hand, and thanks for bringing my amazing friend along for the ride."

"She insisted," the young man said with a little smirk.

Annie tossed the sweatshirt through the open passenger window. "Maybe you don't need a hug, but I sure do. It feels like a lifetime since I last saw you in person. Do you mind?"

It was all the encouragement Lynette needed. Her arms shot back up and she met Annie halfway, catching the shorter woman in a bear hug. In her younger years, she'd have scooped Annie up and spun her in circles, but she settled for a tight squeeze and a moment of rocking to and fro.

Aside from the occasional hug from her mother, Lynette struggled to remember the last time she'd touched another person. Had it been when she'd said her goodbyes to Annie and her other three besties in the Phoenix airport? Their last girls' trip was nearly eighteen months ago, just before the world tilted and sent them all scuttling behind closed doors.

"I've missed you," Annie was saying, her face hidden within Lynette's overabundance of tight silver curls. "Zoom calls can't replace face to face. When Relic told me he was heading over here to give you a hand, he couldn't keep me out of his passenger seat."

The two women separated, though Annie kept one hand on Lynette's shoulder, as if reluctant to end the contact. Relic looked between the two of them, rolling his eyes over their exuberance at seeing each other again.

"Mom, remember, we have to make this quick," he said, a small smile tugging at his mouth. "You aren't the only one excited for a little time with friends. I'm meeting up with the guys out at the lake in a while."

Annie checked her watch. "Oh, right. And I promised Ava I'd watch Nora so she could go on a run before it gets too hot outside."

"Do you still have a full house?" Lynette asked, remembering that all three of her friend's kids, plus a son-in-law and a newborn, had lived with Annie and her husband throughout much of the pandemic. It must have been crowded. Annie's arrangement was in stark contrast to that of her and Donna, ambling around inside their big old house for months on end.

"Our nest isn't empty yet, but my babies are spreading their wings again."

This time Relic didn't bother to suppress a groan. "We're hardly babies, Mom. Other than Nora, that is."

"Sorry, Relic, but Donna still calls *me* her baby, so be prepared to hear that term from your mother for the rest of your life."

Relic shrugged, then gazed around the yard. "Where is Donna? I want to remind her she promised me a batch of her famous chocolate chip cookies when I go back to college this fall."

Another pickup truck, a much newer and fancier one that she didn't recognize, drove leisurely by, catching Lynette's eye. She couldn't make out the driver's face through shadowed glass, but she gave a neighborly wave before turning her attention back to Annie's son.

"Don't worry, Relic. If there's one thing Donna never forgets, it's a promise to a cute young man. You'll get your cookies. Now, I know you said you're in a hurry, so let me show you where I stacked those pine branches."

In what seemed like no time at all, Lynette and Annie once again stood in the driveway while Relic secured a strap over the mound of cuttings in his truck bed.

"Many hands make light work," Lynette said, pulling off her gardening gloves. "Thanks again, you two. Hey, Annie, are you getting excited yet?"

"For our trip to Whispering Pines next week? *So* excited! I love my family dearly, but I think we'd all agree that we've had more than enough months of togetherness. I'm ready for some girl time. How about you?"

Lynette started to shove her gloves into a pocket, but thought better of it given the amount of sticky tree sap on them. She tossed them onto the grass along the drive. "More than ready. We're lucky Renee already had us on her books for the first two weeks in August. When I checked in with her last week, she barely had time to talk. Her repeat customers are returning to Whispering Pines in droves, now that many are more comfortable with getting out in the world again."

Annie handed Lynette the spare set of gloves she'd borrowed and wiped a sweaty strand of hair from her forehead. "It isn't luck. You kept the faith that the Kaleidoscope Girls could stay on track to never miss an annual girls' trip. You asked Renee to make those reservations. But I know lots has changed since you asked her to do that last summer. You've sold your company, bought and renovated this place, and you haven't worked over the past year. Are you still sure you want to have Renee hold the whole place for us? That'll be expensive, regardless of how good of a deal she offered. She still has bills to pay."

Lynette shook her head. Annie was right that she'd experienced plenty of change over the last year, including a surprise hit to her financial situation. She hoped that would turn around. No one needed to know that the chance she'd taken regarding the sale of the company wasn't panning out exactly how she'd planned. She still had money in the bank, but was no longer convinced she could survive the financial demands of her next forty years without working. Besides, fifty was too young for her to retire completely. The year-long break had been nice in many ways, but she missed the stimulation she used to get out of working.

"I was worried that the only way Renee could relax during our visit was if she didn't have other guests to attend to while we were there. She knows *us* well enough now that I don't think she'll feel like she has to play host the whole time. I wanted her to feel like she's getting a bit of a vacation, too. But she actually asked me if I'd mind if she rented out the cabins we won't need. I think she needs the money. She'll have her daughter Julie take care of running the resort while we're there."

"That's good news."

"I think so, too. I do have one request, though," Lynette said. "Any chance I could catch a ride with you out to the resort? I didn't drive during my years in New York, and while I'm comfortable cruising around Ruby Shores, highway driving isn't my favorite thing."

Annie laughed. "Even as a kid, driving wasn't one of your top skills. Wasn't the truck you wrecked during our last month of high school similar to Relic's?"

"Don't remind me," Lynette groaned. "Yes, it was something like this one. I wonder if Storm was ever able to fix it."

"Doubtful," Annie said. "I still get chills when I close my eyes and see that crushed pickup cab from that night. You're lucky you survived."

"I'm lucky I survived both the crash *and* the scene I heard Storm's mother threw afterward," Lynette said.

Despite the day's rising temperature, she couldn't suppress a shiver. Donna had interceded on her daughter's behalf with Storm's mother. Lynette never asked her mother what they'd discussed, but before the cut on Lynette's face had even healed, the mother-daughter duo had packed up and left town. She'd always suspected Donna was running from something again, but her own guilt over wrecking Storm's truck prevented her from asking too many questions.

Relic jumped down from the box of his truck, pulling Lynette's attention back to her driveway. "So, you're the one I have to thank for my overprotective mother, huh? I can't leave the house without her hollering at me to be careful. You really rolled a pickup like mine?"

"I really did," Lynette said. Her hand automatically came up to touch the faint scar on her cheek that would always remind her of that awful night so long ago and the bleak days that followed. Her girlfriends only knew half of what had unfolded back then, and that was how she planned to keep it. "But I suspect your mom would say that anyhow. That's what mothers do."

He grinned. "You're probably right. Now, I hate to rush you two through your trip down memory lane, but I gotta bounce. Ready, Mom?"

"Wait!" Lynette unbuttoned the one pocket she hadn't been pulling things out of throughout her morning. She fished out the cash she'd taken from her purse earlier and thrust the bills into Relic's hand. "I hope that's sufficient."

He gave the money a quick glance, his eyes rounding with surprise. "I can't take this much. It took, like, fifteen minutes, and you two helped."

Lynette shook her head. "That may be true, but you'll still need to take all this to the branch disposal area across town." Then she remembered the heavy statue she'd discovered in the shed earlier. She'd forgotten to ask Relic to help her move it, but it really would be in her way.

"What?" Annie said, eyes narrowing. "I can see there's something on your mind."

Lynette shrugged. "There was just another quick thing I was going to ask Relic to help me with, but I forgot, and now you're both in a hurry, so forget it."

Relic looked at the money once more, shoved it into his pocket, then settled his hands on his hips. "It isn't going to kill Ava to wait a few more minutes for her free babysitter. And my friends won't miss me for a while, I'm sure. What do you need done?"

"But you had plans," Lynette countered, though she was impressed that the twenty-year-old saw the value in an even exchange.

"Work comes first."

Knowing they were wasting time, Lynette bowed her head and motioned toward her garden shed. "Follow me."

Several minutes and plenty of grunts later, the statue stood squarely in the center of Donna's rose bushes. Hot sunshine once again beat down on the girl's copper wreath, now burnished with that blue-green patina. She looked like she belonged there, and once Lynette got the garden shed cleaned out, she vowed to get the water flowing in the pool at the statue's feet.

Relic started his truck and Lynette slammed Annie's passenger-side door before tapping on the roof with her right hand. She might have burned her fingers on the hot metal if not for the gloves she'd pulled back on. "I couldn't have done that without you," she said. Maybe she should give Relic more than the initial fifty. That statue had turned out to be ridiculously heavy.

Annie, ever perceptive, gave her a curt shake of her head. "You gave him plenty. What is it you're always telling us?"

Lynette snorted. This is what she'd missed the most. Time with someone who knew her well and could accurately guess her thoughts. *Just say 'thank you.'*"

"Exactly," Annie said, glancing between Relic and Lynette. "You wouldn't have had to pay him a dime. Ruby Shores is a place where neighbors help neighbors. We don't have much over New York City, but we have that."

Lynette stepped back from the truck so they could leave. She'd held them up long enough. "Annie, you live ten minutes from here. I wouldn't exactly consider us *neighbors*."

"You know what I mean."

She did, and it was one of the many things that had drawn her and her mother back to this small town.

She noticed Relic struggling to see behind him as he backed out of her driveway. His truck wouldn't have backup cameras, being an older model, and her pile of trimmings likely blocked any line of vision out of his rearview mirror.

"Hold up," she warned.

As she walked to the end of her driveway, the same pickup she'd noticed earlier passed her place again. It was heading in the opposite direction and still moving at a slow pace. Once the truck had passed, Lynette gave Relic the all-clear, and she was soon alone again.

If this were New York City, her gut might have warned her it was strange for the same truck to drive slowly past her place twice in such a brief window of time. But this was Ruby Shores. It was probably someone who lived down the street. She hadn't met many of her actual neighbors yet, despite being here for almost a year. But old habits die hard, and maybe that was why she still felt a brief twinge of apprehension.

"You're being ridiculous," she whispered, wishing she could take the big city out of the small-town girl. A trickle of sweat rolled down her back.

She retrieved the keys from the shed and headed back to the box she'd regretfully set aside earlier. After ten minutes with the large ring of keys, she had to concede that none of them would unlock the dusty container. These keys were all too big.

It was probably time to change into something cooler and get back to her main project of cleaning out the shed.

Annie's reminder that their upcoming stay at the Whispering Pines resort was only a week away gave her a new goal. She'd not only empty the shed before their annual girls' trip, she'd get it fixed up, too. That way she could show the other Kaleidoscope Girls real pictures of her miniscule sanctuary that currently only existed in her mind.

If she could build, then sell, a multi-million-dollar company, she could handle renovating her little she-shed.

That meant the mystery box would have to wait until tonight. She was excited to find out what was inside. Whatever it was, someone had deemed it important enough to lock up, and maybe even hide inside a seldom used garden shed.

Chapter Three

Donna downshifted with care as she eased her car up and over the dip at the foot of their driveway. The convertible's top was down and it was starting to sprinkle, but she had to be careful. The small trench between the drive and the road allowed for excess water to run off in the spring and summer months, but it also raised havoc with the undercarriage of her 2016 Mini Cooper.

She pressed the button on her garage door remote. Nothing. The door to the last stall on the right didn't budge. A slap against the yellowed plastic box of the remote did the trick, and she waited while the old door rattled open. A crack of thunder split the air above, startling her. She shoved at the gearshift and punched the gas hard. Her tires squealed as she shot under the door and into the stall.

Another bolt of lightning ushered forth a sheet of rain, and Donna dropped her forehead to the steering wheel in relief. If she'd have carelessly hit Lynette's bicycle in her haste—again—the younger woman would surely threaten to take her keys away.

Unlike Lynette, Donna loved to drive. She'd missed the freedom of being behind the wheel during their years in New York City. She knew her daughter considered her purchase impractical when she bought the bright aqua convertible with her sliver of proceeds from the sale of their company. But a lifetime of practicality had left Donna craving a little excitement.

The color of her Mini Cooper reminded her of warm ocean waters. Her dream of tropical living might be out of reach, but the sight of her car could trick her mind into thinking she was at the ocean instead of driving the quiet streets of Ruby Shores.

Her ears picked up on the increasing noise of the storm beyond the open garage door, and she straightened in her seat. She hoisted and wiggled herself out from behind the wheel, thankful no one was there to witness the struggle.

Despite her car's inconveniently small size—not to mention its inability to adequately traverse the roads during their first Minnesota winter—she refused to follow Lynette's advice and sell it. Lynette seldom drove her Audi. Donna could have asked to use her car in the winter, but she already felt too dependent on her daughter. Maybe one day she could buy a second, more practical car for those days when the Cooper wasn't up to the task.

She slammed her driver-side door. She'd wait till tomorrow to wrestle with the car's finicky top. A quick glance around the stall reassured her that she hadn't clipped anything this time when she'd shot into the garage.

After retrieving her purse from the backseat, she wandered over to the open garage door to look out. Tiny pebbles of hail bounced off the driveway as the heavy downpour continued. This kind of weather made her wish their garage was attached to the house, but that wasn't the way they built homes back then.

She could either rush to the house and risk getting wet, or even hurt, or stay where she was and wait for the storm to subside.

It wasn't really a decision. She wouldn't melt, but she couldn't afford to break a hip if she slipped on wet pavement.

She set her purse on the hood of her convertible, smiling at the contrast between the automobile's white leather interior and its deep aqua body, bringing to mind frothy ocean waves lapping against a white beach. Two of the women at her bridge table had recently discussed an upcoming trip to Bermuda, and Donna listened with a mixture of envy and apprehension. Her nightly dreams often whisked her away to sandy beaches kissed by sparkling waves. But she knew she wasn't ready to board an airplane yet, since the pandemic, and flying was the only practical way for her to travel from the landlocked Midwest to an oceanside beach.

With a sigh, she realized her biggest fear was coming true. She'd waited too long, setting her dreams aside in order to handle the more immediate demands of life.

She should have listened to Sybil.

Years ago, in this very town, she'd come to know and care deeply for Sybil Wall, an elderly woman on her assigned wing at the nursing home where she'd worked. Though Sybil had died in 1994, she was the reason Donna now stood in this dark, musty garage, protected from the storm. This had once been Sybil's home, before it passed to her granddaughter, Raven Black.

The wind shifted direction, pushing rain into the garage and again threatening the pearl-colored leather interior of her Cooper. She hurried to the wall-mounted button to close the garage door, hoping the hail's size and velocity wouldn't increase. It could potentially wipe out the back garden, where she'd spent an inordinate amount of time this summer bringing the roses back to life. The colorful bushes had once been Sybil's pride and joy.

The rain and wind weren't letting up, so Donna flipped on a light inside the garage. Did Lynette even know she was home? She had no doubt her daughter was inside. She seldom left the house these days, except to go for walks.

This weather was not conducive to a stroll.

With the shadows banished from the garage, she picked her way around an old lawn mower and an even older wooden bench that didn't even appear salvageable. They should have thought to drag it out to the curb during the spring cleanup week. Now they'd have to wait another year.

Would she still be here next year?

Donna did her best to banish the unwelcome thought from her mind. She should check on the backyard, but a rough wooden ladder blocked the window. When she moved it out of the way, a sliver stabbed into her left thumb. She ignored it as she squinted through the rivulets of water streaming down the outside of the old windowpane.

A cold droplet of water smacked her forehead. She swiped it away. They really needed to consider replacing the garage roof at some point. There was a reason people referred to these one-hundred-year-old homes as "money pits."

She rubbed at the fog her breathing caused on the glass. With a start, she spied someone standing in the middle of her rose bushes.

"Who in heaven's name is out there in this weather," she whispered.

Lynette had better sense than to stand outside in the pouring rain. The water streaming down the window slowed, and she realized that it wasn't a person at all. It was that statue.

The statue she'd thought still existed only in her nightmares.

"Why is that cursed statue standing in the middle of my rose bushes? I thought that thing was long gone," Donna said through chattering teeth as she dropped her purse in the middle of the kitchen table.

Lynette didn't look up. Donna wasn't even sure her daughter had heard her.

"Where did that come from?" she asked, temporarily forgetting about the disturbing sight amongst the roses as she watched Lynette try to pry the lid off some kind of old wooden box.

When she still got no response, she rapped her knuckles against the tabletop.

Lynette jumped. "Hey! Donna, don't sneak up on me like that. You scared me!"

Donna pulled a chair away from the table and sat, ignoring the outburst. She took a closer look at the box and realized it looked vaguely familiar. She shivered as cold water meandered down her neck. The rain had stopped, but water still dripped from the trees. The large pine that Lynette had trimmed up the day before had splattered her with droplets when she'd passed under it on her way into the house.

"Where did that come from?" she repeated, staring at the box.

"I found it in the potting shed when I started cleaning it out today," Lynette said. "Why would someone keep a locked box out there? I can tell it isn't empty. I've been curious about it all day, but didn't want to quit working out there until the rain chased me inside. Say, I heard you screech the tires again. Good thing I had the sense to move my bike. You didn't run into anything this time, did you?"

Donna sighed. The fact their mother and daughter roles seemed to be reversing was tiring. Lynette scolded her much too often lately. She started to remind her daughter to watch her tongue but bit her own instead. Always the peacekeeper. She didn't want to fight.

"Can I see that?" she said, laying her hand on the lid of the box.

Lynette pushed back with a sigh. "Be my guest. Maybe you can figure out how to open it."

"This looks kind of familiar," Donna admitted, pulling the box closer.

"Really?" Lynette stood and took an empty glass to the sink, filling it with water. "It's pretty old. Do you think it might have belonged to Sybil?"

Donna considered the question. Lynette had spent a little time in this house as a teenager, back when Donna used to help Raven with her grandmother. They'd bring Sybil home from the nursing home so the woman could enjoy a home-cooked meal or read in her small library off the sitting room.

It was unusual, even back then, for an aide to leave the property with one of the patients, but Sybil wasn't your typical resident. One wing of the nursing home bore Sybil's last name, thanks to the sizable donation she'd made to the facility when she retired. She'd come into the money years earlier, when she'd been widowed at thirty-one.

Once a college professor of archeology and ancient religions, Sybil remained a formidable woman until her death, despite the childhood polio that had eventually weakened her legs until she'd become wheel-chair-bound in her eighties.

Donna remembered when Lynette used to say that if she ever had a daughter of her own, she'd name her Sybil. Both of them had enjoyed the old woman immensely.

She shrugged. "If it did belong to Sybil, there's no telling what's inside."

"I was hoping for pirate gold when I first found it, but it isn't heavy enough to be filled with booty," Lynette joked.

Donna didn't find the comment amusing. It wasn't the first time her daughter had hinted about wishing she could find money stashed away in this old place.

When Lynette was working hard on the sale of the business, she had to choose between two very different buyers. Donna had warned her to be extra thoughtful. The decision had ultimately fallen to the younger woman as the majority partner. Lynette picked the underdog, which hadn't surprised Donna.

But it had worried her.

After more than a year, Lynette refused to discuss the tenuous situation anymore, but Donna suspected the required payments were either late or short. She'd noticed her daughter no longer spent money as lavishly as she had when they'd first moved back to Ruby Shores and started renovations on this house.

"Any ideas about how to open it?" Lynette asked, taking her seat again. "I tried everything on that big ring that holds all the other house keys, but none of them worked. Those look like keyholes, though, don't you think?"

Donna agreed, and an idea popped into her head. She stood. "They do. Let me run up to my room. Remember the old jewelry box we found in the library closet? The one engraved with Sybil's initials? I thought it was empty at first, but there was a set of tiny keys in one drawer. I always wondered what they might open. Maybe they'll fit your mystery box. Besides, the back of my shirt got wet when I ran in from the garage. I need to change into dry clothes."

Once upstairs, Donna changed quickly, then rummaged through the many narrow drawers in the vintage jewelry box. Most now contained a jumble of Donna's silver rings, bangles, and pendants she'd collected over the years. One of her duties while helping to run the online business had been to search out talented artisans. Even when they'd failed to establish an official partnership, Donna often purchased unique signature pieces for her own collection.

The set of small keys was in the bottom drawer. She took them back down to Lynette. As she stepped into the kitchen, a flood of old memories poured in, much like the earlier deluge that had held her captive in the garage.

The overhead fluorescent lighting flickered and Sybil's bony fingers twitched against the armrests of her wheelchair. Donna held her breath. A power outage would mean trouble for the residents on oxygen. Her shift was almost over, but they would ask her to stay if this storm wreaked havoc and emergency procedures had to be initiated. She groaned when she remembered she'd left her driver-side window open.

Sweat dampened Donna's neck. Despite intermittent rain showers throughout the afternoon, the oppressive heat continued. Their tiny house would feel like an oven tonight if this weather pattern didn't break.

At least Lynette was away at a fast-pitch softball tournament with her friend Jackie and the girl's family. They were playing in the fifteen-year-old division, and while Donna hated to miss it, no one had been willing to take her weekend shift. Lynette wouldn't be home until

Monday morning.

"Why isn't Raven here yet? She'd never be afraid to go out in a little storm," Sybil said, her voice warbling as she pointed with a gnarled hand at the ceiling. Sybil's voice was getting weaker, but it didn't sound like the storm outside was abating at all. "I need to be home today. It's important. I must read."

Donna dropped to her knees so she could be eye to eye with her favorite resident. "Raven hasn't called to say she isn't coming, so something is probably holding her up. If you want to read while you wait, I'd be happy to go down to the library here and grab one of your old favorites."

Frustrated, the elderly woman waved away her offer with that same gnarled hand. "I don't want to read some silly paperback I've read a thousand times before," she snipped.

Donna smiled at her spunk. She knew Sybil enjoyed books, but the woman loved her usual routine every Sunday of a noon meal and a few hours spent in her old home with her granddaughter even more. Maybe she had a particular book in mind, back in the cozy library that occupied a front corner of her house's main level.

Finally, with only ten minutes remaining in Donna's shift, Raven hurried down the hall toward them. "I'm so sorry I'm late, Gram! My car battery died and I was home alone. I had to wait until my neighbor got home to give me a jump."

"That husband of yours works too much. Who travels for business on a Sunday?"

Raven met Donna's gaze. "She seems more agitated than usual."

Before Donna could respond, Sybil grabbed hold of her granddaughter's hand. "Don't talk about me like I'm not here. Of course I'm agitated. I had plans for today. You know what today is. Or did you forget?"

Her question surprised Donna. At eighty-six, it wasn't like Sybil ever had much in the way of plans, aside from her regular Sunday excursion. But Raven didn't look surprised. Instead, she looked irritated.

"I most certainly did not forget," she said, frowning down at her grandmother. "You'd never let me forget the anniversary of my parents' drowning."

Sucking in a breath, Donna turned to leave. This was not a discussion she wanted to be a part of. Sybil was usually a delight to spend time with, but today wasn't one of those days.

"Wait, Donna," Raven said, the distress clear in her voice. "I know I'm really late today, and you like to spend Sunday evening with your daughter. But with my husband gone and this terrible weather, there's no way I can get Grandma up the back steps and into the house by myself. I know I'm asking too much, but I could really use a hand. It's important for her to be home today."

Home, Donna thought. Did Raven have any idea how lucky she was to have a home with so much history?

Sybil had told her how her husband had opened the first lumber company in Ruby Shores in the 1920s. He'd built a house for his young bride as a clever way to showcase their high-quality products and his extensive carpentry skills. Before landing in the nursing home at eighty-four, Sybil had lived her whole adult life in that house, and even raised her twin grandson and granddaughter there, after their parents tragically died. Now Raven and her husband called it home.

Donna worked hard, often juggling more than one job, but would she ever be able to give her daughter, Lynette, the kind of home both Sybil and Raven had enjoyed?

Remembering how hot and musty her little rental would be, and that Lynette wouldn't even be home, Donna decided it might be nice to spend time in Raven and Sybil's beautiful old house.

She checked her watch. "My shift is about over."

Raven hoisted the strap of her purse higher on her shoulder. "I could pay you."

Donna shook her head. "I'd never take your money. I just meant that it probably wouldn't be a problem to give you a hand tonight. Lynette is away with friends."

Raven breathed a sigh of relief. "You have no idea how much I'd appreciate that."

Sybil dropped her arthritic hands to the wheels of her chair, pushing off toward her room. "I'll grab my purse. There's still so much to do!"

Donna noticed a commanding quality to Sybil's voice that had been missing a short time ago. She glanced questioningly at Raven, but a shrug was her only response.

Thirty minutes later, Donna held a sweating glass of ice water against her forehead. The years had whittled away at Sybil's body, but it still took both women to transfer her from Raven's car, up the back stairs, and into the kitchen without the wheelchair.

Raven didn't look as winded from the exertion as Donna felt.

Once they'd cleared the table following a meal of roast and potatoes, Raven announced that it was time for Sybil to go back to the nursing home. Sybil's anxiety returned. "I must do a reading," she insisted, her bony, swollen fingers turning white as she gripped the edge of the dining table with both hands. "Bring me my cards."

Donna jumped at the loud *crack* of a cupboard door when Raven slammed it shut in frustration over her grandmother's stubborn declaration.

————— ❈ —————

Lightning flashed and a deep rumble of thunder caused the glass win-dowpanes to vibrate. For a moment, Donna was disoriented. Her rec-ollections of that long-ago day included weather almost identical to today's. Had the storm wrapped back around?

Her eyes skipped from the dusty old box in front of a now adult Lynette to the still-damaged cupboard door that Raven had slammed so long ago. The hairline crack in the wood was barely noticeable, but anytime she opened or closed the door, Donna's fingers often worried over it, much like she was doing now with the irritating sliver in her thumb.

She closed her eyes, remembering again how Sybil had sat up straighter in her chair over her granddaughter's impertinence. She'd cleared her throat and released her grip on the table's edge, demurely folding her hands across her lap. Disapproval had been obvious in her unwavering stare. Donna suspected that must have been the same look Sybil had giv-en her unruly college students, decades earlier, if they'd foolishly refused to do her bidding.

"Get my box, Raven," Sybil had ordered.

It was a side of Sybil that Donna seldom saw. She remembered the palpable shift in the energy in this very kitchen. That Sybil was no longer an old, frail woman, reliant on her grown granddaughter to help her escape back to the life she used to live before age had forced her into a small, soulless room, surrounded by other, equally dependent men and women.

"Yes, Grandma," Raven had replied, like a disobedient child.

Once only Sybil and Donna remained in that long-ago kitchen, the same yet different space where she now sat, the old woman had turned her gaze to Donna. Sybil's eyes had looked different, as if the film of the infirmed had been swept away, allowing the older woman to see straight into Donna's soul.

"I need to read your cards," she'd declared, leaving Donna more confused than ever.

Raven wasn't gone long, and when she'd returned, she'd carried a box very much like the one on the table in front of Lynette. It had to be the same one. She could still see the disapproval in Raven's expression as a satisfied grin stole across her grandmother's features. Raven had been out of sorts over whatever was inside the box Sybil was slowly opening.

"Did you find the keys?" Lynette asked, the words cutting through Donna's memories, pulling her back to the present yet again. "While you were upstairs, I ran down to the basement to make sure that new sump pump they installed two weeks ago was working."

"Is it?" Donna asked, doing her best to reacclimate herself to the partially renovated kitchen of today. Now she, not Sybil, was the old woman in the room.

"What, working? It is. We're lucky the contractor thought to check it when I complained about the mustiness down there."

Donna drained her water glass, then placed the set of tiny keys she'd retrieved from her jewelry box in front of Lynette. "Here. I bet these will work. I'm sure they're the same ones Sybil used."

Lynette picked up the keys, then paused. "Hold on. Did you decide that you *have* seen this box before?"

Nodding, Donna pushed away from the table to put her empty glass in the dishwasher. She still felt a sense of unease whenever she allowed herself to think back to the conversation that followed on that long-ago day. And not only the conversation, but how that stormy evening had ended.

"I remember seeing Sybil with it."

Lynette pulled her reading glasses down from the top of her head and bent over the dusty box with the keys. "So this belonged to Sybil. Do you also remember what she stored in here, then?"

Donna had a pretty good idea. "Maybe."

If the same tarot cards Sybil had pulled from this very box all those years ago were still inside, her daughter was going to flip. Things like that had always fascinated Lynette.

Donna had walked away from Catholicism after her fallout with her parents. Leaving the only religion she'd ever known had left Donna feeling lost. It was probably why the discussions she'd had about various religions with Sybil over the years had intrigued her so. Sybil had lived in the largest unit in the nursing home, and it overflowed with books and other items the woman had collected over the years. Sybil often sent books home with Donna, and Lynette would sometimes read them, too.

Had this exposure to other religions fueled her daughter's intrigue with tarot?

Donna had received reprimands from her supervisor for spending too much time in Sybil's room. Her boss complained it was to the detriment of other patients, but since Sybil was a significant benefactor to the nursing home, Donna's job was never truly in jeopardy.

But according to the reading Sybil did for her all those years ago on that stormy Sunday, her life might be.

Chapter Four

Lynette fingered the three small keys on the loop of worn velvet ribbon her mother had brought downstairs. Each key was unique, so they weren't a set.

"I guess it doesn't matter which one I try first."

The third try was the charm. She breathed a sigh of relief at the satisfying *click* she both felt and heard.

"Want to make any guesses as to what's in here?"

Donna shrugged. "I remember one thing that Sybil used to store in there, but Raven hated them, so those could be long gone. Just open it already."

"Now you have me even more curious. I think you're more impatient than me."

Lynette smiled at the same *click* when she twisted the key into the second hole in the box's top. When she tried to open the lid, the tenacious seal held for an instant, then gave way with a sound similar to pulling Velcro apart.

"Boy, this baby might have been practically airtight with this rubber seal," Lynette said. "Whatever someone stashed in here is probably still in decent shape."

She reached in and pulled out a small ivory box that reminded her of the kind that held a deck of playing cards, except slightly larger. She flipped it around.

"Oh . . . wow. *Tarot.*" She glanced up at her mother to find the woman leaning toward her. Her forearms rested on the kitchen table. "Interesting."

The smaller box opened at the top or bottom, like most card decks. Lynette flipped it open on top and pulled out a random card. The top right corner of it was missing. The card was yellowed, its edges worn. She wriggled her eyebrows at Donna and waved the card in her direction, knowing the woman disliked anything mystical. Then she studied the picture on the front of the card.

"I wonder if these are supposed to be two wolves. One is a light color, and the other is black. They are howling at a full moon. A pond of water is reflecting the moon." Two mountains sat in the background while a pair of some kind of posts framed the foreground. She had no idea what any of it meant. "Donna, pull your phone out and look up what this tarot card can signify, will you? It says 'The Moon' across the top."

"I will not. You know I hate that kind of thing. What else is in the box?"

Lynette set the card on the table and pulled her own phone out. "Give me a minute. We have all night. There's no rush."

Lynette did a search from her cell's browser and easily found the answer. After reading a few lines, she picked up the card again and examined it more closely. "I guess this is actually showing three phases of a full moon. It's supposed to represent the three faces of the feminine."

Donna snorted. "This should be good."

Lynette nodded. "The new moon is supposed to represent the virgin whose purpose is unfulfilled. Guess that doesn't fit for either of us."

"Don't be crude, Lynette," Donna said, reaching for the unlocked box.

She pulled it out of her mother's reach. "The full moon represents the mother who has fulfilled her potential. Huh. That makes one of us."

"And, let me guess, the old moon represents the old crone who's all washed up. Does that make one of us or both of us?"

Lynette couldn't tell if Donna's words were joking or self-deprecating. "You tell me. Here, let me pull a card for you."

This time, Donna swiped at the card box, but Lynette again avoided her reach. "Mother, don't be a party pooper."

"You know I hate it when you call me that."

Lynette laughed. "Party pooper? Or Mother? Most moms hate it when their kids call them by their first name."

"Yes, but we're different," Donna said. "All those years of working together changed that for us. I don't want you to pull a card for me. Those things creep me out. With my luck, you'll pull the Death card. If the Grim Reaper is coming for me, I'd prefer not to know."

Lynette pulled a card despite her mother's protests, but checked it before showing it to her, just in case. "It says 'The Hermit.' It's a picture of some old guy with a long white beard. Let me see what that might mean."

Donna reached across the table and picked up the single card, examining it. "At least it isn't a dancing skeleton or something ominous like that. Fine. What is some old hermit supposed to signify? That this represents me, now that we are living in this dinky little town where there's nothing to do?"

When the comment registered for Lynette, she set down her phone to stare at Donna. "Jeez. Is that how you really feel? Do you think I dragged you back to Ruby Shores against your will? Because that isn't how I remember it."

Donna flipped the card back at her. "No. Never mind me. I told you, tarot makes me nervous. Just stop with them already, would you? I want to know what else is in the box."

Lynette weighed her words, trying to decide if her mother really was coming to dislike living in Ruby Shores. It wasn't like they could just pick up and leave again. They had this house to think about now. She picked up the card from where it had landed.

"Honestly, Donna, I think you might like what this one could mean. According to Google, at least, drawing this card can signify a sense of peace and tranquility once one accepts that youth doesn't last forever."

"Great. So it isn't the Death card, but it means I'm potentially on death's doorstep."

Lynette turned her phone screen off and dropped her forehead down to rest on the tabletop. "You are impossible."

This time, when Donna reached across for the larger box, Lynette let her slide it back across the table.

"I'm not impossible," Donna countered. "But those cards are what I remember Raven and Sybil fighting about, way back when. How about we don't go down that same path, and instead see what else is in here?"

"Fine," Lynette said. She straightened, shoved both the Moon and the Hermit cards back in their box, and set the tarot deck off to the side. She should remember to stick it in her suitcase when she packed for Whispering Pines. Her friends would have fun with the cards. If there was time, maybe she'd do a little research on how to do proper readings before leaving on their girls' getaway. "Your turn to pull things from our mystery box."

Donna appeared relieved to move on. "There's a stack of photos in here."

She watched as her mom laid half a dozen photographs out on the table between them. All were black and white, giving some sign of their age. Both women studied them, unsure what, or who, they were looking at. Lynette stood and moved around to Donna's side of the table for a better vantage point.

"Are any of those of Sybil?"

Donna reached for two similar photographs, both of which had a bride and groom in them. One was of the couple by themselves. In the other, a woman stood next to the bride. Donna pointed to the woman, who could have been the bride's mother. "This might be her."

Lynette picked up the photo and flipped it over. Someone had penciled names and *1942* on the back. "Here are names. The top two say Evelyn and Oscar. There's another name under theirs, but the pencil smudged." She held the photograph closer and looked over the top of her reading glasses. "I think you're right. I think it says 'Sybil'!"

Donna held out her hand, and Lynette gave her the picture back. She examined the penciled notation, too. "I wish I could remember what Raven's parents' names were. This might have been them. Raven had a twin brother, too, but the clothes don't look modern enough for the groom to be her brother."

Lynette picked up two of the remaining four photographs and sat back down. "I forgot Sybil was Raven's grandmother and not her mom. But I never knew either of them as well as you did. I was only over here at the house a couple of times when I was in high school. Did Raven have kids? Could this boy be hers? These two pictures seem newer than those bridal shots. The paper is thinner, and the surface is shinier."

This time, when she turned the pictures over, the backs were blank.

"Let me see." Donna wiggled her fingers at her. She studied one by holding it close and moving her glasses out of the way.

Lynette laughed. "I wish we had the same eyesight we had back when I was in high school."

Her mother nodded, then pointed at one of the pictures of the young boy. "Look at that sedan in the background. It looks like the Marquis I used to drive, only newer."

"We never had new cars," Lynette said. "So what model year would you guess this one was?"

"I'm no expert, but I'd guess the mid-seventies, maybe?"

She nodded. "So that picture couldn't be older than that. The boy looks like he's about ten years old, doesn't he? Maybe my age or a few years older? It wouldn't be Raven's brother, then. Maybe her nephew?"

"Listen to you. You sound like a real-life Nancy Drew, honey."

Her comment reminded Lynette of the woman by the same name who they'd met on the beach in Maui during her first big trip with her girlfriends. "Did you know there are some really old *Nancy Drew* books in the library? Those had to have belonged to Sybil, too. Or maybe her daughter read them when she was a little girl. They have blue covers. But now we're getting sidetracked. What if you took copies of these old pictures with your phone and texted them to Raven? I know you have her phone number. She could probably tell us who these people are. I know it doesn't really matter, but I'm curious. If they are some of her family members, she might want the originals back. We could frame a copy of this cool old bridal picture and display it on a mantel in a spare bedroom. Since their family was the only owners of this place before us, the piece of history would be nice."

"I love that idea," Donna said, looking much more cheerful over their discovery of the photographs than she had about the tarot cards. "It wouldn't surprise me if these last two pictures were of this house. One looks like a basement, and I think the other is the very beginnings of a new building. Sybil told me that her husband built this house shortly after they got married."

Donna set the six pictures off to the side, much as Lynette had done with the card deck. "There are a few more things in here. Here's an old-fashioned ring. It might be a diamond. I wonder if it was the wedding ring of the woman in the photographs?"

"Or Sybil's," Lynette suggested. She took it from her mother so she could see it better. "Maybe Raven will know. What else is there?"

Donna pulled a white envelope from the box, her fingers obstructing some writing on the front. Lynette craned her neck.

"What does it say on the front?"

"Hold on," Donna replied, reading the cursive across the front. "It says 'Raven and Gideon.' That was Raven's twin brother's name. I could only remember that it was kind of different, but now I'm sure this was his name."

"Was?"

Her mom nodded. "Was. Raven said he died. Cancer or something. It was a long time ago. Before I knew either her or Sybil."

Lynette sighed. "Poor Sybil. And Raven. So much death. That explains why Raven reached out to you when she was ready to sell this place. There probably wasn't any other family left that might have wanted it. What's in the envelope?"

Donna pulled the back flap free. Someone had tucked it in instead of licking it shut. She dumped the contents into her hand, then screeched when tufts of hair landed in her open palm. She shook her hand, dropping the items onto the table.

"Eww," Lynette said, wrinkling up her nose and leaning closer for a better look. "I bet those are locks of Raven's and her brother's hair. Look! They tied one with a pale pink ribbon. The other is blue. I guess we know why her parents named her Raven. That is some *black* hair. She must have dyed her hair red."

Donna laughed. "I knew the auburn wasn't natural because Sybil complained about it. She told me once that the twins had such beautiful blue-black hair. She never liked that her granddaughter dyed it a different color."

Lynette picked up one of the hair tufts, despite Donna's shudder. "What? It's just hair. It isn't going to hurt us. Anything else in the box?"

Her mother took another look. "Not much. Just a few rocks." She picked them out and set them on the kitchen table.

Lynette exchanged the hair for one of them. "I don't think these are just any old rocks. This looks like a tiger eye. These other two might be rose quartz and amethyst. I always knew I liked Sybil. And that was before I even knew she was into crystals and tarot."

Donna scooped the stones off the table and dropped them back into the box. Then she handed the white envelope to Lynette and told her to put the tufts of hair back. "Give me those tarot cards, too, and we can figure out where to put all this old stuff while we wait to hear from Raven. She may appreciate getting it all back."

A phone rang. Lynette looked around for her mother's cell.

"It's in my purse," Donna said, reaching for her handbag. She pulled her phone out. "I should take this."

"Go ahead," Lynette said. "I'll clean this up. Then I think I'll go soak in a hot bubble bath. I'm sure I stink after a full day of cleaning in that shed out back."

Donna sent Lynette a grateful smile before leaving the room.

Lynette wondered about who might be on the other end of Donna's call. Her mother hadn't seemed to want to specify.

But she was even more interested in the items they'd pulled out of the old box. Especially the tarot cards. Without Donna there to witness her actions, she snapped pictures with her phone of everything in the box except the tarot cards and relocked the box. Then she tucked the tarot deck into a pocket of her jumper.

After she sent copies of the pictures she'd snapped of the photographs to Donna, she headed upstairs with the wooden box and keys. There was an empty dresser in the spare room next to hers. It seemed as good a place as any to store the wooden box, now that they knew what it contained.

Chapter Five

Lynette opened one eye to check the alarm clock on the bedside table. At first, the steady *tick-tock* beat of it threatened to drive her crazy after she'd picked it up at a rummage sale down the block, but she'd liked the look of it. Now she was used to it. But she had to move it closer to her face to make out the actual time without her contacts in.

Six a.m. and cheerful rays of sunshine already peeked around the edges of her curtains. It would be a beautiful morning. She'd planned to work in the shed again, but she'd already skipped her morning walk the day before. It would be too easy to fall out of her daily walking routine if she missed multiple days in a row.

She'd walk, then work. Besides, an idea had come to her in the bathtub last night.

When she got down to the kitchen, she ignored the full pot of coffee Donna must have made. She pulled on her tennis shoes and headed down the back steps. She spotted her mom bent over the rose bushes in the back garden.

"I'm going for a walk!"

Donna kept right on with her gardening. Lynette noticed the white wire running from her ears. She was probably listening to an audiobook while she cleaned up the mess left behind from yesterday's storm. Since

Lynette walked early most mornings, Donna wouldn't worry if she discovered her daughter was gone.

She turned left at the end of their driveway and headed down Breconwood Road. No one was out and about yet, given the early hour. She passed her old friend Owen's house. All was quiet. Owen's SUV sat in the driveway. He'd used it to bring a Shop-Vac over when she'd reached out to him in a panic after accidentally allowing the upstairs tub to overflow.

She walked on, enjoying the summer beauty and still-mild temperature. It felt good to stretch her legs. Muscles she didn't even know she had felt stiff from her work in the shed. If she'd remembered her own earbuds, she might have found a podcast to listen to on the walk. But nature made its own beautiful music, and she was as guilty as most people of not tuning in to it often enough.

Her route took her through several neighborhoods; some were familiar to her, others not at all. She walked past Jackie's parents' place, wondering how Charlotte was getting along on her own now that Glen was living in a memory care unit. She'd half expected to catch Jackie's mom outside, too, tending to her prized tomato plants, but no one was about.

Eventually her feet carried her past the old pizza parlor where she'd worked as a kid. When she'd come back in 2018 for her class's thirtieth reunion with her then boyfriend, Wyatt, she'd been sad to discover the old booths were gone, replaced with rows of washer and dryer units. But now, as she rounded the familiar corner, she discovered that only the laundromat's sign remained. At some point—probably during the pandemic shutdowns—someone had boarded up the windows and secured the front door with a chain. Tall weeds in the parking lot added to the air of neglect and abandonment.

She paused on the sidewalk that rimmed the pitted lot and closed her eyes. She remembered the echo of long-ago voices, and the laughter of unruly children, impatient for their pizza, coupled with scoldings from harried parents. Then there was the banter in the back between the kitchen and wait staff. When she was a senior in high school, this was a special place for her. She'd done her best to avoid spending time at home. It wasn't her mother she had been trying to avoid, but Donna's boyfriend at the time. The grown man who couldn't keep his hands to himself whenever he encountered Lynette alone.

She hated how naïve her mother was back then. If it hadn't been for Storm, her manager and eventual boyfriend, Lynette wouldn't have found the courage to stand up for herself and report the man's inappropriate behavior.

She'd lied to her friends when she told them she never thought about Storm over the years. She thought of him often. She'd even tried to look him up online once, but she didn't find anything. "Storm" probably wasn't his real first name, and she might not have remembered his correct last name.

The effort behind her search was half-hearted, anyway. The last few months of her senior year had been turbulent ones, and her own terrible choices came with serious repercussions for both her and Donna.

Even though they'd moved back to Ruby Shores, the town she'd always considered home, there were some things that were better left in the past.

A garbage truck rolled down the street behind her, and the stench that emanated from it knocked her back into her fifty-year-old self. She turned to continue on her walk and noticed a uniformed woman in a blue top and shorts delivering mail across the street.

"Hey, Carol," she yelled in greeting.

She could tell from the hitch in the woman's step that she'd heard Lynette, but she didn't return the wave or look her way.

What is it with the women in this town? she wondered. Some people seemed so stuck-up, especially the women. Weren't people supposed to be friendly in small towns?

Had she been too abrupt with Carol last month when the woman failed to close the door on their mailbox and their mail fell into the bushes below? Surely the woman wouldn't hold her own incompetence against Lynette, would she?

Her phone vibrated. The incoming text from Kit, about how excited she was getting for their upcoming trip, brought a smile to her face. Screw Carol and her attitude. And screw Lynette's old memories that always made her feel guilty for long-ago mistakes she couldn't change.

The temperature was climbing, and she picked up her pace. She wasn't quite to her destination yet, and she wanted to get home to work on her shed again before it got too hot outside. After three more blocks, she passed below the graceful metal archway that marked the entrance to Shady Acres. The old cemetery didn't actually cover *acres* of land on the edge of town, but this was where Donna said the family had buried Sybil.

If she could find Sybil's grave, her husband would likely be buried beside her, so Lynette could get his name. She might also find the graves of Raven's parents. Maybe even a headstone for her twin brother.

The photographs they'd found had left her so curious.

She could have simply waited for Donna to reach out to Raven, but Lynette had a thing for cemeteries. While the state of the old restaurant where she'd worked depressed her, she felt different anytime she wandered around old graves. She'd read once that people who found cemeteries fascinating were called *taphophiles.*

Donna wouldn't enjoy knowing her daughter was a taphophile any more than she liked her fascination with tarot.

Groundskeepers sometimes maintain listings for graveyards to make it easier for loved ones, or even grave hunters, to locate specific burial plots. Sure enough, Lynette located a binder in a cubby near the entrance. It contained an alphabetical listing of the dead and their corresponding locations within the cemetery. She turned back to the W's, quickly locating the name *Sybil Wall.* She took a picture of the coordinates listed for Sybil's grave and the map of the whole cemetery.

It didn't take her long to locate Sybil's headstone. She remembered that Sybil and her husband were wealthy benefactors of various institutions in town, so the imposing size of the stone wasn't a surprise.

Someone was doing an excellent job maintaining the grounds here, unlike the weed-infested lot at her long-ago place of employment.

She dropped to her knees on the velvety green grass in front of the Walls' headstone. She ran her fingers over the years below Sybil's name: *1899–1994.* So Sybil lived to be an impressive ninety-five years old. She'd have been eighty-nine when Lynette and Donna left Ruby Shores in 1988. Her husband—his name turned out to be Clifford—was born four years before Sybil, but the poor man died in 1930. Lynette couldn't help but wonder what killed a thirty-five-year-old man. Maybe Donna could ask Raven about that, too.

She sat on the soft grass and allowed her mind to drift back to the times she'd spent around Sybil. Her memories were understandably vague, given it was more than thirty years ago now. Still, these snippets of time, locked in her brain, were happy ones.

How long had it been since anyone came here to visit this grave? Did Raven come here before she moved away?

Thoughts of Raven reminded Lynette that she was also here to see if she could find the other graves. She rested a hand on Sybil's headstone, initially as a sign of respect but then to help her get back up on her feet. If Sybil was high above, looking down, she probably smiled at Lynette's grunt.

She checked the tombstone to her left, but those names seemed unrelated. To the right of the Wall tombstone was a more modest headstone, flat on the ground.

"Bingo."

The names matched those penciled on the back of the bridal photos.

According to the granite carvings, Evelyn Wall Gage was born in 1921 and died in 1954. Lynette gasped. Poor Evelyn was even younger than her father was when he'd died. Oscar Gage also died in 1954. He was thirty-six.

Gage must be a common surname around Ruby Shores.

Something else was carved into the stone below the birth and death dates of Evelyn and Oscar, but dried grass clippings and dirt made the inscription impossible to decipher. Lynette tried to clear the debris away with her hand, but the dirt was hard and caked. She was about to try kicking it away when she noticed a nearby water spigot with an empty ice cream pail hanging from it.

Luck was on her side. She hurried over to the spigot and turned the knob, delighted when icy water shot out in all directions. It spattered the front of her tank, but she didn't mind cooling off.

Between the splashes of water and the toe of her shoe, she cleared the stone enough to read the last line.

Beloved parents of Gideon and Raven.

This was the confirmation she'd hoped for. Raven would surely appreciate the bridal pictures of her parents and grandmother.

Feeling proud of her sleuthing skills, she returned the ice cream pail and checked other nearby graves in case they had buried Gideon here, too. But it seemed that, in this regard at least, her luck had run its course.

Was Gideon buried in this cemetery, but in another section? She'd check the list up front again, this time under G for Gage. Or had he died far from here? Maybe he'd been married when he passed, and his body was buried in his spouse's family plot somewhere.

Just before passing under the iron gates of Shady Acres again, she rechecked the list of graves. There was nothing for Gideon Gage, so she tucked the binder back into its protective box and turned toward home.

Her home that once belonged to Sybil and Clifford and their family.

How many people walking the earth today even remembered the Walls?

Who will remember me, and why, when I'm nothing more than a name carved into granite?

Thoughts like those felt too heavy for such a beautiful summer morning.

As her feet retraced the path she'd followed earlier, her mind wandered. Had Raven done any genealogy for her own family? Did the woman have any other close living relatives? While Lynette had always harbored a fascination with graveyards, especially old cemeteries she'd visited in Europe, her interest hadn't extended to genealogy. But digging into Raven's family tree helped Lynette understand how interesting it might be to trace lineages, too.

Raven's situation reminded Lynette of her own sparse family tree.

Raven had lost both her mother and father while she and her twin were still kids. Lucky for them, Sybil was there to raise them. Lynette had Donna, of course, but she'd had no kind of relationship with others in her family. Her mother refused to speak of her own parents, saying only that when they'd kicked her out as a young, unwed woman, their cruel stance meant they'd lost all right to call Donna and Lynette family.

She knew nothing about her biological father.

Growing up, Lynette never pressed Donna on the subject because it had felt disrespectful to do so. As she got older, she rarely thought about the father she'd never met or grandparents who had so easily turned their backs on them.

But a twinge of curiosity, of wanting to finally learn more, had blossomed.

Maybe she'd broach the subject with Donna again. The worst that could happen would be Donna's ongoing refusal to tell her anything. Which would leave Lynette no worse off than she was today.

Besides, she still had Donna, and she'd always known she hit the jackpot with her mother, even if the woman drove her batty some days.

The screen door slapped shut behind Donna.

"I'll love you forever if that lemonade is for me."

Her mother grinned down at Lynette from the top of the back steps. "You better love me forever, regardless. But, yes, I poured this for you. Sorry if it's a tad watered down. You aren't usually gone this long for your morning walks. The ice started to melt."

Lynette reached for the glass. "As long as it's wet and cool, I don't care what it tastes like."

Donna sauntered down the stairs to hand her the lemonade, then sat. She patted the bottom step next to her. "I was getting worried about you."

Lynette joined her mother, thankful for the cool shade provided by the canopy of leaves above. "What could possibly happen to me out for a morning walk in Ruby Shores?"

With a shrug, Donna took back the glass, helped herself to a drink, and returned it. "Not as many terrible things as in New York, but you just never know. Or you could have suffered heatstroke. When will this heat break?"

Lynette set the lemonade on the step between them. "Maybe tonight. More rain is in the forecast. Not that it helped much last night. I can't wait to cool off in the lake out at Whispering Pines."

"What's wrong with the lake right here in Ruby Shores?"

Lynette realized her feet felt like they were on fire. "Nothing is *wrong* with it," she said, grunting as she worked one tennis shoe off with the toe of her other foot. Then she peeled her sweaty socks off and jammed them inside the shoes. "I just meant it will be fun to hang out with the girls and splash around in the water, like we did when we were kids."

She used to love hanging out with her friends at the lake on the edge of Ruby Shores, too, but one terrifying night stole that sense of peace from her. It was a nightmare she'd shared with no one.

Donna nodded, then picked up the sweating glass of lemonade. "Do you mind?"

"*Now* you ask?" Lynette laughed. "Go ahead, I don't mind. I'll get more. I need to go in and shower before I melt. Sorry if I stink."

After another sip of lemonade, Donna waved her free hand toward the garden shed. "I thought you planned to work out there all day today. Why shower now? You'll just get dirty again."

"Mother. I'm hot. And gross. If I started in there right now, the dust would stick to me and I'd come out looking like a shadow at the end of the day. There's one of those big box fans up in the attic. Once I shower and change, I plan to take it out there and set it up on low. The work should be more pleasant that way." She got up from the step but dropped back down when she remembered her trip to the cemetery. "Oh! My walk took longer today because I headed down to the cemetery on the edge of town."

Donna whistled. "No wonder you were gone for so long. Why did you want to go to the cemetery on a beautiful morning like this? That sounds depressing."

Lynette shook her head. "I don't think cemeteries are depressing. I think they're fascinating—unless I have to go for someone's service. Besides, wouldn't you rather go there on a sunny, bright morning versus a dark and dreary evening?"

"I'd rather not go at all," her mother pointed out.

"Fine. Whatever. But I wanted to tell you that the bridal couple in those pictures we found in the box last night were Raven's parents. They're buried next to Sybil and her husband. His name was Clifford, by the way."

"That's right," Donna said with a snap of her fingers. "His name was escaping me. Did you pay any attention to how old her Clifford was when he died?"

Lynette reached for her tennis shoes. "In his thirties. So were Raven's parents. That's way more tragedy than one family should have to bear. Oh, I also looked to see if I could find a headstone for Raven's brother, but I didn't see one. You said he died, too, right? Either they buried him somewhere else, or your memory is faulty."

Donna got to her feet ahead of Lynette, using the handrail for leverage. She picked up the empty lemonade glass. "For Raven's and her brother's sake, let's hope it's my memory. I think I'll give Raven a call, though. I want to tell her about the box, and if I don't do it now I might forget."

Lynette followed her mother up the stairs and into the dim hallway that connected the kitchen to their dining room. "Tell her hello for me. What are you up to for the rest of the day? I'd try to convince you to help me in the shed, but it might get too hot for you, even with a fan."

"You forget I used to dream of living on a tropical island somewhere. The heat doesn't bother me, but I'll leave the dirty work out there to you. We could use some groceries. Why don't I pick up the ingredients for a nice chicken salad for dinner? You'll be hungry later, after all of your walking and work in your shed."

Lynette's stomach growled at the mention of food. If she ate nothing between now and dinner, she'd need more than a salad. But Donna didn't seem to have much of an appetite these days.

It wasn't until she trudged up the stairs to her en-suite bathroom that she remembered her desire to get her mother to tell her more about her grandparents. Maybe even her father.

Doing a little digging into Raven's family history was fun. She'd be turning fifty-one years old in a week. Maybe it was about time for her to know more about her own lineage, too.

CHAPTER SIX

Donna set Lynette's glass on the kitchen counter and re-trieved the lemonade pitcher from the refrigerator. No sense dirtying another glass. She hoped she'd be able to catch Raven on the phone, though she might be at the hospital. A doctor's hours were impossible to predict.

Her hip was bothering her again. She took her phone and lemonade into the sun porch off her bedroom instead of sitting on one of the hard wooden kitchen chairs. The porch would still be pleasant, and she could always turn on the ceiling fan if it got too stuffy.

Her old friend Raven Black picked up on the first ring.

"Donna! What a pleasant surprise! Unless there is something wrong with the house. If that's the case, I don't want to hear it. You and Lynette took it off my hands a year ago. Any plugged toilets or loose window sashes are officially your problem now."

Donna laughed. "Not to worry, Raven. I'm not calling to complain about anything. Are you enjoying Salt Lake? Was it the right move for you and your husband?"

Raven's chuckle sounded staticky. "As far as I'm concerned, it was definitely the right move. I love living close to the hospital in a mainte-nance-free condo. Well, it isn't maintenance-*free*, of course, but from our perspective, anything that goes wrong with the place is someone else's problem. How about you and that brilliant daughter of yours? I know when we last spoke, you worried Lynette was having trouble acclimating to small-town living. Has that gotten any better?"

"I'm not sure," Donna admitted. "In New York, people knew Lynette. I know that seems crazy, given the countless ultra-successful people in the city, but it's true. Here, in Ruby Shores, people have no clue that she used to run such a large-scale, successful online boutique. Or if they know, they don't care. I'm not saying that's wrong, or that people should fight for her attention. It's just different. Maybe she's getting acclimated. She walks almost every morning, which is great for her health and something she never did before. But I worry a little. She has a group of four good girlfriends and the five of them are taking a trip together in a week. It'll be good for her."

"What about you, Donna? I know that moving to Ruby Shores wasn't easy for you, either. I sometimes regret calling you to tell you I was putting the house up for sale. You made me promise to do just that, but you had other dreams for your life. I know you wanted to do lots of travel when you retired. Aside from the whole pandemic mess, have you made any plans? You know, Lynette isn't the only one who can travel with friends."

The reminders of things Donna worried she was missing out on made her uncomfortable. "Raven, I called you with news. Not because I wanted to talk about me or my daughter the whole time."

"Can you hold on a minute, Donna?"

There was a shuffling noise through the phone, along with the distant sound of sirens. Salt Lake wasn't New York, but it was still a city. The sound of sirens around Ruby Shores was so infrequent, Donna noticed things like that now. In years past, her senses wouldn't have even tuned in to it.

"Sorry about that," Raven said, coming back on the line. "I'm glad we moved to Salt Lake, but I am still trying to get used to all the noise. Now, what did you want to tell me? Wait, let me guess. Do you have some juicy gossip about someone in my old hometown? Maybe even that cute, rich guy who lives a block down on Breconwood? The one I told you Lynette should ask out?"

Donna smiled. She knew all about Owen Jameson. "Lynette worked with Owen when they were kids. There's no way she'd ever go out with him. She insists he's always been in love with Jackie, one of her best friends."

"Oh, fine. Forget I said it. I'd never be one to suggest breaking the sisterhood code. My grandma taught me that."

Donna saw an opening. "Speaking of your grandmother, she's actually the reason I called. I found something yesterday that I think you might be interested in. Well, Lynette found the box, but I remembered a set of keys that we needed to open it."

"A box? But we had an estate sale before we moved. I packed up everything I wanted to keep, then we opened the house up with the help of a company that deals in estates. You wouldn't have believed the crowd that showed up. Everyone was curious about the treasures Sybil might have left behind. Remember, she was quite the world traveler when she was younger. Before she took my brother and me in. They picked the house clean—except for the library, which I locked. It didn't feel right to sell off all of Grandma Sybil's books. It felt like those should stay with the house."

"I'm so glad you kept the books. I spend hours in there every week.

Sybil curated an eclectic mix of titles. But Lynette found the box outside."

"Outside?"

"In the garden shed."

Raven didn't speak for a heartbeat. "Oh! I forgot about the shed. I didn't bother to open that up as part of the sale. I figured it was just filled with junk. What was Lynette doing in there?"

It was getting stuffy in the porch. Donna had forgotten to turn on the ceiling fan. She stood and pulled the cord above her head. "Believe it or not, she's turning it into a 'she-shed,' of all things."

Raven laughed. "Because the main house doesn't give you two enough space?"

"That's pretty much what *I* said. According to my daughter, all the space in the main house is actually the *reason* she wants to carve out a cozy little area for herself. Neither of us has ever lived in such a big house before. I think all the open space makes her anxious."

"That's surprising. But, heck, she can afford it, so she should be able to turn our old house into anything she wants."

Donna felt a hiccup of apprehension at Raven's comments about finances, but she'd never admit something so private out loud. "She found an old wooden box on a shelf out there. It took me a minute, but then I realized I'd seen that box before."

Raven let out a low whistle. "I think I know exactly which box you're talking about, Donna. And you wouldn't believe how long I looked for it when we were getting ready to move. I thought we'd lost it forever. Were there still things inside it, or was it empty?"

"Oh, it wasn't empty."

"You have no idea how relieved I am to hear that! Was there a ring inside?"

Donna nodded, then remembered Raven couldn't see her. "There was a ring. It looks old. Or should I say 'vintage'?"

"Was it a single diamond, rather small, with a gold band?"

"Yes," Donna said, doing her best to recollect the details. "A square cut, I believe." She could hear Raven clapping through the phone. "I'm so glad you're excited about this. Was it Sybil's? All I remember her wearing in the nursing home was a plain gold band."

Lynette wandered into the porch. She'd caught her wet hair up in a loose bun on the top of her head. The box fan was in her hand. "Is that Raven?" she whispered.

"Yes," Donna mouthed back, then said into the phone, "Hold on one second, would you, Raven?"

"Hi, Raven!" Lynette said in a raised voice, then said to Donna, "Sorry, I didn't mean to interrupt. I'm headed out to the shed, but would you mind picking up more peanut butter when you get groceries? We're out."

Donna waved an acknowledgment, then shooed Lynette away. "Now, where were we?"

"The ring. Donna, I can't tell you how excited I am that you found it, and that you called me. Grandpa gave it to Grandma Sybil when they first got married. I think it was maybe even his mother's first, but she was dead by the time he met Sybil. Then, when my mother, Eleanor, married, they didn't have money for a ring. Grandma insisted they use the family heirloom as her wedding ring. She didn't like to wear it on her travels, anyhow, because she worried something might happen to it."

Donna loved hearing how generous Sybil was with her daughter. Her own mother had never been that way. Maybe that was one of the big reasons she'd loved Sybil so much. "That is such a sweet story, Raven. And I'm sorry your mother died while you were still so young. You didn't want to wear the ring when you got married?"

"Grandma Sybil offered, but by then I thought maybe the ring was more of a curse than a blessing. My grandfather's mother died young. Shortly after my folks got married, my grandfather died in an accident. Then both my parents drowned. Mother was wearing that ring when they discovered her body. I never wanted it for a wedding ring, but I also recognize the family history behind it, so I wanted to at least keep it. But then I couldn't find it. And Grandma Sybil's memory had gotten so bad, she was no help."

When she'd held the ring the night before, Donna hadn't considered all the potential heartache tied to it. "I'd be happy to mail it to you, Raven. You should have it. There were also a few snapshots in the box. Based on names penciled onto the back, two were from your parents' wedding day."

Raven squealed. "Are you kidding? I remember those pictures! Sybil had similar ones in a frame in her room at the nursing home, but when I went through her personal items after she passed, the photographs were damaged beyond repair. I'm so glad you found more of them! Would you mind hanging on to the things you found? The next time we're in Minneapolis to visit my in-laws we'll drive over to Ruby Shores and pick them up. Plus, I'd get to see you again, which would be so fun."

"Of course. I'll put it all in safekeeping for you. Although there was one item in there that I doubt you want me to save."

There was another voice in the background on Raven's end.

"I'm sorry, Donna, but a patient is waiting for me, so I should go. But you have me curious. What else was in there that I *wouldn't* want?"

"Sybil's deck of tarot cards."

"Well, that stinker," Raven hissed. "She promised me she'd get rid of those things after the fright they caused us that night. She lied?"

Donna laughed. "Apparently. I had the same reaction you did when Lynette pulled them from the box. But Lynette loves them. She's always had a thing for stuff like that. Should I toss them? Or maybe burn them, so they can't come back to haunt you?"

"I don't care what you do with them as long as I never have to see them again. Give them to Lynette, for all I care. I knew Sybil used to keep her tarot cards in that old box, but I didn't realize she stored other things in there, like the photographs and ring. How do you suppose the box ended up in the shed? There's no way Sybil could have put it out there. She wasn't mobile enough anymore. Someone must have helped her. Oh well, I guess it doesn't really matter. Seriously though, Donna, it was so good to hear from you again. I miss our chats. I have to go, but I'll be in touch when we can get back there. You take care of yourself!"

"You, too, Raven. We'll talk soon."

Once the line went dead, Donna set her phone down and settled back into the comfortable wicker settee to sip her lemonade. She could see the rose garden and the back of the statue from her vantage point. Yesterday's storm had knocked a few blooms off, and Lynette and Annie's son had trampled some stems when they put the statue there, but she'd done her best to clean up the damage.

Working beneath that statue under the bright morning sun hadn't bothered her as much as she'd worried it would. If she had her way, they'd banish that statue to the landfill. But it was old and hauntingly beautiful, and probably even valuable, so Lynette would never concede to having it hauled away.

Donna remembered seeing that statue of the girl during her first visit to this house. It was a crisp, cold winter day, and by then Sybil needed some assistance to get around, but she wasn't yet confined to a wheelchair. Donna was there to help Raven get Sybil in and out of the house for her Sunday visit.

Sybil had asked Donna to walk her past the statue, even though it wasn't the most direct path to the house. As they'd stood in front of it, sunlight glinted off the flowers in the girl's hair and the single tear that meandered down Sybil's pale, wrinkled cheek.

"Do you want to talk about it, Sybil?" Donna remembered asking the elderly woman.

Sybil, as Donna had come to know, had a fiery yet calm personality. Her display of emotion on that cold, cloudy day was out of character.

"Isn't she beautiful?" Sybil asked.

Donna turned to the statue of the young girl in the middle of the barren winter garden. "She is. Does she have a story?"

Sybil had flicked the tear away, and a smile stole across her face. "She was a gift. My husband commissioned her for me for our tenth wedding anniversary. Our beautiful Eleanor was eight years old, and Clifford had the artist create this statue in her image. He said it would be so we could always remember our beautiful child like this, when we were old and gray, and she was off living her life somewhere fabulous with a family of her own. He was always a dreamer, and he promised she would be our first of many children. But, a year after Clifford surprised me with the statue, he was gone. Eleanor was our only child. He didn't get to see her build a family of her own. He couldn't have known that I'd be the only one turning gray and decrepit. He never got the chance. Even sweet Eleanor would never have the chance to turn gray. But at least she is here, in my garden. I like to remember her like this. So full of fun and laughter."

Donna remembered the shiver that had raced through her. The statue may have been created in Sybil's young daughter's likeness, but she reminded Donna of a different little girl. One she'd loved with all of her heart. Much like Eleanor, that little girl would never have the chance to grow old.

A clatter pulled Donna out of her memories and back to the porch. Lynette must have dropped a stack of lumber outside the shed. Maybe she should go help her daughter. What other treasures might she be discovering out there that Sybil—or, if Raven's theory was to be believed, someone else—had hidden away?

But she'd gotten up early to work in the garden, and she'd barely slept the night before. Instead of working in the hot shed, she'd allow herself the luxury of a quick nap, then she'd go pick up those groceries, as she'd promised. The breeze from the ceiling fan felt good against her skin, and the scent of roses wafted through the screens. Her eyes drifted shut, and she felt both lazy and comfortable.

Her thoughts returned to the statue, but this time the bowl at the girl's feet overflowed with a deluge of rainwater instead of a dusting of snow. Overgrown rose bushes stood as high as her waist, and lightning flashed off the statue's metal surface. Raven wanted to get Sybil back to the home, but Donna needed a minute to compose herself.

To humor Sybil—and perhaps calm her down on the difficult anniversary of her daughter's death—Donna had finally allowed Sybil to do a reading for her. It was a simple three card spread with the tarot cards, and even though Donna didn't believe in that stuff, Sybil's warning had left her shaken.

As she stood beneath the pouring rain, attempting to pull herself together, Donna struggled to remember the precise names of the three cards. Sybil's message had come as a shock, leaving her with an intense feeling of claustrophobia. The first card Sybil pulled depicted a child, a woman, and an old man. Sybil said it likely represented a child, sitting on a grandfather's knee, while the mother looked on. The man passed traditions on to the child. The next card symbolized successful completion of one thing and the start of something new. According to the third and final card, things were coming full circle. Sybil suggested it might all mean it was time for Donna to go home.

Home . . . ?

Donna didn't think the reading had anything to do with the tiny rental she shared with her daughter. The first card, with the man, could only mean one thing. Panic had sluiced through her veins as the message sank in. Lightning and thunder crashed beyond the windows of Sybil and Raven's kitchen.

Donna had promised herself she'd never have to go home again.

Home wasn't safe. Home was a place of lies and dangerous ignorance. No matter how dire things had gotten for Donna and Lynette through the years, even when there wasn't enough food on the table or money for new school clothes, it was still safer than the home where Donna grew up.

No one, not even her teenage daughter, knew of the letter Donna had received earlier in the week. The one from her mother, begging her to come home. Her father was on his deathbed.

Now Sybil's cards were telling her the same thing.

Were the cards a reminder that the past still held her hostage, and she was selfishly robbing her only daughter of this last chance to meet her grandfather?

The flood of emotions threatened to overwhelm her. She'd run outside, leaving Sybil with her cursed cards still spread out on the kitchen table before her. Donna was oblivious to the sheets of rain and flashes of lightning as she stood in front of the garden statue of young Eleanor. To Donna, the statue was a reminder of her baby sister, the one she'd failed to protect.

The one she'd failed to save.

Had she been fair to blame her father for her sister's death so long ago? She'd been running ever since, but maybe she'd been wrong. She hadn't run because she was pregnant. That came later.

Raven called for her from the house, insisting she come back inside, but Donna needed another minute to collect herself. Sybil's words kept echoing through her brain.

Home ... go home ...

The warning terrified her, and it made her feel exactly like the failure her parents had warned her she'd be.

With the storm raging around her, a blur of movement had caught Donna's attention. She spun toward it, but the ground was slippery with wet leaves and grass. The shadows tilted around her and she felt herself falling. Just before she hit the ground, lightning flashed again, and she thought she could make out the face of a man, or a boy, yelling something to her, before her world went black.

She jumped awake. Her cell phone was ringing. Disgust over allowing the nightmare to return enveloped her, and she swiped at the bead of sweat on her forehead. Those tarot cards were to blame. She'd take Raven up on her suggestion and burn the damn things.

The phone kept ringing. She eyed the screen and took a shaky breath. Dear Chester somehow always knew to call when she needed him the most.

A glance at the back shed confirmed that Lynette wasn't paying her any attention. A cloud of dust erupted from the open door of the shed. Her daughter was busy with her own mission.

Donna allowed the dregs of sleep and the old nightmare to ebb away as she reached for her phone with a grateful smile.

Maybe Raven was right. Maybe it was high time she started pursuing her own dreams.

Chapter Seven

Donna left the house to buy peanut butter and the ingredients for a chicken salad. She came home with a pet cat for her daughter.

Lynette still couldn't believe it. She'd always wanted a cat, but the reality of pet ownership wasn't turning out exactly as she'd expected. Instead of working on her shed, she was prowling the neighborhood because the dang thing had an uncanny ability to escape. She couldn't even call for the cat by name while she searched because she hadn't gotten around to naming her yet.

When Lynette was a little girl, she'd begged her mother to buy her a cat. But Donna always refused. They'd moved around too much, and most landlords didn't allow pets.

Even though it had been years since Lynette mentioned a cat to her mother, Donna somehow believed that now would be the *perfect* time for a pet. She didn't even consult with Lynette beforehand. If she would have asked, Lynette would have simply told her mother to let go of her guilt from all those years ago.

She no longer felt a burning desire to own a cat, although she hoped she'd managed to hide her apprehension from Donna. It would be too easy to become the crazy cat lady . . . holed up in a big old house . . . on a quiet street . . . in Small Town, USA.

Donna hadn't asked, but three days later and after the initial shock wore off, Lynette was already getting used to having the stealthy feline around. The cat was half-grown, but her previous owners had never intended to keep her, so they'd left the naming task for her forever owner.

If Lynette had still wanted a cat, this was the type she would have picked. The kitten was as black as midnight, which fit perfectly with her girlhood dream.

At least, she'd *thought* the kitten was perfect—right up until it ripped the head off Lynette's favorite old toy. Her threadbare teddy bear—the one she used to take everywhere as a child, even to summer camp—was no more. Since moving back to Ruby Shores, the teddy had rested on a rocking chair in the corner of Lynette's bedroom.

Before Lynette, the bear had belonged to Donna as a child.

When Lynette discovered the carnage, she quickly hid the evidence and crossed her fingers that Donna wouldn't notice the bear was gone. She'd located all the bear's pieces except one black button eye. If the stupid kitten ate the button, things might get interesting soon.

Unless she couldn't even find her cat this time.

"Here, kitty, kitty, kitty," she said in a singsong voice, scanning the lawns and bushes surrounding her neighbors' homes.

She'd spied the runaway moments earlier, heading in the general direction of her friend Owen's house. Maybe he'd be home and willing to help her look.

She stepped off the curb to cross another street, and her ankle popped. She recognized the sensation and paused, muttering under her breath. If she ended up with a bum ankle right before her girls' trip, that cat's stint as her pet promised to be short.

A school bus approached from her left, and she waited for it to pass, grateful to take a moment so the pain in her ankle could hopefully fade. The voices and laughter of children floated out of the bus's open windows. School wasn't in session, so the kids must be from a daycare or nearby camp.

Her old summer camp—the one she used to bring her bear along to for company—had ceased operations years ago. Otherwise, she might have guessed the bus held kids from Camp Barefoot.

The bus continued on its way, and Lynette tested her ankle. The pain was gone, so her hunt could continue. If she didn't find that darn cat, how was she ever going to explain to Donna that she'd already lost the only pet her mother had ever given her?

A trio of birds took flight, exploding out of a neatly trimmed hedge up ahead. Had her kitten flushed them out? Lynette already knew the cat loved to slink around under the cover of flowers and plants.

She crossed the street, calling for the kitten again.

That's when she spied her. Barely a blur of a shadow. Lynette would never have noticed the stealthy little thing if she hadn't been looking right at it. The kitten broke free of the hedge, bounced across velvety grass, wove through a flowerbed, and slunk into a dense row of lilacs.

The bushes edged Owen's backyard.

Lynette chased behind her, feeling foolish and inept as she hurried across a stranger's lawn, careful of her ankle. She should just go home, put a bowl of kibble out, and hope for the best. The cat obviously had no intention of letting Lynette catch her. She was probably watching her from Owen's lilac bushes right now, thinking what a fun game this was.

The clang of hammers caught her attention, followed by male laughter. The sounds came from the other side of the lilacs. At least two men were back there, working on something. She recognized Owen's voice and wondered if one or both of his sons were back there, too.

The boys had seemed like nice young men when she'd met them briefly at Jackie's surprise fiftieth birthday party a year and a half ago. Maybe she'd pop over, say hello, and ask them to keep an eye out for her ornery kitten. Then she'd get back to working on her shed. At this rate, it would never be done before she left for Whispering Pines.

She considered going around to the front of Owen's place, but she spied a hole in the bushes and chose the more direct route instead. Was that meowing she heard, just beyond the lilacs? She ducked and stepped into the opening. It wasn't as large as she'd initially thought. Sharp brambles caught in her hair and scraped at her arms and legs.

"If I lose an eye in here, you'll earn yourself a one-way ticket to a shelter, cat," she said, frustration increasing the volume of her words above her intended whisper.

The rubber-soled toe of her left tennis shoe caught, throwing her forward and shifting too much weight to her weaker ankle. She might have stumbled to the ground if a higher branch hadn't jabbed into her hair, catching in the clip on the top of her head. She screeched and reached for her hair, pain causing her eyes to water. With a tight grip on the overhead branch, she regained her footing but struggled to pull her tangled hair loose.

Despite her anguish, she noticed the quiet. No more hammers. Had Owen and whoever else witnessed her complete lack of grace as she'd tried to traverse the lilacs?

"Stop! You're making it worse," a low-pitched, male voice demanded as someone brushed her hands out of the way.

"Oh, crap," she hissed, keeping her eyes shut tight. "I'd hoped no one saw that."

"If it makes you feel any better, Owen ran up to my truck to grab another box of nails. He missed the show. Now stop squirming so I can get you loose."

While she appreciated the help, the man's bossy tone grated. Something didn't jive. The gravelly voice didn't fit with how she remembered either of Owen's boys the night of Jackie's party. This guy sounded like he enjoyed two packs a day, though she couldn't detect the unmistakable odor of a heavy smoker. She opened her eyes to get a look at the man, but he stood behind her, yanking at her hair.

"Ouch! That hurts!"

He chuckled, which only infuriated her further. "I told you to stay still." A branch snapped above. She attempted to pull away, but a heavy hand landed on her shoulder. "You aren't loose yet."

"Sorry," she said, holding as still as she could and feeling like a scolded schoolgirl.

A few more tugs, and her snarled hair tumbled down around her shoulders, obscuring her face for a second.

"Here. Sorry. This snapped," the deep voice said.

Lynette spun and took a blind step backward and tried to push her hair back from her face, instinctively wanting more space between her and the voice. She'd been right. Her rescuer was nothing like Owen's boys. This was an older man. A large, bald man, wearing dark sunglasses, a long-sleeved shirt despite the temperature, and a smirk.

She took a second step back.

"Careful," he said. He thrust his chin toward something over her left shoulder. "If you fall into those roses behind you, it'll hurt worse than the lilac branches."

She tried to glance behind her, but her unruly hair blocked the view. Her curls had to look more like a rat's nest now versus the loosely styled updo she'd started her day with. In her first bit of luck since leaving her house to chase after the kitten, she located a hair tie around her wrist. Even though she refused to cut her silver curls into a shorter, more "age-appropriate" style, she hated it when her hair tickled her face.

Once she'd done what she could to smooth the frizz into some semblance of order, she regarded the man again. He didn't seem to be in a hurry to get back to whatever he'd been doing before she'd caught herself up in the bushes. She glimpsed a large screwdriver sticking out of the front pocket of a well-worn pair of jeans.

"You should be careful with that," she said. "It looks sharp."

His gaze dropped to the tool, then back to her face. "I'm perfectly capable of handling a screwdriver. I think I'm the one who has to keep telling you to be careful. What the hell were you doing in the bushes, anyhow?"

She huffed. "Well, I certainly wasn't spying on you, if that's what you're thinking."

He held up his hands. It was his turn to take a step backward. "I don't recall saying I thought you were spying."

Someone cleared their throat. "Lynette?"

Thank God. "Owen! Am I glad to see you!" Lynette spun again and hurried toward her old friend.

Owen looked between Lynette and the man who'd rescued her, a confused expression on his face. He held a box of nails in one hand and a large hammer in the other. "Lynette, did I miss a call from you? Did you need something?"

She gave a nervous laugh as she reached his side. "No. I wasn't the needy neighbor this time, looking for a tool. I actually lost my cat. She snuck out of the house, and I can't catch her."

The other man chuckled. She looked back at him and then swung her gaze up to where he pointed. "That gangly thing?"

Sure enough. Her kitten sat perched atop some type of wooden structure attached to the back of Owen's house.

"Huh," she said. "How did she even get up there? And what is that thing she's sitting on top of?"

Owen followed their gazes. "It's a half-built pergola. Since when do you have a cat?"

Since Owen had been to her house more than once to help with an odd job here and there, he would know they didn't have pets.

At least they hadn't until Donna brought the little troublemaker home. She confessed as much to Owen while pointedly ignoring the irritating man behind her, even though he'd saved her from the lilacs. He was rude, and probably just some handyman Owen had hired to help with his project.

"What did you say her name was?" Owen asked, wandering over to stand below the post where the cat perched. He dropped the box of nails and his hammer onto the edge of his patio, then straightened to look up at the kitten again.

"I haven't named her yet," Lynette admitted. She walked over to stand beside him. "How are we going to get her down?"

"I have no idea. I can't figure out how she got up there, either."

The other man came to stand on Owen's opposite side. "Maybe you should name her Abracadabra. Or Shazam!"

Lynette bent forward to shoot a glare around Owen at the guy. "Cute. By the way, you didn't tell me your name either."

The guy shrugged. "You didn't ask."

Owen shook his head, looking slightly amused over their banter.

A loud meow pulled their attention back up to the young cat. She was visibly shaking now, as if only just realizing where she was and wondering, too, how she'd get down.

"What are we going to do? If she falls . . ."

Owen gave her arm a reassuring nudge. "She won't fall, Lynette. Cats have crazy balance. Hey, go grab that tall ladder off your truck, will you?"

If the other man's loud sigh was any indication, he probably felt that rescuing one female had wasted enough of his day. He didn't look overly enthused about riding to the rescue of another one, but he turned on his heel and headed toward the front of Owen's house.

"Man, that guy is kind of a jerk, Owen. Who is he, anyway?"

Owen took his eyes off her cat to give her another perplexed look. "You mean Taran? Oh, don't mind him. He's handy on projects like this, so I tolerate him. Hey, didn't he just save you from being abducted by a bush a few minutes ago? I'd think you'd be willing to cut him some slack."

She wrinkled her nose. "Taran? What kind of name is that?"

"Guess it's the kind of name his mother gave him when he was born?"

Lynette wasn't sure why Owen had such a goofy look on his face. Was he enjoying this, despite the precarious position of her new pet?

The cat let out another meow, but it turned into more of a yowl. Her terror was obviously growing over her unfortunate predicament high above their heads. Lynette forgot about Owen and turned all of her attention back to her poor kitten.

"Don't move, honey. Momma will get you down from there. Don't jump!"

The other man returned with a large ladder. "Momma? Lord."

"What are you going to do with that thing?" Lynette asked, ignoring his comment. "This structure can't support that."

Owen helped the man with the ladder. She realized it was actually a tall step ladder, rather than the expandable type like she'd initially thought. She hurried forward and started up the ladder before they even had the thing stabilized.

"Whoa, there! Not so fast," the man Owen had called Taran exclaimed, wrapping his arms around Lynette's waist and setting her back on the ground. "This ladder is tall, but you still won't be able to reach her. I've got a few inches on both of you. I'll do it."

Before she could even protest his audacity, he was halfway up the ladder. She could quickly see that it would be a stretch, even for the taller man, to reach her cat.

"Grab that tarp!" he yelled down.

"Over there." Owen pointed. "I have to hold the ladder. The ground isn't flat here."

"What do we need a tarp for?" Lynette yelled back while scrambling for the blue vinyl sheet Owen had indicated.

"In case I drop her!"

That horrific possibility had Lynette moving even faster. She'd barely gotten back to Owen's side with the tarp and opened it up when a loud yowl from the feline and a muffled curse from the man filled the air.

"Catch it!" Owen yelled.

Later, Lynette could applaud her own heroic efforts and fluidity over scooping up the flailing kitten in the tarp a split second before she would have smacked down onto Owen's trampled grass. But first, she thought she better see to Owen and the man who'd saved her from the bushes. She may have caught the cat, but no one broke Taran's fall, and it was doubtful that he possessed the same nine lives as her kitten.

She set the tarp and her unharmed cat on the ground, whispering a prayer that the foolish kitten would stay put. Then she turned back to Owen and his friend. Both men were on the ground, but at least Owen was sitting up. The other guy was flat on his back.

She dropped to one knee beside Owen. "Are you all right?"

He nodded. "I'll be fine. Caught his damn boot on the side of my head, though. But you better check him. He fell hard."

Lynette scrambled across Owen's matted lawn on her knees. She reached Taran's side just as the man's eyes fluttered open. He groaned and flung a forearm across his forehead.

"Is anything broken?"

The man only grunted. He was hurt, but at least he wasn't dead. She pushed on his chest and stomach, then giggled when she realized how ridiculous her actions must look. It wasn't like she could tell if he had internal injuries just by pushing on different parts of him.

His hand shot back down to grab her by the arm. He grimaced again. "Damn, woman, knock it off. That hurts!"

The movement pulled his shirt sleeve up, revealing a smear of blood. She ignored his complaints and pulled her arm loose so she could grab his wrist, pushing his sleeve up farther to try to find the source.

"You're bleeding!"

He was strong, despite lying flat on his back after a fall from a ladder. He pulled his arm away, but not before she saw something else under the streaks of blood. Tattoos covered his forearm and bicep. She hadn't noticed them earlier because of his long sleeves. But the massive, intricate set of intertwined tattoos weren't what had snagged her interest. It was one silly little mark in particular, on the skin just above the inside bend of his elbow.

The tiny butterfly looked ridiculous on the burly, broad-shouldered man.

The tattoo was also an exact match to the butterfly on her inner thigh.

The muscles in his arm contracted, as if he realized she'd just connected the dots.

She pushed his sunglasses up to get a look at his eyes, then slapped the man's arm and scooted away from him, falling onto her butt. Her kitten, temporarily forgotten, rubbed against her side, as if to either thank her for her world-class catch or offer comfort. But Lynette ignored the cat and the tattooed man, instead pinning her furious gaze on Owen.

"You said his name was *Taran*!"

Owen squirmed. "That *is* his name! I've been in business with the guy for almost thirty years. I know his legal name."

She scrambled up and stood with hands on her hips, still keeping her full attention on Owen. Her cat pressed against her ankle.

"But that wasn't the name he went by when we were kids, was it?"

Owen shrugged. "He made me promise not to say anything to you."

The softly spoken admission hit her like a ton of bricks.

Or a storm.

The man obviously knew who she was. Owen had called her by name more than once. And aside from the silver in her hair, some extra weight, and a few well-earned wrinkles, she was the same girl she'd been at seventeen.

Oh, and my still-perky breasts. But those are none of his business.

"You son of a bitch," she said through gritted teeth. She wasn't even sure if she meant the words for Owen or Taran.

Disgusted, she scooped up her kitten and turned her back on the men, leaving them both on the ground. She'd considered them each a friend, once upon a time, and both had betrayed her, though in much different ways.

But why?

All she knew for sure was that the man on the ground used to go by the name Storm, and it was her turn to walk away from him.

CHAPTER EIGHT

IT WAS WELL PAST midnight and Lynette knew she should go to bed, but recent events wouldn't stop twirling through her mind. Donna had gone up earlier, leaving her alone downstairs.

Eventually, she flipped off the television, throwing the sitting room into shadow. Even though they'd recently released new episodes of her favorite series, the storyline failed to hold her interest.

What she really wanted was a gin and tonic. After yesterday's shock, she decided she even deserved one.

She shuffled through the semidarkness to the kitchen and pulled a crystal highball down from the cupboard with the cracked door. She liked to start her cocktails off with a generous helping of ice. Moonlight illuminated three pastel planters containing herbs on the wide ledge over the kitchen sink. Donna liked to use the fresh sprigs in her cooking. Lynette broke off a sprig of rosemary and nestled it amongst the cubes in her fancy glass.

If she was going to splurge on a cocktail, she'd make it a good one.

She broke the seal on a bottle of Bombay Sapphire that she'd received in a congratulatory gift basket from a long-time vendor to celebrate the sale of her company. The unopened bottle was a testament to her ability to refrain from drinking alcohol whenever she chose.

Or at least that's what she'd keep telling herself.

But this had been no ordinary day. Her past had come back to haunt her, and she deserved a cocktail.

She didn't bother with a shot glass, and instead poured what looked like a reasonable splash of gin. Then she pulled a can of tonic water out of the back of the refrigerator. After stirring the combination as best she could with her index finger, she decided fresh air would provide the perfect complement to the gin and exited the quiet house through the back door.

A bright white moon greeted her, illuminating the path under her bare feet. Despite the wash of moonlight, her midnight-blue peignoir and matching nightie allowed her to blend with the shadows. If anyone happened by or looked out a window, they might not even notice her. Only the silver in her hair might give her away.

Not that anyone should be up at two in the morning.

The icy glass in her right hand felt comfortable—maybe *too* comfortable. She took a delicious sip and recognized the irony of it all. Here she was, right back to making potentially poor decisions now that Storm was back in her life.

Old habits and all.

She stopped on the pathway and dropped her head back, eyes closed, envisioning the moonbeams enveloping her. While she loved sunlight and the warm days of summer, there was a certain magic to a full moon. And here in Ruby Shores, unlike her many years in the city, she could slip outside under the relative privacy of her own backyard to simply bask in its unpolluted light.

A crick formed in her neck and she straightened, wandering over to the statue amongst the roses. Had the young girl there also enjoyed frolicking under the stars? Another sip of her cocktail exploded against her taste buds. She swallowed, and a sigh of pleasure escaped her lips. The *pop!* and *fizz* of the tonic water tickled. It was a pleasant experience. One she'd missed.

The statue girl looked as if she'd been about to execute a pirouette, one slender arm poised gracefully above her head. Her wavy hair, its greenish-copper color bleached to silver, seemed to undulate in the moonlight. But Lynette knew it was simply a trick of the light as the moon's beams plunged through shivering leaves above that dipped toward the statue's extended hand.

The poor girl would remain forever frozen like that, never moving forward.

Lynette shook her head to dispel the hovering sense of melancholy. The statue added the perfect touch to the back garden. She was happy that she'd been able to fix the water pump and fill the basin with water. Its tinkling sounds complemented the chirps of hidden crickets, creating a symphony of sorts in their midnight garden.

Heavy shadows muted her sight but magnified her sense of hearing, and the sensation whisked her mind back in time to the gurgling of another water fountain. Years fell away as she let her mind drift. The peace she'd felt in her moon-washed garden evaporated.

She stood in front of the iconic fountain in Ruby Shores' town square. Gripped tightly in her hand was the mortarboard she'd worn that day for her high school graduation ceremony. Her blood raced at a feverish pitch, driven by excitement, a deep thirst for something, and a primal splash of fear. Her mind galloped, nearly as fast as her blood.

The constraints of high school were officially behind her. The vast world was wide open before her, full of boundless possibilities. It was a time to celebrate—to escape this overload of sensations—but all anyone else wanted to do was go to some stupid chaperoned party.

Of all nights, why had Storm picked tonight to abandon her?

But she knew that wasn't really fair. He hadn't *abandoned* her. In fact, he'd stood up for her just a short time ago. Maybe now her mother's disgusting boyfriend would finally keep his distance.

Tonight had to be special. After all, a girl only graduates from high school once. She'd be a good sport and attend the silly party at the Ruby Shores Community Center so as not to disappoint her friends. But first she'd convince them to take her to meet Storm in the park. He'd promised beer, but he had plans for later that didn't include her. He thought she should go to the after-graduation party, too.

The party was as boring as she'd expected, and the shadow was back again, lingering just beyond her peripheral vision. Her logical mind knew it concealed something with the potential to derail the future she'd always imagined for herself. If she could just keep the shadow at bay, that terrifying thing that lurked within it might dissolve away.

The shadow seemed to be getting stronger every day, threatening to consume her. Being with Storm helped; the beer and the sex meant fun and laughter and light. When she was with him, the darkness couldn't seep through to choke her.

A chaperone called out bingo numbers. Lynette struggled to take a deep breath. If she couldn't find Storm soon, the monsters might finally break free from the shadows. Her friends would be upset, but she couldn't stay.

Escaping the party wasn't hard. She had slipped into a bar next door to use their pay phone, but no one answered at Storm's house.

She'd have to save herself.

Once outside, she spied a truck that she recognized. It wasn't Storm's, but it belonged to a guy who often came to her work. He always sat in her section, ordered a large mushroom-only pizza, and seemed to do homework. She thought he was maybe a college kid, since he didn't go to her school. He'd flirted with her, and even offered her something stronger than alcohol once when she'd complained of boredom. He hadn't ever actually asked her out, but she'd sensed his interest.

It was funny. Even though most considered Storm a "bad boy" type, he was never into drugs. But if Storm wouldn't help her tonight, maybe this guy could. Maybe what he had to offer could keep the shadows away.

She wished she could remember his name as she knocked on the passenger-side window. When he motioned for her to climb in, she did, feeling independent and proud of herself for taking charge.

The air inside the cab was thick. The haze quickly reminded her of the encroaching shadows, and the first whispers of fear tickled the back of her mind. His truck was old, and she had to roll down the window by hand. She lowered it an inch to help clear the air as the guy punched the gas.

They careened away from the curb, the party, and the safety of her friends.

Exhaust from the souped-up engine left a trail of noisy pollution behind them, and she wondered why he'd been sitting there in the first place, outside of a high school graduation party. Was he a dealer, waiting to make a sale?

He passed a joint her way, and she took it, scoffing at herself. She was being ridiculous. This was Ruby Shores. He wouldn't hurt her. The image of her mom's furious boyfriend, locked in a shouting match with Storm, floated before her eyes. Only older men were truly dangerous.

She held the joint to her lips and took a few shallow, inexperienced puffs, then dissolved in a fit of coughing.

She hunched forward, eyes watering. Or were those actual tears? She'd hoped the pot would help erase her fears. He reached over to swat her on the back, but even once the choking subsided, his hand remained there. She could feel the moist heat of it.

The racing of her blood accelerated, but now pinpricks of ice, instead of the familiar fire, jabbed at her extremities.

Soon she could feel a curious mix of lethargy blanket her, quieting the pinpricks, but her gut couldn't be silenced. Two little words churned, over and over.

Get out! Get out!

She finally found that deep breath she'd sought earlier.

Think!

"Hey, thanks for the ride," she said, carefully easing her way closer to the passenger door. The added distance between them caused his hand to fall away from her back, but only for a second. He reached for her knee, and the way he squeezed and massaged her leg made Lynette feel like vomiting.

Where was Storm? Why wasn't he here to protect her?

You have to save yourself!

Why couldn't she even remember this loser's name?

"Drop me at the gas station on the corner here, will you? I need to run inside and buy some tampons. I left the party early because I got my period, but my friends are coming to get me soon."

The boy, who now looked even older than before, smirked in her direction. Had the textbooks been for show? Was he some pervert teacher from a nearby town?

"What's wrong, little girl? Not so high and mighty now, are you? I think that's a lie, and I'm calling your bluff. You're a tease, aren't you? How about if you and I head out to the lake instead? I know this perfect little picnic spot. And if you aren't hungry, we can use the picnic table for something other than food."

The hand on her knee moved higher on her thigh and squeezed tight. He was no longer groping her. He was restraining her.

How could she have been such a fool? Hadn't her encounters with creeps her mother brought home taught her anything? Those men pretended to be upstanding citizens, but they were someone else, even some*thing* else, when their masks fell away.

Think!

Then it dawned on her. She had actually learned one important thing from those disgusting men. Those types of guys always thought they were so clever, and they often underestimated girls like her.

She had to let him think he had the upper hand. She'd need to play along, instead of fighting him, and watch for a way to save herself from what she knew had quickly become a very dangerous situation.

Biting her lip to keep from cringing, she slid across the bench seat toward him. Her foot kicked something on the floor and it clanged against the door.

You can do this!

She casually draped her arm across his lap. Would he see right through her act? When her elbow brushed against his arousal, she nearly fainted with fear.

You can do this, she kept repeating in her mind.

She was back to only being able to take shallow breaths, but she focused on those, doing her best to tamp her panic down. The lights of

Ruby Shores faded behind them. This road was familiar to her. She'd traveled it countless times with her friends on trips to their favorite beach.

She knew of the picnic area overlooking it, too, and was terrified that it would all be deserted at this time of night.

The awful man turned his truck onto the old rutted path leading to the picnic area. Everything was dark beyond the reach of the headlights. The pickup bounced over the rough ground, throwing her forearm against the front of his jeans. He groaned and released her thigh to press her arm more tightly against his lap. His other hand gripped the steering wheel.

"Shit, girly, I'm going to show you what it means to be with a real man tonight," he said, a disgustingly excited quality to his voice. "I know you've been sleeping with that long-haired creep you work with. Oh . . . you tried to hide it, didn't you? But trust me. He was just a warmup for tonight."

The man's mention of Storm helped clear her mind, and she remembered something important. Storm lived on this lake with his mom and baby brother. She'd been to his house a handful of times, but only once when his mother was home. He'd introduced her as his girlfriend, but the woman had been cool toward her.

Was Storm back home yet? Probably not. When they'd met for beer at the park before the graduation party, he'd told her he was going out with buddies tonight. She'd been mad, but he'd convinced her she should spend her graduation night with her friends and he'd call her tomorrow.

Oh, why didn't I listen to him and stay at the party?! Bored *is so much better than* dead.

Would this man kill her? She knew it was possible.

Storm's house wasn't far from the beach. Less than a mile. If she could get out of this truck, she could probably find it, even at night. He'd told her once that they never locked their garage. Maybe she could hide in there, if his mom wasn't home and able to help. The woman might not like her, but surely she wouldn't refuse to help a young girl in need.

She slid forward on the seat when he slammed the brakes and threw the truck into park. She fought her gag reflex as he ground his hips against her arm, now caught between his crotch and the steering wheel.

If she let him drag her out to a picnic table, she'd never be able to fight him off.

He'd left the headlights on; moths danced in their glow. It was like he wasn't even afraid of getting caught. That was probably because they were out in the middle of nowhere. No one was going to pop up and save her, and he knew it.

As he reached for his door handle, she grabbed his hand.

"Look," she said, nodding her head toward the front of the truck. "The bugs are terrible out there. Besides, I'd much rather lie down on this soft seat in your truck than a hard, splintery picnic table."

He stared at her in the dim light cast by his dashboard, as if deciding whether he could believe her. If she was going to sell this, now would be her only chance. She released his hand and slid hers up under his shirt, caressing him. His stomach felt soft; wiry hairs covered his chest.

Storm, the only other male she'd ever touched in a similar fashion, felt so different. *He* was different. Storm would never hurt her. This man might kill her . . . but first he'd rape her. If he sensed any fear in her, he'd pounce, like the animal he was.

She forced her hand down toward his waist, where she made a show of not having enough room to wiggle her hand beneath the leather strap of his belt.

"Slide over this way so I can climb on top of you," she demanded, trying to sound breathless.

He chuckled. "That sounds even better than you underneath me." He glanced toward the picnic tables out there in the darkness, then he swiveled his head to check all around them. "Fine," he moaned, killing the engine and lights, then sliding far enough away from the steering wheel to pull her onto his lap.

It was as if the world beyond the truck windows faded into nothing. The only sound was the ticking of the engine as it cooled and the panting of the man beneath her. Her breathing came hard now, too. She'd let him think she was hot for him.

Her mind raced as he thrust his thick tongue into her mouth. It took every ounce of her willpower not to either bite it or puke. She let him kiss her while she tried desperately to think of a way out of the truck before things went any further.

She pulled her face back just enough to rest her nose against his. "I want to take my jeans off. They're in the way."

He let out a whoop and pushed her off. "About damn time," he said, tossing off his shirt and unbuckling his belt. "You've teased me for months. You finally figured out what you've been missing, didn't you?"

"I did," she said. She pulled her top off but left on her bra. Then she unzipped her jeans and made a show of wriggling them down her hips and thighs. She moaned. "They're stuck on my damn shoes."

She bent at the waist and reached for the floor under the guise of removing her shoes. Her fingers searched for and found the metal item she'd kicked earlier. It felt like a wrench of some sort, heavy and cold against her palm. Holding it tight, she kicked her jeans away so they wouldn't interfere with what had to come next.

The man beside her wasn't worried she'd try to escape now. He'd pushed his jeans down to his knees. Moonlight revealed the maniacal light in his eyes, sending a chilled dagger of fear down her spine.

She angled her body toward him and crawled back onto his lap, keeping her right hand and the only chance at escaping behind her back. She was careful not to let the tool smack against the steering wheel. The air in the cab grew thicker with heat and danger, despite her window still being down a little. A white moth had found its way inside, landing on the glass just behind her attacker's head.

She kept the wrench as far away from their bodies as possible and distracted him with her lips and tongue.

When she sensed his complete abandonment to his repulsive desires, she trailed kisses down his neck and onto his chest. The salt of his sweat reinforced her panic. She stole a look at his pasty face. His eyes were shut, his mouth slack in anticipation of what he thought was coming.

The white moth fluttered in front of his temple, as if giving her a target.

Hoping she had enough leverage, she swung the wrench at his head as hard as she could. It connected with a dull *crack*, and his head fell back against the seat. The moth landed silently on his forehead as blood began to trickle.

The man didn't try to flick it away. He never even uttered a word.

Clouds parted above the pickup truck as she scooted away from him. Stronger moonlight shone through the windshield, reflecting off the dash. It gave her just enough light to see the trickle of blood grow and ebb down the side of her attacker's face.

Was he . . . dead?

If not, she still wasn't safe. She dropped the wrench and it clanked against the steering wheel before falling to the floor. She groped around in the semidarkness for her clothes and tiny purse, then shoved the passenger door open and hopped to the ground.

Run!

But if she'd killed him, she needed to make sure she left nothing behind that could identify her. It was self-defense, but would anyone believe her? Hadn't she willingly gotten in the vehicle of a near stranger?

She dressed quickly and used the hem of her shirt to wipe the door handles on the passenger side, both inside and out. She heard a shallow, pained gasp and eased the door closed as quickly and quietly as possible.

Not dead.

At least not yet.

She turned to run toward Storm's lake house, unsure whether her shaking legs would support her, when she remembered the wrench. She couldn't leave it behind. Her fingerprints were all over it. Besides, if he woke up and came after her, he might even use it on her.

"You can do this," she said, whispering the words aloud now.

She dashed around the front of the silent hulk of the truck and pulled the driver's door open, half expecting the man to pounce on her. But despite the one moan, he hadn't moved. Maybe she'd imagined it. She found the wrench, closed the driver's door as quietly as possible, and again used her shirttail to wipe the outer handle clean.

Free.

She was almost safe. Now she just had to find her way through the darkness to Storm's house.

Something furry wove its way between her ankles, drawing a gasp out of her. Her eyes fluttered open.

The ugly truck was gone, banished back to the place where her night-mares dwelled. In the moonlight, a young girl once again stood frozen in a basin of babbling, bubbling water.

A soft meow pulled a smile from Lynette.

"Darn it, cat, you need to quit sneaking out of the house like that," she whispered.

She downed the rest of her gin and tonic, scooped up the long-legged kitten with her free hand, and held the purring pet against her thundering heart.

"Thank you for not running off again," she said. "It's like your black fur disappears in the shadows out here and I'd never find you."

The kitten rubbed her head affectionately under Lynette's chin. It tickled. Her giggle helped to dissipate the remaining negativity she'd conjured up by diving deep into one of her darkest memories.

Storm's reappearance might be the catalyst behind Lynette's justification for the gin and tonic, but she couldn't blame him for the terrifying nightmare she'd lived through on that long-ago night. Her mistakes were what led to both the attack and the accident that had come later.

She turned back toward the house, keeping a tight grip on her pet, thankful for the distraction she provided. "I suppose it's about time I named you. I think Ebony would be the perfect fit. How about you?"

The moon had continued its descent while she'd stood in the garden, lost in her long-buried memories, and it no longer illuminated the path for her. But she didn't need it. She knew her way home.

girls' trip

WHISPERING PINES

2021

Chapter Nine

LYNETTE JERKED AWAKE WHEN the car's momentum slowed.

"Morning, sleepyhead," Annie said, grinning as she flipped on her blinker. "Or should I say 'good evening'? I can't believe you slept most of the way. Were you out late on a hot date last night?"

"I wish," Lynette said. She rotated her head from side to side and rolled her shoulders to dispel the tightness in her neck. "No, no dates for me. I painted the inside of my new she-shed and stayed up way past my bedtime. I'm sorry I wasn't good company during the drive."

Annie turned onto the gravel lane that Lynette remembered would lead them straight to Renee's lodge. Keeping one hand on the steering wheel, Annie cracked open each of their windows. The fresh scent of pine wafted in, dispelling the last dregs of sleep from Lynette's mind.

"It looks and smells different in August than it did in January, doesn't it?" Lynette said.

Annie gazed at the scene beyond the windshield. "It was beautiful in winter, but this is like being plunged into the heart of a forest. Have you ever seen so many shades of green?"

Something scampered across the path in front of them. Annie dynamited the brakes. Even though they weren't going fast, Lynette had to grab the dash to keep from smacking her forehead.

"I told you not to put your shoulder belt behind your back when you were trying to get comfortable earlier," Annie said.

"Did you have to hit the brakes that hard?" Lynette rolled her eyes at her friend, then checked her throbbing finger. "Great, I split my nail."

"I'm sorry, Lynette, but I would have hated to hit that little critter. I think it was a squirrel. Hey, when did you give up the acrylics?"

Lynette tried to chew off the jagged part of her fingernail, but she'd need a clipper to do a decent job. "About the same time I gave up New York City."

Annie nodded absentmindedly, then pointed ahead toward Kit's Mustang. "Look! Jackie and Kit beat us here! They better not be having fun without us."

Given that they'd planned to be at Renee's resort for a little over two weeks, including three weekends, Lynette doubted she and Annie had missed much already. She wondered whether her friends were waiting inside the main lodge, just beyond the parking lot, or if everyone was enjoying this beautiful evening outdoors. They'd spent all of their time in the lodge during their earlier winter visit. Renee had created a delightful atmosphere inside, conducive to facilitating retreats, but Lynette was looking forward to exploring the whole resort this time.

"I guess I'm not surprised to see other vehicles in the lot," Annie said, pulling next to Kit's red vintage Mustang and cutting the engine. "I know you told her to go ahead and rent out the extra cabins."

Annie's memory was spot on. When Lynette reached out to Renee to finalize their trip plans, it was a relief to hear there was interest from other guests in renting out the extra cabins during the Kaleidoscope Girls' stay. As long as Renee saved the very best cabins for the four of them, it was nice not to have to shoulder the extra expense.

A year ago, Lynette had offered to rent out the whole resort during their stay. She'd been on a high following the lucrative sale of her business. But she wasn't feeling as flush these days. Receipt of scheduled payments from the new buyers was in jeopardy, though she had no intention of telling anyone about her money troubles.

Lynette nodded. "Last summer we still had so many questions about the pandemic. Lots of things have changed since then. Renee felt comfortable opening the resort again this spring, and since she'd refused to charge us the normal rental rates, I knew she could use the extra income. I hope you don't mind that we changed our plans a little."

The two women stepped out of the car and slammed their doors. Despite the many vehicles, no one else was nearby at the moment.

"Of course I don't mind. Unless that means Renee is going to have to work while we're here. That wouldn't be as much fun for her."

Lynette walked to the back of Annie's vehicle and rapped her knuckles on the trunk lid. "We talked about that, too. Her daughter, Julie, will be the contact for any other guests, and her sister Val is actually cooking for us. Remember how we had to email Renee a list of some of our favorite meals and breakfast items? Val was going to do the shopping beforehand, and even stock the refrigerators in our cabins."

Annie finally found her key fob in her purse and popped the trunk. "Perfect! I remember you mentioning Julie's name. We'll all throw money in for the food, right?"

"Yep! No worries."

The main lodge door opened, followed by squeals and laughter.

"The gang is all here!" Renee cried.

She rushed toward the two latest arrivals with open arms. Jackie and Kit weren't far behind. Hugs and exclamations of excitement rang out.

Kit pulled back first. "Maybe we should be a little careful. Did you all test before you came?"

"Yes, ma'am," Annie said. "We all followed your directions, Miss Scientist, and we all passed with flying colors."

"That's Mrs. Adams to you, chick," Kit replied. "And sorry, I just had to check. It's been a strange eighteen months since we were all together the last time. Reflex."

"I'm just so glad things are getting back to normal," Renee interjected, taking the heavy duffel from Lynette so she could keep pulling luggage from the trunk. "Whatever 'normal' even means these days. Hey, I have an idea. Why don't you hold off on the luggage? It's a beautiful evening. I thought you might like to take a tour of the grounds and cabins before it gets dark. The last time you were all here was the middle of winter. Things look different this time of year."

Lynette took her bag back from their hostess and tossed it in the trunk again. "I was just commenting on that to Annie on the way in—right before she slammed on the brakes and almost put my head through the windshield. I can't wait to explore!"

Annie came over and slammed her trunk, narrowly missing Lynette's head. "I told you. I didn't want to hit the squirrel."

Renee giggled. "Remind me to tell you my squirrel stories some time. Now, come on. We're wasting daylight."

Lynette congratulated herself as they roamed the grounds of Whispering Pines alongside Renee. It was hard to beat the lush beauty of Hawaii, and the sunny February warmth of their Arizona girls' trip had easily trumped the muck and slush of New York City. But this tranquil getaway would provide a much-needed balm for their pandemic-weary souls.

The beach and lake, only a short stroll from the lodge, looked so different without the heavy cloak of wind-sculpted snow and fractured ice. Lynette kicked off her sandals and let soft waves lap against her ankles. The sand's texture differed from the white sand beaches on Maui, reminding her instead of long-ago days at summer camp. When she closed her eyes, she could almost hear the chatter and laughter of their youth.

"Promise me we'll spend plenty of time out here on the beach," Kit said, bending to pick up a rock. With a flick of her wrist, she skipped the flat stone across the surface of the lake, where it bounced a handful of times before sinking.

Renee laughed. "You haven't lost your touch. And I promise you'll get as much beach time as your little heart desires. Now, come on. I'll show you the cabins."

While Lynette had glimpsed the log-sided cabins from a distance during their first visit, everything looked so much more cohesive now. The cabins blended harmoniously with the green grass, summer flowers, and leafy trees. Before, the dark cabins had looked stark, almost out of place, against their bleak surroundings.

Only the towering pines that lent the resort its name were unchanged, regal and green regardless of the season. Lynette spun in a slow circle as she walked, wondering what secrets the timeless sentinels could whisper about the antics of countless vacationers over the decades. If only the trees could talk. Had Renee's Aunt Celia planted any of the pines, or did they pre-date her, too?

She bumped into Annie, knocking her friend off the path and into a bordering flowerbed.

"What is wrong with you, Lynette?" Annie yelped, sidestepping a clump of vibrant Gerbera daisies. "Watch where you're going!"

Lynette grimaced. "I'm sorry, Annie. I wasn't watching where I was going. This place is just so beautiful!"

Annie tiptoed out of the flowers and back onto the path. She gave Lynette a playful poke in the side. "I forgive you. But only because it's such a pretty evening. Besides, you probably owed me after I almost slammed your head into the windshield earlier."

"Renee, you married Matt here, right? That must have been so pretty."

Their tour continued. Renee led them past three cabins circling a large firepit ringed with stone, then pointed down a path that led into the woods with a promise to show them her new house later. She showed them both a larger cabin and a smaller unit along the tree line, sharing various tidbits of the resort's history with her friends as they walked. After taking them back to the duplex that was tucked away on the other side of the lodge, they looped back to the firepit area.

Annie skipped up the steps of one of three small cabins closest to the resort's main firepit. "I'll take this one!"

"Are you sure?" Kit said. "It's smaller than those first two Renee showed us."

Annie shrugged. "I love campfires. If I stay in this cabin, I can sit out by the pit as late as I want without having to take a long walk in the dark when I'm ready to go to bed. Besides, I know we agreed that two of us would share that big cabin back there, but to be honest, I'm still a little traumatized by how full our house was for most of the last twelve months. I'd love to have a cute little place all to myself. If you guys don't mind, that is."

Renee held up her hands. "I already rented two of these out, but I was planning on one of you taking the third."

"Kit and I will take the big cabin," Jackie said. "There's plenty of space for both of us, and we know we room well together. After all the quarantine time, we have lots of catching up to do. And I saw the way Lynette's eyes lit up when you said there are rumors that the third cabin back there is haunted. Would you want to stay in that one, Lynette?"

Lynette was delighted with the way the sleeping arrangements were working out. "Would I want to? Absolutely! I was hoping I could be in there. Renee, isn't that the same one you sometimes rent out for bridal couples, too? Maybe I can have a little fun with some local spirits, but also absorb a little lucky romance juju. I'm on a full year dry spell at this point."

"You poor thing," Renee said. But she didn't look at all sympathetic.

"Oh, shut up. Just because you are the little wifey-poo to the sexy local sheriff and probably enjoying hot sex every night, you don't have to rub it in."

Just as Lynette was saying this, the door to the cabin next to Annie's opened and two preteen boys scampered out and past them, mortified expressions on their faces.

The women tried to hold in their laughter, but only Kit was successful. "You idiots are going to traumatize those boys!"

"They hear worse in the halls of their school every dang day. Trust me," Annie assured her as the boys jogged out of earshot. "Now, back to the topic at hand . . . How *is* the sex, Renee?"

Renee's bottom lip popped out in a pout. "Practically nonexistent. At least since May. We had to make the economically responsible decision to move Julie and Robbie back home. They weren't too happy about it either. They'd enjoyed a year of complete privacy in the two sides of the duplex."

Annie shuddered. "We just managed to kick all our kids except Relic out. Why are you bringing yours back?"

"Because I need to rent out the duplex to help keep this place going," Renee admitted. "We lost a full year of income because of the shutdowns. We've never rented out the duplex before, but we started to this summer."

"Hmm," Lynette said, gazing around the grounds. "That would explain the number of cars in the parking lot. I was struggling with the math. Even if you, Matt, and both your kids each had a car, I was only seeing three other cabins here that we aren't taking up."

Renee shrugged. "We do what we have to, right? Even if that means sacrificing passionate sex with the spouse for the summer months."

"There's always the beach, when everyone else is asleep," Kit suggested, earning herself a high-five from Lynette. "And yes, I admit Dean and I have had to get more creative, too, with a teenager in the house."

Footsteps behind them announced more campers, and they exchanged pleasantries with a young couple that wove around them and went into the third cabin by the firepit.

Lynette sighed. "They're going to have cabin sex. I just know it."

Renee shushed her.

"What? Fine. Enough talk about sex. It's depressing, anyhow. It may be eight at night, but I'm hot. Do you have anything cold to drink?"

Lynette hated how their joking around about sex brought to mind the tattoo she'd spied on Storm's inner arm. She had yet to mention it, or Storm, to her friends.

"I sure do," Renee said. "In fact, Val put together a yummy charcuterie board to welcome all of you. There's a tall pitcher of tea in the fridge, too, and chilled wine. It's all in the lodge. I'd have had you over to the house, but Matt is working a late shift tonight, so he might still be sleeping. And Robbie's been home all day, so the kitchen is probably a mess."

Lynette looped her arm through Renee's, turning her toward the lodge. "Stop apologizing, Renee. This is supposed to be vacation time for you, too. I know that might be easier said than done, but let's at least try."

Renee matched her steps and the rest of the Kaleidoscope Girls fell in line behind them. When their hostess dropped her head to Lynette's shoulder, a powerful wave of well-being made her squeeze her old friend's arm. She was glad she'd kept in contact with Renee over the years, even if it was sporadic. They would all have lost out if Renee wasn't still in their lives.

"The resort grounds look beautiful," Lynette said.

Renee raised her head and patted Lynette's arm. "Thank you. I will pass your compliment on to my son. Robbie worked hard out here this year, keeping everything top-notch. It's important that we get people back into the habit of renting from us every year. Repeat customers are our mainstay."

"As they are for almost every business."

"Except for the business my middle kid is in," Annie chimed in from behind them.

Lynette released Renee's arm and turned to face Annie, walking sideways. "Is Colton back to work at the funeral home, then?"

"He is. Careful, Lynette. We aren't as nimble as we used to be. When I walked backward like that on Camelback, I darn near broke my neck."

With a laugh, Lynette saluted her friend and spun around to face forward. "I suppose repeat customers aren't exactly a thing for funeral homes."

"Knock it off, guys," Jackie said, reaching around them for the door into the lodge's kitchen. "I'm so done with talk of death and dying. We've all had to endure too much of that over the past year and a half. You'll ruin my appetite. And if Renee's sister is as good at making meat and cheese trays as she is at baking those delicious granola bars of hers, we are in for a treat."

Renee held the door so Jackie and the rest of them could file into the lodge. "Trust me, Val is a wizard in the kitchen. She'll fatten all of us up over the next two weeks."

Inside, the kitchen was brightly lit but empty.

"She's not here?" Lynette asked. She was looking forward to meeting this talented sister.

"Nope," Renee said. "She still has four boys at home, so she got as much ready this afternoon as possible. We're all set for the weekend, and she plans to come back out on Monday."

"Her kids aren't back in school, though. Will she bring them, too?" Annie asked.

"I sure hope not. They're good boys, but they are boys. The oldest is not quite sixteen and her baby is ten. Not a baby anymore, I guess, but that little Jake of hers is something else. My dad was feeling brave and offered to help Val out with them on and off over the next couple of weeks. Her husband, Luke, works during the week."

Jackie opened one of the many upper cabinets and started pulling out dishes. It surprised Lynette to see how comfortable she looked in the lodge's kitchen. "Jackie, did you sneak in here and work during that

January retreat we came to a couple of years back?"

She laughed. "No. We were getting things out for our snacks when you two arrived. That retreat was three solid days of pampering. Sneaking into a kitchen to work wasn't even on my radar."

The five women worked to set out the tasty-looking treats Val had prepared. The group's time together in Maui and then Arizona had helped them each claim their areas of expertise, or lack of, in the kitchen.

"Fill a plate, pour a drink, and let's head up to the library. There's a window air-conditioning unit up there. I turned it on a couple hours ago," Renee said.

Fifteen minutes later, all five women relaxed on the comfortable chairs and sofas in Renee's library. Empty plates littered the tabletops in front of or beside them as they sipped at their refreshments.

"If I lived out here, I'm not sure I'd ever leave this room," Lynette declared, wriggling even deeper into the cozy chair she'd claimed. "This room has the same vibe I'm going for in my little she-shed, actually, though a fireplace isn't really in the cards. I wish I had pictures for you, but I haven't made as much progress on it as I'd hoped."

Annie laughed. "Aren't there, like, four fireplaces *inside* your house?"

"Five, actually," Lynette clarified, raising her nearly empty glass of sweetened tea in a toast. "But who's counting?" She winked.

Jackie set her empty wineglass on the table at her elbow. "Why would anyone need five fireplaces in a single-family home, no matter how big it is?"

"Minnesota winters can get cold," Kit offered.

"Don't remind me!" Jackie said. Her words trailed off in a yawn. She checked her watch. "I don't know about the rest of you, but I'm exhausted. I know it isn't even nine yet, but we have two full weeks of fun ahead of us. Would it offend anyone if we called it an early night?"

Lynette almost protested. She wasn't one bit tired. But then she remembered she'd stolen an hour of sleep on the way to Whispering Pines. Besides, she was excited to check out the cabin she'd be calling home. She gathered her plate and glass and followed her more agreeable friends out of the room.

Renee moved to close the library door but paused. "I should turn off the air. Give me a minute, will you?"

Everyone held up. Kit wandered over to a full wall of photographs.

Lynette didn't remember them from her time upstairs during the winter retreat. "Those weren't here before, were they?"

Jackie shook her head. "I remember there being some old framed pictures downstairs, just inside the front door to the lodge. But I don't think they're still there."

Renee returned, closing the library door, and caught up with Kit in front of the wall of framed photographs. "This display is new. Well, it was new that summer after you guys were all here. There were so many neat old pictures hanging down there, but it was always so dark and hard to see them. Then one fell and I cut my foot on the broken glass. That sucked, but the stitches were the push we needed to move them all up here. Plus, we added a bunch of new ones. There's a lot of Whispering Pines history on this wall. We didn't hang all the old ones back up, but the extras are in a new photo album on one of the library shelves."

The more vintage photographs interested Lynette the most. They reminded her of the bridal pictures she and her mom had discovered in the wooden box from the shed. "Are all these old black-and-white shots of your relatives, Renee?"

"Most of the really old ones are of the resort's earliest guests. As far as relatives go, it would pretty much just be Celia in the older ones."

"The infamous Celia?" Lynette asked, even more intrigued.

"The one and only. Here is one of my favorites of her," Renee said, pointing to a picture of a woman with an old-fashioned hairdo, smiling into the camera.

"She was pretty," Annie whispered.

"She was, but she was so much more than that, too. I'll tell you all about her life around the fire over a bottle of wine one of these evenings. At least what I know of it, that is. She led a fascinating life."

Lynette started at the top left corner of the large display and let her eye travel along the rows of framed photographs. "I like the way you've paired old and new shots of similar composition. This outdoor wedding shot has to be from the forties, given the women's dresses and the men's suits. Wait, is this colored picture from *your* wedding, Renee? You positively glowed!"

Renee grinned. "It was definitely one of the best days of my life."

"Wow," Kit said, pointing at another of the older pictures. "Check out the classic Ford in this one."

Jackie laughed and accused Kit of a lack of appreciation for any kind of romance.

She shrugged. "What can I say? I'm a car girl. Here, I'm going to snap a picture of this and send it to Dean and Isaac. They can tell me the make and year of it. Wait, you don't suppose anyone tucked the car away under a dusty old tarp here at the resort somewhere, do you?"

Renee moved over to Kit's side again and gazed at the picture. "Unfortunately, no. That would be worth a pretty penny these days, wouldn't it? That girl is Celia. The other three must be friends of hers. I wonder how old they were when this was taken."

Jackie motioned toward another of the older framed pictures. "Here are the same group of girls, splashing in the water along the beach. Check out those swimsuits! Forties again, Lynette?"

Lynette nodded. "Right around there. Maybe they were college age. Didn't most women only go to college back then to find a husband?"

Renee grunted. "Probably, but not Celia. She never married. I didn't get the impression that she felt like she'd missed out by not having a husband, either. But I guess I never came right out and asked her that."

"Life is simpler without a husband," Lynette said.

"It sure was," Kit laughed, raising her left hand. Her diamond wedding ring twinkled in the fading sunlight that still seeped through the large windows overlooking the lake. "But I don't regret giving up 'simple.' "

The women quieted but didn't immediately move away from the wall of pictures.

"Is this my cabin?" Lynette asked, pointing to two framed pictures, side by side. One was black and white; the exterior looked shabby. The other was a newer, colored photograph; there was snow on the ground.

"For the next two weeks," Renee confirmed.

"Is that *blood* in the snow in front of it?" Annie asked, moving to stand closer to the framed picture.

"Would it help amp up the whole 'haunted' bit if I said it was?" Renee said with wide eyes. Then she laughed. "I think you might need new contacts, Annie. Those are rose petals. We went all out decorating it for my sister and her husband a few years ago."

"Val?"

"No, Jess. She married her new husband, Seth, in a holiday ceremony. I worried they'd get cold out here in December, but they stayed warm."

Lynette raised both arms high. "Stop right there! No more talk about sex!"

Everyone laughed.

"I like all these modern shots, too, Renee," Jackie said, still perusing the wall. But then she yawned. "Man, I'm going to fall asleep on my feet."

Renee clucked her tongue. "All right, ladies, I'm calling it. Let's go put the food back in the fridge and you can all get settled in for the night. We can help you with your bags, Annie and Lynette, since we interrupted your unpacking when you first got here. Is everyone still fine with making it an early night?"

Lynette thought about her quiet little cabin on the edge of the woods and the mysterious events that Renee had hinted at. Yes, she was ready to go explore it on her own. Was there any truth to the rumors, or was it simply a product of years of speculation, enhanced to tease apprehensive campers with good old-fashioned ghost stories?

She'd keep an open mind. And who knew? Maybe it would be her turn by the end of their stay to infuse the cabin's checkered history with even more mystery.

Chapter Ten

L YNETTE WOKE TO SOMEONE banging on her cabin door, but she refused to open her eyes. Had she gotten even two hours of sleep?

"Lynette, are you in there? Come on! We're having breakfast on the beach!"

She rolled onto her stomach and smashed her pillow over her head. "Shut up, Jackie! You'll wake the dead."

The knocking continued.

"Grr . . . fine," Lynette moaned as she tossed her pillow to the floor and pushed into a sitting position on the bed.

As she allowed her eyes to drift open, she surveyed her bedroom through wild, steel-gray curls. Light washed across the floor. She hadn't bothered to close the curtains the night before, since her bedroom window faced the woods.

The outer door crashed open. Her head swung toward the noise in time to see the door rebound against the kitchen wall.

"Oops," Jackie giggled. She stepped inside, a wicker basket in her left hand.

Lynette flopped back onto the bed, eyes closed again. The top of her head grazed the headboard, but not hard enough to hurt. "I locked that door. How did you get it open?"

Footsteps skipped toward her. "Renee told me where she stashed a hide-a-key."

Lynette fumbled around for her second pillow, intent on muffling her friend's screeching voice, but came up empty-handed.

"I see you kicked your pillows off." Jackie dropped onto the bed and stretched out next to her.

"You aren't going to let me go back to sleep, are you?"

"Of course not. Get up," Jackie insisted. "This is the first day of our vacation and we're going to make the most of it."

Lynette felt a hand pat her thigh, and she knocked it away. "You know you're a pain in the butt, right?"

The weight next to her disappeared, and a pillow smacked her in the face. "But you love me, anyway."

The sound of a drawer sliding open brought her back to sitting. "Get out of my stuff!"

"Hush," Jackie said. "Aren't you Little Miss Tidy? Clothes put away already and everything. My rooms are a mess. It's already heating up outside. It'll get hot. Since we're eating on the beach, do you want shorts or capris?"

"What I want is to brush my teeth, use the bathroom, and drink some coffee. Must we dive right into the day?"

Jackie tossed underwear and a pair of denim shorts her way, then held up an orange T-shirt. " 'We are the granddaughters of the witches you couldn't burn,' " she read aloud. "A little early for your fall wardrobe, but this will do."

Lynette caught the shirt when Jackie tossed it, too. "I saw it online and thought it was cute," she grumbled, then crawled out of bed with a sigh.

"You'll have to be sure to wear that on Halloween when you hand out candy. It'll make the kids think twice about you."

Lynette snagged a hair tie from the bedside table, along with the rest of the clothes Jackie had thrown at her, and shuffled past the irritating woman for the bathroom.

"Get out. I need ten minutes."

She could hear the dresser drawer slide shut in the bedroom, and then Jackie followed her into the main room of the cabin. "You have five. And if you're late, we won't save you any coffee."

It was the perfect thing to say to get Lynette moving.

Old friends always knew how to motivate each other.

More than five minutes later, but less than ten, Lynette sauntered onto the beach, her cheap flip-flops kicking up sand. Her four friends were already there, laughing and shoving pastries into their mouths.

"We are *not* going to have an early roll call every single morning," she warned, wagging a finger at them as she joined the group on the sand.

"Good morning, sunshine!" Renee smiled up at her. "Sleep well?"

"Don't get me started." Lynette plopped onto one of two wool blankets spread out on the sand and eyed the thermos in Renee's hand. "There better be coffee in that."

Renee handed it to her, along with a paper coffee cup. "No worries. We have plenty."

She shot Jackie a look as she poured herself a cup, then took a large gulp of the black, steaming liquid. After the sting of the heat passed, Lynette let her head fall back, inhaling deeply. The earthy scent reminded her of the wet morning back home when she'd started on the old garden shed, except here the fragrance was even bolder. A pelican flew in a graceful arc, high above them.

"I'm feeling better."

Jackie laughed. "Good. For a minute there, I was afraid I'd woke a hungry bear instead of my friend. Why are you so tired? We all turned in early last night."

Lynette took another big swig of coffee, then reached into a nearby sack and pulled out a soft, gooey Long John. Peanut sprinkles rained onto her lap. "I couldn't sleep. I swear, the edge of the horizon was turning gold before I finally dozed off."

Kit removed a round donut with white frosting from the bag.

Annie gasped. "Does that have jelly in it?"

"Sure does," Kit said, handing it to the other woman. "You can have it. Jelly-filled aren't my favorite. Besides, I already ate one donut. I probably don't need another."

After accepting the sugar bomb, Annie turned to Lynette. "Did those ghosts Renee mentioned keep you up?"

Lynette snorted. "The opposite. I was hoping to hear something, or at least *sense* it, but all I heard were animal noises coming from the woods behind me."

The pastry only made it halfway to Annie's mouth. "Animal noises? What kind of animal noises? Like bears?"

They all laughed as Annie swiveled on the blanket to stare into the heavy tree line behind them.

Renee poured herself some coffee. "The occasional bear does wander into this area, but we've only had one cause any trouble. Somebody didn't latch the cover on the dumpster behind the lodge and a bear knocked it open. What a mess! We didn't actually *see* the bear, but it left plenty of evidence behind."

"Are they dangerous?" Annie asked. A thin line of frosting arced across her upper lip.

After screwing the top back on the thermos, Renee shrugged. "They are wild animals, so yeah, they can be dangerous. Just be smart and don't leave food or garbage lying around. If you're really worried, I think I have some bear spray in my office in the front of the lodge. You can carry it in your pocket. But I never bother."

Annie still looked doubtful as she finished off the rest of her donut. Red jelly smeared her fingertips.

"The totem pole looks perfect mounted there where your sidewalk runs into the beach, Renee," Kit said, nodding toward a carved wooden post. "Mine is still sitting on our front patio at home. Isaac swears it wards off evil spirits and germs. When none of us got sick during quarantine, he said it confirmed his theory. Aren't you glad you brought one back from Maui?"

Renee pulled her knees to her chest and allowed her coffee cup to dangle from her fingertips. "*So* glad. I think of that trip almost every time I walk past it now. That was a wonderful vacation. I only hope you have half as much fun here as we did in Hawaii and Arizona."

Lynette caught a wistfulness in her tone. "You aren't seriously worried that we won't enjoy ourselves here, are you? This place is a little slice of paradise! Look how calm the water is out there. It's like glass. And I loved that we could just drive here. Still not comfortable with the idea of climbing back into an airplane yet, but I'll get over it."

"That surprises me," Jackie said, dumping the cold dregs of her coffee into the sand. "You've traveled all over the world, Lynette."

"A lot has changed during the past two years," she replied.

Even more had changed than her four friends would guess, but she wouldn't get into that and risk ruining this peaceful Saturday morning. Her discontent might not be real if she didn't put it into words. She'd been so sure she'd love living in their big, beautiful home in Ruby Shores, but her confidence in that was slipping away. She was lonesome, bored, and she didn't even want to allow her mind to puzzle over her potential financial concerns if the sale ultimately fell apart.

A slight breeze ruffled the once smooth surface of the lake, as if her thoughts stirred the surrounding energy. She noticed a loon far out on the water. But a blur of movement shifted her gaze to the left, where two brightly colored butterflies danced above the picnic basket.

"Oh look, butterflies!" Jackie said.

Lynette was happy to have her thoughts interrupted. The fluttering insects reminded her of a similar picnic in their recent past, though that was beside a different lake and the sun had been higher and hotter. She jumped to her feet and waved her arms up and down, like wings. "Ladies! What does this remind you of?"

Annie grinned, wiping her sticky fingers on a paper napkin. "Summer camp?"

Laughing, Lynette dropped her arms. "Well, kind of. I was thinking about our picnic lunch we had, out on Owen's old summer camp land, the weekend of our class reunion."

Jackie nodded. "Except that was a white butterfly and wine instead of monarchs and coffee, but yeah, I see the similarities. I also remember how all of you were pushing me to chase my dream of building something of my own after I missed out on that promotion."

Kit sighed. "And to think I was still hemming and hawing about marrying Dean back then. What was I so afraid of?"

Lynette laughed. "Marriage. The very idea still terrifies me, but I'm glad you don't feel like you made a mistake. I also remember how we all dove into the water, intent on finding us some of those diamonds.

Remember Counselor Wendy telling us about the diamonds in the falls when we were kids? I'd like to point out that we have, in fact, found our own diamonds at this point." She raised her wrist and jiggled her diamond tennis bracelet, then pointed at the ring fingers of Kit, Annie, and Renee, plus the diamond studs in Jackie's ears.

"We've come a long way, baby," Jackie said, showing off her earlobes.

Renee looked a little lost. Then Lynette remembered she wasn't at their reunion weekend. "I'm sorry, Renee, I forget you weren't at our reunion. But you must remember Wendy and the diamonds?"

Renee nodded. "Don't worry about it. I understand that the four of you have more history together. Besides, you'll probably get sick of hearing me talk about all my old memories of out here, too. So I apologize in advance if I bore you. But there is just something special about this place. I hope you feel that, too. Something that makes the good times even more memorable."

Lynette sat back down on the blanket, then reached over to grab hold of Renee's ankle. "Hey, girl. What do I always say?"

Renee frowned. "Just say 'thank you' . . . ?"

This pulled a giggle out of Lynette. "Well, yeah, I say that all the time, but that wasn't what I meant. *Stop apologizing.* That was something I noticed in my business. Women have this annoying habit of always saying we're sorry. Men don't do that. We need to stop. Except for when it actually needs saying. But not for every little thing."

"Fine," Renee said, making a hand motion as if locking her lips closed. "In that case, I'm going to share so many of my fun old memories over these next two weeks, and no matter how sick you get of hearing about them, I will not apologize."

The other women all assured her they'd love to hear more.

"Where should I start?" Renee asked.

Lynette gazed around. "Start with this beach. What are some of your happiest early memories of hanging out down here? You used to come here as a kid, too, right?"

"I sure did," Renee said, grinning. "There are so many memories, I wouldn't know where to start. But, let's see . . . All right, do you remember that colored picture of a little kid's sand bucket on the wall in the lodge? We didn't talk about it, but maybe you noticed it."

Lynette didn't remember, but both Jackie and Annie nodded.

"I finally threw the rusty old thing out last year. It had sat on a shelf in the office since the eighties. But after I cut my foot on some broken glass only a few feet outside my office, I removed all hazardous items from the area."

"What's the story behind the bucket, then?" Kit prodded.

Lynette always loved the way Kit could keep their conversations on track.

"You wouldn't believe it."

"Try me, Renee," Lynette said. She believed most things.

"Fine. But there are ghosts involved."

She rubbed her palms together. "Perfect."

Renee laughed. "Well, during our first summer vacation at Whispering Pines, we spent most of our time down here on the beach. I was ten. That means Ethan, my big brother, was eleven. I remember how mad he was that he had to miss his baseball tournament back home to come to Aunt Celia's resort. Jess would have been about eight, and Val was a bratty five-year-old."

Lynette reached for the thermos again. This wasn't feeling like a quick conversation. "Where do the ghosts come in?"

"You're going to have to wait for it, and I'm not going to apologize," she said with a wink. "I can't remember the exact order of events, but I think I fell in love for the first time in my life the same day we found that bucket."

Annie pulled her sweatshirt off. The temperature was continuing to climb. "Keep talking," she said, tossing the garment to the side.

Renee didn't need further encouragement. "There was another boy out here that summer. He was traveling with his grandparents. No brothers or sisters. He was Ethan's age, and they started hanging out and fishing together. He was *so* cute. Man, I haven't thought about him in years. I wonder what ever happened to him . . ."

"He's probably bald with three ex-wives and a beer belly that would interfere with your sexual pleasure," Kit offered, maintaining a deadpan expression.

That stopped Renee cold. Then she laughed. "If that's the case, I'll keep Matt."

"I'd keep Matt regardless," Jackie teased.

The conversation brought forth memories of Storm again for Lynette. It was probably the "bald" comment. Or maybe it was the mention of falling in love for the first time. The man in Owen's backyard was much bigger than the Storm of her youth, and his handsome black hair had disappeared, but he certainly wasn't rocking a beer belly. Was he divorced? Or married? She had no idea. It was going to be tough to keep her recent encounter with Storm to herself. Her friends would eat the story up if she shared how she ran into him.

Renee was talking again, and she tried to pay attention to what she was saying. Her friend still hadn't gotten to the ghost part yet.

"Sorry, that sent us off on a tangent," Renee said. Then she gasped and covered her mouth when she realized she'd apologized again. "The boy's name was Brandon, and he's part of the story. If I remember right, we were building sandcastles down here. Of course, Ethan had to turn it into a competition. When we were kids, everything had to be a competition. I think it was his way of trying to assert some dominance, since his sisters outnumbered him," she said. "Now, let me get back to the bucket. I think it was Jess who dug it up. It was buried right over there, and it was obviously old, so it had to have been under the sand for a long time. At the beginning of that vacation, an old guy who worked for Aunt Celia had told us that there were two little ghost boys that have roamed around out here for years, causing all kinds of mischief. And get this . . . he'd specifically said they liked to steal toys and bury them in the sand!"

Kit squished her face up in obvious disbelief. "He probably buried the bucket to mess with you."

Renee spread her hands out, palms up. "Maybe. But I like to believe it was the ghost boys. Their names are Albert and Arthur."

"The ghosts have names?" Annie said. She didn't look as doubtful as Kit. "You say that like they're still haunting the resort."

"They are." Renee winked. "Actually, legend has it that the boys got lost in the woods around here years and years ago. They found their bodies in a cave. Now, the spirits of the little imps still hang around here, causing trouble."

Annie shook her head. "I bet the bears got them."

Jackie shoved her in the shoulder, laughing. "Oh, stop. The bears aren't going to get you. Go on, Renee."

Renee laughed. "Let's see, what came next? Sand caked the bucket, so I guess we brushed at it with our hands. I remember it was a hot and windy day. Some of the sand got into Val's eyes." Renee gazed out over the lake, lost in her memories. "She screamed and bawled, sending both Mom and Aunt Celia running to help. They carried her up to either the lodge or our cabin—I can't remember which. As they were running across the grass with her, Mom yelled back at us to stay out of the water."

Annie took another peek into the white pastry bag but, not finding anything tempting enough, rolled the top back down on it. "Let me guess. You didn't listen."

Renee shrugged. "I can tell you work with kids. You're partially right. *I* listened, and so did Jess, but Ethan didn't. Then again, I guess he didn't feel like he had a choice."

"Why not?" Lynette asked. She was still hoping to hear more about the ghost boys, but she was becoming invested despite herself.

"I'm getting there. Be patient. Cute Brandon was fishing out on the dock." She pointed at the old wooden dock that jutted into the water off to their right.

Lynette was confused. "I thought he was building sandcastles with you."

"No, but he was close by," Renee clarified. "Not long after those three disappeared to get the sand out of Val's eyes, Brandon started yelling something. Turns out one of our plastic blowup rafts had blown into the water. I can still see it, the bright pink of it, bobbing on the waves out there."

Lynette followed Renee's finger with her eyes. "Your brother went out to grab it?"

"He did, even though we were yelling at him to stay out of the water. I wasn't too worried about what Mom would say about him going in. She was pretty distracted and much more worried about Val than the rest of us, but I didn't want to disappoint Celia. As a kid, I always wanted to impress her. But Ethan didn't listen. He waded out into the water. Problem was, it was windy, like I said, and he couldn't move as fast as the raft. He eventually caught it, but he'd reached deep water by then, and it didn't take us long to realize that he was struggling to get back. The waves were really high way out. This is a big lake, and it can be deceiving. Remember that if you take any of the boats out while you're here."

"How did he get back? Did you all get in trouble?" Kit asked as she slid her sunglasses off the top of her head onto her nose.

"Brandon saved the day," Renee said, a wide grin making her look like a kid again. "And he had my heart. He jumped in, swam out to Ethan despite the now obvious danger, and helped him get back to shore. He'd captured my undying love . . . until he had to go home early when he broke his leg. But before that, once he'd rescued Ethan from the lake, I suppose the two of them felt invincible. They snuck into the woods later that week, even though the grownups had warned them to never go into the trees without an adult. Believe it or not, we think they found that cave where Arthur and Albert supposedly died. The idiots stood on top of it. Brandon fell in and hurt himself, and it was Ethan's turn to save him. Aunt Celia was so flustered, waiting for them to be found. Honestly, I think that was the most upset I remember ever seeing her."

Lynette considered this. "She probably didn't want to double the number of ghost boys roaming around out here."

"Right!" Renee said, motioning at her with both hands. "I never thought about it like that. Wouldn't *that* have just ruined this place for everyone? Seriously though, Celia never would have forgiven herself if something happened to Ethan out here."

When she paused in her storytelling to catch a breath, the haunting call of the loon, far out on the water, filled the silence.

The sound provided the perfect backdrop to Renee's story. Lynette could feel her own grin widen.

Maybe a few mystical spirits actually do still roam the woods around Whispering Pines, after all. I'll have to consult the tarot cards about the ghost boys.

Chapter Eleven

BY THE AFTERNOON OF Lynette's second full day of vacation, she could begin to feel the stress of the past few months melt away beneath the hot sunshine. Spending the previous day on the beach and around the resort with her dearest friends was providing a balm: a soothing and easing of her troubled mind.

The heat must have worn her out, too, because she had enjoyed her first good night's sleep of eight solid hours in a long time. She had woken feeling well rested and ready for another relaxing day outside. The old saying that laughter was the best medicine was true. And today was shaping up to be just as beneficial to her troubled soul.

Jackie, on the other hand, seemed to be experiencing a different kind of day. Instead of relaxing like the rest of them in one of the two canoes, she was determined to master the art of paddleboarding.

As Lynette watched Jackie struggle with the board, she sensed her friend was going in the minute the woman's feet tipped the board ever so slightly to the right. The universe loves balance, so Jackie's body tried to compensate with a dip to the left. The seesawing motion escalated quickly, ending in a graceless splash into the previously calm waters between the two canoes.

Lynette let out a bark of laughter.

Kit smirked. "Gravity wins again."

"I warned you to keep that beast as flat as possible," Renee said to a spluttering Jackie. "It isn't very forgiving."

"You don't say," Jackie spat out.

Lynette watched as her dripping-wet friend attempted to hoist herself back up onto the blue fiberglass board, but it was too tippy. The dock they'd launched their mini–boat parade from looked toy-sized. They'd floated out farther than she'd realized while Annie shared funny stories about her granddaughter's monkey-like climbing adventures.

"Maybe little Nora could show you how to climb back onto that thing," Kit suggested from her front seat in the other canoe. Renee sat behind her, having insisted she was the best one suited to steer the heavier old boat.

Jackie flipped Kit off for the less-than-helpful comment, which subsequently threw the poor woman off balance again, and in she went, all the way under the water.

Lynette took pity on her and used her oar to guide the lighter-weight, newer canoe over to Jackie's side. Annie didn't seem inclined to help from her position in the back, but it wasn't hard to maneuver it alone.

"Matt sure gave you a nice birthday present here, Renee," Lynette said, appreciating the ease with which she could single-handedly propel the red canoe forward. "Here, Jackie, grab my hand. It's too deep out here. You aren't going to drown with a life jacket on, but I don't think you're going to be able to climb back up on that board. I'll help you crawl in here instead."

Lynette felt her canoe tip back and forth, much as Jackie's board had a minute earlier. "Sit down, Annie! Are you trying to send both of us into the water, too?"

"Me?! If you try to haul Jackie into this canoe, we're going over for sure!"

Lynette stuck her hand down near Jackie's head but glanced toward Renee for assurance that this was the best course of action. Renee lifted her oar out of the water and placed it across her lap. Kit followed suit behind her, a marginally concerned expression wiping the grin off her face.

"This is exactly why I leave paddleboarding for the kids," Renee said. "They can scramble on and off that thing, no problem. Me? Not so much. Just be careful, Lynette. Jackie is probably strong enough to climb into your canoe with some help, but Annie's right. You could tip."

Jackie slapped Lynette's hand away, let go of the paddleboard with her other hand, and lunged for the side of the newer canoe. Annie dropped to her butt with a shriek while Lynette grabbed hold of both sides of the canoe, doing her best to counteract Jackie's weight.

There was a second or two when it felt like Lynette was fighting a losing battle, but it was their lucky day. Jackie hadn't mastered the paddleboard, but when she hooked her right leg over the edge of the canoe, she was strong enough to haul herself up and in. She landed on the bottom of the canoe in a spreading puddle of water, right between Annie and Lynette.

Annie hollered again as she lunged for the beach bag she'd brought along. "Jackie, you're going to soak our snacks!"

Jackie's answering grunt told Lynette the woman couldn't care less about food right now. She struggled to sit up, then sighed in frustration when Renee yelled to grab the paddleboard before it floated away.

Lynette retrieved her oar from the bottom of their canoe where she'd dropped it while trying to hold the boat steady. She fumbled it as she swung it over the side of the canoe, and it slid through her hands. Something on the shaft caught on a ring and pulled it right off her finger. Both the ring and the oar plunged into the lake and out of sight.

It was Lynette's turn to shriek.

"What now?" Kit asked, shaking her head at them from across the expanse of water between the two canoes.

The oar popped back to the surface. Lynette scrambled to retrieve it, careful not to send their boat rocking again. Holding her breath, she prayed that whatever her ring had snagged on still held her sentimental piece of jewelry against the oar shaft.

It did not.

"Oh no!" she spit out.

The ring was gone.

"Don't worry about the paddleboard, Lynette. This boat is heavier, but I can still move fast enough to catch it," Renee said, using the oar in her hand to push the other canoe toward the board as it floated away.

"It's not the *board* I'm worried about!"

The canoe rocked underneath her again as Jackie tried to get situated. "What's wrong, Lynette? Did you hurt your hand? Is that why you dropped the oar? Things got a little crazy there for a minute."

Lynette held up her hand for Jackie. Her reddened ring finger throbbed. The unyielding silver—pulled off so abruptly—left a mark. Tears gathered deep in her throat and her eyes stung. "My hand will be fine. But my ring . . . it's gone."

She couldn't quell a hiccup.

"Which ring was it?" Jackie asked, wiggling closer so she could better see Lynette's naked finger.

"Jackie, I'm not going to tell you again—sit still!"

Even Lynette had to grin at Annie's tone, despite the pain in both her finger and heart.

"Aye aye, captain!" Jackie said. "Or should I say Captain Granny? Jeez, if you yell like that at your granddaughter to sit still, she must be terrified of you!"

There was much laughter, but Lynette sobered quickly.

"My ring. It somehow caught on the oar and it fell off. Into the lake. I'll never find it now."

"Was it a special ring?" Renee yelled, still trying to retrieve her floating paddleboard.

Lynette sighed. "It was. My mom has a matching one. We both put them on years ago, when she got so sick with cancer. We'd met with a holy woman who blessed them shortly after the diagnosis. They were meant to help support healing. I feel terrible about losing it. I haven't taken it off in years. Maybe the sunscreen I put on before we got out on the lake seeped under it. What will Mom think? What if her cancer comes back now?"

Renee and Kit had reached the paddleboard and hauled it up onto their canoe. Once it was more or less secured, Kit swiveled to look at Lynette again. "Oh, honey, you know that isn't the way things work. Your mom will be fine. She *is* fine. Whether you take that ring off has absolutely no bearing on her health. Intellectually, you know that."

"Spoken like a true scientist," Jackie said. She didn't sound like she found Kit's assurances any more helpful than Lynette did.

Lynette knew her friends didn't believe in things like spiritual blessings and good luck charms. At least not in the way she always had. But she was too upset to try to convince them otherwise. "I hope you're right, Kit. Renee, your kids don't scuba dive, do they? I'd pay them good money to come out here and look for my ring."

She thought Renee looked sympathetic when their gazes met across the water, but her friend shook her head. "The water is extremely deep out this far, Lynette. None of us have scuba diving equipment, but I had guests a few years back who tried going out to explore around the lake bottom near the resort. They reported back that it gets super murky where the water's deep. I'm afraid that ring is gone forever. What if you had another one made to look just like the old one? If you've worn it that long, surely you have pictures of it? Your mom would never have to know."

Lynette considered Renee's suggestion. Getting a new ring made to look like the old one might work, and maybe Donna would never have to know, but *she* knew. It wouldn't be the same. She'd lost the talisman she'd been convinced had helped keep her mother healthy.

Not that her friends would understand.

She nodded back to Renee. "Maybe. We'll see. But any chance we could head back to shore now? My finger hurts. Ice might help."

In reality, her heart was hurting more than her finger, but it sounded like a good excuse to get off the water. She wasn't having fun anymore.

By later that afternoon, Lynette had made a decision. Despite losing her special ring, she wasn't going to pout. It would be a waste of this precious time with her friends.

When mosquitoes threatened to ruin their beautiful day outside, Renee invited them over to her screened-in patio for wine and crackers. It reminded Lynette of the porch at her own house that Donna loved so much.

Matt wasn't home. Even though his shift wasn't supposed to start until later, as the county's sheriff his help had been needed for a possible drowning at a nearby lake. Lynette shivered when Renee explained where her husband had disappeared to. Her overactive imagination pictured her lost ring, floating down to settle on the chest of a drowning victim.

"Maybe I *will* have a little of that wine," she said, hopeful that one glass would help banish the terrifying image from her mind.

Both Renee and Annie looked surprised.

"I thought you said you didn't plan to drink anything stronger than lemonade on this trip," Annie said. "I hate that even one cocktail can give you a migraine these days."

Renee pulled the wine bottle out of the silver ice bucket. "If you're sure you want some . . ."

Lynette was sure.

The migraine story was one she'd used to fend off offers of alcohol. She purposefully ignored the tiny voice in the back of her mind, warning her it was a bad idea to take another chance.

Isn't this how it always starts? With just one?

As far as she knew, Renee was the only one of her friends who knew she'd spent a month, years ago, in a rehab facility. She didn't consider herself an alcoholic; it had just been a dark period, right around the time it seemed that her mother's cancer treatments weren't going to be enough to save her. But Lynette had learned the tools to pull herself back from the edge, and Donna beat cancer.

It wasn't like she hadn't had any alcohol in the years since. She could handle a drink now and then.

Maybe her refusal to treat herself to a cocktail once in a while was part of the reason she found life in Ruby Shores so boring. Meeting a man for drinks in New York City or participating in a toast to celebrate a major milestone in her old business used to be fun. Just because Wyatt, the man she'd dated longer than most, told her alcohol turned her into a shrew, it wasn't reason enough to give up the fun altogether.

As she took the first tart sip of the wine Renee handed her, she remembered how impressed her friends had been when she'd shown up to their class reunion weekend with Wyatt. The girls had only seen what was on the surface. Sure, he was younger and had a sexy way about him, but they didn't know how deeply he'd hurt her when he walked away—not once, but twice.

Intent on keeping thoughts of yet another ruined relationship at bay, she downed half of her wine. Then she remembered Wyatt's pictures from their reunion weekend. She set her glass down and jumped to her feet.

Both Annie and Renee looked at her in surprise.

"I'll be right back," she said. She ran into Kit and Jackie on her way out. "I'll be right back," she repeated, hurrying to her cabin.

The girls were going to love those pictures.

Five minutes later, she rushed back onto the porch with a large envelope. The conversation she'd interrupted ended abruptly, as if they might have been talking about her.

They stared as she waved the envelope in the air before again reaching for her wineglass. She emptied it in one big gulp, pretending not to notice how guilty they looked. A glow was already washing through her veins after that first glass of wine.

"I brought you all a present," she said, ripping open the envelope to pull out a small stack of five-by-seven photographs. "Do you guys remember when Wyatt took these?"

Curiosity replaced the concern on a couple of their upturned faces.

Renee looked confused. "Wyatt?"

Lynette paused. "Oh, that's right. You never met Wyatt. I brought him home for our class reunion. Annie took us out on her pontoon that weekend. Wyatt is a photographer, and he got some cute shots of us. I forgot all about them until I was unpacking some old boxes last week. Yes, I admit, I'm still not completely unpacked, even though we moved a year ago."

"Actually, I think I remember you mentioning him when we were in Hawaii," Renee said. She pulled a second wine bottle out of the bucket and refilled Lynette's glass.

"You are the perfect hostess, Renee. I'm only sorry I don't have any pictures for you."

Renee sank onto the empty wicker rocker. "Don't worry about it. I know I'm not quite the full-fledged Kaleidoscope Girl that the rest of you are."

Jackie, who was sitting on the end of the sofa closest to Renee, reached over and gave their hostess a side hug. "That is ridiculous, Renee. You are a Kaleidoscope Girl, through and through."

"Yes, you are," Lynette said, and she meant it. Renee was a loyal friend. Unlike Wyatt who had turned out not to be.

She handed two prints to each of the other three women who'd been on the pontoon that day. They laughed all over again, remembering the fun they'd had that weekend. Even Renee seemed to enjoy herself.

Lynette took a sip from her wineglass, then raised it in a toast. She gave a little whistle to snag their attention. "Here's to spending time with the four best women on Earth. We've all made it through some difficult times, and we have the scars to show for it, but we are always better when we're together. This is like summer camp all over again. But for adults. With wine."

They met her toast with cheers and laughter, and as she looked from friend to friend, she hoped this was the beginning of a new, better chapter in her own life.

Chapter Twelve

Renee glanced out the kitchen window at the sound of tires on the gravel drive. She always felt a thrill of relief when her husband returned home from a shift. She had thought she understood what she was signing up for when she married a man in law enforcement, but the worry was even more constant than she'd expected.

She dropped her pen onto the notepaper that sported her long grocery list and poured a hot cup of coffee for Matt. He'd need it.

After tightening her robe, she stepped outside to meet him. The early morning dew tickled her bare feet. Birds twittered, announcing a new day.

"Aren't you a sight for sore eyes," Matt said. "But I might be even more relieved to see that steaming cup of coffee in your hands than your beautiful face."

Renee handed him the mug, noting that his eyes actually looked sore. His haggard expression matched the news she already knew was coming. "I'm sorry the rescue wasn't successful."

He took a long drink of coffee before responding. He grimaced at the heat of it, then sighed. "You already heard, huh? I thought they were going to keep it out of the press until they could notify his family. The guy was from out east somewhere. We're still trying to piece together what happened."

Nodding, Renee threaded her arm through her husband's, nudging him toward the house. "There are no secrets anymore. I saw a post on social media. Do you want some breakfast? I could make eggs."

He shook his head, then drained the rest of his coffee and handed the empty mug back to her before opening the door into their kitchen. "I'm not hungry. I just need sleep. It would be even better if you'd come back to bed and snuggle in beside me. You know I always sleep better with you there. What are you doing up already? It's barely six."

Renee released his arm and preceded him into the house. "As tempting as that sounds, I'm afraid I have too much to do. Val is waiting for my list of what we want to eat this week before she can go to the grocery store. She had us well stocked with meals for this past weekend, but not for the full two weeks of the girls' visit."

She sat back down to her list. After pouring himself a glass of orange juice, Matt wandered back to stand behind her. He rested a hand on her shoulder while he drained the glass, then dropped a kiss on the top of her head. After a tough day—or in this case, night—at work, he was often more affectionate. She knew the horrors he witnessed from time to time helped him appreciate what he had to come home to.

He must have glanced at her list, because he snorted and squeezed her shoulder. "This is what I was afraid of. I know you were excited to have your friends stay here, but does it even feel like a vacation to you? And didn't you say it's your turn to plan next year's trip? When do *you* get to relax?"

She patted his hand on her shoulder. "I don't mind. It feels good to have people around here again. I just hope they're having fun."

He squeezed her again, then stepped away and pulled his shirt out of his waistband. She watched as he unbuttoned his shirt, and when he caught her looking, he wriggled his eyebrows at her. His grin eased some of the exhaustion from his features. It wasn't hard to read his mind.

Laughing, she took one last look at her list and pushed it away. "The kids are both still asleep."

Matt shrugged. "We've kind of mastered the art of keeping quiet."

"Not really. Besides, you just said all you wanted to do was sleep. I know that look. You aren't thinking about sleep anymore."

He reached for both of her hands and eased her up out of her chair. "Oh, I still need to sleep. But first, I just want to enjoy the thrill of being alive for a few minutes. You wouldn't deny me that, would you?"

She allowed him to pull her close and slipped her hands under the white V-neck tank he always wore under his uniform, running her fingers up his flat abdomen. "Val is going to be mad at me if I don't get her that list by seven. She wanted to run to the store before her boys get up and Luke has to leave for work."

He pulled her close and nuzzled her neck, coaxing a giggle from her. "Stop," she whispered. "That tickles! You're acting like a newlywed."

"I think four years still qualifies for newlywed status. Don't you?" He rested his forehead against hers and breathed deeply. "You smell so good. Come back to the bedroom with me for just a little while. Please?"

As if she could deny him when he asked like that. But her cell phone in the pocket of her robe vibrated with a text.

He must have felt it, too. "Val can wait. Oh, that reminds me. George called me this morning."

She pulled her face back a few inches. "He already called this morning? But it's so early. Why is my dad bothering you at the crack of dawn?"

Matt chuckled. "He wasn't bothering me. He knows my night shifts usually end around six. He was just checking to see if I'd be home later this afternoon. Said something about unloading a trailer and he could use some help. He knows you're busy with company."

She took two steps back, and her husband's hands fell away. Mention of one's parents was a surefire buzzkill. "Unloading a trailer? Of what? I don't know anything about that."

But Matt wasn't to be dissuaded. He caught her hand and turned them toward their bedroom. "I don't know either, and right now I don't care. I'll be here to help, but only if I get some rest. To do that, I need you to come back and sing me a lullaby."

She laughed. "A lullaby, huh? Is that what we're calling it these days?" But she allowed him to pull her out of the kitchen. Then she stopped. "I better lock the kitchen door. God knows my friends wouldn't think twice about walking in here looking for some early morning coffee."

Matt released her and finished pulling off his uniform top. "Good point. I love those ladies, but right now you are the only one I want to see. Don't be long."

Renee hurried back to the door and flipped the lock. She took a quick peek out the window. They had built their house back in the trees, but they kept a path clear so she could see a bit of the resort from here. All looked quiet.

She sometimes felt like an outsider when hanging out with her friends, given how much better the other four knew each other, but she always felt right at home in her husband's arms.

"I think it's so sweet that the two of you still act like newlyweds," Kit said between bites of her chef salad. "Dean doesn't even look at me like that anymore, and we haven't reached our two-year anniversary."

Renee smiled, remembering her earlier conversation with Matt. "What do you mean? We're hardly newlyweds. It's been four years already since we got married."

"That's not what it looked like this morning."

She set her iced tea down. "This morning?" She heard Annie giggle and swiveled her gaze to her left. *Busted.* "Were you spying on us this morning? I *told* Matt it was a good idea to lock the door!"

Kit slapped the table and pointed at Jackie and Lynette. "See? We told you so!"

"I just thought you were trying to make me feel even worse about my romantic dry spell," Lynette said, jabbing a fork in Kit's direction.

Renee's confusion morphed into frustration. "Do you four want to let me in on your little secret? I'm feeling left out again."

The second the words left her mouth, Renee regretted them.

The smile fell from Lynette's face. "You feel left out? Oh, honey, we never want you to feel like that. You're one of us. You know that. The five Kaleidoscope Girls, forever!"

"Never mind," she murmured.

Why did she have to open her big mouth? She'd tossed and turned with worry over Matt most of the night. Sometimes she said things she regretted when she was tired.

But Lynette wasn't one to let something go. She set down her fork and reached across the table toward her.

Renee hated the flush she could feel creeping up her neck. "No, seriously. Forget I even said that. Come on. This is supposed to be a fun day for shopping and lunch. Did I show you the shoes Jackie and I found when you two were in the bookstore?"

Lynette wriggled her fingers at her. She wasn't to be deterred.

Now Renee worried she might have hurt all their feelings. She sighed, placing her hand reluctantly in Lynette's.

"Look, Renee," the other woman said, clasping her fingers tightly. "You are every bit as important to me as these three are, and I know they feel the same way. Just because you didn't go to high school with us doesn't diminish the importance of our history together. And how much we mean to each other now, as grown-ass adults."

Annie and Jackie nodded and layered their hands on top of Renee's and Lynette's.

Only Kit hung back. Always the more practical and straight-talking of the five, she shook her head. "I am so sorry, Renee. I was just teasing. We weren't spying on you. You told us you get up early when Matt works a night shift so you can make sure he gets home all right, and we needed coffee. We were going to come steal a cup from you before he got home. But then we saw you step outside in your robe when he drove up. We remembered he'd left early last night to go help at a possible drowning, so we hightailed it out of there to give you privacy. Regardless of how that rescue turned out, he obviously had a long night. You looked so welcoming toward him, and we didn't want to interfere. That's all I meant by my earlier comment."

She sounded sincere, and Renee didn't want to cast any shadows over their day. She eased her hand out from under the others', dismissing the whole discussion. She decided to diffuse the tension with humor. "And here I was, worried that you saw him rip my robe off the second we reached the kitchen. The poor man can hardly keep his hands off me."

Annie covered her ears, pretending she didn't want to hear. "Don't rub it in," she cried.

"Fine," Lynette said as everyone's laughter died down. She was the last to pull her hand back. "I'll forget what you said about feeling left out, but only if you share a little more about your love life with your sexy sheriff husband."

Renee grinned. "The only way I'd even consider doing that is around a campfire, when the shadows hide my blushing cheeks—and with plenty of wine involved."

Jackie raised her glass of soda, as if in a toast. "I'm sure we could arrange that."

Later, in the clothing boutique at the end of Main, Renee's cell phone chimed. Everyone was still laughing at Annie in the chunky ivory sweater that she was trying on. Its knit sleeves reached her knees. Renee glanced at her screen, then dropped the phone back into her purse.

"I'm sorry to break this up, ladies, but Matt just sent a text. My folks and sister are at the resort, and they could use a little help. We should get back."

They'd all piled into Renee's vehicle for their day of shopping, so they wrapped things up at the boutique and climbed back into the car. When she pulled into the lodge's parking lot thirty minutes later, a pickup sat off to the side with a construction trailer hooked to the back. The trailer bore her brother's company logo. The back cargo door was down and a half-dozen sizable boxes crowded around the end of it.

She spied a family playing on the beach, but no one else was in sight.

"Is that them?" Jackie asked, pointing toward the truck and trailer.

"Yep. That's Dad's pickup and Ethan's trailer, but I don't know what could be in all those boxes." She parked and turned off the vehicle. "Matt said Dad needed help to unload something this afternoon. Let's go see what's going on. Maybe they're all in the lodge."

The five headed inside. They found Renee's sister Val and her mother, Lavonne, in the back kitchen, but neither Matt nor her dad.

After a round of introductions and hugs, Renee opened the refrigerator.

"Don't worry, I got everything you asked for," Val assured her. "Even though you were late sending me your grocery list this morning."

"Imagine that," Annie mumbled.

Renee rolled her eyes and Jackie, Kit, and Lynette all grinned. Val and Lavonne kept pulling food out of the bags of groceries strewn across the massive kitchen island.

"You're keeping track of your receipts so we can reimburse you, right?" Kit asked.

Renee wondered if Kit still felt bad for upsetting her earlier and was now trying to make it up to her by steering the conversation away from anything that might embarrass her in front of her family.

"You bet I am," Val said with a nod. "I have four boys between the ages of ten and sixteen at home. School starts next month. I can't afford to foot your grocery bill, too."

Kit wagged her head. "I can't imagine *four* of them. I have one and, I swear, our cupboards are bare the next day after we grocery shop. I have two younger brothers, but I never realized how hard it must have been for our grandparents to keep enough food in the house."

Lavonne looked curious at Kit's comments, and Renee realized her own mother didn't know Kit's history. She'd fill her in later.

"Mom, thanks for helping Val with the food. We really appreciate it. But I'm dying to know what the deal is with those boxes and the whole trailer thing. What gives?"

The older woman folded the last of the empty paper grocery bags and carried a whole pile of them over to the large recycling bin in the corner. "What gives is a little surprise. Val, can you get the rest of this? I'd like to take the girls out back and find your father. He and Matt might need some help, too."

"Sure, go."

Renee nodded appreciatively to her little sister and followed Lavonne out the lodge's back door. She spied her father and husband near the firepit, working on something. Whatever it was looked red, but she couldn't make out anything else. "Are they building something?"

Lavonne grinned back at her, but kept walking. A quick peek over her shoulder told Renee that her friends were following along behind, also looking curious. Unable to wait any longer, Renee skipped ahead.

Matt was holding what looked like the bottom half of a chair. Her father was bent over him with a ratchet.

"What are you guys doing?" she yelled before she'd reached them.

George straightened at the sound of his daughter's voice, a hand going to his lower back. "Well, hello, kiddo. We were wondering if you'd get back in time to help."

She glanced between her father, her husband, and what she could now see was indeed the bottom half of a chair. It was one of those heavy-duty, Adirondack styles—the kind she'd been wanting for the resort, but she could never justify the cost. Meeting Matt's eyes, which thankfully didn't look as tired since he'd gotten some sleep, she smiled.

"Did you get these for me?"

Matt straightened. The chair base remained in one piece, so they must have been working on it for a while. "No. I had no idea, other than George saying he needed a hand this afternoon, like I told you earlier. This is all his doing."

Lavonne cleared her throat as she reached Renee's side. "To be clear, it's technically not *his* doing. It's Celia's."

"Celia's?" Kit repeated as Renee's friends joined them.

"As in your famous *Aunt Celia*?" Lynette asked.

George tossed the ratchet onto the dirt at his feet and eased himself down onto the grass. "I need to rest a minute. And as far as Celia goes, I think my big sister was more *infamous* than famous, but yeah, she's behind this."

Renee really needed to get to bed earlier tonight. She kept feeling like she was out of the loop today. "Celia?" she repeated.

"You better explain, Dad," Val said, surprising them all with her appearance. "What? The food is all put away, and I didn't want to miss this."

George smiled. "I'll explain, but why doesn't everyone have a seat before I get a kink in my neck from looking up at all of you? Sorry we don't have the chairs put together for you yet, but the grass is dry."

"If I get down there, I'll never get up again," Renee's mother said. "My knee doesn't bend like that anymore. I'll stand. Go on, George."

While everyone else settled on the grass, Matt jogged to the side of Annie's cabin. He returned with a collapsible chair and opened it for his mother-in-law.

"I want one of those," Lynette said, watching him wistfully.

"The chair?"

Lynette laughed. "No, the man, Renee. Not yours, of course. I'll find my own."

"You wanted red, right, Renee?" George said, pulling everyone's attention back.

"Red? Well, yes, I've been drooling over red Adirondack chairs online for quite some time, Dad. But how could you possibly know that? And what does Celia have to do with these chairs mysteriously showing up today?"

Val snorted. "We *all* knew you wanted them. You mention it often enough. But you were too cheap to buy them for the resort."

"Not too cheap. I was just trying to be an *astute* business woman, Val. The woman Celia expected me to be."

A few snickered at the bickering sisters.

"Dad?" Renee said, needing an explanation.

George nodded. He bent one knee up and rested an arm across it, looking uncomfortable. "Maybe the ground wasn't such a good idea. I'll be brief. Renee, I want you to know that I'm confident Celia would be proud of everything you've accomplished out here at Whispering Pines. You not only brought it back from the brink of ruin, you have made it even more than a family destination by incorporating your off-season retreats into your business plan. Celia would certainly have loved that idea."

"So she sent me new red chairs from the grave? Come on, Dad, what gives?"

He shook his head. "Renee, sometimes you're as impatient as she used to be. I'm getting to it. Now, you've done great things out here with the gift Celia left you. Your two sisters and your brother are making the most of their inheritances, too. But we've never talked much about how your mother and I are trying to maximize the gifts Celia left to us."

Renee gasped. "Wow. You're right, Dad. I guess I just kind of assumed that if Celia left you and Mom anything, and maybe Uncle Gerry and Aunt Letty, you were choosing to keep those details private."

"And you'd be right, dear," Lavonne said. "We don't plan to get into details now, either. For heaven's sake, George, get to the point."

"I would if all of you women would stop interrupting me."

Val laughed. She didn't look as confused as Renee felt. Maybe she already knew the story.

"Part of my inheritance from Celia included a few certificates of deposit," George explained. "My sister probably thought that, given our age, relatively risk-free investments would be best for us. Anyhow, a certificate was coming due, and instead of reinvesting it right now, we decided to cash it in and put it to good use. Because, as we all know, we can't take it with us."

Renee hated it when her beloved father made off-hand comments about his mortality. As if sensing her unease, he gave her a wistful smile.

"Did you decide to split the proceeds four ways?" Renee asked. It seemed the most logical path.

"That would be the fairest," Annie chimed in.

"And life's always fair, right, Annie?" Lynette said. But her expression suggested to Renee that her friend didn't believe a word of it.

George shrugged. "No, it wasn't a huge sum of money, and splitting it four ways would make it less impactful. There will be additional money in the future, and your mother and I will decide who might benefit from it most. Right now, we think that person is you, Renee."

Renee wasn't comfortable with his thought process. "Matt and I are doing fine, Dad. Yes, things are tighter out here after losing a full year of income last year, but things are looking much better this summer."

"Can I try to explain our rationale, George?" Lavonne asked, looking between her husband and Renee.

"Go for it."

Her mother took a deep breath. "While dear Celia left Whispering Pines to you, Renee, no one can deny that we *all* benefit from your work to get it up and running again. This place has become a peaceful getaway for the whole family. You seldom let us pay to stay out here, which is kind of you, but it doesn't help keep the lights on. Your father and I wanted to figure out some way to help support you. We don't need the money personally. I guess you could say we want to keep Celia's legacy going strong. She was one of the most generous women I've ever known, and we can keep that generosity flowing. A dozen new chairs isn't an earth-shattering gift, but they will spruce things up out here."

She paused to look around, then continued. "We thought maybe you could split them up, with six down on the beach and six around the firepit, but you can divvy them up however you choose. Now do you understand why we said they are actually from Celia?"

A wave of gratitude washed through Renee. "I understand perfectly. This is all very generous of you. And Celia. I love how you are keeping her legacy alive."

"She deserves nothing less," George said.

Lynette, who was sitting next to Renee, lay back to stretch out on the grass. "Skip what I said a few minutes ago about wanting a helpful man in my life. I want to be like Celia, and like both of you, Lavonne and George. I want to give. I want to do big and little things that make a difference."

Jackie raised a hand. "Me, too!"

Annie stood back up. "I think our age is showing, friends. Because all of this talk about leaving a legacy is resonating with me, as well."

Kit held a hand out to Annie. "Help me up. Let's get these chairs built first, then we can figure out ways the Kaleidoscope Girls can save the world."

Renee laughed. "I love your practicality, Kit."

"And I'd love to relax in these amazing chairs around the fire tonight while you make all of us jealous with tales of your red-hot sex life, Renee," Kit said.

Renee ducked her head, embarrassed, and Val groaned.

"On that note, I am out of here," her youngest sister said. "I have a dinner to prepare, and the last thing I want to listen to is disgusting stories about my big sister's sex life."

Renee felt a strong arm around her waist, and she buried her face against her husband's chest. "I swear, Matt, I never agreed to disclose anything private around the fire tonight!"

She felt him laugh. "Honey, you are almost as red as your new chairs. But relax. I know you'd never share anything with your besties that would make them feel so jealous and inadequate."

"Stop!" Renee heard Lynette yell. "No more sex talk!"

Everyone laughed, and Renee was reminded that while she might question whether she was a true part of the Kaleidoscope Girls, she never had to worry about her relationship with her husband. He'd never allow anything to come between the two of them.

CHAPTER THIRTEEN

D ONNA PUSHED HER CUP away. "If I drink any more coffee, I'll float away. I can't believe we've talked for two hours. Charlotte, you probably had other things you needed to do today other than sitting here, jibber-jabbering with me."

The woman across from her grinned. "Honestly, Donna, now that poor Glen is in the memory care unit, I can afford this luxury. But you're right. I do need to pick up a few groceries, and both Hoover and Nikki will have to go outside before too long."

Charlotte reached for her purse, but Donna quickly nabbed their ticket. "My treat. You drove, I'll pay. Hoover and Nikki?"

"Thank you, dear. You don't need to buy my coffee, but I appreciate it." Charlotte grinned. "Ah, yes, Hoover and Nikki. The dynamic duo. Nikki is Jackie's border collie. I'm puppy-sitting for her while our daughters are off on their girls' trip. And Hoover is the little dog Glen brought home a few years back, after a friend of his died suddenly and there was no one else to take her. She's a quarter of Nikki's size, but she more than makes up for it in attitude. I don't know what I'd do without her. Do you have any pets?"

Donna shrugged, setting her small handbag next to their empty coffee cups. "No, but I surprised Lynette with a cat recently. I'd have been happy to watch Ebony, too, while Lynette is off with her friends, but she arranged for Annie Pierce's son, Relic, to take care of the cat during the two weeks that she'll be away, since he's already mowing our grass. She must not trust me to look after Ebony. Which is ironic since the little stinker snuck out on her last week."

Charlotte shook her head. "Don't you hate it when your kid treats you like a feeble-minded old woman?"

"With a vengeance. But we better get going, or those dogs will make a mess on your carpet. We hate to prove our children right." Donna stood and looped her handbag over her shoulder. She waved their ticket at Charlotte. "We should do this again sometime. Even two hours wasn't enough time to catch up."

"Maybe Patsy was on to something when she suggested we form our own little girls' club, just like our daughters did when they were kids."

Donna glanced back at the woman for a second, careful not to bump into a table on her way to the register at the front of the café. "I agree. Maybe we could even crash their little reunion at that lake resort. I hate to miss Lynette's birthday. It'll be the first time I'm not with her to celebrate."

Charlotte caught up to her as she handed the ticket to the hostess. "You can't be serious! Lynette is fifty years old. You two have never been apart for her birthday?"

Charlotte's surprise reminded Donna just how lucky she was to have a relationship with her grown daughter that most mothers only dream of. "Fifty-one, but that's right. This will be a first."

Charlotte slowed and pulled to the curb in front of the stately old house that Donna and Lynette called home. As Donna opened the passenger-side door, she spied a young man jogging around the north corner of the house.

"There's Annie's youngest now," Charlotte said. "Donna, I've always admired this house, but I've never been inside. We'd have loved to buy in this neighborhood, but we could never afford it on a principal's salary. What is this style of architecture called?"

"Um, I believe the proper term is 'American Foursquare.' At least that's what the handyman Lynette hired to help us with the crushingly long list of projects around here told us. Give me a minute, Charlotte," she said, managing to climb out of the front seat without grunting, and slammed the door behind her. "Is everything all right, Relic? You look upset."

Relic slid to a stop, still near the house, and pointed to the phone at his ear. She hadn't realized he was talking to someone. She overheard him tell someone to hurry, then he stuffed the phone away and jogged across the lawn toward her.

"Hey, Mrs. Howe. Am I happy to see you!"

Donna opened her mouth to correct him, but snapped it shut just as quickly. She'd been no one's wife, ever, but the boy wouldn't care. "What is it? Are you having trouble starting the lawnmower? Lynette mentioned the starter might need to be replaced, but I don't think she's gotten around to it yet."

He shook his head. "It's too wet to mow. I stopped by to change the kitty litter and check the house. Dad told me to be sure to go down into the basement, given all the rain we've gotten. Good thing I did. Did you know there's at least a couple inches of standing water down there?"

Donna gasped. "In the basement? Obviously I didn't know there was water down there, child! Do you think I'd be out for coffee if I knew there was water down there?"

Relic took a step back.

A steadying hand dropped onto her shoulder. "Hello, Relic. I don't know if you remember me, but I'm Jackie's mom, Charlotte. Jackie is one of your mom's good friends?"

Realizing Relic was only trying to help, Donna inhaled deeply. "I'm sorry. I didn't mean to yell," she apologized. "You better show me. Thank you, Charlotte. We'll take it from here. I know you need to get going."

"Don't be silly, Donna. I'm not leaving you with a mess on your hands. The dogs will be fine for another hour, and I can buy groceries tomorrow." She turned her attention back to Relic. "Lead the way, young man."

He nodded and turned back to the house. "I just called my dad. He's on his way over to help, too."

Donna had to hurry to keep up with him. "It's Tuesday afternoon. Isn't Henry at work?"

Relic nodded and reached for the door. "Yeah, but he said he could come anyway. I didn't think I should tackle this by myself."

Donna didn't like the sound of that. The new sump pump must have failed.

The second Relic yanked the door open, a bundle of black fur streaked past them into the spent peony bushes lining the house's foundation.

"Grab the cat!" Donna screamed.

Charlotte launched into action. Despite her ivory linen slacks, the woman dove in, sending stems and leaves rustling. Brown petals fluttered to the ground. One loud meow followed two quick grunts, then nothing.

Donna glanced frantically between a shocked Relic and Charlotte's hunched back. It was all she could see of the woman in the bushes.

Then came a cackle. "I got you, you little minx," Charlotte laughed, a note of triumph in her words. "I have her by her collar, but if you two don't give me a little help here, she might try to scratch my eyes out!"

"Grab the crate," Donna said, pointing at the portable cat transporter just inside the door.

Relic moved fast, but by the time he got to Charlotte, she'd straightened, ducking her head from side to side. It wasn't the cat's claws she was trying to avoid, but her tongue.

"Aren't you a sweet little thing," she cooed, petting the cat's long black fur. "What's your name?"

Relic dropped the small crate onto the grass, shaking his head at the pet Lynette had hired him to watch in her absence. "Ebony. You know, because her fur is so black? I think Lynette should have gotten to know her better before giving her a name. *Licorice* would have suited her better. She licks everything."

"Thanks for catching her, Charlotte," Donna said. She sighed with relief. "You surprised me. I don't think I could have moved like that."

Charlotte grinned as she handed the cat to Relic. "My little Hoover likes to sneak out once in a while, too. Let's just say Ebony here isn't the first animal I've had to snag from the bushes. Now, let's go check that basement."

———— ❦ ————

"We're going to need more than buckets and rags to clean this up," Relic's father said. "Do you ladies have a Shop-Vac around here?"

Donna sighed. She knew Henry was right, but they didn't own one. The basement had three inches of standing water in it. Thankfully, Lynette had noticed a dampness on the basement floor when they'd first moved in, so they'd decided not to keep much down here. Instead, they'd used the attic for storage.

She'd need to walk down to their neighbor Owen's house, a block over, to see if he was home so she could borrow his. *Again.*

This was yet another example of why she missed her old life in New York City. When you lived in an apartment in a high rise, water in a basement was never your concern.

"I'm sorry, Henry. We don't. But we've borrowed one from our neighbor before, and he told us we could use it anytime. I'll walk over there to talk to him. Lynette has his phone number, but I don't."

"I'll come with you. If we can catch him, I'll carry it back. Shop-Vacs are clunky," Henry said. "Relic, go out to the garage and see if you can find a big broom. Maybe even a squeegee."

Donna scanned the mess again. "Do you think I should call Lynette?"

Henry considered it, then shook his head. "It'll just ruin the trip for her. Relic and I can help you clean this up. I'm glad you don't store much down here. Do you use that washer and dryer over there?"

"No. The previous owners installed a new set in what used to be a butler's pantry, off the kitchen."

"That's good," Henry said. Donna could feel him looking more closely at her. "This isn't as bad as it looks, Donna. Don't worry."

She straightened her spine. He was right. They could handle this. Lynette needed a break from household disasters.

Footsteps above reminded her that Charlotte was still upstairs, probably looking for the flashlight she'd sent her after just before Henry arrived. "Come on then," she said, trudging back up the stairs. "Relic, if you find the items your father asked for before we get back, run upstairs and grab a pile of towels from the linen closet, too, please. The ones on the lowest shelf are meant to be used as rags."

In the kitchen, she discovered Ebony, sitting on the chair that Lynette normally used, keeping an eye on the chaos. Charlotte was rooting around in the broom closet.

"Charlotte, we have to run over to see if we can borrow our neighbor's Shop-Vac to suck up that water. Why don't you go on home now? These two gentlemen will help me take care of this."

Her friend glanced at her wristwatch, then ran her hands down the front of her pants. "I probably should do that. But promise me you'll call if I can be of any help. And I expect a tour of this place the next time I come over. From what little I've seen, it's as lovely as I'd imagined."

Donna took a deep breath. "I promise. Thanks again for the fun afternoon. We'll get together again soon, I promise."

Donna covered the block between their home and her friendly neighbor's as quickly as her seventy-two-year-old knees would allow. She hated to keep Henry away from his work any longer than necessary, though he'd assured her it wasn't a problem.

When she turned into the driveway, Henry stopped. "Wait. Isn't this Owen Jameson's place?"

She nodded, not surprised that Henry would know Owen. Lynette had told her they'd all been friends when they were kids. But then she remembered Henry didn't grow up around here. "How do you know Owen?"

"I don't know him well, but I visited with him at Kit and Dean's wedding. You know how those ladies can take forever when they start gabbing. We talked fishing after everyone else was gone, while we waited for the bride and her tribe to wrap things up."

Donna laughed. "Sounds about right." Unfortunately, she'd missed Kit's wedding. "Those girls sure can talk."

The whine of a saw cut into their conversation and Donna spied two vehicles up ahead in the driveway. "Good. Looks like we might have caught Owen at home."

"Sounds like someone is working out back," Henry said as they walked toward Owen's house. He let out a low whistle when they came abreast of a shiny pickup truck. "Damn, nice truck. Owen's?"

She laughed again. She knew nothing about trucks, but she had to agree. It was *pretty*. "I have no idea. I've never seen it before."

Donna stopped to catch her breath. A man shouted something out back, followed by the sound of hammering.

Henry noticed her fatigue. "Stay here. I'll go see if it's him back there."

She didn't argue. Her right knee felt like someone was stabbing it with an ice pick. "If you don't mind."

The quick smile he shot her told her he didn't, and he hurried around the corner, out of sight, much as his son had done when Donna first arrived home from her coffee date.

She turned her attention back to the handsome vehicle Henry had admired. Out-of-state plates, so it probably wasn't Owen's. Maybe it belonged to one of his two boys. If she remembered right, one was a young doctor. She wasn't sure what the other did for a living. How much did a pickup truck like this even cost? Probably two or three times more than the Mini Cooper she'd splurged on. Her imagination took flight, dreaming up possible professions of someone that could afford a vehicle like that.

"Donna, I hear you have a little water problem over at the house."

She spun toward the voice, disoriented for the briefest of moments when pulled so abruptly from her thoughts.

Owen strode toward her, a friendly smile on his face.

She noticed, again, what a handsome man he was. Why was it that some men got more attractive with age? She had even mentioned Owen to Lynette, to which her daughter only laughed, making some comment about his heart belonging to another. Donna assumed she was referring to Jackie, his old high school crush, and let it go. Her daughter was never receptive to her dating advice. Not that she could remember Lynette going out on a single date since they'd been back in Ruby Shores.

Henry and another man followed behind Owen.

"I don't know that I'd call it a *little* problem, but Henry was kind enough to come over to help. I didn't realize that the two of you know each other."

Owen nodded. "Met him at that wedding your daughter and her friends talked me into letting them hold out on my land by the lake. Hard to believe that was almost two years ago now." He turned toward Henry. "You ever follow up with that other guy about the fishing? Because we are having zero luck around here lately. What the heck was his name?

Renee's husband, I mean."

"Matt," Henry supplied. "And no, but it's funny you should ask. Just last month I asked Annie to get his phone number for me from Renee, and she did, but then I forgot to give him a call."

Donna noticed the other man was hanging back a bit. He wore dark sunglasses and a baseball hat pulled low. He was a large man, standing with legs apart and thick arms crossed over his chest. Owen wore a tank top, but the mystery man was in long sleeves, despite the August heat. While he didn't fit the image of the wealthy investment banker Donna had conjured in her mind, her gut told her he was the owner of the fancy pickup truck.

Then she remembered Henry needed to get back to work, so she got down to business. "Any chance we can borrow that Shop-Vac of yours again, Owen? I hate to be a bother, but . . ."

Owen waved away her words. "You aren't a bother, Donna. That's what neighbors are for. All those years of city life must have made you forget that. Stay right here and I'll go grab it."

The man Owen hadn't bothered to introduce held up one hand. "We can just drive my truck over. I've got an industrial-sized vacuum in the box already. I bought it to do some work out at my lake place."

"Even better," Owen said. "Let's go."

"I certainly don't expect all of you to help with the water," Donna protested. "I was just hoping to borrow your tools."

Owen stepped around her and opened the back passenger door of the snazzy truck. "What kind of people would we be if we left all the hard work to you? Besides, we just finished up on my new deck and pergola out back and we were about to break for a beer. Got any cold beer in your fridge over there?"

Donna tried to remember if she had anything at the house to offer these men. Lynette didn't like to keep much alcohol in the house and never drank beer, but Donna thought she might have picked up a case of it for the crew that fixed their roof earlier in the summer. Hopefully there were a few cans left.

"If I don't have beer, there might be a bottle of red wine in the cupboard."

The unnamed man shivered at her mention of wine.

Her primary concern at the moment was that Owen appeared to expect her to climb into the backseat of the monstrous truck. There were no running boards, and the odds of her gracefully reaching the seat were about zilch.

As if he'd realized Donna's dilemma over climbing onto the backseat by herself, the owner of the truck gave Owen a light shove to move him out of the way, then placed one arm behind Donna's back and the other at her knees. He scooped her up and deposited her on the black leather seat as if she weighed nothing at all.

"Th . . . thank you," she stuttered, to which he simply grunted and slammed the door.

"Let's go," she heard him say to Owen and Henry.

Within two minutes, they were pulling into her driveway. The men talked fishing during the short drive over, and Donna noticed the driver was finally taking part in the conversation.

Before she could worry about how she'd get out of the truck without doing a face plant, Owen opened her door and offered her a hand down. "Can't let him show me up," he said with a wink.

This Shop-Vac was much larger than the one they'd previously borrowed from Owen, and within an hour, mere shadows of moisture remained on the basement floor.

The three men, plus Relic, joined Donna at the kitchen table. Ebony snubbed them when Relic set her on the floor, sashaying out of the room as if she had better things to do.

"Are you twenty-one yet?" Donna asked as she held a beer in Relic's direction.

"Close enough?" he suggested, glancing between her and his father.

"He was a big help," Donna said to Henry. "I don't mind if you don't."

"Fine," Henry conceded.

The driver of the pickup and supplier of the handy-sized vacuum crumpled his beer can and burped. Relic giggled.

"Jesus, Taran, did you inhale that thing? And where are your manners?" Owen chided.

Donna wondered again about the man Owen had finally introduced while they worked down in her basement, but she didn't want to prod. One rude individual at the table was enough.

She could have sworn the man's cheeks reddened at Owen's reprimand. One side of his mouth twitched up in a grin. "Sorry, ma'am. Been a while since I enjoyed a refreshment in the presence of a lady."

She somehow doubted he'd ever spent much time around *ladies*, but he hadn't really offended her. Taran had been a big help. Before she could tell him she forgave him for his rudeness, he spoke again.

"Actually, Jameson, you aren't the first person to *scold* me for belching in this kitchen."

"You've been here before?" Donna asked, surprised. "Do you know my Lynette?"

The man took his dark glasses from where they hung from the neck of his shirt and slipped them back on before answering. "I was just a kid. Doubt I was even ten. The old lady who lived here used to feed me chocolate chip cookies and lemonade. I think I shoved a half a dozen of those delicacies down my throat at a time. I knew better than to burp at the table—my momma raised me right—but it slipped out. And do you know what she said?"

Everyone stared at the man with a mixture of amusement and confusion over this surprise admission.

"What did she say?" Relic asked, enjoying his seat at the table with the grown men.

"She said that was the best damn compliment I could have given her."

Donna once again felt like the world was out of focus, but the feeling passed in a flash. She couldn't have said what brought on the feeling. Relic dissolved into laughter and Owen popped the back of Taran's ball cap up, knocking his sunglasses sideways.

"Watch it, man," he growled, swatting Owen's hand away.

Donna narrowed her eyes at the two men. "How long have you two known each other? You act like brothers, but I remember you saying you don't have any, Owen."

"Too damn long," Taran said, getting to his feet.

Henry caught Donna's eye and shrugged, as if to say he wasn't sure what to make of Taran, either.

Everyone else rose, and the men headed for the back door.

"I wish there was some way other than beer that I could thank you for all the help," Donna said, trailing behind them while also keeping a wary eye out for Ebony. She didn't want the cat to sneak out again. But the feline seemed to have disappeared, hiding away in the bowels of the old house.

"Think nothing of it," Owen said, holding the door so Donna could follow them out into the side yard. "Say, Henry, I'm serious about the fishing. Gage here has been complaining that there isn't any decent fishing left in the state of Minnesota anymore, and he'll be taking off again in a couple weeks, so I'd love to prove him wrong. What do you think about giving Renee's husband a call? Maybe we could get something lined up."

Henry nodded. "I think I'll do that. Give me your number, and if I hear anything promising I'll be in touch. Maybe we can carve out a couple days before you head out, Taran, and go drown a few worms."

Donna watched as Henry and Owen exchanged numbers, and then all four drove off in the vehicles they'd arrived in. Their brief comments about a fishing trip reminded her of her earlier discussions with both Patsy and Charlotte about possibly organizing a little getaway sometime. How was it that men could so easily throw something like that together, while women got tangled up in the details?

She started back toward the house with a sigh, but remembered she hadn't grabbed the mail that morning. Charlotte had arrived before the mailman. She smiled as she changed directions, heading for the front of the house and the pretty black mailbox attached to the house's front gate. Lynette joked that the box, which sported an iron bird perched on the top, looked like something that belonged on a witch's house.

"My girl's imagination runs to the eclectic side," she murmured, and a twinge of loneliness hit.

She noticed a thick envelope jutting out of the mailbox. Her smile morphed into a grimace when pain shot up from her knee again. Maybe she should go see that orthopedic doctor Lynette had been suggesting. But a visit to the doctor would have to wait, because she had an idea.

She just hoped her scheme wouldn't get her into trouble.

Chapter Fourteen

Lynette arranged one more red chair around the firepit. "You said ten, right? Because I doubt we could squeeze any more in than that."

"Right," Renee said. She dropped a stack of firewood next to the existing pile. "There. This should be enough wood to hold us for a while. If we need more, Matt would probably be willing to grab us some before he heads in to work. Thanks for bringing four chairs up from the beach. I know they aren't light."

"Hey, anything to get out of dish duty."

Laughing, Renee dropped into the closest Adirondack. "I couldn't agree more. We'll leave the washing and drying to Jackie, Kit, and Annie. Knowing Val, she's already prepping our breakfasts and lunches for the next couple days. I can't believe it's already Wednesday. Two weeks sounded like such a long time, but now our vacation is already almost half over! It makes me sad."

Lynette eased into the chair next to Renee. "It makes me sad, too. But it was nice to just hang out yesterday and today. This trip is different from Hawaii and Arizona. Those were amazing, but this one is so laid back. It feels good. The rain doesn't even bother me. A girl can only take so much beach time. Although, when I was a kid, I probably never imagined saying those words out loud."

Renee rested her head against the back of her chair and looked to the sky. "A few rainy days are nice. But I'm glad the weather cleared for tonight. I've actually been looking forward to giving you a chance to get to know my family better. I know you met Val and my folks on Monday, but there's nothing like a visit around a campfire to get to know someone. By the way, I think my niece Lauren has a little crush on you."

Lynette unzipped her sweatshirt. With the rain moved on, the early evening sun still offered some heat. "It was cute the way she insisted her mother move so she could sit by me at dinner. I hope I didn't disappoint her, now that I'm just a middle-aged woman with a cat, living in little Ruby Shores, instead of a fashion mogul in New York City."

Renee brought her head back up to look at Lynette. "Don't do that."

"Do what?" Lynette asked, surprised by the clip in her friend's tone.

"Belittle yourself. Just because you sold your company doesn't mean you are a different person. If getting laid off from my corporate job taught me anything, it was that we are so much more than our jobs. We can't let our careers define us. You are still the same smart, creative woman you were when Lauren first read your name in the online fashion reports that she follows so closely."

Lynette pulled her sweatshirt off completely. It might not be the sun making her so hot. She'd thought she was done with hot flashes, but maybe not. "You give me too much credit, Renee. You have no idea what my days look like now, compared to two years ago."

"So tell me," Renee said.

"I'd hate to bore you."

Before Renee could challenge her further, voices approached from the direction of the lodge.

"Saved by the crowd," Lynette joked.

"We aren't done with this conversation yet," Renee said, pushing out of her chair. "Man! Don't tell Mom and Dad I said this, and I really love these new chairs, but *dang* . . . they are hard to climb out of."

Lynette's arms and back were already aching from carrying four chairs, one at a time, up from the beach. She might need a hand to get out of her chair at the evening's conclusion.

Renee turned toward her approaching family and friends. "Val, did you remember the s'more stuff?"

"Sure did, sis," Val said, holding a picnic basket aloft.

Lynette recognized the basket from the beach picnic on their first morning back at Whispering Pines. "You are spoiling us, Val. In case your sister doesn't tell you how amazing you are often enough, please know how grateful we are for you. You have incredible skills in the kitchen."

Val dropped the basket of supplies near the chair Renee had just exited and then sat in the one on Lynette's opposite side. "I appreciate that, Lynette. But I'm done with my duties tonight. We'll let Renee handle the s'more making.

Everyone else reached the firepit and settled into the remaining chairs. Lauren sat in Renee's old chair, to Lynette's right, until Val pointed at the nearby basket and warned her that the chair came with responsibilities.

"Fine," the young woman huffed, moving around the still-cold firepit to sit next to Julie, Renee's daughter. She pulled her phone out. A pout marred her youthful features.

Lynette noticed that Julie also seemed more intrigued by whatever was displaying on her phone than the people around the firepit.

"Today's youth," she whispered to Val. "Is there any hope for our future?"

Val took a moment to consider the question before nodding. "I do worry about kids' social skills. And I'll lump my four boys into that generalization, too, though my youngest two don't have phones yet."

"It would have been fun to meet your kids. And your husband. What are they up to tonight?" Lynette asked. She accepted a dripping bottle of water from Renee as the woman made her way around the circle of chairs with a cooler.

Val took one, too. "Believe it or not, Luke, my husband, had promised to take Dave, our oldest, driving. Dave wants to schedule his license test before winter."

"Probably a good idea."

Jess, who'd been visiting with her mother in nearby chairs, must have overheard. "What's a good idea?"

Val swiveled toward her other sister. "Luke's helping Dave practice driving tonight so he can take his test before the roads get icy."

Jess shook her head. "I am so thankful that those days are behind me. Student driving almost killed me." She looked across the firepit toward her daughter and lowered her voice. "Don't tell Lauren I told you this, but she didn't pass her permit test until her third try. You don't have kids, right, Lynette?"

Lynette nodded, but before she could say anything, Val gave her sister a friendly tap on the knee. "Oh, but my dear sister, you forget. The whole 'student driver' thing isn't over for you yet."

Jess tossed her hands in the air. "And that is just one more grudge I can hold against my dear ex-husband."

"You might need to explain that to Lynette," Val said.

"Actually, Renee mentioned you adopted a young child that your ex fathered," Lynette spoke up. "As a childless woman, I have to admit that sounds either incredibly brave or stupid of you."

Jess coughed when a plume of ashes wafted toward her face. Jackie gasped the second she realized what had happened when she threw the first log into the pit.

Lynette waved her discarded sweatshirt to clear the surrounding air. "Don't mind Jackie. She's always been inept at starting campfires. When we were kids at camp, they had a session about safety and tried to teach us the correct way to start a fire to cook with or keep warm."

"And I admit I couldn't quite master it back then either," Jackie finished for her. "But I didn't think we wanted to sit around a firepit without a fire."

Renee finished handing out refreshments and returned to her chair. "I forgot about that. If I'd remembered, I'd have assigned Jackie a different job."

Lynette laughed, then turned her attention back to Jess. "I thought maybe you'd bring your little one tonight. What's her name?"

"Harper. And I might have let her come along, but I had to take her to the clinic this morning. Ear infection. So my hubby offered to keep her home with him tonight so I could enjoy myself. None of us got much sleep last night."

Val twisted the top off her water bottle. "I may have four young male drivers in my future, but at least they're all past the earache phase. Or I sure hope they are."

Lynette was enjoying visiting with Renee's sisters. It was fun to pick out their similarities, while also seeing how unique each was from the other. Renee used to talk about her sisters and brother in the letters she'd write her, back when they did a better job as pen pals. "So, Jess, you have Harper and Lauren. And—sorry, I forgot your husband's name. What does he do?"

"I have a twenty-six-year-old, too. Nathan. My husband is Seth. He owns his own business. Actually, that's how I met him. Through his business, I mean. Our aunt—the same one who passed Whispering Pines on to Renee—left me an ownership share in a few different businesses."

Their aunt Celia sounded more and more intriguing to Lynette all the time. "Wait. Your aunt was a partial owner of your current husband's business? How the heck did that happen?"

A cloud of smoke obscured Jess's face for a second.

"Jackie, are you trying to kill us?" she laughed, waving ineffectively at the wafting smoke before turning her attention back to Lynette. "Seth was actually the grandson of one of Celia's best friends."

That made a little more sense. She nodded. "And what is his business?"

"Well, he sells vintage architectural pieces that he rescues from old buildings facing demolition. He finds them in other places, too. He also works in stained glass. She—Celia, I mean—helped him get one of his first stained glass gigs when he was younger."

At the mention of stained glass, Lynette's mind immediately went to the circular window at the landing of her staircase back home. "Stained glass, huh? As in, full windows?"

"Yes," Jess said. "Why?"

"Well, I have what could be an amazing circular window in my house. Just the other night, when it was storming outside and I was sitting on the bottom step with my cat, I imagined how incredible the window could look when the lightning flashed. But, sadly, it's boarded up. A stained glass window would look amazing. Replacing the glass is on my honey-do list, but since I don't currently *have* a honey, it's hard to get things crossed off."

"Ouch!" Kit yelped. A molten gob of white goo flew off her shaking hand and into the fire.

Lynette hadn't noticed that Renee had pulled out the marshmallows and started roasting some until Kit's little outburst. Annie looked up from her phone at the screech and caught Lynette's eye.

"You are as bad as the kids, Annie. Put your phone away."

"Sorry, Lynette. Since when are you the phone police? And speaking of phones, have you talked to your mom today?"

Lynette sighed. She was just about to ask Jess if her Seth might give her a bid to replace the broken window. Jess was already visiting about something new with Val.

"One second," she said, holding a finger up to Annie. "I'm sorry to interrupt, Jess, but I have a quick question. Do you think Seth might be able to replace my broken window? I really want stained glass in there, but I don't know anyone who does that kind of work."

Annie slapped her hands on the arms of her chair in excitement. "Lynette, what if you had a kaleidoscope-type design made for your window? Wouldn't that be cool?"

"I actually love that idea! Jess, could Seth do something like that?"

Renee handed another marshmallow to Kit. "Seth is very talented. I bet he could make a kaleidoscope window."

Jess nodded. "He probably could, but he's pretty swamped. Might take some time to get him over to Ruby Shores to have a look. But I can mention it to him. Renee will get you his number."

"Perfect! It's all right if it isn't right away. I've gone a year with it like that already. A few more months won't matter."

"Maybe the window broke in the storm that damaged my grandma's house," Kit chimed in. "Remember that, Jackie? Your Owen came to her rescue."

"You four need to quit calling him *my* Owen," Jackie said. She poked at her fire with the long metal rod Renee kept near the firepit for that very purpose.

"Lynette, you should call home," Annie said. "Henry just sent me a text. So, no, I wasn't just playing on my phone and ignoring all of you."

Lynette's mind connected some dots. "Wait. Did Henry have news from Relic? Relic is checking my house everyday so Mom could just do her thing while I'm gone. My cat is all right, isn't she?"

"What's your cat's name?" Val asked.

"Ebony. I haven't had her very long. She's young and naughty. She likes to sneak out of the house. I hope she didn't get away from Relic. I did warn him."

Val snickered. "That sounds familiar. I don't have a cat, but our dog, Storm, was the same way. She was always sneaking out of the house when she was a puppy. The boys were terrible about latching the door."

Lynette felt torn between Annie's nagging to call home and Val's discussion about pets. Maybe home could wait for another minute. "What did you say your dog's name was?"

"Storm."

"It is not!" Lynette cried. "You won't believe this, but my first boyfriend's name was Storm."

"That's kind of crazy," Val said. "But *my* Storm is a girl. And before you even ask, the answer is no. I didn't name her. The boys did. With a name like that, I'm guessing your first boyfriend wasn't your typical boy-next-door kind of kid?"

"Not at all," Lynette laughed, allowing her mind to travel back in time again. "No one would have ever accused Storm of being typical. He was actually my manager at a pizza place where I worked when I was a senior in high school. We ended up going to prom together. He was only two years older than me. These girls here were all a little scandalized by my dating him, but I asked him anyway."

Kit finished licking the marshmallow goo from her fingers. "I always thought you went with him because you knew we might not approve. Actually, do all of you know that Renee came to prom with us? Her date was this kid named Owen—he was more of the typical boy-next-door type. But, alas, they didn't click, and we all knew why. Owen was in love with Jackie here. Still is, too, if you ask me."

"Storm was so *hot*," Annie chimed in. "My parents would never have allowed me to date someone like him in a million years. Lynette, you were so lucky Donna didn't care. And don't forget to call her! When Relic checked on your cat and house yesterday, he found water in your basement."

All the titillating memories of her younger self with handsome bad boy, Storm, fled her mind. "Seriously, Annie? You couldn't have led with that minor detail? And my phone is back in my cabin. I need to run and grab it."

Annie held her hand out. "Wait. It isn't an emergency or anything. Henry said he and a couple other guys helped your mom clean everything up. I just thought you might want to touch base with her when you have a minute."

Lynette paused, torn between leaving the fun of the campfire to call her mother and waiting until morning.

"I'm sure Donna would have called if she was worried about the house," Renee added. "Here, have a fresh s'more. Call your mom in the morning. It's too beautiful of an evening to ruin it with bad news."

Renee was right. Donna would have called if the water problem needed her immediate attention. "That does look tasty," she said, accepting the sticky treat and sitting back in her chair. "You're right, Renee. No more bad news tonight! I'm going to assume my house is as right as rain again."

"Until it rains again," Val said with a wink. "Sorry. Bad joke. But I couldn't resist."

A touch at her elbow made Lynette jump. She hadn't even noticed Lauren move away from her chair on the other side of the pit. "Girl, you scared me!"

"I'm so sorry, Lynette," Lauren said, keeping her voice low as she crouched down behind Lynette's chair. "But I thought this might be something you'd want to see right away."

The urgency in the younger woman's voice set Lynette's pulse racing yet again. *What now?* she thought, awkwardly reaching back for the girl's phone with her left hand, since her right was full of graham crackers, chocolate, and dripping marshmallow.

She squinted down at the phone screen, immediately recognizing the two faces smiling back at her. They were the two women she'd sold her company to. The women she'd taken a chance on, despite the strong objections of both her lawyer and her mother.

One quick glance at the headline told Lynette she probably shouldn't expect the second-to-last payment she was due anytime soon. Maybe never.

She hated it when Donna was right. Had Lynette misplaced her trust and faith? If the article was accurate, the idiots were in danger of running her previously stellar company right into the ground.

Chapter Fifteen

F OLLOWING PHONE CALLS TO both her lawyer and Donna the next morning, Lynette felt marginally better about her house situation, as well as the bad press Lauren had showed her by the campfire.

It was a relief to learn that her lawyer had indeed received the scheduled payment from the sale on Lynette's behalf since they'd last spoken and deposited it into her account. He was curious if a packet he'd sent the previous week from New York to Lynette's home had arrived. There were things he needed to discuss with her, but he was confident these items weren't material in nature.

When she'd talked with her mother, Donna confirmed the arrival of a large envelope from Lynette's lawyer. It was waiting for her on her desk in their home library. She'd gone on to convince Lynette that their home was fine, despite the water Relic had discovered in the basement. Their friendly neighbor, Owen, who they'd borrowed tools from in the past, had kindly helped with the cleanup, along with Annie's husband and son. Donna seemed less interested in discussing things on the home front. She wanted to hear all about Whispering Pines and whether her daughter and friends were having fun.

Feeling better about things back home, Lynette vowed to have a fun day. When Renee gently rapped on her cabin door around nine, she was game to put on hiking clothes and head into the woods with her old friends. Jackie and Renee set a quick pace for the other three.

"Hey, Jackie!" Lynette yelled. "Guess who helped Mom clean up the mess in my basement?"

"How would I know?" Jackie snapped over her shoulder.

Lynette stepped around a fallen log and hurried to catch up with her. "Jeez, what has you so uptight this morning? You used to smile when someone mentioned Owen."

Jackie pushed her hair back off her forehead. "But you *didn't* mention Owen. You were making me guess. I hate guessing games. Man, it's so hot! I should have stayed in bed."

Lynette could tell something was up with Jackie, and she sensed her friend wasn't in the mood to make small talk. She slowed her steps just enough that Jackie and Renee were soon out ahead of her again. She didn't want to catch Jackie's crummy mood.

Crabby or not, Jackie was right about one thing. It was already hot, even in the woods, despite the early hour and shadowy path. She hung back and allowed herself to focus on the beauty and peace around her. Walking through the dense trees was so different from her morning strolls through Ruby Shores.

"Renee, any ideas for what we'll do when we get back from our walk?" she eventually asked. "I might need to stay out of the sun. I saw on my phone this morning that it could reach a hundred today. That's blistering hot, even by the water."

Renee slowed so Lynette could catch up to her. "Actually, I do have a plan for later. It's a surprise. I'm not sure if everyone will think it's fun, but I bet you will."

"Oh, I like surprises!" Lynette said. She checked behind them and noticed Annie and Kit were discussing something. Jackie was still out ahead, and the distance between her and the rest of their small hiking party was growing.

"Jackie seems uptight this morning," she said to Renee. "I have no idea what's bothering her, but I think she might need some space today. Annie and Kit probably have lots to talk about, now that Kit is raising Isaac. Since Annie is both a high school principal and a mother of three grown kids, I'm sure she has plenty of advice to offer. They could talk all day."

Renee nodded and swatted away a bug, then started moving again. "Jackie will tell us what's going on when she's ready. I understand why Kit might be looking for guidance, too. Big life changes like she's going through are tough to navigate. They took in a teenage boy at the same time they got married! That's a lot for anyone to deal with. I feel like life keeps me caught up in one big change after another, too. It's been that way ever since my first husband died."

"How many years ago was that? My heart broke for you when I read your Christmas letter that year," Lynette said. She remembered receiving Renee's unusually brief note. She'd canceled her holiday plans for that evening and stayed home in front of her Christmas tree with a glass of wine, mourning a man she'd never met. Grieving for her old friend's excruciating pain.

"He died in 2005. Sixteen years is a long time. There were still some good times, after losing Jim, but raising two kids as a single, frazzled mother often felt like one crisis after another. But we made it."

The life Renee described was so different from Lynette's. She could barely imagine what her friend's day-to-day life looked like in those ensuing years. "But you conquered all, and now you are a superwoman, running a beautiful resort and retreat business with your handsome husband. The troubles are behind you."

Renee nodded but said nothing more on the topic, so Lynette walked alongside her in silence, taking in the natural beauty all around.

Something off in the trees caught her eye. "What's that?"

"What's what?" Renee said, slowing. She sounded like her mind was somewhere miles from the woods at Whispering Pines.

Lynette stopped. "There. It looks like . . . an old clothesline?" She laughed. "But that can't be right, not out here in the middle of nowhere."

"Believe it or not, that's exactly what it is. An old camper used to be parked out here. We stumbled across it a few years back. Well, Lauren and Harper were the ones to find it, actually."

Curious, Lynette strode toward the tilted metal pole. "Hey, Jackie, wait up! Come back here! Renee, isn't Harper pretty young? Like three or four? A few years ago means she was a baby back then."

Renee followed her. "Remember how Jess's ex-husband fathered a baby with his mistress? That crazy, incompetent woman showed up out here one day, totally unexpected, and tried to take Harper. Lauren was here at Whispering Pines, alone, babysitting her new half-sister. It was a cold and rainy day, not hot like today. Lauren was terrified. She ran into the woods with Harper to try to lose the woman. Jess realized the girls were missing, and a few hours of complete chaos followed. Matt and a deputy helped find them, thank God. They were hiding inside the camper that used to be out here."

To Lynette, it sounded like something out of a horror movie. "Wow! Maybe life outside of the Big Apple isn't as boring as I always thought."

"I've never even been to New York City, but trust me when I say that my life has *not* been boring."

"Oh, Renee, you really need to visit New York someday. We'll go together, and I can show you all my favorite things. But what happened to the camper? The trees and underbrush are so thick out here."

Renee nodded as Jackie, Kit, and Annie all joined them at the same time.

"Camper? There used to be a camper here? Where did it go?" Annie asked, spinning in a slow circle.

"Val convinced a bunch of guys to help her yank it out of here." Renee pulled her phone out of the pocket of her hiking shorts and checked it. "Dang. I'm sorry to cut our hike short, ladies, but I just got a text from Julie. She's having trouble with our credit card machine and one of our customers is trying to check out early. I better get back. Besides, the mosquitoes are vicious today."

"But what did Val want with an old camper? Do they take it camping? I don't understand how they even got a camper out of here. Or in," Kit said, looking as curious as Lynette felt.

"I'll tell you the entire story, I promise. Or Val can. It's really her story to tell, anyway. Ready?"

Jackie, still unusually quiet, nodded and headed back in the direction they'd come. "Ready. I need to call my mom, anyhow."

"Is everything all right?" Annie asked, hurrying to catch up with Jackie.

"No. It's my dad. He fell yesterday. Mom called late last night to let me know, but she said he was going to be fine. I just worry, you know?"

Lynette's thumb rubbed against the empty spot on her finger where she used to wear the silver ring she'd lost in the lake. "I do know what you mean, Jackie. I hate that our parents are getting older. But if any of you tell Donna I said she's old, I'll never speak to you again."

———— ❦ ————

Lynette helped herself to a handful of pretzels from a bowl on the coffee table in Jackie and Kit's cabin. Voices floated over to her from the kitchen counter where the two were busy layering cold cuts and cheese slices on homemade bread. Jackie seemed to be in a better mood. Lynette could only catch every third word or so of their conversation over the hum of the air-conditioning unit in the window. She wandered over to stand in front of the cool stream of air, munching the pretzels.

After hanging with Kit and Renee in the lodge for most of the day to avoid the sun, she'd slipped back to her own cabin midafternoon for some solitude. It had been stuffy inside, but a ceiling fan positioned over her bed and a smaller window unit than this one had kept the temperature bearable. She'd only meant to rest for a few minutes, but sleep finally found her. When she woke, the fan above was motionless. When the bathroom light wouldn't turn on either, she knew she'd blown a fuse. A lukewarm shower had revived her, but this cool air felt heavenly.

"I hope you like turkey or ham," Kit said as she placed a tray of sandwiches next to the pretzels.

Lynette turned to her friend. "Either is fine. Where do you suppose Renee and Annie are? Didn't we agree on 6:30?"

As if her words had conjured up one of the missing Kaleidoscope Girls, the outer screen door into the cabin's enclosed porch squeaked open and slapped shut. Annie's voice reached the living room before she did.

"Tell me you didn't start the party without me!"

Kit laughed. "It's never a party until you arrive, Annie. You're just in time for sandwiches."

"Perfect," Annie said, stepping into the front room and kicking her sandals off next to the inner door. "I'm starving. And sunburned."

Lynette picked a sandwich off the top of the pile, then took a closer look at their latest arrival. "God, Annie. Are you just coming in from the beach now? I couldn't take any more sun today."

Annie nodded, but walked right past the food for the kitchen. "I probably should have done that, too. I need something cold to drink. Where's Renee?"

The entire kitchen was easily visible from the living room, and Lynette saw Jackie spin away from the refrigerator with two bottles of beer in each hand. She kicked the door to the fridge closed with one foot. "How about a beer?"

"Yes, please!" Annie cried, taking both of the bottles from Jackie's left hand and giving one to Kit. "But we need an opener."

Jackie held one of the remaining two bottles toward Lynette. "Beer?"

She shook her head. She hadn't enjoyed an icy beer since high school. If she was going to splurge and allow herself a cocktail or two, it would have to be something tastier than beer. She'd already overdone it once on this vacation with the wine.

"Save it for Renee. I'll get some ice water."

Annie slammed a drawer. "Speaking of Renee, I thought she'd be here already," she said, popping the top off her beer.

Jackie used the opener next. "She was here, but then she said something about forgetting to bring over the surprise, and she ran out. That was about five minutes before you got here, Lynette."

Lynette wandered to the kitchen and flipped open a few of the upper cabinet doors before finding a water glass. "Renee has these cabins well stocked. Oh, and remind me when she gets here—I think I blew a fuse in my cabin, and I'm not sure how to fix it. I need to ask her. Even though I hate making her do any work for us. It's supposed to be her vacation, too."

Annie took a sip of her beer, then used it to point to a small sign posted on the wall in the kitchen. "What if you tried that number? Her daughter, Julie, might answer. Maybe she can handle it without bothering Renee at all."

"That's a good idea," Lynette said. Once she'd dumped ice into her glass and filled it from the tap, she pulled out her phone.

She'd just finished talking to Julie when the outer screen slapped shut again.

"Sorry I'm late!" Renee yelled as she hurried into the front room. "Tell me the party didn't start without me."

Lynette laughed as she watched Renee set a small wooden box on the coffee table next to the food. She loved how they often said the same things, like both Annie and Renee had when they got to Jackie and Kit's cabin a little late.

It was another perk of a long, comfortable friendship.

"I can't believe you kept these!" Lynette cried, fingering her way through the stack of letters. The contents of the box turned out to be Renee's promised surprise.

Renee placed her empty paper plate on the floor next to her rocking chair, then used her foot to push off the coffee table, setting the rocker into motion. "We can thank Mom for that. I had no idea she kept that box after I moved out."

Jackie returned to her spot on the couch next to Lynette after putting the extra sandwiches away. She nodded toward the box. "I love that you two kept your promise to each other to stay in touch after summer camp. Are those all the letters Lynette sent you through the years?"

"I wish," Renee said, shaking her head. "I'm not as much of a pack rat as my mother. When I moved here, to Whispering Pines, from Minneapolis, I tossed a lot of stuff, including any newer letters. But Mom was careful to keep things that were important to each of us kids after we moved out. They still live in the same house where I grew up. They've updated our bedrooms, but we each have a few shelves of our old things in closets throughout the house."

Lynette couldn't imagine having full shelves of things from her girlhood days. She and Donna had moved around too much for that.

She pulled out the envelope at the front of Renee's box. "I bet this is the very first letter I ever sent you. The postmark says October nineteenth, 1982."

Jackie leaned over to look. "I've always loved your handwriting, Lynette. Your cursive is a little fancier these days, but I'd recognize your writing anywhere. I wonder if my girls could even read this, since it's in cursive."

Annie grimaced. "Don't get me started. I hate that the school systems have moved away from teaching cursive in the lower grades."

Lynette pulled the torn flap out of the back of the old envelope. She'd licked and sealed it shut nearly forty years ago. She laughed as she pulled out a folded piece of paper and four small, rectangular pictures fluttered into her lap.

"I forgot I sent you school pictures of everyone! Do you guys remember how we always had to file down to the gym to get these pictures taken during our first weeks of school?"

Kit snatched the photos out of Lynette's hand. "These are too funny! I forgot you had braces, Annie. If these were taken at the start of seventh grade, we were twelve, right? You look about eight years old in this one."

Annie shrugged. "What can I say? I was a tiny yet mighty gymnast back in those days. Puberty was slow to find me."

Kit groaned as she gave the pictures back to Lynette. "Lord. My hair was awful! No wonder kids used to call me Carrot Kid!"

Renee smiled. "I knew Lynette would get a kick out of reading some of these old letters, but I'm glad the rest of you might enjoy them, too."

"These are priceless, Renee," Jackie said. "If we see Lavonne again while we're here, we'll have to be sure to thank her for saving them. When my mom cleaned out my room, she didn't do as good of a job picking out the important things to keep for me."

Lynette scanned the letter she'd written so long ago. "I love my descriptions of our school days. Moving from room to room between classes was a big deal for us." She folded the lined notebook paper back up along the well-worn creases and stuffed it back in the envelope, along with the school photos. "I still can't believe you kept these."

"Well, I kept the ones you sent me during junior high, high school, and then the first couple years of college. While I wish I'd kept everything, it is nice to have these," Renee said. "Pick another one!"

Lynette worked her way through the stack, smiling at the various dates, pen colors, and variety of envelopes. "I remember how I used to love finding funny cards to send you." Her fingers stilled on an envelope dated from May 1988. The specific day wasn't legible. "Maybe I talked about prom in this one."

"Oh, the heartache," Renee said, clasping at her chest in mock despair. "That was a tough couple of months for me. First, the guy I'd dated throughout most of my senior year broke up with me. He turned out to be such a jerk. I remember thinking he was calling to ask me to prom, but he broke things off. I wanted to *die*. He probably didn't want to spend the money. But then, my old friend Lynette here stepped in and saved the day. My prom dress didn't have to go to waste, after all. I just knew going to the prom with all of you was going to be perfect. I was so young and dumb, thinking it would be a night of romance and magic."

Jackie pulled the envelope from Lynette's hand. "But the way it turned out, Lynette was the only one who seemed to find any romance that night. I remember how my date was more concerned with his track buddies than with me. Kit would have preferred to be there with her student teacher than her science nerd date, and Annie went with an underclassman."

"I object!" Annie said, holding up her empty beer bottle. "Elliott was nice. And a good kisser. I did enjoy *some* romance that night. But our little Lynette here couldn't keep her hands off her date. Not that I could blame her."

They all laughed as Annie fanned herself.

"And my date only had eyes for Jackie," Renee added with a shrug.

Jackie opened the letter. "How about if I read this one out loud? Lynette might paraphrase or leave out some good details if we let her read it to us."

"Do *not* read that out loud," Lynette said, trying but failing to remember what she might have said to Renee. She reached for the envelope, but Jackie held it away.

"Fine. I'll just share the juicy bits."

Annie got to her feet. "Hold that thought, Jackie. I need to use the bathroom."

"All right. But hurry."

Lynette watched Jackie's face as her friend read the letter to herself. What had she told Renee about that awful last month of her high school days? Had she dared to reveal more to Renee, the girl she hadn't known quite as well as Annie, Kit, and Jackie? Things happened during that last month of high school that she'd thought she would never share with anyone . . . like the man who attacked her on the night she'd wrecked Storm's truck. Now, all these years later, she couldn't be sure she was remembering things quite right.

At one point, Jackie looked up from the letter to catch Lynette's gaze. "I'm so sorry you had to go through that crap with your mom's boyfriend," she said.

Donna's poor choice of men wasn't one of the topics she still refused to discuss. Her friends already knew the stories about Donna and her boyfriends. While those situations had undoubtedly left Lynette with a few emotional scars, she liked to think she'd overcome them.

"Stop talking!" Annie yelled from the back of the cabin. "I can hear you!"

Kit tucked her foot underneath her bottom. "You guys had better wait for her. I think our little Annie always had a thing for Lynette's boyfriend, Storm, and she doesn't want you to reveal anything about him when she isn't in the room."

Annie hurried back into the room, shaking her hands as if the bathroom might not have a hand towel—or she was just in a hurry. "Go ahead, Jackie."

Jackie shrugged. "It isn't a long letter. You wrote this after a late work shift, Lynette, and it was the day before we graduated. Donna was at a fortieth birthday party for someone named Raven, so you must have been home alone. You apologized to Renee for spending a little too much of your time on our prom night with Storm, and you worried she didn't have fun with Owen."

Relief washed through Lynette. The terrible events of graduation night hadn't unfolded yet when she'd written this particular letter, so her secrets were safe.

"A *little* too much?" Annie repeated, interrupting Lynette's thoughts with a giggle. "Lynette, you bailed on all of us! We'd probably still be grounded if my parents would have caught you sneaking back into the house so many hours after curfew."

"I forgot about that," Jackie laughed. "It actually surprised me, though, when you and Owen didn't hit it off. You two could have made a cute couple."

Kit leaned forward and stared at Jackie. "You are so full of shit, Jackie. You know *exactly* why that didn't happen."

"I have no idea what you're talking about," Jackie said as she folded the letter back up, though that was obviously a lie.

Lynette decided to let Jackie off the hook, so she picked up on a different thread from the letter. "You guys won't believe this, but the woman named Raven that I mentioned in the letter is the same person I bought our Ruby Shores house from."

Annie reached for a pretzel. "Oh, sure! Raven Black. But what was her mother's name? I forgot that's who owned your house before."

Lynette took the envelope from Jackie and put it back in the box, then set the whole thing back on the coffee table. "Her mother died when she was young. The person you're thinking of was Sybil Gage, Raven's grandmother. Donna met them both when Sybil was a resident at the nursing home where she worked."

"I didn't really know either woman, but Sybil was a relatively well-known college professor when I was a new teacher," Annie said between nibbles of a pretzel stick. "Raven was the only female family practitioner in Ruby Shores for years. I hated to see her move away. Remind me again where she and her husband moved to, Lynette?"

Lynette was happy to steer the conversation away from the shadows that still haunted her from that time in her life. She told her friends more about both women and the fun memories she had of Sybil and her house, and even shared about the mystery box she'd discovered in her garden shed.

The conversation continued to ebb and flow, as it always does between old friends, weaving between memories of long-ago days and newer life developments.

The box of old letters reminded Lynette that even though old secrets sometimes try to poke their way back to the surface, she was a master at pushing them back into the dark.

Chapter Sixteen

LYNETTE KICKED OFF HER sandals and walked out to the end of the dock. The weathered wood on the platform felt slightly grooved underfoot. She imagined the indentations were the result of each tiny impression left behind by countless previous visitors to Whispering Pines. When she closed her eyes, her mind could hear snippets of laughter and conversations between friends and lovers, swept away on the wind and circling back, across space and time, for her ears only. It made sense that they could have left physical impressions, too.

Thankful for the Adirondack chair at the end of the dock, she sank into it, unconcerned about the puddle of water that still clung to the seat. The scorching heat of the previous day had made it difficult for her to enjoy any beach time, so today's rain shower provided welcome relief.

She yawned. Nightmares had again interfered with her sleep the night before.

How could it already be Saturday? The first half of their vacation at Renee's resort had passed too quickly.

A car pulled into the lodge's parking lot, drawing her attention away from the water. She watched from her vantage point, far out on the dock, as two adults and three small children climbed out. They were too far away for her to make out any details, but this had to be the family Renee was worried might not show up.

While her friend hadn't come right out and talked specifically about any concerns she might have over the resort's long-term viability, Lynette sensed an unease in her. She should make a point to speak to Renee alone on the topic. If there was a problem, maybe she could help. She knew Renee was currently spending a couple hours after lunch in her resort office, doing bookwork. Kit and Annie had given Renee a hard time about working on vacation, but Lynette understood the demands of owning one's own business. Jackie seemed to, as well.

Lynette's eyes turned to the gravel road the car had just traveled, and she wondered whether Jackie was on her way back from her run yet. She'd eaten little at lunch because she wanted to get in some exercise and enjoy the cooler weather. Jackie claimed to have little time to run or go to the gym, given her own small business she continued to work to grow.

She wasn't sure where Kit and Annie had disappeared to. Wherever they were, if they were together, they were probably discussing kids again.

The rhythmic sound of waves lapping against the dock pulled Lynette's attention back to the lake at her feet. A boat cut toward a far-off shoreline, to the northeast of Whispering Pines, and she wondered if Robbie was captaining it. Renee shared stories the night before last about some of her son's experiences acting as a fishing guide for interested resort guests.

Lynette loved to hear about entrepreneurial endeavors that her friends' children were pursuing. She'd had many conversations with Annie's daughter, Ava, about the online children's clothing business the young mother was still interested in pursuing.

Waves continued to lap against the dock's supports, even though the fishing boat was far away. If the dock and shoreline hadn't blocked the ripples, how far could they have traveled?

She used to think her own business was like the flowing water. Her efforts grew a business that employed many and helped countless women feel pretty when they donned their clothes or accessories.

She never had the chance to be a mother like her four best friends, but she could at least act as a mentor to their kids if they had an interest in business.

What kind of mother might she have made?

Everyone, even her own mom, thought Lynette had consciously chosen to never have children. Maybe they assumed it never happened because she remained single. She doubted anyone other than herself ever wondered if that long-ago night when she'd crashed Storm's truck was the real reason she was never able to conceive.

She relaxed and allowed her eyes to drift shut, half expecting to catch the whispers of laughter on the wind again. Instead, what floated to her were scenes from her reoccurring bad dream. Maybe if she allowed herself to remember those darkest of days, she could release the pain they still caused her, once and for all.

The nightmare, fueled by her memories, always kicked off with the same scene in her mind. She supposed she should be thankful that they didn't pick up inside the truck, or as she swung her makeshift weapon and cracked it against that evil man's skull.

No. It was after, when the glow of the moon above chased back the shadows just enough to allow her to run away from the truck, through the dark night, and reach Storm's lake house. The dreaded sound of footsteps behind her never materialized. There was no sound at all. It was as if a vacuum had sucked away all the sound on Earth, other than her own labored breathing. Even her pounding on Storm's back door, the door that she knew led into the house's kitchen, was soundless. Her lungs ached, her legs trembled, and her fists throbbed, but no one came to the door. She thought a light may have flipped off inside, but she couldn't be sure.

Headlights swept across the lake house's exterior, throwing light across two large garage doors. She dove behind a bush that flanked the kitchen door, panic sluicing through her. But the headlights continued on. It wasn't her attacker. She tried banging again, then jiggled the locked doorknob.

As she'd feared, Storm wasn't home, and his mother and baby brother must be gone, too.

The hoot of an owl shattered the silence as the wind picked up around her. She thought she could hear waves crashing down on the other side of the house, but maybe it was just her own blood pounding in her ears.

Maybe she could get into the house—and to a phone—through the garage. The house was large, at least two or three times bigger than the tiny house she lived in with her mom, and it blocked the moon. But she tried to picture what the headlights had briefly revealed. Keeping one hand against the house, she hurried toward the garage doors. Around the corner was another door. Was that the one Storm had meant when he said they never locked it?

She had to force herself to move carefully, and even now, all these years later, her fingers tingled with the feel of rough stucco, a wooden doorframe, and the cold metal of the first garage door. She had nearly fallen when her right foot caught on something in the darkness. The owl hooted again, and the hum of insects seemed to magnify.

I'm coming for you . . .

She shook her head to dispel his evil hiss. "It's just your mind playing tricks on you," she whispered into the dark.

Finally, her fingers felt the corner of the garage, and when she turned, light from the moon revealed the door she hoped would give her access to the house. The doorknob didn't turn smoothly, but with some force it ground around and she opened the door. The lock probably didn't even work. With a sigh of relief, she slipped inside, pulling the door shut quietly behind her. A tiny nightlight, plugged into an outlet near the floor to the right of the door, provided enough light so she could see Storm's truck right in front of her.

Someone must have picked him up.

Was there any way he'd left his keys inside?

The only time she'd ever noticed him store his keys in the visor was the last time he'd brought her here. It was the same visit where his mother had so obviously snubbed her. She crawled up onto the driver's seat, cringing as the creak of metal echoed all around her. She flipped the visor down, and she heard the clank of something fall, but the nightlight did nothing to cut the darkness inside the truck's cab.

A wave of panic, much like the lake waves she thought she'd heard moments earlier, washed over her. She froze. The shadows she'd fought so hard to ignore, to squelch in any manner she could, closed in, and suddenly she knew. This was her punishment for being so stupid. For ignoring her mother's constant warnings since before she'd even gotten her first period.

In the inky black of the pickup truck—the comforting scent of pine emanating from the thick collection of air fresheners she knew hung below the buttons of the truck's old radio that would forevermore remind her of Storm—her mother's words echoed.

Lynette, never, ever have unprotected sex with a boy. The last thing you want is to end up pregnant.

And there it was. The monster she'd known was lurking just on the very edge of her conscious mind. She was probably pregnant. Her period was almost a month late and her boobs hurt. Her mother was going to kill her.

Unless her attacker found her first.

This realization jolted her back, and she knew she had to find Storm. He'd know what to do. He had protected her before, and he'd do it again. But, in the meantime, she needed to protect herself.

She groped around on the floor below the steering wheel and found the keys, remembering that Storm kept a garage door opener in his glove compartment. She fished it out. The truck started after a second turn of the key. Holding her breath as the heavy door behind her rumbled open, her overloaded mind convinced her that the other truck was going to pull into Storm's driveway at any moment, blocking her in. The second she had enough clearance, she threw the truck into reverse and shot out of the garage, tires spinning.

It wasn't until she'd reached the end of the short road that ran from Storm's house to the main road that she remembered she hadn't thought to shut the garage door. What would Storm think when he got home and realized his truck was gone?

But then something else registered in her rattled brain. Storm's mother's car was parked in the stall next to his. She hadn't been able to see it in the dark garage, hadn't even thought to check for it, but the truck's headlights had swept over the vehicle when she'd raced out of the garage.

As she punched the gas and took the corner too fast, two different questions slammed into her brain. If Storm's mother was at home, why had she ignored Lynette's cry for help? And was the woman, even now, calling the police to report the theft of her son's truck?

The shadows closed in again from all sides, and she had to shake her head to clear her vision and keep Storm's truck on the road. She'd almost made it, but unless she kept her wits about her, danger still lurked. If she could just find Storm, he'd know what to do.

Where had he said he was going tonight?

Her mind was acting like a toddler in a bouncy house, catapulting from one thing to another: terror that her attacker would find her, Storm's reaction if she told him she thought she was pregnant, whether the police were on their way to arrest her for stealing the pickup.

How had things gotten so messed up? How could she fix things?

What if she'd killed the man who was attacking her?

She needed to get a grip on her runaway thoughts if she was going to see this evening through in a way that wouldn't blow up the life she and her mom had carved out for themselves.

Out on the open road, there were no obstructions to the moonlight. It illuminated her path forward, and the shadows retreated. The rest of the world slept, and she slowed the truck to a more manageable speed. It was unlikely she'd be able to find Storm until tomorrow.

The needle on the truck's fuel gauge was deep into the red zone, so she wouldn't get far before she ran out of gas. Could she find Jackie and the others? Maybe they'd be at Annie's by now. But if the party was over, Annie's mother had probably realized one of her daughter's friends had slipped out.

She wouldn't put her friends at even more risk of getting into trouble because of her selfishness.

Was there enough gas for her to get home? Her mother never got home until the sun was peeking over the horizon when she worked a night shift. If Lynette headed there now, she could pretend she'd gone straight home from the party. She could even claim a migraine forced her to leave the party early. No one ever had to know that she'd jumped into the vehicle of a near-stranger. That he'd had horrible plans for her, and she'd been stupid enough to trust him.

Another glance at the dash made her realize the gas was even lower than she'd initially thought. Tomorrow was payday, and Storm probably had to wait for his next paycheck to fill up. Was that emergency twenty-dollar bill still tucked away in the zippered pocket of her purse?

After a moment of panic, she realized she still had her purse looped across her body, but she'd caught the strap in the seatbelt. If the cash was there, she'd pull into that old truck stop on the outskirts of town and pray it was still open.

She released her seatbelt and snapped open her purse, fumbling for the pocket zipper with one hand while keeping a tight grip on the steering wheel with the other and both eyes on the road. Her slowly developing plan would fall apart if she hit a deer or ran off the winding road.

Her fingers found a folded piece of paper that felt like cash. She pulled it out and held it high so the moonlight could allow her to see if it truly was her emergency stash. But a light flashed in the truck's rearview mirror. To her horror, she saw a set of headlights closing in on the road behind her. All thoughts of twenty-dollar bills, gas, and even home fled her overtaxed mind.

She couldn't see what type of vehicle it was, but she knew. She knew in her gut she hadn't killed him, and now he was coming for her again. This time he wouldn't be stupid enough to let her escape.

She punched the gas on Storm's old truck. The motor was powerful, and she tried to convince herself that she was pulling away from the headlights.

"Keep your eyes on the road, keep your eyes on the road," she chanted, her words echoing around the empty interior.

But her traitorous gaze refused to focus on the road. She kept checking the mirror, afraid the headlights would overtake her.

Are they getting closer?

Then the truck's engine faltered. The motor belched and sputtered. Lynette's right foot pushed harder on the accelerator, her attention further splintered. The road curved to the left, but the truck stayed on its forward trajectory.

She'd missed the curve.

For a split second, she had the sensation of flying. Silence replaced the hum of the tires across blacktop. Later, she wouldn't be able to say how long she hung there, suspended in the air.

But what goes up must come down, and the truck landed with a bone-crushing *thud*.

Then she was spinning. Around and around she went, and her final thought before the shadows closed in for good was a realization that this must be how it would feel to be stuck inside a spinning kaleidoscope.

"Lynette! You fool! You're going to get struck by lightning, sitting out on the end of the dock like that!"

Her eyes flew open at the panic in Renee's shouted warning. Waves crashed in front of her, and it took an extra heartbeat for Lynette to realize where she was. Just then, the sky above opened up and a deluge of rain crashed down on her, bringing her back to full consciousness.

She must have fallen asleep. A storm had rolled in while she'd been tossed around in the same old nightmare that she never managed to escape.

"I'm serious, Lynette!" Renee yelled from shore. "Matt just called and said we're under a severe thunderstorm warning! We need to get inside. That white patch out over the water means hail is moving this way!"

Between the rain and the increasing howl of the wind, Lynette struggled to get out of the deep-seated chair. Once on her feet, she teetered for a second as the elements buffeted her, and she envisioned plunging into the angry water below the dock.

She managed to stay upright and stumbled back around the chair, and she was halfway to the beach when she skidded to a halt in horror.

"Renee!" she screamed at her retreating friend.

Renee threw her hands up and stopped, turning back to face her. "What?!"

Lynette waved her right arm toward the lake. "I saw a boat out there! Is Robbie out there with guests?"

"No! Unlike you, he pays attention to the weather. They beat the storm back and they're all safely inside. Now, let's go, before it gets any worse!"

Lynette ran the final length of the dock and sprinted across the sand. Just as she reached the point where the beach met the grass, a bolt of lightning and nearly instantaneous thunder cracked overhead. The blinding light bounced off the twisted wooden smile on the frozen face carved into Renee's Hawaiian totem pole.

Lynette yelped, stumbled ahead, and just caught herself before falling face-first into the wet grass.

Chapter Seventeen

T HE STORM LEFT AS abruptly as it had come. By seven, the weather had cleared enough to allow their evening barbecue to proceed as planned.

Kit moaned over the heaping spoonful of baked beans she'd just shoved into her mouth, and Lynette grinned. "I told you they tasted like heaven."

Once Kit swallowed, she smirked. "And you were so right. Val needs to write a cookbook. Man, I'm sure I'll have gained ten pounds by the time I get home next week. But I might think twice before making these at home for Dean and Isaac."

"Why?" Lynette asked, not following Kit's logic. "They'd love 'em!"

"Exactly," Kit said, scraping another spoonful from her plate. "They'd eat too many beans, and I'd have to put up with their farts for who knows how long."

Lynette shuddered. Donna would never pass gas around her. Yet another reason to limit the men in her life.

"Any word on your dad, Jackie?" Annie asked.

"Mom was right," Jackie said. "He's fine. The fall didn't cause any serious damage."

Renee plated the last of the burgers and closed the grill lid. "Thank

"

God for that. Eat up, ladies! There's plenty."

After making room for the hamburgers on the still-damp picnic table, Renee squeezed onto the bench between Lynette and Annie. "I'm so glad the storm moved on so we could still have our picnic. Wait until you taste the cherry pie Val baked for us."

Annie grabbed the ketchup bottle and dumped a big dollop onto her burger. "Speaking of Val, tell us her story about the camper!"

"Or, if you want to wait to let her tell us about that, I remember you mentioning a story you wanted to tell us about squirrels," Kit said, laughing as she pointed at an industrious squirrel climbing up a nearby tree with a nut in its mouth.

Renee spied the squirrel and shook her head. "Since Val will be out here again before you all go home, ask her about the camper. The squirrel story is cute . . . and then not so cute."

Lynette was confused. "Cute, then *not* cute?"

"It starts out funny," Renee said, helping herself to some beans. "It happened the very first time I came out here again, after I found out Celia left Whispering Pines to me. Winter still had a grip on things. Well, early spring, but the ice wasn't off the lake yet. So it looked different from the trips I remembered when we came here as kids."

Lynette understood that. "That's how I felt when we drove up here last week. It looks so different now versus when we were here for the winter retreat."

"Right," Renee said. "I didn't come alone. Some of my family came, including Jess and my brother, Ethan. Dad and Julie, too. Anyway, we were all looking around the place. This was before I updated the lodge. Most of the pictures you saw on our new wall upstairs were still hanging by the lodge's front door. In fact, I was checking them out when Jess screamed."

Annie added more ketchup to her plate. When Lynette grimaced, she shrugged. "What? I like ketchup. Go on, Renee."

Renee laughed. "As I was saying, Jess screamed. She'd made her way farther back into the lodge. We all just figured she'd found a mouse or something. But it was actually a family of squirrels, living in the sink of an old bathroom that doesn't even exist anymore since the remodel. We think the little critters crawled through a broken window. We had to keep the bathroom door shut tight until we could move the squirrels and fix the glass. To be honest, I'd have reacted the same way, but we'll probably keep teasing Jess about that scream of hers for the rest of her life."

Jackie, always the animal lover, smiled. "I'm just glad you relocated the squirrels."

"Well, we did, but I'm afraid one of them still met his or her ultimate demise later that year."

"That sounds ominous," Lynette said. "I take it this is the not-so-funny part?"

Renee had to use her napkin to shoo away a hovering fly. "It is. But first, that nest of squirrels popped up in my dreams. I remember enjoying a perfectly delicious kissing scene in a dream that morphed into a nightmare when I discovered a nest of them in a cabin. Come to think of it, it was your cabin, and your bed, Lynette."

Lynette choked on her bite of pickle. "There were squirrels in my bed?"

"There sure were," Renee confirmed. "But only in my dream."

"Well, that's a relief," Lynette said with a shiver. Her friends probably thought it was an act, but really it was her attempt to banish any thoughts of her own nightmares about her secret attacker.

"There was another actual incident, though, that didn't have as happy an ending for the squirrel. I joke about it being part of the original family of squirrels, but I suppose it could have been. Who knows?"

Lynette was careful to swallow her next bite of pickle before prodding Renee on. "What was the incident?"

"Something happened later that summer when we had a bunch of people out here. It was actually after a barbecue kind of like tonight. We still aren't sure how it happened, but I found a dead squirrel in the middle of my kitchen floor in the duplex. I lived in there before Matt and I built our new house."

Jackie's face fell. "How did a squirrel end up dead in the middle of your kitchen?"

"We never did figure it out. Someone might have simply left a door open, and it was sick. It could have crawled in there and died," Renee said, though she didn't look convinced. "I had more squirrel nightmares after that. It took me a couple years before they didn't make me nervous anymore, running around here. I try to focus on the funny part of discovering them in the lodge and Jess acting like a sissy, and forget about the other thing."

Lynette pushed her plate away, deciding she'd eaten enough. All the talk about squirrels may have chased away her appetite. "Well, I'm certainly glad to hear those squirrels never actually infested my cabin."

"If you'd seen the shape of your cabin before we fixed it up, you might not be so confident in that statement," Renee said with a twinkle in her eye.

Lynette maneuvered her legs out from under the picnic bench and stood. "Speaking of my cabin, I have a little surprise in my suitcase. Sit tight while I go grab it, all right?"

"Let me guess," Kit said with a grin as she scooped out another helping of beans. "You have the letters Renee sent you when we were kids."

Lynette snorted. "I wish! All I have from my childhood is that little teddy bear I used to bring to camp. And now that I think about it, I don't even have that anymore. Ebony ripped its head off. But don't tell Donna. It would crush her."

"That'll be fun for them," Annie was saying as Lynette rejoined her friends at the picnic table a few minutes later.

"Who is going to have fun doing what?" Lynette asked as she placed the vintage box of tarot cards on the picnic table and sat down again.

Annie reached for the box. "Renee just told me that Matt got a call from Henry. Something about coming out here to fish with him and Robbie. I guess Matt mentioned Robbie's fledgling guide business when they visited at Kit and Dean's wedding. I think Relic wanted to come, too, but he won't be able to this time."

"He also mentioned maybe bringing Owen," Renee added.

"Owen always loved to fish," Jackie added.

"The guys are coming here? To Whispering Pines?" Lynette asked. "No men are allowed on our girls' trips!"

Lynette's mind raced back to the scene in Owen's yard. Storm used to like to fish, too. If he was still in Ruby Shores, would Owen dare bring him on their impromptu fishing trip? That would be the fastest way to ruin her time at Whispering Pines. But she couldn't check. She didn't want to even mention the man's name—*either* of his names—to her girlfriends.

Renee laughed. "Don't worry. I made that abundantly clear to Matt. He agreed. If they can line up their schedules, he promised that we won't even know they're on the lake. They'd meet at the boat landing. It'll be like they aren't even around. They'd tent at the public campground on the other side of the lake."

"Just as long as my husband doesn't think it's all right to show up here. I love him dearly, but this is our time," Annie said, turning the box Lynette had brought over in her hands. "What the heck are these, Lynette?"

Lynette wriggled her fingers at her. "I'll show you." When Annie handed the box of cards back, she pulled the first few cards out and fanned them in her hand. "They're tarot cards."

Kit set down her spoon, finally giving up on the beans. "Tarot? Come on, Lynette. Don't tell me you're getting into that nonsense now?"

Lynette didn't appreciate her friend's condescending tone. "God, Kit, for once in your life, could you set aside your snooty scientific attitude and live a little? Why don't I pull a card and see what the spirits want to tell you?"

"Nope. Not interested. And I live plenty, thank you. That stuff is just silly."

Unlike Kit, Annie and Jackie looked curious about the cards.

Renee's expression was harder to read. "Where did those come from? They look really old."

"Where they came from is actually part of why I brought them. Believe it or not, I found them."

"You *found* them?" Kit repeated.

"What, did you think I conjured them up out of thin air?" Lynette said, half kidding but still annoyed with the skeptic in their group.

"Sure, that's what I thought, Lynette," Kit said. Her sarcasm wasn't hard to miss.

"Knock it off, you two," Renee said. "You are worse than Julie and Robbie when they get going."

Lynette took a deep breath. Renee was right, of course. "I'm sorry, Kit. I found these in a locked box in the garden shed I'm converting."

"Was there anything else in the box?" Kit asked. By her tone, Lynette thought she was probably sorry to have argued, too.

More flies were landing on the leftovers of the meal, despite Renee's ongoing efforts to ward them off. A rumble of thunder, far off in the distance, warned that the stormy weather wasn't over yet.

Lynette put the loose cards into the box, shoved them into the large pocket of the raincoat she'd grabbed from her cabin, and stood. "I really thought it would be fun to play with these cards a little. Why don't we put all the food away first, and then head up to the library before we mess around with them? Kit, I promise not to be offended if you decide to turn in early instead of joining us."

With a deep sigh, Kit rose, too, and replaced the cover on the bean pot. "I'm sorry. I don't want to miss anything. If I promise to behave, can I come, too?"

Lynette doubted Kit could hold her tongue, but she didn't want her to miss out either. "Fine. But if you're a smart aleck, don't be surprised when you wake up with a fresh wart on the end of your nose tomorrow morning."

"Many hands make light work," Renee said. She hung the dishtowel she'd used to dry the last of the dishes on a hook at the end of the large kitchen island in the lodge. "Thank you, ladies. Now, let's have some fun! I'll admit, the sight of those cards freaked me out for a minute, Lynette. I guess I'm overly superstitious. But it'll be fun. What if we dim the lights, light some candles in the library, and turn on some music? You know, set the stage."

Kit shook her head, but when she caught Lynette's eye, she held her index finger up to her lips.

Lynette laughed. "That's right. Hush."

Jackie rolled her eyes, grabbed Annie by the hand, and pulled her toward the stairs. "Come on. We'll leave these children to their antics and go find a decent playlist for the evening's festivities."

Annie, allowing herself to be pulled, grabbed an open bottle of wine left over from dinner on the way out the door. "Someone should bring glasses! Unless you want to just pass the bottle."

Ten minutes later, all five of them sat in a semicircle of chairs and love seats they'd rearranged in the upstairs library. Soft candlelight cast the only light in the room, and piano music added the ambiance Renee had suggested.

Lynette pulled the entire stack of cards out of the box, shuffled it a few times, and fanned them out on the table between them. "True confession time. I have no idea how to read tarot cards. But I'll wing it. I'll pull one card for whoever wants to go first. Then we can use our phones to look up what it might mean. Just some harmless fun." She glanced at Kit. "I think I see a little blood on your lip."

Kit's hand flew to the corner of her mouth, then a knowing smile bloomed. "Cute. You got me. Yes, I'm biting my tongue. But I won't break my promise to behave."

Lynette winked at her over the cards, then clapped her hands. "Who's first?"

Jackie and Annie both raised their hands. Renee did, too, but much more tentatively.

"Why don't I pull one for Annie first? Or else she'll find some way to complain that I'm not being fair," Lynette said. "Then we'll see what the spirits have up their sleeve for you, Renee."

Annie bounced in her chair. "You know me so well, Lynette!"

Everyone laughed, then Lynette waved the palms of her hands over the cards and mumbled something, trying desperately not to laugh. Then she swayed.

"Pick a damn card already," Kit insisted, drawing laughs all around.

"Fine," Lynette said. She picked one at random from the far right side of the fan and held it up for all to see. "Let's see what the Universe wants to tell Annie. I pulled the Queen of Pentacles card for you. Well, I suppose that could mean they recognize you as a queen in your world. Probably appropriate for someone in charge of a whole high school. See, Kit, do you believe now?"

Kit pulled her phone out of her shorts pocket. "Oh, shut up, Lynette. Why don't we see what the so-called experts say the card really means?"

As she scrolled on her phone, Lynette leaned toward Jackie. "See, Jack, I told you we'd convert her to the dark side."

Jackie hunched her shoulders and let out a cackle that would make any self-respecting witch proud.

"You're all nuts, you know that, right?" Kit said, never looking up from her phone. "Huh. Well, that's interesting."

Annie leaned toward her. "What? What does it say?"

"It says that if this card appears in a reading, it may mean you need to pay particular care to your own needs and indulge your sexual desires right now."

Jackie's cackle turned into a deep belly laugh, and she threw herself back against the love seat.

"It really says that?" Annie asked. She wriggled her eyebrows. "Interesting. Maybe I'll have to tell Henry to swing by if he comes to the lake to fish."

"Or you could text that sexy ex-husband of yours—you know, the *pilot*—and have him fly over tonight. He might be better equipped to satisfy you." Lynette kept her face as neutral as possible as she teased Annie. "You know what I always say. I'm sure that little love triangle the three of you kicked off years ago is still smoldering. And while Henry is a nice guy and all . . ."

Annie smacked her over the head with a throw pillow. "That's an awful thing to say, Lynette!"

Jackie wiped tears off her face, still hiccupping, but the laughter was under control. "I've always wondered—*hic*—what Michael was like in bed."

Annie's swing missed its mark this time. Jackie was too quick for her.

"Guys!" Renee jumped to her feet and yanked the pillow out of Annie's hands. "You're going to knock a candle over and burn the lodge down, and then the spirit of my dear Celia will haunt your asses for the rest of your lives. Knock it off! You really should take this all a little more seriously. Now that we know Annie has a libido issue, pull one for me."

Annie denied the accusation.

Once everyone settled down again, Lynette pulled another card.

"It better be a good one," Renee warned.

Lynette kept the card face-down. "Should we go with this one, or do you want me to pull a different one?"

Renee looked from the mystery card in Lynette's hand to the slightly mussed fan of the remaining cards. "I'll pick one for myself. I've learned that I'm in charge of my own destiny."

"Boom!" Annie said, smacking her hands against the coffee table like she was playing the drums.

Renee pulled a different card, keeping it face-down, and handed it to Lynette.

Lynette shook her head. Something didn't feel right. "I don't think that's how this is supposed to work . . ."

"Lynette, you just said you don't really know what you're doing. I think that card I just gave you is the one I'm meant to see."

Against her better judgment, Lynette took Renee's lead. "Fine, if that's what you want."

"It's what I want."

Lynette turned the card over. Someone gasped, but no one said a word.

Candlelight danced across the image of a skeleton holding a large scythe, riding atop a black horse.

Even in the dim light, Lynette could see the blood drain from Renee's face.

"I don't want to play anymore," Renee said. Her voice was little more than a whisper.

A flash of lightning overpowered the glow from the candles, and Lynette had to agree with her friend.

When someone flipped the lights back on, even Kit looked a little pale.

Chapter Eighteen

Lynette grinned at Renee and Annie as they twirled across the sand. Annie's kaleidoscope-patterned cover-up billowed around her as she danced to yet another song from a playlist that captured many of their favorites from high school.

"I don't need anything but a good time, either," Kit said beside Lynette, watching them shimmy to one of Poison's classics. "Jackie, go dance with them! I can tell you want to."

Jackie laughed. "The only way I'm getting out of this lovely chair is if Renee has some Joan Jett on her phone. I'm surprised the Wi-Fi works so well down here on the beach."

"Remember when we used to bring big boom boxes to the beach when we were kids?" Lynette said, enjoying both the beautiful day and the companionship of her friends. "Hot sun, rock and roll, cold beer . . . I didn't think life would ever get any better than that."

Kit dug her toes into the sand, then kicked a little spray of it into the air just as Renee and Annie collapsed onto their backs in a fit of giggles as the drummer's crescendo faded away. "My memories from back then aren't all sunshine and roses."

"To be honest, mine aren't either," Lynette agreed. "But the music always brings all the best memories to mind."

Kit seemed to consider this, then nodded. "It is hard to wallow in the crap memories when I picture Annie jamming out to a little Bon Jovi in the backseat of my Mustang."

Jackie wriggled her way out of the Adirondack chair. "Some of my very best memories include your Mustang, Kit. I'm so glad Dean fixed it up for you. Tell me you're driving us to dinner in it tonight!"

"Our options are my Mustang or Annie's sedan, so yeah, I'm happy to drive. We'll celebrate Lynette's birthday in style!"

Lynette squirmed. "I meant it when I said we don't have to celebrate my birthday tonight. Or we could do like we did in Arizona and celebrate *all* of us turning fifty-one. Every birthday is a blessing, you know."

Jackie pulled off her white cover-up and tossed it onto her chair. "Isn't that the truth? But no, not this time. Annie got to be the birthday girl in Maui, all by herself. You made a special trip home to Ruby Shores for that surprise fiftieth Owen threw for me. And since it was actually Kit's birthday in Arizona, she got a little special attention. So today is your turn."

"But what about Renee? Her birthday is in May. We've never all been together for her birthday," Lynette said.

Kit unzipped the beach bag next to her chair and pulled out a sun hat. "There's always next year. Maybe we'll have to plan our girls' trip for May. Then we could have a big birthday party for her, on *her* actual birthday."

Jackie gazed down at them both, her expression skeptical. "Annie probably can't get away in May."

Kit kicked another tuft of sand. "That's a problem for another day. Are you going for a swim, Jackie? I thought you'd only get out of your chair for a little Joan Jett."

"Changed my mind. Anyone want to race? We could reenact the way we kicked Ivory's butt at summer camp that time. Wasn't that the same summer we first met you, Kit?"

"It was," Kit said, jamming the hat onto her bright hair. "Back then my hair color didn't get any help from a bottle. Now it does, so I need to protect it from the sun. I'm going to have to pass on a race."

Jackie turned away. "You wouldn't have to if you let it go natural like our birthday girl. Her hair is still gorgeous."

Lynette felt a twinge of pleasure. She liked her own silvery curls, too. It might be one of the few things she still loved about her natural body, but at least it was something.

As Jackie reached the edge of the water near the old dock, she bent and picked up a pair of sandals. "Hey, Lynette, aren't these your sandals? What are they doing out here?"

Lynette smacked her forehead. Her hair might still be her crowning glory, but sometimes her brain failed her. "*That's* where they are! I bet I looked for them for twenty minutes this morning and couldn't remember where I put them."

Secretly she blamed her forgetfulness on the vivid nightmare she'd endured on the dock yesterday, just as the storm rolled in.

Jackie shrugged and dropped the sandals onto the dock. "I'll bring them up to you after my swim. Or you can join me."

"Nah, I'm good," Lynette said, relaxing back into her comfortable chair.

"I'm glad to see Renee doesn't still seem upset about that card you pulled for her last night." Kit kept her voice down so Renee couldn't hear her.

Lynette looked to Kit. "To be clear, *she* pulled that card. I'd already pulled a different one for her. By the way, I love your hat. It's cute."

"Thanks," Kit said, tipping her head in Lynette's direction. "And you're right. She pulled the Death card. Were you thinking the same thing when she flipped it over?"

Lynette sighed. "Probably. My first thought was of Matt. I've never even been married, but I imagine it's terrifying to be married to a police officer. Especially in this day and age. Do you think she thought that, too, and it scared her?"

"Yeah, I do. When we got back to our cabin last night, we actually did some research about tarot," Kit admitted.

"Wait . . ." Lynette laughed. "You and Jackie researched tarot readings last night? I thought you hated that stuff."

"I never said I hated it. I just said I didn't believe in it. Still don't. But that doesn't mean I'm not willing to research more about it. I'm a scientist, after all. I love research."

Lynette returned her gaze to the water. Jackie was swimming perpendicular to the shore now; her strokes looked smooth and strong. Renee and Annie were fiddling with the music, their voices too low to hear. "That is such a Kit thing to say. Did you find anything interesting in your research?"

"We did. The Death card doesn't actually signify that someone is going to die. It's more about transformation and change."

"Hmm," Lynette said, considering this. "You should tell Renee that. It would probably make her feel better."

Kit relaxed her head against the back of her chair and slipped the hat down over her eyes. "I already did. Why do you think she's smiling and dancing now?"

———⁂———

Lynette pulled her door shut and put on her seatbelt. "These belts must be new."

Kit turned the key in the ignition. "They are. Dean and Isaac are on a mission to make these old classic cars as safe as possible. Isaac thinks his mother might have survived the car crash that took her life if the old Camaro she was driving would have had air bags."

"This thing has air bags now?" Lynette asked. The dash looked the same to her as it had when they were teens.

"No," Kit laughed. "The belts were an easy fix. Retrofitting for other kinds of safety equipment is a whole different ballgame, but Isaac has his sights set high."

Annie's head popped up between the two in the front seat. "I don't understand why I'm always stuck in the middle of the backseat."

Kit and Lynette both laughed, then Lynette playfully shoved Annie back with a hand to her forehead. "Pretend you are royalty and we are your chauffeur and bodyguard."

The banter and visiting continued amongst the five friends during the twenty-minute drive from Whispering Pines to the cute new restaurant on the water that Renee's daughter had recommended.

When they arrived, Renee let out a whistle from behind Lynette. "Looks like Julie's recommendation was a good one. This place is darling," she said as she climbed out of the backseat. "Let's hope the food is tasty, too."

Lynette slammed her door, then linked her arm through Renee's. "The company is excellent, and that's all that really matters. Besides, if the food is awful, I bet your sister has yummy snacks tucked away in the fridge at the lodge. That can be our backup."

They filed inside, and the pleasant surprises continued. Renee's daughter had called ahead and reserved them the best table in the place, with a beautiful view of the lake beyond.

Once seated, Lynette allowed herself to enjoy one gin and tonic. This was her birthday celebration, after all.

"I forgot my readers," Jackie said, holding her menu away from her face. "Why do they have to make the print so small?"

Renee pulled a set of glasses off the top of her head. "Here, use mine. I already know what I want. Julie said their special is walleye, and I've been hungry for fish lately."

Jackie accepted the reading glasses with a thankful smile. "Maybe if the guys catch something, we can wrap up our vacation late next week with a fish fry."

"No boys allowed! Except Matt and Robbie, but they don't count," Lynette reminded them all, to which everyone again agreed.

"But we'd take their fish," Jackie said as she looked over Renee's glasses at Lynette. "Men have to be good for something, right?"

"Spoken as a true divorcée," Annie pointed out just as the waiter arrived.

The food turned out to be as tasty as Julie had promised, but Lynette still thought Renee's daughter had seemed overly pushy in getting them away from the resort for the evening. She was probably getting a little tired of them all. Renee said that Julie loved to be left in charge of the resort. This was her chance.

Once staff cleared their dishes, Renee insisted they order dessert. "I'm sorry we don't have a birthday cake, Lynette. I'll find you one for tomorrow, since Monday is your actual birthday. But I'm in the mood for a little cheesecake."

Her phone vibrated on the table.

"Jackie, can I have my glasses back, please?"

Lynette grinned as she sipped her decaf. Passing reading glasses back and forth wasn't something any of them would do if they were here to celebrate her twenty-first birthday instead of her fifty-first. She watched as Renee read the text. Her friend seemed to stiffen.

"Is everything all right, Renee?" she asked. The image of the tarot card from the previous evening floated into her brain.

Renee glanced up, then set her phone face-down on the table again. "Of course. Julie just wanted to loop me in on something. Now, where were we?"

"Lynette was just going to tell us how she's feeling about being back in Ruby Shores," Annie said.

Lynette watched as a different server brought everyone but her and Kit fresh cocktails. "Kit, I can drive us back if you want a second drink."

"Thank you, but no. I'm good with water. But I like Annie's suggestion. How are you settling in, Lynette? Do you enjoy living in Ruby Shores in your big, beautiful house?"

Do I? Lynette wondered. Sure, there were things she loved about life in a small town, but there were still days when she felt like a square peg in a round hole.

"Do I enjoy it?" she repeated, gazing from face to face. "I guess I do. Most of the time. To be honest, sometimes I think Donna has settled in better than I have. I thought it would be so easy. But the days can be long. And lonely. I've never lived in such a big house. Overall, I suppose it's good."

"That isn't exactly the ringing endorsement I was hoping to hear," Renee said.

Lynette shrugged. "It's an enormous change. These things take time. But I get to see our Annie here, once in a while."

"Now that the world is getting back to normal we have to make a point of getting together more often," Annie said. She took a quick sip of wine, then asked, "How is your shed remodel coming along?"

"Not as quickly as I'd hoped," Lynette admitted with a laugh. "But if this last year has taught me anything, it's that house-related projects always take twice as long and cost three times as much as a person plans for."

"I may live in an apartment for the rest of my days," Jackie said. "Home ownership isn't all it's cracked up to be."

"Lynette, you mentioned a cute contractor who had worked on your bathroom remodel last year. Did anything come out of that?" Annie asked.

While the question seemed to pique everyone's interest, Lynette was afraid she was going to have to disappoint them. "Sadly, no. Turns out the guy already has a husband. I think I'm getting rusty in the romance department."

Their desserts arrived amongst their laughter.

"I have faith in your ability to hook another hot Romeo, Lynette," Kit said. "You might just need to be patient. If you are still interested in male companionship, that is."

Oh, I'm still interested, she thought. But when the vision of one particular *hot Romeo,* as Kit had suggested, came to mind, she hastily pushed it away. *Been there, done that.* History had taught her some painful yet valuable lessons, and she wasn't one to repeat prior mistakes.

Besides, Storm—or was it Taran?—was probably long gone by now.

"Oh, do tell," Kit said. "I know that little grin."

"I don't know what you're talking about," Lynette shot back. She did her best to relax her face into a neutral expression. She had no intention of telling her friends about her run-in with Storm, so she decided to change the subject. "Fine. I'll be patient in my quest to dip my toe back into the dating pool. But, speaking of pools, that reminds me. Annie, I got the old fountain working on that statue you and Relic helped me drag out of the shed."

"I forgot about that!" Annie said. "Was Donna okay with the way we stood her up in the middle of her rose bushes?"

Renee paused, the forkful of cheesecake just shy of her mouth. "You made your poor mother stand in the middle of a rose garden? Why, for heaven's sake?"

The question stumped Lynette for a beat. Then she laughed. "We stood a statue of a girl in the middle of Donna's roses. But it was a little weird, actually. She seemed upset about the statue, even though she'd seen it before. Not sure what that was about, but she got over it. Maybe she likes it better now that the fountain part is working."

After eating her bite of cheesecake, Renee grinned. "That makes more sense. You'll have to text us pictures of your shed when you get it done. I'm not sure how soon I'll be visiting Ruby Shores. How is everything else, Lynette? Have you acclimated to not working every day? Do you miss it?"

"Say, what was it Lauren saw online regarding your old company?" Jackie interjected. "I hope it wasn't anything that could still affect you."

Lynette considered whether this was a topic she might divulge more about. She decided it couldn't really hurt. "If I tell you something, you have to all promise not to mention any of this to Donna," she said, making eye contact with each woman at the table.

Everyone promised.

"Lauren stumbled across a brief article on a fashion newsletter about labor-related complaints at my old company. I'm hoping that either there's no truth to any of it, or the women I sold it to are smart enough to see their way out of the trouble. The sale happened during the worst of the pandemic upheaval. I sold it to two women I hired on at the company years ago. My other option was to go with an interested venture capital group. That was the avenue Donna would have preferred. It certainly seemed less risky. But people took a chance on us, back in the day, and I thought it was important to pay it forward."

Renee pushed her empty dessert plate out of the way. "Your middle name doesn't happen to be Celia, does it? Because that sounds exactly like something she would have said. I've always thought the two of you would have had plenty in common."

Knowing Renee had always considered her Aunt Celia to be one of her favorite people, Lynette took that as a compliment. "Thank you for that, Renee. Mom was right, though. The deal I selected was risky, and not all the scheduled payments have come in on time. The new owners have caught up now, but to be honest, the delays have even caused me some headaches with cash flow. When I talked to my lawyer yesterday morning, he'd received the latest installment. Hopefully that's a good sign. I'm optimistic I'll receive the rest of the money they owe me, as agreed."

Maybe if she said it often enough, even she'd believe it.

Jackie shook her head. "Do you know how proud we all are of the successful life you built, Lynette? As a former corporate employee turned small business owner myself, I have a new appreciation for how hard it is to be an entrepreneur."

Lynette was feeling uncomfortable with all the attention she was receiving. As she searched for a different topic she could bring up, Renee's phone vibrated again.

"Ladies, if you are finished with dessert, how about we move this party back to the resort?"

Kit dropped her linen napkin onto the tabletop. "Is everything all right?"

"Of course," Renee assured them. "Julie could use a little help, just for a minute, and then we can get back to celebrating Lynette's birthday."

Lynette took one last sip of her cooled decaf and rose. "This was celebration enough. But I wouldn't mind some time around the firepit again. I'd love to hear more about Celia, Renee."

If the ongoing chatter in Kit's Mustang during their drive back to Whispering Pines was any indication, Lynette suspected it might be a late night. Not that she'd mind. Maybe if she was tired enough, she could enjoy a dreamless few hours of sleep for once.

A parked minivan in front of the lodge looked vaguely familiar to Lynette when they pulled into the parking lot at Whispering Pines. Maybe it belonged to some late-arriving guests, and this was what Julie had reached out to Renee about.

"That's weird," Annie said, leaning forward from the backseat again. She pointed at the van. "That looks just like my folks' van that we used in Arizona, doesn't it? Strange."

"Huh," Lynette said. "I thought it looked familiar."

Everyone climbed out of the Mustang. Renee led the way, but when she reached the front door to the lodge, she turned to face them. "Actually, Annie, that *is* the same van."

"What?" Annie asked, looking between the lot and Renee.

Lynette took a step closer to the van. A cactus made up part of the design on the front license plate. "Why are Annie's parents at Whispering Pines? Did something happen back home?"

Renee shook her head. Lynette thought she looked nervous. "Annie's folks aren't here. Just her mom, Patsy. Donna and Charlotte, too. Maybe even my mom, but I don't see her car yet."

Lynette opened her mouth, but before she could ask more questions or point out that mothers weren't any more welcome on their girls' trips than men, the front door of the lodge burst open.

"Surprise!" Donna yelled. A paper cone birthday hat dangled from one hand and a wineglass occupied the other. "You didn't actually think I'd let you turn fifty-one without me, did you? I've never missed one of your birthdays, and I wasn't about to start now!"

"Renee?" Lynette muttered, just before a gaggle of soft arms enveloped her in a cloud of perfume and the hint of alcohol on her mother's breath.

Chapter Nineteen

"*Surprise!*"

Lynette threw her hands up in the air, pretending to be shocked over the noises and sights before her. The real surprise had come the previous evening when they'd returned to Whispering Pines to find Donna, holding a birthday hat. Folding tables and chairs, bright decorations, and far too many people all littered the expanse of lawn between the resort's main firepit area and the beach. She didn't even recognize everyone. A gold tablecloth draped over one long table at the edge of the grass. Neatly stacked black paper plates and napkins stood ready at one end. A black-and-gold garland draped across the front and read *Happy Birthday!* There were even lights strung up high between a few trees. She didn't remember them being there before; they'd make this area glow when night fell.

Despite the vast differences between party venues, it reminded her of the surprise birthday party Owen and Jackie's mother, Charlotte, had thrown for her friend's fiftieth a year and a half ago.

As if she could read her mind, Jackie wrapped an arm around her shoulders with a laugh. "Yes, you might recognize some decorations. Apparently, Mom threw everything in a box after my party and saved it. When Donna came up with this hair-brained idea to throw this party to-

"

gether so quickly, dear Charlotte offered up most of this. Look, Lynette, I know you weren't thrilled to find our moms here at the resort when we got back last night, but remember . . . you promised to be a good sport."

Lynette squeezed Jackie's hand, then pushed her arm away. "I'll behave," she whispered before turning to the larger crowd. "All of you do realize that the surprise came last night, right? You already told me to expect cake and balloons today."

Donna finished setting a tray of treats on the table, then approached Lynette with her hands extended. "Thank you for humoring me, dear." She clasped both of her daughter's hands in her own. "You know how I like surprises. And I couldn't bear the thought of missing your birthday."

While still a little irritated over Donna's completely unexpected appearance at the resort, Lynette knew her mother meant well. She hadn't even realized the two had never spent one of Lynette's birthdays apart until Donna had pointed it out. Lynette might not have many people in her life, but Donna had always been there for her, and she needed to do a better job of feeling grateful for that fact.

She pulled her mother into a quick hug, then stepped back. "I don't even know who some of these people are!"

Donna laughed, then swept her arm toward the mingling crowd. "Whoever could make it from Renee's family is here, and I know you haven't met all of them. Plus, we opened it up to other resort guests. We didn't want anyone to feel excluded. Now, come on, let me introduce you to some of my new friends!"

Lynette sighed, but allowed herself to be dragged from person to person and group to group. Donna had always been the more outgoing of the two of them, and since moving back to Ruby Shores, Lynette's circle had shrunk significantly. But she'd promised to play along, so she put on a brave smile and accepted birthday wishes from friends and strangers alike over the next hour.

Once they'd spoken with everyone, Donna pulled her toward a ring of lawn chairs in front of the food table.

Renee's mother patted the chair next to her. "We saved this one for the birthday girl. Have a seat."

Before releasing her hand, Donna took a closer look at her fingers. "Lynette, I just noticed you aren't wearing your ring. Did you leave it at home?"

That didn't take long, Lynette thought, cringing inwardly.

She was still upset about losing her special ring in the lake, but she'd hoped Donna wouldn't notice. She considered lying, but what would that accomplish? The ring was gone, and there was no way she'd get it back.

"I'm so sorry, Mom . . . I wish I would have thought to leave it at home for safekeeping, but you know how neither of us likes to take it off. Well, we were boating out on the lake, and the sunscreen I'd put on must have gotten under it, because it slipped off. We were in deep water, and . . . I'm afraid it's gone."

Maybe if she didn't know her mother almost as well as she knew herself, she'd have missed the shadow that passed over her expression. Donna shook her head. "Oh dear. That's a shame. But accidents happen. I'm only glad it was just the ring that you lost. Remember, you aren't the strongest swimmer, Lynette."

Donna was right. There'd never been time or money for swimming lessons, though Lynette liked to think her abilities in the water were sufficient enough to at least keep herself alive. She also suspected her mother's comment was meant to divert attention away from her disappointment over Lynette carelessly losing such a special piece of jewelry.

"Maybe we can have a duplicate made using yours as the pattern—we could even have that one blessed, too," Lynette suggested.

"Don't be silly. The ring did its trick, and that darn cancer of mine is long gone. Now, sit by Lavonne here and enjoy your party. I'll go get us both something to drink. What would you like?"

Lynette glanced around the lawn and at all the people there to celebrate with her, and she felt that old familiar craving for a gin and tonic. Light on the tonic. But she'd already had one the night before, and she didn't feel like tempting fate with more alcohol at the moment. "If there's iced tea, that would be perfect. Thanks, Mom."

Donna finally released her hand and headed for the refreshments.

"Your mother is a delight," Lavonne said as Lynette sank into the chair beside her. "I feel so lucky to finally meet all the mothers of the infamous Kaleidoscope Girls. It always felt a little strange to me, not to have ever met any of them. I always made it a point to get to know the parents of my children's friends."

Lynette was about to point out that Kit's mother wasn't in attendance when a boy ran by and tripped over Lavonne's foot. Lynette noticed a knee brace on the woman's extended right leg. The boy, who looked to be around ten, skidded to a stop.

"I'm sorry, Grandma! I hope I didn't hurt you," he said. His concern appeared real to Lynette.

Lavonne reached out and snagged the boy's hand. "Jake, you need to slow down. I'm fine. But what are you doing, running through the middle of the birthday party? If you want to run, go run in the sand. By the way, have you met Lynette, our guest of honor? Lynette, this is Jake. Val's youngest."

"And Grandma's favorite," the boy added with a teasing grin, revealing a mouth full of metal. "Actually, I'm *everyone's* favorite, since I'm the baby of the family."

Based on the grimace that replaced his smile, Lynette guessed Lavonne must be giving the boy's hand a reprimanding squeeze. But she also suspected the charming kid probably was indeed a family favorite.

"Jake, we don't play favorites around here."

Young Jake bent over his grandmother and dropped a quick kiss on her forehead before jogging off with a wave and a smile.

"He is totally your favorite," Lynette whispered to Jake's grandmother.

"He is an awful lot like his Grandpa George," Lavonne replied with a wink.

Lynette took this to be an indirect affirmation of Lavonne's true feelings for the boy. Then she remembered that this was the woman who'd so graciously held on to the letters she'd sent to Renee. "Say, Lavonne, I wanted to thank you for keeping those letters I exchanged with Renee when we were kids. *And* to think to give them to her so we could read through them here. They were the catalyst for such a fun trip down memory lane. I wish I'd have kept Renee's letters to complete the set."

Lavonne gave one last shake of her head as she watched her youngest grandchild disappear from view before returning her full attention back to Lynette. "I'm delighted to hear that. We still live in the same house we raised the kids in, and every closet, nook, and cranny in the place feels so stuffed with junk that I sometimes consider purging most of it. But then something happens, like the joy you girls found from reading through the letters, and it reminds me how important some of that old stuff really is. The value of it lies in the memories it can spur. It's only junk if there are no important memories attached."

Lynette's mind flitted back to the old wooden box she'd pulled out of the shed. The things inside must have held a similar kind of value for Sybil to lock them away like that.

Donna returned with three plastic cups of iced tea, handing them each one. A woman in the chair on the other side of Lynette excused herself and Donna took the seat before anyone else could claim it.

"Who was that?" Lynette didn't recognize the departing woman.

"One of the resort guests," Donna said. She settled into the chair and took a sip of the ice-cold tea. "Oh, that's good. It's hot today."

It was hot again. Lynette thought it was perfect lake weather. "I still can't believe you pulled this off, Donna," she said, looking around them. "How did you manage it?"

Donna paused for one more sip before responding. "Well, I guess it started last week when I had a coffee date with Charlotte."

Lavonne shifted in her chair to better face the birthday girl and her mother. "Is that something you do often? Get together, I mean."

"No," Donna admitted. "I've thought of reaching out to both Charlotte and Patsy since we moved back, but then it was difficult because of the pandemic. It wasn't until more recently that it was even possible."

"The months of isolation were horrible, weren't they? And to think, a year ago we were all still stuck at home," Lavonne said. "Now, remind me again what Kit's mother's name is, would you? When I said earlier how nice it's been to meet the other mothers, I forgot she isn't here. Were all of you close through the years?"

Lynette searched the crowd for Kit, finding her seated at the edge of the grass with Annie and Jackie. The three were laughing about something. "Her name is Mia. Kit's mom, I mean. She was never a big part of

Kit's life, at least when we were all in school together. Kit's grandparents raised her. But Mia is back in Ruby Shores now."

"That's right," Donna confirmed. "To be honest, I was a little nervous to call Mia, but I actually did reach out to her."

"You did?" This surprised Lynette.

Donna nodded. "Well, I didn't have Mia's number, but I had Hazel's. Hazel is Kit's grandmother," she explained to Lavonne. "She's in her nineties and still as spunky as ever. To answer your earlier question, I'd term all of us mothers as more of acquaintances versus friends. In Kit's case, Hazel was always our contact person, not Mia. The woman suffered substance abuse problems and was absent for most of Kit's growing-up years."

"Did you end up talking to Mia, then?" Lynette asked.

"I did. And I actually feel like she might have agreed to come with us to Whispering Pines. But Hazel had an important doctor's appointment. Mia didn't feel she should miss it."

Lavonne looked around the crowded lawn. "It seemed as if you were having lots of fun with Charlotte and Patsy last night, though. By the way, thank you for allowing me to bunk with the three of you in the duplex."

Lynette swirled the tea in her plastic cup to distribute the melting ice. "I still want to hear the story behind how you worked this out with Renee to make this party happen."

Donna nodded. "As I was saying, I grabbed coffee with Charlotte last week. It was something we'd meant to do for some time. We found so many things to talk about, and two hours passed quickly. It was so nice to get out of the house and visit with another woman again."

"Do you mean it was great to talk to someone other than just me?"

Lynette asked pointedly.

"You know I love you, dear," Donna said. "We wouldn't be here if I didn't. But if you want to hear this, quit interrupting."

"Fine." Lynette felt like a scolded child instead of a woman turning fifty-one.

"We started talking about how lucky the five of you girls are to have each other. About how much fun it would be to travel with friends again. I used to do that when we still lived in New York and I had a couple girlfriends nearby, but we've fallen out of touch. I also realized that this might have been the first time I'd be apart from you on your birthday."

"Which is baffling for me to think about," Lavonne interjected. "But I suppose I haven't missed many of my four kids' birthdays either."

"See," Donna said, holding a hand out toward Renee's mother. "I started thinking that maybe it was high time I travel again, and it might even be fun if the mothers of the Kaleidoscope Girls looked into some trips of our own. But then Charlotte dropped me back at the house after coffee, and we had that whole mess with the water in the basement. I forgot about my idea until later that night."

"Let me guess. You called Charlotte back and got this thing rolling," Lynette said.

"I sure did. Charlotte was game, but before I even called Patsy, I thought I better check with someone here at the resort. Renee would have been the obvious person to call, but I didn't have her phone number. So I went online and found a contact number for the resort. I reached Julie, Renee's daughter, and told her what I was thinking. It just so happened that some guests had to check out early last week, which left the duplex free. And here we are."

Lynette considered the abbreviated recap of the timeline. "When did

Renee find out about this, then? She obviously knew you were here when we got back to the resort last night. And she never said a word."

"You can blame me for Renee's secrecy," Lavonne said. "Julie thought Donna's idea sounded fun, but since she'd never actually met her—or any of the other mothers, for that matter—she called me to see what I thought. We looped Renee in a couple days ago, but I swore her to secrecy. I'm glad to see she can keep a secret."

"Oh, she kept it, all right. It floored me to find you all here," Lynette said. "But I'm honored. Donna, you've always made my birthdays special, but this is over the top. I've never had such a big party thrown in my honor."

Donna held up her cup of tea and tapped it against Lynette's. "I'd say it's about time, then."

Lynette's birthday party wound down by early evening. Resort guests had wandered back to their cabins or other activities, and Renee's extended family had scattered, except for Lavonne.

Lynette picked up a half-eaten bag of chips and a nearly empty tray of cookies from the food table.

"Oh, no, you don't," Jackie's mother said. She took both items from Lynette's hands. "This is *your* party. That means you don't have to clean up."

"But I can help. What else am I going to do?"

Charlotte shook her head. "No. I insist. Lynette, we are at a beautiful little lake resort on an even more beautiful summer evening. Don't tell me you can't find something to keep yourself occupied."

Charlotte wasn't going to give up.

Lynette glanced around. Renee stood on the path leading back to their house, discussing something with Matt; he was in uniform and likely headed to work. She spied Kit and Jackie breaking down tables while Annie lugged away an armful of collapsible lawn chairs.

That morning they'd discussed making an early night of it, since they'd all stayed up late the night before, catching up with their mothers. Maybe she'd head back to her cabin and find something to do. It was too early to go to sleep, but she could read. She'd already finished the one novel she brought on the trip, but she was struggling to get into the murder mystery Jackie had lent her.

"All right. Well, thanks, Charlotte. Thank you for not only giving me a pass on cleanup duty, but for helping with this whole surprise visit. I think I'll head up to the library then and find a new book to read."

"That sounds perfect," Charlotte said. "I've had so much time alone lately, I've gotten back into reading, too. First we moved my husband, Glen, into a memory care unit. Then everyone was stuck at home for all those months. I'd forgotten how relaxing it can be to get lost in a good book. Enjoy."

Charlotte loaded her arms up with as many party things as she could carry. Once she was out of sight, Lynette did the same thing. If she was going to the lodge anyhow, there was no reason to go empty-handed.

"Thanks again for everything, Donna," Lynette said when she found her mother in the lodge kitchen. She deposited the leftover paper products onto a space on the island. "I tried to help clean up, but Charlotte told me that wasn't allowed."

"Yet you brought things back here anyhow, I see," Charlotte said with a laugh.

Lynette shrugged. "But that's it. I'm going to go up to the library and find that book, then I plan to go read in my cabin. I just hope it isn't too hot in there tonight."

"Doesn't your cabin have air?" Lavonne asked as she piled leftover buns back into their original plastic bag.

"Yes, but it's not working, so it's been warm the last night or two. Don't worry. It's fine. I like hot weather."

Lynette left the kitchen just as Jackie stepped out of a nearby closet, wiping her hands. "There, we've got all the tables put away. Did I hear you say your cabin is hot?"

"It has been. Remember when I blew that fuse a few nights ago? It might have been a power surge. Something damaged the unit. But I don't want to bother Renee with it. I told Julie, and she'll get it handled."

Kit joined them in the hallway leading to the stairs. "Come stay with us if your cabin is too hot."

Lynette shook her head. "There's a fan right over my bed. I'll manage. But thanks. I'm going to grab a book and do some reading. I am peopled out for the day."

They both laughed.

With one foot on the bottom step, Lynette turned back to her two friends. "I'll tell you what. If it's uncomfortable inside my cabin and I'm not ready to sleep yet, I'll come read in your screened-in porch for a while. But I'll be so quiet that you won't even know I'm there."

"Sounds good," Kit agreed. "My plan is a cool soak in our clawfoot tub and an early bedtime."

Jackie closed the closet door. "And I have to do some online book-keeping. Did I tell you guys I have two part-timers working for me now? They won't be happy if they don't get their paychecks on time. Funny that it doesn't matter if I'm on vacation. People still need to get paid."

"One perk of business ownership," Lynette laughed. "I'll see you both tomorrow."

Lynette headed upstairs to the library and picked out a promising paperback. She also stumbled across a thick scrapbook of old pictures. Renee had mentioned they'd put one together with the extra pictures that didn't make it back up on the wall in their new photo gallery. This must be the album. She was sure Renee wouldn't mind if she borrowed it, so she took that back downstairs with her, too.

She'd reached the bottom of the stairs when the kitchen door swung open. Both Charlotte and Donna came through with arms full of bags and tubs.

"I wish you'd let me help," Lynette said when she saw their struggle.

"Nonsense," Donna said. "It's still your birthday. Tomorrow you can help."

"But I thought you were going home tomorrow?"

Her mother laughed. "Don't worry, we are. I just meant that your birthday is over tomorrow and things can go back to normal. Say, that reminds me. Will you follow me out to Patsy's van? I brought that packet from the lawyer that you'd asked about. If I wait to give it to you before we leave tomorrow, I'll probably forget."

Lynette understood Donna's logic. Personally, she'd already forgotten about the packet. "Will do. That way I can hold the door for you both, too."

Five minutes later, Charlotte was back inside and Donna stood with

Lynette in front of the lodge.

"Thank you again, Mom. Today really was special. I'm sorry if I was a little rude last night. It was just such a shock to see you."

Donna laughed as she handed her daughter the old leather Louis Vuitton bag Lynette used to take to the office every day. "Here's that paperwork. I understand your reaction. These trips serve as special times for you and your friends. To be honest, I worried you might *stay* mad at me for crashing like this."

Lynette took the bag. The handle felt familiar, comfortable even, in her hand. "Wherever did you find my case?"

"On the top shelf in that little library closet. Finding it brought back so many memories," Donna said. "I don't think a day went by when you didn't carry that thing back and forth between your apartment and the office. I'm glad you kept it."

Lynette placed the novel and scrapbook she'd borrowed from the library inside the bag, then ran her free hand over the well-worn leather. "Someone recently told me that the only true value of older things are the memories they evoke. I suspect that even applies to a vintage Louis bag."

Donna nodded. "We made lots of wonderful memories working to-gether over the years, didn't we, honey?" Then she inhaled deeply. "I love the way the air smells around here."

Looking around, Lynette agreed with both points. "We made lots of amazing memories. Not just for us, but for our employees, and even our customers. But speaking of work, that reminds me of something else that I wanted to discuss with you."

Holding up one hand, Donna shook her head. "If it's about the sale of the company, I've suspected for a long time that the buyers might not be paying you on time. I don't want to talk about anything that will steal any joy from today, though, so why don't we just wait and discuss this when you get home?"

Lynette let her arm straighten so her bag rested on the ground. "How could you possibly know anything about that, Mother? Only my lawyer knows about the late payments, and he'd never betray client confidentiality."

Donna's eyes narrowed. "Need I remind you that no one on this earth, not even your friends here, know you better than I do?"

"I suppose that's true," Lynette admitted. "I don't want you to worry about that, though, because I have it under control. In fact, there should be a copy of the latest payment—which my lawyer told me came in on time for once—in this packet." She tugged on the strap of her bag.

Donna looked to the bag and then back to Lynette's face. "If it isn't about the sale, then what is it?"

"Hopefully it's nothing serious. But a few nights ago, one of Renee's nieces, who loves fashion, showed me a very unflattering article that's circulating about how the new owners treated staff as the pandemic dragged on. It also mentioned quality concerns with their merchandise."

Her mother crossed her arms and tapped one toe. "Lynette, we sold the business. It sounds like they are back to making their payments on time. With luck, that will continue. Remember how we talked about your need to let go of your attachment? The company isn't your headache anymore."

It was Lynette's turn to take a deep breath. She remembered the early days, when the company was her baby, instead of a headache. She held the fresh, pine-scented air deep in her lungs for an extra beat. "I'm trying, Mother."

"I suppose that's the best I can hope for out of you. I know better than anyone how much of your life that endeavor cost you."

Lynette looped the strap of her bag over her shoulder. "I don't regret it."

"Nor should you. You built something to be proud of. But it's time to move on and enjoy the abundance you earned. Now, I better get back inside before my new friends have everything all cleaned up for the party I invited them to."

Donna walked toward the door, and Lynette turned to the sidewalk that circled around the lodge.

"Mom, wait. I have to ask. We both worked really hard for a long time on our business. Do *you* regret any of it?"

As she reached for the doorknob, Donna sighed. "How could you even ask me that, Lynette? Working alongside you was the greatest honor of my life. I think I'm probably the luckiest woman on Earth to have a daughter like you."

Lynette watched as the door closed behind her mother, considering her parting words. "No, Mom, I'm the lucky one."

Chapter Twenty

"LAVONNE, PLEASE THANK YOUR grandson for getting this fire going for us tonight. It's the perfect way to end the day," Donna said. She jumped when a rogue ember landed on her cotton-covered thigh and quickly brushed it away. "But it's a good thing I wore these old-lady shorts today. It was too hot for pants, but if these shorts weren't this long, that spark would have burned me."

"I'll be sure to pass your thanks on to Robbie," Lavonne assured her as she glanced at Donna's leg.

Donna looked around their deserted surroundings. "Where do you suppose the others disappeared to?"

"Do you mean Patsy and Charlotte? They mustn't be back from their evening stroll yet. They headed out while you were outside with your daughter. Charlotte invited us to walk with them, too, but my knee is in tough shape. I apologize if you'd have liked to go along. I thought it might be fun to spend some time around the fire enjoying this beautiful sunset. But that didn't sound like any fun by myself!"

Donna laughed. "A relaxing sunset sounds like the perfect way to end a very busy day. I have one knee that gives me trouble once in a while, too. Why don't we get to know each other a little better before they get back?"

"I'd like that," Lavonne said. "I've spent countless evenings sitting right here through the years, and neither the view nor the conversation gets old."

"Can you reach that poker? If we adjust this log a little, the fire could last us until bedtime. Unless you're a real night owl."

Lavonne had to stretch to reach the long metal rod. She handed it over to Donna. "If I'm having a good night, I can sometimes make it until midnight, but that's about my limit."

Donna stood and rearranged the logs to allow for more airflow. "That should do it, although I'm no fire expert." She stood the poker up next to her chair and sat down again. "You are so lucky to have a place like this for your family. I've only been here for one day, and I already feel calmer inside."

"That might have more to do with successfully pulling off this impromptu trip and your daughter's birthday party," Lavonne said. "But you're right. People often comment that there's just something a little magical about Whispering Pines. I worry it might be too much for Renee, though."

Donna scanned the area again, this time taking in the cabins, lodge, and beach. Beyond her immediate view, there was also Renee's new home and the duplex where the four mothers were staying. "It has to be an incredible amount of work to keep this place up."

"Work *and* money," Lavonne added. "Renee had a long-term career in a corporate job. She never loved it, but at least it was a steady income with benefits. In fact, she was still working at her job when Celia decided to leave this place to her. Renee got laid off from that job, but not until after Celia died. I often wonder what my sister-in-law was thinking when she decided Renee was the right person to leave this resort to. Plus, that was before Renee met Matt, so she was the single, widowed mother to two teenagers, too. She and Celia were so different."

Donna couldn't help but smile over her new friend's concerns. "Oh, Lavonne, as mothers, we never stop worrying about our kids, do we? It took me a long time before I was comfortable with the risks my Lynette was taking in building her business. Well, I suppose that technically it was *our* business, but I played a more minor role. I always worried how she'd handle failure."

"But I was under the impression that your company was very successful. Lynette didn't fail."

Donna had to whisk away another floating ember before it landed on her arm. "Right, she didn't. And Renee won't either. This Celia you all talk about. She never had a husband, right? Or kids of her own?"

"That's right. She was only responsible for herself. Well, and her mother, I guess. Her mother and stepfather were in a terrible accident when my husband and their other brother were still young. The stepfather didn't make it. Celia gave up on some of her big dreams to help raise the boys and nurse her mother back to health."

It was fun for Donna to hear some of this Celia woman's backstory. "Even if she wasn't ever a mother, she was still a caregiver. Plus, I'd say that if she never married but still wound up owning a place like this, she found financial success."

Lavonne nodded. "She was an amazing woman. I can't even imagine the level of discrimination she would have faced in the business world, but she persisted and eventually flourished. Oh, and I almost forgot—her own father died in some kind of accident when Celia was only five or six. There was another girl in the family, too, but she died of a weak heart at eighteen. My George doesn't like to talk about that. I can't imagine how awful it would be for a child to lose a sibling."

Donna shivered at Lavonne's words, despite the toasty warmth of the fire and the warm air of the mid-August evening.

Lavonne must have noticed her visceral reaction. She reached over and touched Donna's hand. "Oh my. Is that something you've had to endure, too?"

This woman was certainly perceptive. Donna wasn't used to anyone noticing her upset. But ever since she'd come home to find that darn statue standing in the middle of her rose garden, thoughts of her long-dead sister were never far from her mind. "It isn't something I talk about. *Ever.* Lynette doesn't even know."

"Your own daughter doesn't know you lost a sibling? Why in heaven's name would you keep something like that from her?"

She shrugged. "It sounds kind of silly when you pose it that way. You said Celia's sister died of a weak heart. That is certainly tragic. My little sister's death was tragic, too, but it wasn't unavoidable. Violence killed her."

Lavonne gasped. "What happened, Donna? How old was she when she died?"

The old familiar panic rose in Donna's chest, threatening to cut off her air supply.

"I could apologize for asking, Donna, and we could let this conversation turn to something much less painful, but something tells me we shouldn't do that. I can see in your expression how hard this still is for you. But if you never talk about it, how can you heal?"

She snorted. "It all happened over fifty years ago. Everyone involved is dead now. Except for me."

"All the more reason for you to talk about it," Lavonne said, grabbing hold of Donna's hand. "Secrets are like poison. Why would you do that to yourself?"

The words made Donna wonder. Had she been poisoning herself for years with the knowledge of how her father had caused her sister's death?

"I never wanted Lynette to know the truth."

Lavonne gave her fingers another squeeze, then relaxed back into her red chair. "I suppose I understand why you wouldn't have wanted to go into detail with her about something so horrific when she was a child. If you don't want to share the specifics of your sister's death, Donna, I understand. You mentioned violence. Just tell me that whoever hurt your sister paid the price for whatever it was they did to her."

Donna sighed. "As far as I know, he never did. Not in this world, at least. To be honest, the moment we turned away from Irene's grave after her funeral, I ran. I ran and I never looked back. My parents insisted it was a terrible accident. That she fell down the stairs, hit her head, and never woke up."

A door slammed nearby. Donna whipped around, but relaxed when she saw it was a man she didn't know exiting the cabin next to Annie's.

"He? You didn't believe it was an accident? Do you think your father hurt your sister?"

Donna pressed a hand to one eye. She could feel a migraine coming on. "I know he did. My father was an angry man with a hair-trigger temper. I lost count of the number of black eyes my mother tried to explain away. To her credit, I know at least one or two of those happened when I'd misbehaved and she was trying to protect me. He only ever hit me once, but I stood up to him. I don't think anyone else ever had, and it was the last time he laid a hand on me."

"Do you think your mother was afraid to take you and your sister and leave him? Were there any other kids?"

She grabbed the poker again. This conversation was making her nervous, and she needed to stand. "No, it was just my sister and me. If Mother ever considered leaving him, she never told me. Her parents raised her to believe men had the right to treat women however they choose."

Sparks flew as she took her latent frustration out on the burning logs.

"Did your father move on from you to your sister?"

She spoke the words so softly, Donna almost missed them.

"It wasn't that straightforward. Maybe if it had been, I'd have found the courage to take my sister and leave. But she was always more forgiving of both of our parents than I was. We only talked about the abuse and our father's anger a few times, and she insisted I was overreacting. I should have trusted my gut. It told me otherwise. But we stayed. Then, one night, Mother and Father were fighting again. I was so sick of their theatrics that I stayed in my room with a pillow over my head, doing my best to ignore them. I wish my sister would have done the same. But even the pillow couldn't muffle their screaming. They were getting louder, and I was almost ready to run upstairs and tell them to be quiet before the neighbors heard everything. That probably would have shut them up because the only thing either of them really cared about was appearances."

She took a hot breath. Even decades later, the scene was still vivid in her mind.

Lavonne gave her the space to collect herself.

"Then I heard my sister's voice, begging Father to let go of Mother. There was a different type of scream then, and I couldn't tell if it was Mother or Irene. I ran out of the room just in time to see my sister fall over the banister at the top of the stairs. I was too late to save her."

This time, Lavonne's gasp was exactly what Donna had expected.

"And yes, before you even ask, it was as awful as you might expect. Everything after that was a blur."

The two women sat in silence, both trying to process the long-ago tragedy.

"What *does* Lynette know?" Lavonne eventually asked.

Donna dropped the poker and collapsed back into her chair. "She thinks I ran away from home because I was pregnant with her and my parents cut me out of their lives."

"Were you pregnant when you left?"

"No. I was a virgin when I left. But I was such a mess, and had no way to support myself, that I suppose I confused sex for love. It was the end of the 1960s and I was only eighteen years old when I left home. I knew the trauma over my father's abuse and my sister's death had me all screwed up, and for two years I left a string of losers in my wake. When I realized I'd ended up pregnant, I knew I couldn't go back home. I'd slammed that door and locked it tight. There were some tough years ahead, but things got better when we ended up in Ruby Shores."

Approaching footsteps cut off Donna's next words.

"Sorry we took so long!" Patsy said.

Both Patsy and Charlotte stepped into the firelight. That was when Donna noticed that night had fallen while they'd talked. "We were about to send out a search party for you," she lied. Everything except her own painful history had faded from her mind once she began sharing her secrets with Lavonne.

Instead of calling her a liar, Lavonne played along. "Yes. If you hadn't gotten back in the next five minutes, I was going to call my son-in-law to bring in the reinforcements to find you."

The women laughed, and Donna was thankful the mood had lightened.

Charlotte handed her a light jacket. "I saw this on your bed and remembered you were in shorts. I thought you might get chilly."

The small, kind gesture brought a tear to Donna's eye. She was constantly being reminded why her daughter cherished the friendships with her four friends so dearly.

"See, I was right. You're so chilled your eyes are watering," Charlotte said with a quick wink before taking a seat.

Charlotte understood, too.

Once the other two women joined them, the conversation floated between a variety of lighter topics. When the topic of grandchildren came up, Patsy mentioned how much fun it was to be a great-grandmother, too.

"And don't forget your promise when we were all together for that fun Thanksgiving dinner at Annie's house," Donna said. "I get to act as an honorary great-grandmother to little Nora, too!"

Patsy laughed. "That is perfectly fine. I think Nora will be very accepting of the wide variety of grandparents she's inherited. My daughter's complicated love life makes for quite the blended family."

"At least she *has* a love life," Donna said. "I always liked her first husband, but I understand that not all marriages will last. I hadn't met Henry until that Thanksgiving. He seems fine, too. And Henry was certainly helpful last week when we had water in our basement."

"Way back when all that started between Annie, Micheal, and Henry, I warned her that she was playing with fire. Moving in with two male roommates," Patsy said, shaking her head as if she'd known the arrangement was doomed from the start. "Of course, she insisted they were just friends and she'd never let it go beyond that."

Charlotte laughed. "As they say, live and learn. I had my doubts, too, when my Jackie married Todd. Turned out I was also right to question my daughter's judgment, but we wouldn't have Hailey and Mackenzie if they wouldn't have married."

"Jackie has twin girls, right?" Lavonne asked.

"Right. I'm sorry, Lavonne, I forget you might not know as much about the girls' lives as the rest of us."

Lavonne made a dismissive gesture. "Don't worry about it. To be honest, sometimes Renee feels a little left out, too. It bothers her, but I understand. This has just been so fun. I hope I have the chance to get to know all of you, and your families, a little better in the future. So, Jackie divorced. Does she date?"

The question pulled a groan from Charlotte. "She does not. But I wish she would. Maybe she wouldn't spend so much of her time worrying about me, now that my Glen is in a facility because of his dementia."

Donna's thoughts drifted to Owen. He was always so helpful when either she or her daughter needed anything in their new roles as home-owners. "Why don't Jackie and Owen take a chance on a real relation-ship? Lynette insists they should try."

Charlotte nodded enthusiastically. "I used to wonder the same thing. But my daughter is pig-headed."

"He's a handsome guy," Donna added, though Charlotte didn't seem to be the one who needed convincing. "But I'm one to talk. Poor Lynette. I don't think she's gone out on a single date since we moved back to Ruby Shores. I sometimes blame myself and my horrendous dating history for her apparent aversion to any kind of long-term relationship."

Lavonne tapped the arm of her chair. "We can't blame ourselves for our children's misadventures in romance. At least that's what I keep telling myself. Our son is divorced and is the primary parent to his three kids. Renee's first husband died, and until Matt came along I never thought she'd make the time to find someone new. Our youngest is still married to the father of her four sons, but it isn't easy. And don't even get me started on Jess."

"Lavonne is right," Patsy chimed in. "Annie never listened to my dating advice. Our other daughter was a wild one, and then she did an about-face and married an uptight preacher. The man is difficult to tolerate."

Donna laughed. "He wasn't the most pleasant person at Annie's Thanksgiving table."

Patsy gave her a thumbs-up.

"Maybe Kit was the smartest one of the group," Charlotte said. "She held out until a couple years ago in the marriage department, and as far as I know, she's quite happy with Dean. But Lavonne, if you knew more about Kit's parents' story, even you would lay the blame for her hesitancy at their feet. I guess the bottom line is that we never finish being mothers."

Donna had to agree with that sentiment. "That was something Lavonne and I talked about while you two were walking. She worries about Renee and the pressures of keeping this beautiful resort running. My Lynette gives me plenty to worry about, including whether our move back to Ruby Shores was really right for her. Charlotte, you seem at least marginally concerned about Jackie, too."

"And I worry about my Annie's ability to keep everyone in her blended family happy—and on speaking terms," Patsy added.

Heads nodded around the fire, then the conversation died off for a moment. Donna shivered as the fire burned lower. Since no one was yawning yet, she pulled another log off the pile and added it to the firepit while the other three women seemed lost in their thoughts. Once she'd stoked the fire again, Donna sat and looked at each of them, wondering how much they'd all given up over the course of their lives for their loved ones.

"Do you ever get sick of only thinking about the well-being of our families?" she asked. "Our grown kids? Your grandkids?"

All three women looked her way, and she could see each was considering her question.

"I'm not ashamed to admit that I still have dreams I'd love to pursue," she continued. "Are we too old to do that now? We're all in our seventies, right?"

"That's an interesting set of questions, Donna," Lavonne said. "Whether or not we're too old . . . I don't think so. By now you've all heard of Celia, right? Well, she lived to be in her nineties, and she was still working and doing fun things with the resources she'd built for herself, right until the end."

Donna liked the sound of that. "That's great. Okay, keep going, Lavonne. What's one dream you still want to chase? I hope you have more than one, but we might run out of wood if we stay up *all* night talking."

Everyone laughed, then turned expectant eyes back to Lavonne.

"I guess the thing that pops into my mind relates to Celia," she said. "On the one hand, even though I loved Celia and respected her for all her accomplishments, I did feel like I lived in her shadow. I'm not sure I ever made a difference in anything—at least not the way Celia did."

They countered her statement with one "No way," a "Boo!" and even a couple of hisses.

"Why do we sell ourselves so short?" Charlotte asked. "Lavonne, you just finished telling me you have four grown children, and if they are all as amazing as Renee, I'd say you've accomplished plenty. And then there are all your grandchildren. I've always felt that raising kids is the most important work anyone can do. Nothing affects the world more. I think that's why I fell in love with my husband, too. He had plenty of flaws, but the one thing we always agreed on was providing a stable environment for our children. But . . . and we need to remember this . . . we've raised our kids and done what we can for them. I think Donna is on to something. If we still have unrealized dreams inside us, we better get to it. Time's a-wasting!"

"Fine," Lavonne conceded. "I won't argue with any of that, but my dream is still somewhat related to Celia. She left an incredible legacy. Money can't buy happiness and all of that, but it can really help those in need. I want to use the resources we still have—including our inheritance from Celia—to keep helping others. To keep Celia's legacy alive."

Charlotte raised her eyebrows. "I think that is a wonderful dream. Before you even decide who to point to next, Donna, I'll volunteer. My dream was always to escape the terrible winters in Minnesota. We'd planned to go south for a few months each winter after Glen retired, but we never got around to it. Then he got sick. Part of me would feel guilty for leaving him now, but I could remind myself that I'm not getting any younger, either. Sadly, he wouldn't miss me at this stage, and it would only be for a month or two to start. Maybe when I get home tomorrow I'll start doing some research. You ladies have inspired me!"

Patsy clapped her hands. "I can help you out with that dream, Charlotte. We have a second home in Arizona. You probably know that, since Jackie stayed there with Annie and the other girls for their fiftieth birthday celebration. The neighbor to our south down there called last week and is looking for a renter for next winter. It's small, so it wouldn't be too expensive, but it's cute. If that interests you at all, I can get you his phone number."

"Please!" Charlotte said. Her face glowed in the fire's light.

Donna steepled her fingers and rested her chin on top of them. "I'd move away."

Her simple statement had all heads swerving in her direction.

"Do you mean, like . . . just for the winter?" Patsy stammered. "It is a nice break to get away for a few months."

"No. I mean that my dream for many years has been to live in Europe during the summer months and then somewhere with pure white beaches and bright blue ocean waves in the winter." Donna could hardly believe she'd said the words out loud, but knew she had based on the stunned expressions of the other women.

"Why did you move to Ruby Shores with Lynette, then?" Charlotte asked. "And why did you buy such a big house? I mean, it's beautiful, but it's also old and *huge*. None of that jives with what you just said your dream was."

Donna didn't have a good answer. "I'm not really sure. Escaping New York was our immediate focus. Ruby Shores felt like the safe bet. The pandemic was still picking up speed and there were so many unknowns. But for the past few months, I've been worried that it might have been a mistake. Not that I can do anything about it now. I made a commitment to Lynette, and I need to stick with it."

"But you're the one who wanted to talk about dreams. Why would you do that if you thought yours was unattainable?" Patsy said.

A chill passed through Donna, so she pulled on the jacket that Charlotte had brought her. "I guess I'm either a glutton for punishment or I want to live vicariously through you."

Patsy made a sound of disgust. "That's not good enough, Donna. I haven't gone yet. My dream is to get back to traveling, and not just with my husband. I love him, but getting out of town with a bunch of girlfriends is so different. I used to do that many years ago. In fact, Annie told me once that my trips were her inspiration behind these annual trips they take now. But my old group is all gone. My friend Betsy was my last hope, but she passed when I was on an anniversary cruise with my husband. So I have a proposition for you three—and Kit's mom, too, if she's interested."

Donna had a good guess what Patsy was about to suggest.

"I think this quick little getaway to Whispering Pines should be the first of many trips we take together! But given that we have at least twenty years on those privileged little Kaleidoscope Girls, I think we probably want to go more often than once a year. Donna, we could consider somewhere tropical or even Europe for you. It isn't the same as actually living there, but it might be the next best thing. And it would get you out of Minnesota, Charlotte. This doesn't tie quite as nicely with the dream you mentioned, Lavonne, but maybe we could do one volunteer trip a year or something, in addition to traveling for fun."

Excited chatter erupted amongst the four following Patsy's suggestion. Donna felt her own spirits lift in a way they hadn't for a long time.

"Where could we go first? And when?" Charlotte finally asked, loudly enough to cut through their twittering.

Donna raised a hand. "If the weather is as tough this winter as last year, maybe we could get away for the holidays. Or at least right before, so we can still be with our families for Christmas. I have this friend, his name is Chester, and he loves to travel. He told me once that the Biltmore home, just outside of Asheville, North Carolina, is magical at Christmas. Would something like that interest anyone?"

The other women all raised their hands high in the air.

"But let's not tell our daughters about this yet," Patsy said. "I'd hate for them to crash our fun!"

"You are brilliant, Patsy," Charlotte said, giving the other woman a high five. Then she swung around and pinned Donna with an inquiring gaze. "Now, Donna . . . let's talk about this Chester fellow."

Chapter Twenty-One

Lynette closed the door to her cabin, not bothering with the lock. She felt perfectly safe at Whispering Pines—and besides, the temperature inside would scare anyone away, whether friend or foe.

At first, her cold shower kept her comfortable enough to sit at the small kitchen table and peruse Renee's scrapbook. After studying the additional photos, she switched to reading a book. Even though the first few pages of her borrowed novel proved promising, the air inside her tiny cabin had begun to feel oppressive. Since there was no screened-in porch, it was time to head to Jackie and Kit's unit.

She paused at the base of her cabin's stairs to look back at the small structure. The setting sun reflected off cheery red trim that contrasted nicely with dark wood siding. Annuals cascaded from the flower box lining the single front window. All together, it created a welcoming scene.

It made her think of her small garden shed back home. It wouldn't take much more work before that facelift was also complete.

The buzz of insects filled the warm, humid air. She'd placed one of Renee's new red chairs in front of her cabin days earlier in the hopes of a relaxing evening or two outside, but the mosquitoes would eat her alive. Thankfully, she'd already warned her friends she might borrow their screened-in porch for the evening.

She wondered if the cement sidewalk beneath her bare feet was once nothing more than a dirt path, back in the days of the earliest photographs of Whispering Pines that she'd found in the scrapbook. Or maybe stones or bricks once led the way, replaced over time with a more practical surface. Convenience over charm had its place, but what had this place looked like fifty or even a hundred years ago? She'd have to ask Renee about the resort's origin.

The walkway to Jackie and Kit's cabin passed behind the three cabins closest to the firepit, and she wondered whether Annie was relaxing inside her unit. Hopefully her friend was enjoying some well-deserved alone time.

Lynette caught a whiff of burning wood. Someone had lit the firepit. She spied Donna and Lavonne sitting there, talking. Their voices floated her way, but she continued on, liking the idea of her mother forming friendships with the other moms.

When she reached her destination, she didn't see either Kit or Jackie. Both were probably inside, doing their own things, too.

She knew that not all of their future girls' trips would be long enough to enjoy plenty of both togetherness and alone time, but the ease with which they could bounce between the two was a definite perk of this vacation. Since she'd already mentioned relaxing on their porch, she was as quiet as she could be as she let herself in.

A yank on the chain hanging from the center of the porch's ceiling fan created a pleasant stir to the air. A long wicker sofa ran parallel with the front of the porch, its back against the screen. Comfortable pillows beckoned, and she realized no one walking by would even see her if she laid on the couch. Heck, maybe she'd even fall asleep here. A light breeze and the fan were already helping to lower her body temperature.

Once settled, she opened her novel and searched for the paragraph where she'd left off. It was almost too dim to make out the words, but she ignored the little lamp next to the sofa, enjoying the solitude.

A voice reached her, and the word "magical" distracted her from her reading. She closed the book and let it rest on her stomach. It felt good to just relax.

Then she heard her mother's voice on the breeze. "Oh, Lavonne, as mothers, we never stop worrying about our kids, do we? It took me a long time before I was comfortable with the risks my Lynette was taking in building her business."

Lynette smiled. She was familiar with her mother's concerns. "*Our* business, Donna," she whispered.

She really shouldn't eavesdrop. It wasn't polite. Donna and Lavonne deserved their privacy. She opened the book again, found her spot, and started to read. It was a romance, so she already knew the couple would end up together in the end.

Then Lavonne's voice cut into her concentration. "Celia gave up on some of her big dreams to help raise the boys and nurse her mother back to health."

She closed the novel again and set the book on the floor. Despite Renee's promises to tell them more about her aunt, they hadn't talked in depth about her yet. She doubted Lavonne would share any secrets with Donna that Lynette wasn't supposed to hear, so she gave herself permission to close her eyes and listen. If the two women were discussing anything they didn't want others to hear, they would have taken their conversation back to the duplex for privacy, right?

Lynette smirked. *Fine, maybe I'm rationalizing a little.* But what could it hurt?

Lavonne was still talking. "I can't even imagine the level of discrimination she would have faced in the business world, but she persisted and eventually flourished."

Lynette shifted from her back to her side on the couch to make it a little easier to hear the conversation happening over by the fire. Renee's mother shared some of the personal tragedies Celia suffered during her younger years that had to have made her life difficult. Even though Lynette had always been an only child, she couldn't imagine the pain of losing a younger sister, only eighteen years old. How could someone get through something so horrific?

Realizing she'd lost the thread of their conversation again, Lynette tried to tune back in. The noise of the ceiling fan was making it a little difficult.

"It isn't something I talk about. *Ever.* Lynette doesn't even know."

Her mother's words brought Lynette up to a seated position, her ears straining to catch every syllable now. It was wrong to keep listening. She knew that. But it was like a person's reaction when they pass a mangled vehicle on the freeway. You know you should look away, but you just can't help yourself.

"My little sister's death was tragic, too, but it wasn't unavoidable. Violence killed her."

Lynette shot to her feet and reached for the chain on the fan. It wobbled when she yanked it harder than necessary, desperate to cut off the steady whoosh of the fan's blades.

Little sister?

What little sister?

Her mother had a *sister?*

Even from this distance, she heard Donna snort. "It all happened over fifty years ago," she was saying. "Everyone involved is dead now. Except for me."

Dead?

"I never wanted Lynette to know the truth."

Too late, Mom, she thought. And then: *I need to stop listening.*

Lavonne's calming voice reached Lynette. "If you don't want to share the specifics of your sister's death, Donna, I understand . . . Just tell me that whoever hurt your sister paid the price for whatever it was they did to her."

"As far as I know, he never did. Not in this world, at least. To be honest, the moment we turned away from Irene's grave after her funeral, I ran. I ran and I never looked back."

Irene? Who was Irene?

"I know he did," Donna was saying in answer to some question Lavonne had asked. "My father was an angry man with a hair-trigger temper. I lost count of the number of black eyes my mother tried to explain away."

Mom's father is my grandfather, Lynette thought, covering her mouth in horror.

"To her credit, I know at least one or two of those happened when I'd misbehaved and she was trying to protect me. He only ever hit me once, but I stood up to him. I don't think anyone else ever had, and it was the last time he laid a hand on me."

Lynette grabbed one pillow from the sofa and hugged it tightly against her stomach. She'd waited her whole life to learn more about her mother's family.

She grimaced. *Happy birthday to me.*

She wished now that she'd never asked her mother about her childhood. She must have caused the woman so much pain, forcing her to remember these horrific things, even if she'd never actually opened up to Lynette about them.

"Then I heard my sister's voice, begging Father to let go of Mother. There was a different type of scream then, and I couldn't tell if it was Mother or Irene. I ran out of the room just in time to see my sister fall over the banister at the top of the stairs. I was too late to save her."

Lynette stood again. She stepped to the screen door, her eyes on the back of a cabin that stood between her and Donna. An almost overwhelming impulse to run to her mother's side washed through her, but she couldn't move. She didn't dare, since she wasn't supposed to be hearing this conversation.

"She thinks I ran away from home because I was pregnant with her and my parents cut me out of their lives."

Lynette realized she was suddenly part of Donna and Lavonne's conversation again.

Her mother was still talking. "I was a virgin when I left. But I was such a mess, and had no way to support myself, that I suppose I confused sex for love. It was the end of the 1960s and I was only eighteen years old when I left home. I knew the trauma over my father's abuse and my sister's death had me all screwed up, and for two years I left a string of losers in my wake. When I realized I'd ended up pregnant, I knew I couldn't go back home. I'd slammed that door and locked it tight. There were some tough years ahead, but things got better when we ended up in Ruby Shores."

String of losers . . . ?

The jumbled, stolen pieces of her mother's conversation fell into place.

How much of my life is a lie?

She jumped at the sound of a door opening.

"Lynette, what the heck are you doing, standing out here in the dark?"

She spun to face Kit. The backlighting made it impossible to read her friend's expression.

"Umm . . ." Lynette struggled to form a cohesive sentence.

"Are you all right? Why don't you come inside?"

She shook her head and turned back toward the firepit. "I have to hear the rest of this."

She could have tried to pretend she was doing something other than eavesdropping, but Kit would probably see right through her lies. Besides, she had to listen for any other secrets her own mother might feel inclined to share with nearly complete strangers.

"Hear what?" Kit asked.

Lynette heard her step onto the porch and pull the door shut behind her.

"Jackie is clicking away on the computer back in her room," Kit said. Her voice sounded abnormally loud in the hush of the porch.

"*Shh!*" Lynette hissed. "My mom is out by the fire, talking to Lavonne."

Kit took a step forward to stand next to her. She was wearing a flowered wrap robe and a towel around her hair. "And you're, what . . . trying to listen to what they're saying? From here? In the dark?"

At least Kit was whispering now. Lynette ignored the judgment in her tone.

"Yes, and trust me when I say I'm not proud of myself, but the conversation has been incredibly *enlightening* up to this point. You can either stay here and shut up, or you can go back inside."

Lynette could feel Kit's gaze through the semidarkness, but she didn't care. There seemed to be a larger variety of voices coming from the direction of the firepit now.

"Is Annie out there with them?" Kit asked.

Despite everything, Lynette couldn't help but grin at Kit as her friend turned her head and leaned closer to the screen, as if also trying to hear what was being said. "I don't think so. That's Patsy talking. I never realized how similar they sound. She just said how much she loves being a great-grandmother."

Kit chuckled. "Fine. This sounds pretty harmless. But let's sit down at least. I don't want someone to walk by and catch our two shadows standing here, eavesdropping."

They hurried over to the couch where Lynette had laid down to read earlier.

". . . I warned her that she was playing with fire. Moving in with two male roommates."

Kit poked Lynette. "That's Patsy, and she's talking about how she warned Annie not to live with Henry and Michael after she moved to Minneapolis. Remember how Annie met both of them on that mission trip she took after college?"

"I remember," Lynette whispered. "But hush. We might miss something good."

She caught Charlotte's distinct laugh, then her voice. "As they say, live and learn. I had my doubts, too, when my Jackie married Todd."

"Good thing Jackie isn't out here," Kit whispered. "I wouldn't want her to hear her mother say something unflattering."

You have no idea, Lynette thought. But she intended to keep the things she'd heard earlier to herself, at least for now.

Lavonne was talking now. "Don't worry about it. To be honest, sometimes Renee feels a little left out, too. It bothers her, but I understand."

"Aww, I hate that she feels that way," Kit muttered. "I never want Renee to feel left out. I know she told us she does sometimes, but it must be worse than we thought if she told her mom."

Lynette nodded.

"Dang. I can't quite hear everything they're saying," Kit whispered. "They should talk louder."

Lynette held a pillow to her own face to stifle the sound of her laughter.

"I know, I know," Kit said. "I was too quick to judge."

Then they heard Lynette's mother say, "Why don't Jackie and Owen take a chance on a real relationship?"

Kit giggled. "See, even Donna thinks Jackie should finally test the waters with Owen!"

"I used to wonder the same thing. But my daughter is pig-headed."

"Oh, Charlotte thinks it, too!" Kit giggled again. "All right. I'll admit that this is kind of fun."

Lynette didn't respond. What she'd overheard earlier was anything but fun—not that she had any desire to share that part of the conversation with Kit or anyone else. Then she cringed when she heard the next words that floated over to them. Donna was talking again.

"But I'm one to talk. Poor Lynette. I don't think she's gone out on a single date since we moved back to Ruby Shores. I sometimes blame myself and my horrendous dating history for her apparent aversion to any kind of long-term relationship."

Lynette tossed the pillow she'd used to stifle her earlier giggles onto the chair on the other side of the porch. "I'm not averse to a long-term relationship!" she hissed. "I just haven't found the right guy yet."

"Hmm," was all Kit had to say to that.

"We can't blame ourselves for our children's misadventures in romance."

"Who said that?" Kit asked.

Lynette wasn't sure, but then Charlotte started talking again.

"Maybe Kit was the smartest one of the group. She held out until a couple years ago in the marriage department, and as far as I know, she's quite happy with Dean."

Kit stood and executed a deep curtsy. The towel unraveled from her hair and fell to the porch floor. "Are you listening to this, Lynette? Remember, Mother knows best. You guys thought I was a scaredy-cat, but it sounds like I was just smart."

Lynette scooped up the towel and snapped it at Kit in jest. "I don't know, Kit. I've avoided marriage altogether. Maybe *I'm* the smart one." She swung the towel at her friend again, but this time Kit snagged it back.

"Can you imagine the five of us at their age, sitting around the fire like they're doing now, picking apart the lives of our kids?" Kit said. "I wonder what will be happening in Isaac's life in twenty years."

Although Lynette didn't have kids, the question was an interesting one. Even Annie's granddaughter would be a young adult in twenty years. The thought made her shiver.

Time passes too quickly.

She recognized the sound of her mother's voice again. "Do you ever get sick of only thinking about the well-being of our families? Our grown kids? Your grandkids?" There was a pause, then she went on. "I'm not ashamed to admit that I still have dreams I'd love to pursue. Are we too old to do that now? We're all in our seventies, right?"

Kit froze. She must have heard Donna's question, too. "That's weird. I was just wondering what it would feel like to be seventy."

"Shh! I want to hear this," Lynette said, hushing her noisy friend yet again.

"By now you've all heard of Celia, right?"

Lynette pointed toward the fire. "That's Lavonne."

"I know," Kit said. She sat next to Lynette again.

Lynette strained to listen. She really wanted to hear what else Lavonne had to say about Celia.

"Well, she lived to be in her nineties, and she was still working and doing fun things with the resources she'd built for herself, right until the end."

Kit nodded through the shadows, as if also encouraged by Celia's longevity, and they heard Donna prompt Lavonne to tell them her dream.

"I guess the thing that pops into my mind relates to Celia," Lavonne said. "On the one hand, even though I loved Celia and respected her for all her accomplishments, I did feel like I lived in her shadow. I'm not sure I ever made a difference in anything—at least not the way Celia did."

Kit made a clucking noise. "That's sad."

Charlotte must have felt the same as Kit, because Lynette heard the woman interrupt Renee's mother. "Why do we sell ourselves so short? Lavonne, you just finished telling me you have four grown children, and if they are all as amazing as Renee, I'd say you've accomplished plenty. And then there are all your grandchildren. I've always felt that raising kids is the most important work anyone can do. Nothing affects the world more."

Lynette struggled to pick out a few more sentences before Lavonne chimed back in. "Fine, I won't argue with any of that, but my dream is still somewhat related to Celia. She left an incredible legacy. Money can't buy happiness and all of that, but it can really help those in need. I want to use the resources we still have—including our inheritance from Celia—to keep helping others. To keep Celia's legacy alive."

In that moment, Lynette knew she'd have given Lavonne a pat on the back for harboring a dream like that. She often felt the same pull; she often worried she was falling short.

Jackie's mom went on to talk about how she used to dream of escaping Minnesota in the winter. Lynette wasn't surprised when Annie's mom mentioned their second home in Arizona and something about a neighbor.

Kit shifted on the sofa next to her. "I figured Patsy might have some ideas when Jackie's mom started talking about going south in the winter. I loved their house in Arizona. That was a birthday I'll never forget."

Lynette nodded. That had been a glorious trip. But she was dying to hear what her mother might say about her own neglected dreams.

"I'd move away."

She felt Kit's hand on her arm. "Wait. Who said that?!"

"Donna," Lynette whispered, praying Kit would be quiet. Had she heard her mother correctly?

"Do you mean, like . . . just for the winter?" Patsy stammered. "It is a nice break to get away for a few months."

"No."

Lynette tried as hard as she could to hear her mother's words.

"I mean that my dream for many years has been to live in Europe during the summer months and then somewhere with pure white beaches and bright blue ocean waves in the winter."

"Oh, man . . ." Kit muttered. She no longer sounded as enthusiastic about their spying.

"Why did you move to Ruby Shores with Lynette, then?" Charlotte asked. "And why did you buy such a big house? I mean, it's beautiful, but it's also old and *huge*. None of that jives with what you just said your dream was."

Lynette felt like the porch was spinning out from under her.

"I'm not really sure," she heard Donna admit. "Escaping New York was our immediate focus. Ruby Shores felt like the safe bet. The pandemic was still picking up speed and there were so many unknowns. But for the past few months, I've been worried that it might have been a mistake. Not that I can do anything about it now. I made a commitment to Lynette, and I need to stick with it."

Kit squeezed her arm. Lynette had almost forgotten her friend was there with her.

"She doesn't really mean it," Kit said, her voice rising above a whisper. "She's probably drinking wine."

"But you're the one who wanted to talk about dreams." Patsy's voice floated through the screen. "Why would you do that if you thought yours was unattainable?"

Regret welled up in Lynette. She should never have listened to this private conversation between her mother and her new friends. She could picture Donna's answering shrug to Patsy's question before her mother even replied.

"I guess I'm either a glutton for punishment or I want to live vicariously through you."

Kit grabbed Lynette's hand, stood, tugged. "We should go inside. We weren't meant to hear this."

Lynette pulled her hand away. "It's too late now. We might as well hear them out. Go inside if you like."

Patsy was talking again. "... Annie told me once that my trips were her inspiration behind these annual trips they take now. But my old group is all gone. My friend Betsy was my last hope, but she passed when I was on an anniversary cruise with my husband. So I have a proposition for you three—and Kit's mom, too, if she's interested."

Kit hadn't left Lynette, so she heard the mention of her own mother. "And here I thought everyone forgot about Mia. You know what she's going to suggest, right?"

"I can probably guess," Lynette said.

"I think this quick little getaway to Whispering Pines should be the first of many trips we take together!" Patsy said.

"Yep, there it is," Kit said. "Somehow I'm struggling to imagine my mother doing anything with Donna, Charlotte, Lavonne, and Patsy."

Lynette was having trouble concentrating. Kit's comment regarding Mia didn't surprise her, given the complicated mother-daughter relationship the pair had always endured. But prior to overhearing Donna's comments tonight, she thought the relationship she enjoyed with her own mother was special. Maybe even bulletproof. Suddenly, she worried everything they'd built rested on a shaky foundation of lies. Even her own lineage was something very different from what Donna had always led her to believe. Did her mother even know which of her "string of losers," as she'd so eloquently called the early men in her life, had fathered Lynette?

Her mind drifted back to the sunny morning when she'd visited the cemetery on the edge of Ruby Shores, intent on learning more about Sybil and her family. Even in death, their love and support were obvious.

Lynette remembered walking back out of those iron gates toward home, intent on asking her mother to tell her more about their family.

Now, here she was a week or two later, feeling like she'd give anything to erase the truth.

This time, when Kit tried to pull her to her feet, Lynette allowed it.

"I'm sorry you had to hear that, Lynette."

All she could do was nod and follow Kit into the cabin's front room. She went to close the door behind them—she'd heard more than enough—when she heard one last thing out of Charlotte.

"Now, Donna . . . let's talk about this Chester fellow."

Chapter Twenty-Two

L YNETTE WOKE TO THE incessant buzz of her cell phone.

"What time is it?" she groaned. As she fumbled for the phone on the bedside table, she knocked over her half-empty water glass from the night before, drenching everything. She gritted her teeth to cut off the litany of swear words that threatened to make her head feel even worse. At least the vibrating would stop if the water shorted out her phone.

But replacing it would just be another headache. She better find the towel she'd dropped somewhere around here after the second cool shower she'd taken before bed.

Her hands skimmed the foot of the bed in search of her towel, but the single thin blanket and top sheet were in a tangle. Giving up on finding it, she used the hem of her over-sized sleeping T-shirt to dry her phone off as best she could. It was a good thing she'd opted for the water-resistant case. The buzz had stopped, but it started up again in her hand.

"Hey, Annie, what's up?"

Even to Lynette's own ears, her voice sounded like she'd swallowed glass.

"Well, good morning. Don't you sound chipper this morning?" Annie said, sounding much too bubbly.

Lynette pictured her friend's peppy smile and fought the temptation to throw her phone across the room. Maybe that would accomplish what the water hadn't.

"This is how I sound after tossing and turning all night. If you're just calling to chat, I'm hanging up now. I want to go back to sleep."

"Oh, I'm sorry you had a rough night," Annie said. "Night sweats again?"

Lynette lay on her back, kicked what remained of her covers off the bed, and eyed the rotating ceiling fan above. "Oh, it was a sweaty one, but only because my air is still out. Annie, what do you want?" She thought she heard a cupboard door close. "Where are you?"

"In my cabin. Since I went to sleep so early last night, I woke before the sun was up," Annie said. "I opened a window, and the birds sounded so lovely. I went down on the beach and sat on the dock to watch the sunrise. It was the perfect way to start the day. I'm starting a pot of coffee now, but then I'm running over to the lodge. Mom, Donna, and Charlotte are loading the van to go home. I saw Jackie walking back toward the duplex with her mom. Maybe she forgot something. But anyway, that's why I'm calling. I thought you might want to run down and say goodbye to everyone, too."

Lynette's head throbbed at the reminder of the reason behind her sleepless night. The heat wasn't to blame; the culprit was Donna, and she knew she wasn't ready to face her mother just yet. First, she needed time to process everything she'd overheard the night before.

"Lynette? Are you still there?"

She used her free hand to rub her left temple. "Have you talked to Kit yet this morning?"

"No, why? I thought she might still be sleeping."

Lynette let her hand fall back onto the mattress. "You woke *me* up?!"

"Kit's mom isn't even here! Fine. I don't really care whether you come see them off with me. I was just trying to be nice, but I'm hanging up now so you don't ruin the start of a perfectly nice day for me."

She felt a twinge of guilt. "I'm sorry, Annie. I have a banging headache."

But Annie, always true to her word, had already hung up. That was the thing about Annie: You could always trust her to tell the truth.

Unlike my own mother.

In the room's quiet, she heard a dripping sound. Then she remembered the mess she'd made with the spilled water. "Crap!"

She rolled off the bed and found her bath towel hanging on the back of a small wooden rocker in the corner of the room. Once she'd used it to mop up the floor and dry the table, she tossed the towel onto the rocking chair again and stumbled for the kitchen.

Annie had mentioned coffee. Maybe a fresh, strong pot of her own would help.

Fifteen minutes later, she eased into the Adirondack chair in front of her cabin, hoping to allow enough time for the first cup of coffee to take effect before she had to talk to anyone else.

A soft yellow sun glowed in the azure sky, making Lynette wish she'd grabbed her sunglasses on the way out the door. At least it was cool yet, though the air was heavy with humidity. Dew on the grass tickled her feet, and she suspected her shorts would be damp when she stood. She focused on the solitude as she took another sip of black coffee. The tension in the back of her neck eased. Ten more minutes and she might even be headache-free.

Her phone vibrated in her pocket, interrupting her peace. She pulled it out, vowing to smash the phone once and for all.

It was her lawyer.

Since it had only been a few days since their last conversation, there was a strong likelihood she'd soon need something stronger than coffee for this headache.

"Hello, Kevin. Please, I'm going to warn you I'm already nursing a potential migraine here. So if you are calling me again so soon with bad news, I'm going to beg you to reconsider."

Because she'd worked with Kevin for many years, how he reacted to her request would immediately tell her whether she should go back inside and grab a dose of her headache medication now. If he chuckled, she'd be safe.

He didn't. "I'm afraid this can't wait, Lynette."

She sighed. He was using his lawyerly tone, which meant she might as well get this over with. "Fine. What is it?"

"Have you read the packet of information I sent? I think you might still be away on vacation, so I wasn't sure."

She hadn't pulled the envelope out of her Louis Vuitton bag since stuffing it inside. "Donna gave it to me last night. But I haven't opened it. I didn't realize it was time-sensitive."

"Nor did—"

Static came through the line, making it impossible to hear what the lawyer was saying.

"Great," she said, pushing herself out of her comfortable chair to see if she could find a stronger signal. "Hold on, Kevin. I'm having trouble hearing you."

She left her coffee cup on the wide arm of the chair and took a few steps away from her cabin, which snuggled up against the tree line rimming the resort. Another bar appeared in the top right corner of her phone.

"Can you hear me?"

"I can. Can you hear me?"

Lynette grinned, despite the pain in her head. "We sound like a TV commercial. What were you saying about the packet, Kevin?"

"Actually, don't even bother to read that one. What I sent was a copy of the original sale agreement with an updated payment schedule to show that they'd caught up. However, your buyer's attorney reached out to me late yesterday afternoon. Lynette, they are requesting some modifications to the terms previously agreed upon."

Lynette allowed her head to drop forward, and she rubbed the back of her neck. "Can they *do* that?"

"It's unusual," he said. It sounded to Lynette like he was rustling through paperwork. "But we talked about the risks you would accept around the deal terms. You were optimistic about the buyers' ability to make the required payments, even though I cautioned you that I didn't love leaving them with some wiggle room. An out. Pardon the jargon."

Her lawyer's statement was correct, even if it stung to hear it. Neither her attorney nor her mother had wanted her to sell to her two old employees. She'd wanted it to work out so badly for the two women, having mentored them herself through the years, that she had gone against their advice. "What do you mean when you say an *out*?" She emphasized the last word with air quotes, even though her lawyer couldn't see her. "How bad is it, Kevin?"

There was more static, so she moved again.

"Lynette?"

"Yes, go ahead. I can hear you."

"I'm not sure yet. Instead of one last payment to you in six months, they've asked for a one-year deferment, and then monthly payments until they pay you in full. We would, of course, impose a fair level of interest and a penalty on the late payments, but if you agree to the amendment, they wouldn't be in breach of contract. Remember, we knew this could happen."

She cleared her throat, frustrated at the admonishing tone that was creeping into his voice. "And if we don't accept?"

He paused, as if worried how she'd take the answer.

"Kevin?"

"Yes . . . well . . . a few different things could happen, none of which would be desirable for either party. It sounds like they are suffering some significant financial challenges at the moment. Some employee issues have also surfaced. I worry that if you force their hand, they may have to shutter the business."

Lynette sank onto the grass. Her legs no longer felt reliable. "That's not acceptable!"

His grunt was humorless. "I thought you would say that. Listen, I felt it was my responsibility to loop you in on this immediately, but they've given us a month to respond. Are you still at that ocean resort?"

"It's a lake resort, but yes. I'll head home on Sunday. Will you be sending me new papers to sign? Do I need to fly to New York to figure this out?"

The moment the words were out of her mouth, she realized her old habits of flying anywhere on a moment's notice, regardless of cost, might no longer be feasible. The final agreed-upon original payment was also supposed to be the largest, and now it was at risk.

"I don't think that will be necessary," Kevin said. "But give me a few days to work on this and we'll talk again next week. I really am sorry to have to call you with this news, Lynette. I hope I didn't just ruin the rest of your vacation."

Lynette grunted. "Kevin, I'm afraid you're going to have to get in line for that."

***

Twelve hours later, Lynette joined her friends around the firepit where their mothers had spent the previous evening. A little of her gin and tonic sloshed out onto her hand as she sank into another of Renee's new red chairs. "These suckers are comfortable, but they are a nightmare to get in and out of," she said, careful not to spill any more of her drink.

"Where have you been hiding all day, Lynette?" Kit asked. "I thought you would join us on the beach. It wasn't so hot today."

Lynette shook her glass to help the ice inside keep her favorite cocktail cold. "I woke up with a headache. Took me most of the day to shake it. A few things have come up over the past twenty-four hours that gave me plenty to think about, too. I wasn't in the mood to socialize."

She didn't miss the concerned looks her four friends exchanged.

"But don't worry," she continued. "My head feels fine now, and I've put all that other nonsense out of my mind for the moment. It'll still be there for me to deal with when I get home."

Jackie handed her a bag of sunflower seeds. "Here. I know you've always liked these. They go better with whatever is in that glass than a s'more would."

Annie waved a metal roasting stick in their direction. "But if you want me to whip one up for you, just let me know."

"What's in the glass, Lynette?" Renee asked.

"Gin and tonic," Lynette said, giving her glass another shake. "And it's tasty. Nobody is allowed to judge me, either. I'm on vacation. Now, what were you lovely ladies discussing when I arrived a few minutes ago? I heard Kit laughing. Oh, and if anybody plans to tell any deep, dark secrets tonight, keep your voice down. You wouldn't believe how far sound travels out here."

She gave Kit an exaggerated wink. They'd promised each other not to mention the conversations they'd overheard the mothers having the night before.

"Lynette, are you drunk?" Kit asked.

"Don't be ridiculous. How can you even ask that?" Lynette demanded.

Maybe a little, she thought. Not that she wanted any of her friends to know this wasn't her first drink of the evening. Especially Renee, since she was the only one who actually knew about her struggles and rehab stint.

Kit shrugged. "Sorry. We're all adults here."

"That's right," Lynette said, waving her index finger at her. "Seriously, what were you talking about a minute ago?"

Renee looked unsure for a moment, then relented. "I was telling them about how I used to try to impress Celia when we'd visit here as kids."

Lynette relaxed in her chair and let her eyes go to the top of the tall pines above them. "I'm going to guess that whatever you did to impress her worked, because she left this amazing place to you."

"That's nice of you to say, Lynette. We always got along. She kind of felt like a much older sister to me, even though she was actually old enough to be my grandmother."

"We've heard bits and pieces of what she left to others in your family, but why don't you recap it," Jackie suggested.

"Sure," Renee said. "As you know, Whispering Pines passed to me. She left her house and some rentals to my brother, Ethan. It took us a few years to get around to cleaning out her attic. We all went in there together and decided who got what. Ethan didn't want to make those decisions alone. There were so many neat things up there. We even found a gorgeous wedding dress, tucked away in an old trunk. It was in pristine condition. Celia never married, so no one actually wore it until my sister Jess married Seth."

Lynette poured a handful of sunflower seeds out and tossed some into her mouth. Her creative self tried to imagine the vintage gown that Renee described. "I remember a picture from your wedding on the wall in the lodge, but was there one from your sister's wedding, too? I'd love to see the dress."

Renee shook her head. "They didn't get married out here, but they did honeymoon in your cabin."

Lynette remembered Renee telling them the honeymoon part when they'd first arrived. Then she had another thought. "Lauren is Jess's daughter, right?"

"She is, and I already know where you're going with this. Yes, Lauren loved that vintage gown. In fact, it wouldn't surprise me if she'd ask to wear it for her own wedding someday. Not that she's engaged or anything now. But there were some other vintage dresses up there, too. Maybe Celia wore them when she was a young woman. Lauren kept those. They aren't formal gowns, but they really are beautiful. Maybe she could show you those someday. I know you two share a love of fashion."

"I would like that," Lynette agreed.

The conversation continued to flow amongst the five women. Renee provided them with a summary of Celia's generosity, as well as many of the high points of her life and career.

"That reminds me," Renee said later, the fire having died down to mere embers between them. "We also found a newspaper article about Celia in her job. If I'm remembering right, she was in her thirties when they featured her. What she accomplished was so unique for women back then. That was the focus of the piece. I'll have to find it again and let you read it. I think I tucked it into the blue trunk in my living room. We pulled that trunk out of Celia's attic, too. It's the one that held the wedding dress. You'll need to be sure to read the article, Lynette. I see so many similarities between you and my aunt. You were both incredibly successful businesswomen."

The past tense Renee used grated on Lynette's already taut nerves. The gin wasn't helping her relax as much as she'd hoped. Maybe one more would do the trick. She should probably stop, but too many bombshells had landed smack dab in the middle of her life lately. Her mother, the one person she trusted more than anyone else on Earth, had lied to her about so many important things. The business she'd worked so hard to build over decades was possibly imploding at this very moment, and if she didn't make some big concessions, she would face a very different financial future than the one she'd imagined.

Even Renee thought she was washed-up. Hadn't she practically said as much?

Maybe Annie sensed Lynette's distress, because she changed the subject. "Say, Renee, I understand Matt and Robbie are taking my husband fishing for a couple of days, starting tomorrow." She was trying to roast another marshmallow over the dying fire. "Henry thought Owen might come, too?"

"That's what I hear," Renee said. "But don't any of you worry. I reminded Matt that we don't allow boys on our girls' trips, so they won't be swinging by here at all. The closest they might come is way out there on the water. Robbie thinks he's found the best fishing spots right now. But I guess we'll see."

The mention of Owen brought Storm to mind for Lynette. She pictured the man, flat on his back on Owen's grass, how the tiny butterfly tattoo on his inner arm had practically rippled when he'd flexed.

She shuddered, pushing the thought away. If any of these women found out Storm was back and she hadn't mentioned it, they'd tease her as mercilessly as everyone teased Jackie about Owen. That was the last thing she needed right now. She already had plenty of other things on her plate to worry about.

With her luck, he might come knocking with his hand out, looking for reimbursement for the truck she'd totaled more than thirty years ago.

One last nightcap suddenly sounded like the perfect way to end a dreadful day.

CHAPTER TWENTY-THREE

L YNETTE DROPPED HER BAG onto the sand and pulled out a beach towel.

Annie glanced up at her. "If you're going to lie down on your back like this, I should warn you. This position hurts more than it used to."

After smoothing her towel out next to Annie, Lynette glanced at Kit and Renee, relaxing in nearby chairs. She noticed Jackie's mystery novel in Kit's lap.

"What do you think?" she asked, nodding toward the book.

Kit picked it up. "I like it. Thanks for passing it on to me when you couldn't get into it. The only trouble was I couldn't put it down last night. I'm tired today."

Lynette could relate. Sleep was even harder than lying flat on her back on the sand would be. Her night cap hadn't even helped. Maybe if she took a dip in the lake, then lay down in the hot sun on her towel, she could doze off. She couldn't see whether Renee's eyes were closed behind her dark sunglasses, but she did detect the soft purr of a snore. Given the woman's lack of response to Lynette's arrival, beach naps were possible.

Kit nodded, smiling at Lynette's appraisal of Renee. "She hasn't moved in twenty minutes."

"Maybe we should splash her. If only I had a bucket," Lynette teased.

"That's a bad idea," Annie said from her towel. She didn't bother to open her eyes this time. "You know—paybacks and all."

"I suppose I shouldn't tempt fate," Lynette said. "There's always karma to consider. But doesn't she look too darn peaceful?"

Kit set the mystery on the arm of her chair, shaking her head. "I think it's exhaustion more than anything. She's always worried about Matt when he's on duty. It wears on her. But he's fishing with the guys right now, so she can relax."

"That would be hard," Lynette said. She kicked her sandals off. "I'm going to cool off, then try to take a nap, too."

"Check on Jackie while you're out there, will you?" Kit said with a nod toward the water. "She's been out there for a while, as per usual. Between all her swimming and running, one would wonder if she might be getting in shape for something in particular."

"Or some*one*." Lynette winked.

She wandered to the water's edge. The cold water felt luxurious against her hot skin. A nap on an inflatable raft out on the lake sounded even better than a towel on the sand. If only she had one.

She pushed off once the water reached her waist, dog-paddling in Jackie's direction. Jackie was swimming perpendicular to the shoreline. She supposed it was like swimming laps, but lake-style. Once her friend got close, she yelled hello.

Jackie flipped onto her back and waved. "Coming out to join me? The exercise feels good after so much sitting and eating."

"No, I'd probably get all turned around and get myself into trouble out here. Like Renee told us Ethan did when they were kids. I've never been as strong of a swimmer as you. If I was, I'd try to talk you into diving with me to find my lost ring. My finger feels naked without it. But since that isn't even remotely possible, I just got in the water to cool off and say hi."

Jackie grinned. "If Renee thought finding your ring was possible, I promise I'd try. But she said it was too deep in that area. Hey, you seem to be in a better mood today, though. I was worried about you after last night. Is everything all right?"

Lynette nodded, almost gulping lake water. Her arms and legs were tiring from swimming in place. "Fine. Or they will be. I just got some upsetting news from my lawyer yesterday. But I don't want to get into it now. Like I said, I'll deal with it when I get home."

A boat must have gone by out on the lake somewhere, because a series of swells moved through. A wave splashed into her mouth. "I better get back before I drown," she said, coughing. "Be careful."

"I will!" Jackie laughed. "You, too. I have five more passes to do, then I'll come join you bathing beauties on shore."

Lynette turned to head back, and another wave hit the back of her head. She gave up on trying to keep her hair dry and switched to a crawl stroke instead. Her hair would be impossible to deal with later, but for now, she'd enjoy the cold refreshment of the lake.

By nightfall, Lynette's worries were back. Donna had sent her a text, reporting that everything at home—including the basement and Ebony the cat—was fine. But she couldn't find their old teddy bear. Did Lynette have any idea where it had disappeared to?

Lynette imagined her response: *Why yes, Mommy Dearest, I know exactly where the teddy bear is because I hid his body, along with his severed head minus one black button eye. I guess we both have our share of secrets, don't we?*

She'd always known how important that bear was to Donna, though she had never really understood why. Now she had to wonder if maybe it had something to do with the horrors she had overheard Donna share with Lavonne. Could the stuffed animal have belonged to Donna's long-lost sister, once upon a time?

Despite having fallen asleep on her towel next to Annie after her short swim, the fire smoldered on in her brain. The rest hadn't helped. When she'd suffered anxiety like this in years past, only gin had helped to snuff the flames. Two quick shots of the stuff before dinner had helped her navigate the conversation around the picnic table, and the wine she drank with her steak had helped her relax even more. She had a good buzz going now, but she doubted her friends could even tell.

She'd grown good at hiding it over the years.

The rational part of her brain knew that turning to alcohol was one of the worst things she could possibly do. She'd worked so hard to put her addictions behind her. But wasn't logic the thing that had gotten her into this mess to begin with? When she could no longer stomach the pressures of running her company, her employees' desire to buy it had seemed like the perfect solution. But look at it now.

Moving back to Ruby Shores, and bringing Donna along, had made sense, too, when the pandemic spread through the city. Not only that, but Donna told her she thought moving was a good idea, and Lynette had foolishly assumed her mother was sincere.

Lynette felt a confusing mixture of guilt for holding her mother back from living her own life and anger at her mother for the lies.

Donna had spent her entire life supporting Lynette. She'd worked tirelessly to provide for her when Lynette was young. Even once her daughter had become an adult, Donna continued to do all she could to make life easier for her.

But how could Donna be so deceitful about how she herself had grown up?

It was late, and all four of her friends had gone to bed an hour ago. Lynette wasn't one bit tired. She felt compelled to head back out to the dock. Clouds had moved in during dinner and light sprinkles had left the beach deserted before moving on. Moonlight chased back the shadows and danced across the rippling surface of the lake.

She ignored both chairs, choosing instead to get down on her stomach near the end of the dock. When she rested her chin on her hands, she could watch the dark ripples disappear beneath the dock. The wind picked up, coaxing the ripples into waves, and Lynette reached for the dancing water. For a split second, she wondered what it would be like to slip below those waves. To just . . . disappear.

The flask she'd shoved into the front pocket of her jeans jabbed her hip bone, forcing her to sit up. She really shouldn't think such ridiculous thoughts. Life was hard. That wasn't anything new. It had always been hard, but she was a fighter, not a quitter.

She spun the top off her flask and took a swig, coughing over the straight gin. Tomorrow she'd need to find a liquor store. The bottle she had stashed in her suitcase was empty now. How was that even possible? She couldn't possibly have downed the whole thing by herself.

But she didn't have a car here and she doubted any of her friends would give her a ride.

A ripple of light on the waves drew her gaze upward. She studied the shadows and crevices of the moon, thinking back to some of the times she'd basked beneath its magical glow. Her friends teased her all the time about being part witch. She liked to play along, but on nights like this, she wondered if there was some truth to it all.

Or maybe she was just drunk.

But was that really such a bad thing? Without the sharp edge of panic slicing through her thoughts, she could consider all her options for dealing with the problems bubbling up in her life.

Her butt and back ached. The chair would be more comfortable than sitting on the unforgiving planks of the dock. She stood, but her foot knocked over the flask she'd neglected to close.

"What's the matter with me?" she said, but only the wind answered back, and its words were in a language she couldn't quite decipher. "I keep spilling things."

Then she remembered Renee mentioning a fun little bar that she and Matt would boat to for a burger and beer once in a while. The five of them had even talked about taking one of the resort's speedboats over there for their last supper before they headed home.

She giggled at the notion of a "last supper" as she tipped the last few drops of gin left in the flask into her mouth. Now she really was out, and unless she kept this buzz going, everything would come flooding back to her.

She preferred this haze to reality.

Renee's bar probably offered off-sale, too. Maybe not bottles of gin, but beer would do in a pinch. Sadly, she didn't know how to drive a speedboat, and fortunately she wasn't so drunk that she didn't know her limits.

Then she remembered how easy it had been to maneuver Renee's new canoe across the water. Would it be hard to find the lakeside bar if she took out the red canoe?

Suddenly, a quick boat ride to restock her gin supply seemed like a much better plan. If she had to ask to use someone's car tomorrow, there would be questions. She loved her friends, but they could be incredibly nosy. Renee might even resist the idea.

Convinced she'd devised a better plan, Lynette set the now useless flask on the chair. She'd laughed when she'd discovered it in one of her cabin's kitchen cupboards. Who used a flask anymore? But it had served its purpose. And hopefully it would again soon.

On her way to the area where Renee kept her boats, she remembered to grab her shoes from the sand at the foot of the dock. It wasn't like she could go into the bar barefoot, could she? Sometimes she surprised herself with how smart she really was.

When she reached the small inlet where the resort's boats were tied up, she saw that both speedboats were gone. Good thing she'd already decided a canoe would work better.

When they first took the canoes out, Renee put Lynette and Annie in the red one. She'd said it was newer, and easier to navigate. Had Matt given it to her as a present? Lynette couldn't quite remember the details, but she was sure Renee would want her to use the red one tonight.

Safety first.

Speaking of safety, she should probably wear a life jacket. But there weren't any in either canoe. Oh well—she could swim; she didn't really need one. Good thing she'd tossed her phone onto the kitchen table, back at her cabin, deciding instead to put the flask in her front jeans pocket. At the time she'd been thinking she didn't want to get any more bad-news phone calls, but now she wouldn't want to risk getting it wet, either.

It was a pleasant night, and the water didn't look too rough. Just some waves. One quick trip to the bar along the water and she'd be back before anyone even missed her.

Unless there weren't any paddles either. Without paddles, she'd be out of luck. She checked inside the red canoe again.

"Yes!" she cried.

Clips held two paddles in place, one on each side. If she was better with them, she'd have tried using both to speed up the trip. But again, she knew her limits. Besides, it would be nice to have a spare, just in case she dropped another one.

It took more muscle than she'd expected to pull the red canoe down to the water's edge. For a moment, she worried her plan might be squashed. She supposed it made sense to pull them far up on the shore so they wouldn't float away if rough weather moved in, but it sure was inconvenient.

Lynette took pride in her gift of tenacity, and mere minutes later, she was paddling away from shore. When Renee had told them about the bar and restaurant, she'd pointed toward the north. How hard could it be to find? It wasn't like she was driving without a map on a maze of back country roads. There was only one shoreline.

Her arms felt strong, and she dug deep, gliding smoothly past the dock. A moonbeam glinted off the flask she'd left behind, and she smiled. As long as she got back before the moon got much higher, her little flask could act like a lighthouse, beckoning her back home. She paddled on, keeping an eye on the shoreline, thankful for the bright moon above.

Then, without warning, everything around her dimmed, and for one heartbeat, she lost sight of the tall pines rimming the shore.

The moon could be fickle.

The haunting cry of a loon split the night air. Lynette searched for it, sure it was floating somewhere close on the reflective surface of the water, but it eluded her. Then another far-off sound tickled her ear.

Thunder.

She felt the very first prickle of fear. If more clouds moved in, she'd lose her light.

The idea of paddling around on the water in the dark, possibly through rain and wind, had her digging deeper. She could still see the tree outline, though it appeared smaller now. Was she angling too far to the left, out into deeper water? It was hard to keep her bearings.

She spun around to look behind her, debating whether it might be wise to abort her mission, but all she could see was water and moonlight. Where was Renee's dock? The pinpricks of light from the cabins? The glow from the streetlight in front of the lodge?

A fat drop of rain landed on her right hand. She stared down at it, and the extra-pale skin on the finger where she used to wear her silver ring glowed back at her.

Then two more drops hit her on the top of her head and a shoulder. The rain increased, and it was as if tiny daggers fell on her, cleaving straight through the gin haze she'd surrounded herself with and shattering her cocoon of safety.

Why hadn't she thought to check the weather before going out on the lake? Especially alone, and at night.

Her mind conjured up Renee's earlier warning about how dangerous the lake could be if you didn't respect it. Just as the last of her friend's words of caution played out, the moon disappeared behind a thick bank of clouds and the rain poured down in earnest. Her sense of direction deserted her. She couldn't help but wonder if her silver ring was right below the canoe now, stuck in the muck created by the dead and decaying.

Maybe when Renee had pulled that Death card from the tarot deck, the Universe had meant it not for Renee, but for Lynette.

Chapter Twenty-Four

RENEE DROPPED HER RING of keys onto the top step of Lynette's cabin. The rain made them slippery, and there were so many resort keys; the ring was cumbersome to hold while also trying to open a door.

"Is she in there?" Annie yelled from the grass in front of the cabin.

"Here," Jackie said, pushing the ring back into Renee's hands. "She's not answering, but she might be asleep."

"Or passed out," Renee muttered. "What possessed her to drink like that again? I thought she was doing so well lately." She felt Jackie push closer, as if trying to shelter from the downpour under the overhang of the cabin's roof. She fumbled through the ring again, trying to find the correct key. "This would go quicker if you quit bumping into me."

"Sorry. The rain is so cold. What if Lynette *isn't* in her cabin, sleeping it off?"

Renee refused to even consider that. Frankly, there weren't many other decent places Lynette could take shelter from the weather. New guests were already settled in the duplex that Donna and the other moms had left. She kept the lodge locked when no one was using it, which was the case at this ungodly hour, and they kept all the sheds and small outbuildings around the resort locked, too, for safety reasons.

But Jackie kept insisting, that as she closed the windows in their cabin when far-off thunder threatened to usher in a rain shower, she had heard Lynette yell something.

She'd sent Kit to double-check the lodge while they looked in Lynette's cabin, but something told her Lynette wasn't over there.

As she fumbled for the correct key again, she couldn't help but wonder how Matt, Robbie, and the other anglers were faring in their tents. Maybe it wasn't even raining at the campground on the other side of the lake. For their sake, she hoped that was the case. Tenting in the rain wasn't as cozy as holing up in a comfortable cabin.

Lynette has to be inside, she thought.

Between the noise of the storm and all the wine Lynette had put down at dinner, she must have passed out. While the run to Lynette's cabin through the rain hadn't been fun, it was probably a good idea to check up on her, even if Jackie was wrong about the shout she thought she'd heard. Tomorrow she'd talk to Lynette about her drinking. She had genuine concerns about her old pen pal.

She finally found the correct key again and shoved it into the lock, holding tighter this time. The door swung open and Jackie pushed past her, heading straight for the cabin's single bedroom. The kitchen light glowed. No one was in the two outer rooms or the bathroom. Annie and Kit both ran inside and into the tiny kitchen, past Renee, as she dropped the keys into the pocket of the sweats she'd pulled on over her shorty pajamas.

"Is she here?" Kit asked. The rain had plastered her wet hair against her skull. "You were right, Renee—you locked the lodge up tight."

"She's not here," Jackie said, rushing back out of the bedroom. "Her bed is messy, but I don't know if she even made it today."

Renee spied an empty gin bottle in the sink. She crossed over to it and held it up for the others to see. "I don't like this. Could she have left the resort?"

Kit shook her head. "Not unless she took one of your vehicles. When I checked the lodge, I saw both Annie's car and my Mustang in the lot."

Thunder cracked above, rattling the windowpanes.

"Dean is going to kill me if it hails on my Mustang after he just put all that money into fixing it up," Kit added. She hurried to the single front window and pulled up the shade. "It's really coming down out there. Maybe Lynette got into the lodge some other way."

"Maybe you forgot to lock one of the doors, and she let herself in, then locked it behind her. Lynette always locks doors. All those years of city life, I suppose," Annie said, shaking rainwater from her hands.

Annie's suggestion wasn't impossible, but it was a stretch. Renee knew no one wanted to even consider that Lynette might be outside somewhere. Maybe she should call Matt. Since they were tenting, she was sure he was monitoring the weather. He'd know whether this storm was supposed to continue for much longer or if it would clear. Summer storms were usually short-lived in Minnesota.

"What if she was stupid enough to go for a walk in the woods in the dark?" Kit said. "Bears are nocturnal."

Renee held up a hand. "Stop. I need to think. If Lynette did something to put herself in danger, we need to find her. Fast."

"Call Matt," Jackie said.

"I was just thinking that, too," Renee admitted, pulling her phone out. "Let's hope he has decent cell service at the campground."

She stepped away from the others as their nervous chatter continued.

Matt picked up after she'd held her breath through two ring tones.

"Hey, babe. Everything all right over at the resort? A couple of the guys talked about doing some night fishing, but I'm glad they decided against it. It's really coming down out—"

"Matt," she said, cutting him off. "We might have a situation over here."

"What happened?" His tone shifted. She thought the background noise from his end of the call might have even quieted.

"It's Lynette. We can't find her."

Jackie, Kit, and Annie came over and stood quietly beside her, though Annie's toe was tapping like crazy.

"What do you mean, you can't find her?"

Renee rubbed at her forehead in frustration. "She was drinking. That was the first thing I noticed that seemed off about her. She doesn't really drink much anymore, but yesterday and today seemed different, even though I think she was trying to hide the fact that she was drunk."

"Okay . . ." he said, drawing out the word. "But this is supposed to be a vacation for all of you. It's all right to blow off a little steam."

"I know that," she snapped back. She instantly regretted it, but Lynette's disappearance had her nerves stretched thin. Her gut told her something was very wrong. "I'm sorry. I'm scared. I wouldn't have called you if I wasn't really worried. We ate at our house this evening, then we visited on the porch, but we've been together for a week and a half now. There's still plenty to talk about between us—"

"Renee," Matt said. "Get to the point, please."

"We were all tired, so we turned in. Jackie and Kit watched Annie go to her cabin, but Lynette is staying in the Gray Cabin. She insisted she could get herself home safely. You know it isn't far."

"The Gray Cabin?" Kit whispered.

"That's what we call the little cabin Lynette's in," Renee clarified, holding a hand over her phone for a second.

"But she didn't get there?" Matt asked.

"Maybe not. We aren't sure." She turned on speaker mode and held the phone out for everyone to hear. "Jackie and Kit thought she had. But before Jackie went to bed, she went to close the windows in their cabin since it was threatening to rain. She also went out onto their screened-in porch to pull the sofa back from the screens a little so it wouldn't get wet. That's when she heard someone yell the word 'yes.' She thought it might have been Lynette. The rain came, and she was uneasy, so she ran to Lynette's cabin. The lights were on, but the door was locked and Lynette wasn't answering. Jackie came and got me. We've been looking ever since, but we can't find her."

She caught her breath.

"And you're sure she didn't just pass out on her bed?"

"No. I used my key to get into her cabin. Her bed is messy, but she isn't in here."

"Did you check the lodge?"

Jackie started shifting her weight back and forth. "What, does he think we're idiots?" she whispered.

"No, I don't think you are idiots," Matt said. "I'm just trying to assess the situation."

Annie shoved at Jackie's arm.

"Guys, focus!" Kit scolded.

Renee switched the phone off speaker and put it to her ear again. "Matt, we'll check everywhere we can think of again, but I'm terrified. What if she went for a walk in the woods? She was drunk, and she's always liked to go for walks in the dark. She loves being out in the moonlight."

"Is there any chance she went out on the lake?" an unfamiliar voice asked.

The very idea sent a blade of fear through Renee. "Who said that?"

"A friend of Owen's," Matt said. "You don't know him. But Renee, is that possible?"

"The lake?" She hadn't even considered that possibility.

Jackie shook her head. "She isn't a strong swimmer. She wouldn't be that dumb."

"But she *was* pretty drunk," Kit countered. "Look, guys, Lynette overheard some things that hit her pretty hard the other night. She asked me not to say anything, but I know it really hurt her."

"Renee," Matt said, pulling her attention back to her phone. "We can be there in twenty minutes. Fifteen if we hurry. I'm sure she's all right, but she might have wandered off into the trees or something, and it would be best if we got her inside in this weather. It sounds like you could use some extra hands."

"Don't patronize me, Matt," Renee said. It was easier to yell at him than to consider that Lynette might be in real danger.

"I'm not, hon, I swear. But I don't want anyone to go down by the water alone. Stay paired up if you go outside. Recheck the buildings, too. We'll be there as quick as we can."

She nodded to her phone, then, feeling stupid, ended the call and shoved it back into her pocket. "The guys are coming to help us find her."

"Good," Jackie said.

Annie and Kit looked relieved to hear it, too.

Renee took a deep breath. She would let Matt take over the search once they arrived, but in the meantime, it was up to her to find Lynette while also avoiding spreading a sense of panic amongst her other guests. "Jackie, come with me, down to the water. I want to check the canoes. God forbid she was stupid enough to take one of them. Kit and Annie, I need you to go back to my house, wake up Julie, and make sure Lynette didn't circle back and fall asleep on my porch or something. My daughter sleeps hard and will often miss phone calls. She can help you double-check the lodge, any outbuildings, that kind of thing. By then the guys should be back. Now go."

A full twenty minutes later, Renee paced impatiently in front of the lodge, waiting for signs of Matt's truck. When headlights finally shone through the trees, heading in her direction, she could have dropped to her knees with relief.

Her husband's pickup came into view, followed by a second truck that she didn't recognize.

At the sound of the trucks, the others joined her on the sidewalk, Julie now with them. No one cared that the rain continued to come down in sheets.

"Did you find her?" Matt asked the second he jumped from his truck.

Despite her panic over Lynette, an awful memory flashed into Renee's brain from their first Halloween at Whispering Pines. When her world felt like it was crashing in around her then, Matt had come to the rescue.

Could he do it again?

She shook her head, praying her legs would keep her upright. "Matt, the new canoe is gone."

Instead of falling into panic mode like she'd done, Matt gave a small shake of his head and caught her up in his arms for a brief hug. "Don't worry. We'll find her. She couldn't have gotten far," he whispered in her ear.

When he stepped back, a man Renee didn't recognize was standing beside him. "Any chance someone screwed up and didn't tie it down? Could it have blown into the water? Floated away?"

The implication that she wasn't competent to maintain things at her own resort rankled her already frazzled nerves. "I never go to bed without ensuring we've properly secured everything," she said through clenched teeth. "And you are?"

Annie stepped up to her side, squinting at the mystery man. "Are you Owen's fishing buddy?"

The man smirked. "Amongst other things."

Renee wasn't sure what that was supposed to mean, but the man appeared unsettled.

"I know you," Annie said, stepping closer to the man. "But you've changed."

Matt looked between Owen's friend and Annie. "Someone want to clue us in, here?"

Renee shifted to see the rest of Matt's group standing farther back. Though she hadn't seen Owen since their senior prom, she recognized him. Henry was there, too, standing near Robbie.

Jackie and Kit stepped forward, too. Only Julie stayed back.

When Jackie got a better look at the stranger, she tilted her head, then walked toward Owen. "Care to explain why you brought *him* here?"

Owen took one reflexive step back. "Hey there, Jackie. I didn't intentionally bring him here. We're just a bunch of guys on a fishing trip, here to help you look for Lynette."

The mention of their missing friend's name was like a slap, reminding Renee of the real crisis at hand. She really didn't care who the guy was; she just wanted to find Lynette.

She turned back to Matt. "Lynette must have taken the canoe out."

He didn't look convinced. "Why would she do that in this weather?"

"The storm didn't roll in until after everyone was back in their cabins. Or *should* have been back, at least. Something was up with her. She wasn't acting like herself, and she drank too much. Maybe she was feeling trapped here, without a car."

"So she stole a canoe and went out by herself on a dark night?" the mystery man said. "Sounds like something Lynette would do."

And then Renee knew, too. "Wait . . . *Storm?*"

The guy snorted. "Name's Taran."

"Come on, Gage," Owen said. "Enough already. I don't know why you asked me not to be up front with everyone, but all that matters now is that we find Lynette. If she really went out on the water, she could be in real trouble."

The man dropped his head for just a moment, then turned to face Renee again, hand extended. "Hey there, Renee. It's been a long time. You've got a good kid here. Robbie put us onto some nice fishing holes today, and your husband is a great host. But why don't we hold off on any more catching up until after we find that old friend of yours? We all know how accident-prone she is."

Matt raised a hand. "I'm not sure what the hell you all are talking about, but it'll have to wait. If you've checked all the potential places she could be right here on the resort, I think we're left with the options of *woods* or *lake*. Since we took both of the resort's speedboats fishing and left them back at the campsite, we might have to start with the older canoe to go out and do a quick first pass. I can call someone to get over here with a faster boat, but that'll take a little time. Julie, you stay here in the lodge, just in case she comes back. Renee, do your other guests know what is happening? Is there any way Lynette might be in one of their cabins?"

"No. She doesn't know anyone else out here. The other guests don't know she's missing, and I was hoping to keep it that way."

Matt considered this, then sighed. "I'm afraid it'll be much more effective if you can yell her name while you search for her. You can deal with any freaked-out guests later, I suppose. Maybe Lynette fell and hurt herself. She might yell out if she hears you."

"She has a weak ankle," Kit offered.

Renee closed her eyes. She hoped and prayed Lynette was just inside the edge of the woods, sitting down and waiting to be rescued.

"I need one person to come with me in the canoe," Matt was saying. "Preferably someone strong enough to help paddle, as we'll want to move fast. Everyone else, except Julie, should form a search party and head into the woods. Robbie, you probably know those areas best. You can lead them. Stay together. We don't need to lose anyone else tonight."

The man Renee had known as Storm said, "I'm going with you, Matt."

Matt looked skeptical. "You sure? It's dangerous on the water in the dark. I know the rain seems to have moved off, but there's no telling what other surprises the weather has in store for us. The forecast promises storms for most of the night, and you don't even know Lynette. Or maybe you do?"

He nodded. "I actually knew Lynette back when we were kids. Come on. That woman is a magnet for trouble."

Matt nodded, then turned to his stepson. "Robbie, there are a bunch of life jackets from earlier today in the box of my truck. Grab me two, would you?"

"Better make that three," Storm said. "If Lynette was dumb enough to go out in the canoe, she probably didn't bother with a life jacket, either."

Chapter Twenty-Five

R AIN CONTINUED TO PELT down on Lynette. The moon had deserted her, snuffed out by the clouds. The occasional gust of wind rocked the little boat. She huddled on the floor of the canoe in a growing puddle of water. What she wouldn't give for a jacket or a tarp so she'd have at least a little protection from the elements. Or a bucket to bail water out of the canoe if this rain kept up.

As she lay curled up in a fetal position, one thing became crystal clear: This was the Universe's way of reminding her it was never safe for her to drink alcohol. She'd done stupid things while drunk before, but nothing as foolish and dangerous as this.

She jolted upright when a scraping sound reverberated through the bottom of the canoe. The rain had stopped, too. Had she dozed off and drifted onto the shoreline? There was just enough moonlight for her to make out the black silhouette of a naked tree branch to her right.

She grabbed for a section of the horizontal tree. Thin, bone-dry sticks broke off in her hand and scraped against the canoe as she fumbled for a thicker branch. Now she regretted leaving her phone behind. Even if there was no signal out here, making it impossible to call for help, the built-in flashlight would have been useful.

Her mind scrambled to pick the best course of action. Could she hold on to the branch of this dead tree until morning, when her friends might notice she was missing and send help? It was unlikely that anyone would miss her tonight. She had no idea if it was still the middle of the night or edging closer toward morning. All she knew for sure was the bone-deep exhaustion that was settling over her, and she didn't trust her grip.

The bottom of the canoe was still bumping against something, and since the part of the tree she held was dry, she knew she'd reached shore, even though she could see very little. Did she dare put her foot down, over the side of the little boat, to test how shallow the water was here?

The branch she held cracked, and a wave bounced the canoe against the branches. The screech of wood against metal sent a shiver down Lynette's spine, reminding her that she needed to save herself. No one else was coming for her.

Her best bet would be to get out of the boat and onto solid ground. Keeping her tenuous grip on the tree, she got to her feet, fighting for balance with the wobble of the boat. She gripped the opposite side of the canoe with her free hand and took two tentative steps toward the narrower front. She didn't want to let go of the tree, since it was probably still attached to the shoreline, but getting her body wedged between the boat and the tree would be undoubtedly painful, and probably dangerous.

The opposite side would be her safer option.

Without giving herself a chance to chicken out, she released her death grip on the prickly branch, stood up straight to catch her breath, then sat on the bench seat closest to the front of the canoe and swung her left leg over the side.

At first, her foot dangled in the air, telling her nothing, so she shifted her weight to the left, stretching her toes toward the water. She reached her foot down until waves lapped at her calf, but if the murky bottom was close, she still couldn't feel it. She pulled her leg back in, sat back up on the bench again, and leaned over the side with her left arm this time, testing to see if she could feel the bottom that way.

This would all be so much easier if the moon would show itself again!

She reached farther, sure the bottom had to be close. But her movement coincided with a gust of wind, and as water blew off the dead tree behind her onto her back, a wave hit the canoe, and Lynette heard a screech as the whole world tipped to the left. It wasn't until the water fully enveloped her that she realized it was *her* screeching.

Her body took over when her mind faltered, and her sandaled feet found enough traction to allow her to stand. She'd poked her head and shoulders above the waterline when something smacked her hard on her right shoulder, knocking her under the water again.

Pain shot through her body like fireworks, but self-preservation can be a funny thing, and the next thing she knew she was sitting on solid ground with only her lower legs still floating in the water. Her fingers clasped what felt like long, wet grass, and she paused there long enough to catch her breath.

A break in the clouds allowed enough moonlight to stream down for her to see the canoe, now at least ten feet from shore, floating away.

"No!" she yelled. Dismay flooded through her already overwhelmed senses as the red canoe bobbed away atop the choppy water, its size diminishing.

Moooo . . .

Lynette spun away from the water toward the completely unexpected yet undeniable cry of an animal. But all she could make out behind her was a gentle, grassy slope. The combination of the angle of the earth and the low light didn't allow her to see far.

Another animal cry reached her ears.

"Cows?!" she said, scrambling to get to her feet on the slick bank.

As she stood, she could again make out the hulking shape of the fallen tree the canoe had snagged against to her right. Moonlight glittered atop angry waves on the lake, and she had to push her snarled, dripping curls away from her face to better see what lay to her left: an undulating mass of dark shapes, tucked against what appeared to be a grove of trees. Then she caught the unmistakable odor of manure. Not even the fresh rain was enough to mask it.

She'd reached land, but her luck hadn't deposited her onto shore near her intended destination or even a nearby resort.

At least she hadn't washed up in the middle of the cattle herd, she reasoned. Though given their increasing level of bawling and movement, some in the crowd of massive animals sensed her as potential danger.

She was no longer at risk of drowning, but if she didn't find shelter, she might get trampled to death by a stampede of livestock. Could the fallen tree offer her enough protection? It was the most obvious choice, so she hurried up the shore toward the exposed roots of the tree, but she didn't get far. Three or four steps in, she slipped in the mud and went down hard. An all-too-familiar pain shot up her leg, and she knew instantly that she'd rolled her weak ankle again. Straight on the heels of that realization came the stench.

That wasn't *mud* that she'd slipped on.

Giving herself a second to catch her breath, she listened for the cows. They continued to bellow, but it didn't sound like any of them were moving in her direction. Clouds continued to drift high above, and the moonlight flickered, but it didn't completely desert her.

She stood again and, keeping as much of her weight as possible on her good ankle, hobbled around the tree. At least here pesky branches didn't obscure the thick trunk, and it provided her enough support to advance up and around it to the far side. Water lapped higher here, and she had to move farther up the grass toward a trio of other trees. At least these still stood tall, and once she reached them, the ground below felt more stable and relatively dry. The noise from the cows wasn't as loud here. This area might provide enough protection until dawn, when she'd be able to see more of her surroundings.

Her injured ankle wasn't going to allow her to go any farther.

She sank down on a small outcropping of rocks at the base of the largest of the three trees. Her imagination threatened with images of spiders, snakes, and other terrifying inhabitants, so she closed her eyes and willed her mind to a different place.

She imagined herself back in the long-ago days of summer camp, where she'd wiled away the days with her best friends, before the demands of everyday life descended with adulthood. The memory involved a day trip their camp counselors had taken them on to a local dairy farm. Perhaps it was the smear of manure that undoubtedly covered the right side of her jeans that pulled that memory to mind. She remembered how laughter filled the air as Jackie and Kit sat side by side on milk stools, trying but failing to follow the farmer's directions on how to milk the patient dairy cow that stood above them.

The sound of male voices pulled her from her stupor, and a brilliant flash of light practically blinded her. She threw a protective arm over her eyes and struggled to understand what was happening. Once her eyes had again adjusted to the darkness, she used the sturdy trunk of the tree to stand. Her one ankle throbbed, and she bent her leg to keep all the weight off it while she scanned the area.

At first nothing seemed to have changed, but then she saw something out on the water. A light, almost like that of a lighthouse, skimmed in an arc across the water in her direction. A voice yelled her name.

"Here!" she screamed. "I'm up here!"

She tried to step toward the water, forgetting about her worthless ankle, and she went down again. Stars danced before her eyes as she rolled onto her back and tried to breathe through the pain.

"Lynette?!"

"Yes! I'm up here, by the trees!" she yelled, praying whoever was out on the water could hear her. She thought it might be Matt. But how was that even possible?

This time, she couldn't get up any farther than her knees, but it was enough for her to make out what looked like two small boats on the water. One floated behind the other, connected by some kind of rope. When the light again flashed in her direction, this time it stayed on her.

"We see you, Lynette! Are you hurt?! Just stay there! We'll come to you."

She collapsed back onto her bottom, overwhelmed with relief. Now she was sure it was Matt's voice. Hadn't Renee said he and her son were out fishing with Annie's Henry? She must have roped them into searching for Lynette. As she waited for them to reach her, she remembered how everyone had teased Henry and Annie for needing to be rescued from a ditch in a snowstorm the winter before their trip to Arizona.

Now it was her turn to be rescued by her friends.

She was going to have to figure out a way to make it up to them all. Exhaustion overwhelmed her. Her rescue was imminent, and she wasn't about to die beneath the hooves of an angry mob of cows. She lay on her back as she waited, already trying to form the apologies she'd need to make to everyone involved.

The sound of a boat hull scraping against a shale-covered shore reached her, along with urgent yet hushed voices. She'd officially survived her own stupidity, and she knew she would be forever grateful to her rescuers. With one last, steadying breath, she sat up to greet them.

But only one head popped up in the moonlight as someone approached from down below, and she felt another rush of disorientation.

How?!

"Damn, Lynette, looks like you haven't outgrown your tendency to attract trouble," a still-familiar voice said, confirming what she thought she was seeing. "At least this time I'm around to save you from yourself."

Matt had stayed behind to hold the canoes as Storm rushed forward to collect Lynette.

Storm ignored her when she insisted she could walk. They both knew she couldn't. As he struggled to deadlift her off the ground, grunting and slipping, her cheeks burned. She hoped he didn't notice in the moonlight.

Matt had set his searchlight on the front of the canoe to make it easier for Storm to see his way back. She caught the speculative look Renee's husband gave them both when Storm dumped her on the front seat of the rescue canoe, but then he took over. He did his best to make sure her injuries didn't extend beyond a rolled ankle. Once he was satisfied, he tossed a blanket over Lynette's shoulders and motioned for Storm to climb in before grabbing the light and taking up the position at the rear of the canoe.

Lynette knew she should be grateful, but it was hard to think straight. She held the blanket tightly around her, doing her best to ignore the man sitting directly behind her.

"I need you to brace yourself, Lynette," Matt said. His voice was firm yet reassuring. "We're going to row hard to get you back to the resort as quickly as possible. I know you're freezing, and your friends are a wreck. Are you ready?"

She nodded, unable to form words. She no longer feared for her safety—unless her friends were mad enough to hurt her—but her teeth were chattering too hard to talk.

The canoe lurched backward from shore, then swung around, cutting through the dark water. It wasn't long before the glow of lights from Whispering Pines appeared. As they grew closer, she scanned the shoreline for Renee and the others. She spied a small group of people jumping and waving in their direction at the same time their whoops reached her ears.

"Looks like your fan club is waiting for you," the man directly behind her said.

The blanket fell from her shoulders when she waved back at the four figures on the shore. Then she noticed a few more people streaming across the shadowed beach.

"I called Robbie and told them they could call off their search of the woods. That we'd found you," Matt said, as if in explanation.

A search of the woods? She was going to have even more apologizing to do than she'd initially thought.

The telltale scrape of sand against the canoe bottom reached her ears just as the rain started up again. Low rumbles of thunder had followed them across the water, so more rain wasn't a complete surprise. Hopefully this meant the welcoming committee wouldn't stay long, once they were sure both her and her rescuers were safe. That might give her until morning to form the proper apologies she knew she owed to everyone.

One of the men behind her flipped on a flashlight. Lynette could see Renee wade into the water and grab hold of the canoe to stabilize it.

Kit rushed forward and pulled Lynette into an awkward hug. "You are such an idiot," she whispered, for Lynette's ears only. "But I've never been so glad to see you."

Lynette knew that Kit was the least prone of all the Kaleidoscope Girls to displays of emotion, so she put her arms around her dear friend and squeezed tight. She felt terrible for scaring everyone so badly.

The boat tipped back and forth below her as Matt and Storm both got out.

"We've got it from here, Renee," Matt said.

Lynette saw him drop a quick kiss on Renee's forehead. She looked pale, as if Lynette had practically scared her to death.

Kit scurried out of the way, and Lynette grabbed both sides of the canoe for balance. Her blanket fell away. "I'm really sorry for scaring everyone," she said through clenched teeth, knowing her apology was only the first step in making it right with everyone after her foolishness. The shivering seemed to be getting worse, so she tried to wrap herself in the blanket again.

"She could be going into shock," Matt said as he tossed the rope that was tied to the front of their canoe to Robbie. "We need to get her somewhere warm."

Lynette nodded and stood, remembering this time not to put any weight on her bad ankle. Before she could figure out how to get out of the canoe, powerful arms picked her up. Her face smashed against a wall of flesh, and she knew it was Storm that held her again.

At least he didn't grunt this time.

She pushed against him, but he didn't loosen his grip. "Knock it off, Lynette. You can't walk on that ankle of yours. Renee, where should I take her?"

Mortified, Lynette recognized the truth in his words. She could hear a brief discussion going on around her, but the blanket had fallen over her face and, grateful for the glimpse of privacy, she left it there. Or was it her hair? Maybe if she pretended she wasn't actually in Storm's arms, that she was really asleep in the bed in her little cabin and this was nothing more than a nightmare, she'd wake up to bright sunshine and nothing worse than a nasty hangover, with no apologies needed.

Suddenly, there was nothing supporting her, and she was falling. She screeched in alarm, but just as quickly, she found herself atop that very bed.

"We can take it from here," Renee said. "The rest of you, get out. Matt, it's too late for you guys to drive back to your camp, so can you find a place for everyone to sleep tonight? I'm sorry we pulled you away from your fishing trip."

Someone might have suggested a different course of action, but Lynette only heard parts of the conversation.

"I'll sleep in here with her. If she seems to have trouble warming up and settling down, I'll call you, Matt, and we can take her in to get checked. Her ankle is probably just sprained. It always gives her trouble."

Is that Renee talking?

The voices faded, and the next thing Lynette knew, someone was tugging at her sandals.

"Come on, girl. You smell like the butt of a cow, and you are not crawling under my sheets until after we get you out of these clothes and into the shower."

Yep. Renee.

Lynette's eyes snapped open, and she could see both Renee and Jackie at her feet. Kit stood over her with arms crossed, shaking her head in disapproval.

Annie walked in with a stack of clean towels. "They're all gone," she said. She set the stack down on the dresser and snapped a towel open. "Now, get up, Lynette. We've got you."

Chapter Twenty-Six

L YNETTE STRUGGLED TO OPEN the back door to the lodge's kitchen while also staying upright on crutches. She'd never mastered their use, despite being forced to use them in the past, thanks to her weak ankle.

The door swung inward. "Morning, Lynette. I thought I heard someone out here."

"Hey there, Val! I wasn't expecting to see you on a Thursday morning." Lynette smiled appreciatively at Renee's youngest sister, then hobbled through the open doorway. The delicious smell of bacon and coffee gave her spirits a kick. "But my stomach already says 'thank you' for making us breakfast. You've spoiled us throughout this whole vacation. My poor armpits can tell I've gained at least five extra pounds during my time at Whispering Pines."

Val closed the door behind them and followed Lynette into the kitchen. "It's my pleasure. I love cooking for big groups. Coffee?"

"Please!" Lynette looked around the empty kitchen. "Where is everyone? Renee left me a note saying to come to the lodge for breakfast before the guys head back out to fish again."

"They're setting up the table in the main room out there."

Lynette couldn't help but wonder whether Storm was still around, but she didn't want to ask. She was embarrassed to see him after the previous night's debacle. "How can I help?"

Val pointed to a nearby stool. "First, you can get off the crutches and give your sore arms a break. Renee told me what happened last night when she called this morning."

Once settled, Lynette breathed a sigh of relief and stacked the borrowed crutches against the island. "These are Robbie's, aren't they? I sure appreciate that he thought to drop them off last night. I wouldn't be able to get around without them. He has a few inches on me, so walking with them is a little difficult, even after I adjusted them. But enough about me. Tell me what you've been up to, Val."

Val grinned as she pulled a pan of fresh caramel rolls from the oven. "I think I'd rather hear about *your* escapades. Renee might have let it slip that the big bald guy she introduced me to when I got here this morning not only rescued you last night, but that he used to be your high school sweetheart?"

Lynette choked on the coffee she'd just sipped. The hot liquid dribbled down her chin and onto the island. "I'm sorry. Toss me that towel, would you? There is no way Renee used the term 'sweetheart' when talking about Storm."

"I might have improvised," Val admitted. After placing the rolls on the island in front of Lynette, she handed her a towel.

The door between the kitchen and the rest of the lodge swung open and Renee's son strode in. "Val, we need to eat and get back out on the water! Can I take the food in?"

"Why so impatient, Robbie? Relax and say hello to Lynette. I've never known you to pass on seconds on my caramel rolls."

He moved to the pan of rolls and swiped his finger across the top before either Val or Lynette could catch him. "Shit!" he yelped, jumping in pain.

"See, I told you not to rush," Val said, running a dishrag under water and handing it to her nephew. "Put this on your finger, go back out there, and tell everyone we'll eat in five minutes. I need to pull the bacon off the griddle yet."

The young man gave Lynette a quick smile and nod, then strode back out of the kitchen, mumbling under his breath.

After taking another sip of coffee and swallowing it this time, Lynette turned her attention back to Val. "Say, I've been meaning to ask you about your protein bars. Have you had any luck getting them into some of the larger grocers around Minnesota?"

Val shook her head as she scooped dripping slices of bacon off the griddle on a side counter. "Summer was crazy with the boys under foot, and now we're getting ready for back-to-school. We've got four kids going to three different schools, from fifth grade up to a junior in high school. At least we don't have a senior yet. I know how much work that last year of school can be. And I'll get to do it four times! But I'm not complaining. I'll start working on my business again in September. All I managed this summer, aside from feeding all of you, were a few craft shows. I have this great old Airstream camper that I use to sell our baked goods from, alongside my mom. We usually wrangle two of the boys to come along and help."

Lynette shook her head in awe, watching as Val placed the sheet pan full of bacon next to the rolls and gave a large kettle of scrambled eggs on the stovetop one last stir. "You are certainly efficient. Hey, was that the camper you pulled out of the woods? We went for a walk and stumbled across an old campsite. Renee told us a little about it, but insisted she'd leave the telling of the full story up to you."

Val brushed her hands together. "Yep, that's where I found my camper. I'll tell you what. I know we talked before about you giving me some pointers about product distribution. After I make it past back-to-school season, I'll call you. We'll talk all things bars and campers. How's that sound?"

"Val?!"

The shout from the other room sounded like Robbie again.

"I hate to stand in the way of men and their fish," Val said. "Let's get the animals fed."

The breakfast Val provided was delicious, but Lynette could only pick at hers after offering another blanket apology to everyone. She felt awful for worrying her friends and interrupting her rescuers' fishing trip. After being so outspoken about not allowing any of the men to crash their girls' trip, they ended up riding in to her rescue. What bothered her the most was how Matt and Storm had risked their own lives to go out on the lake on a dark and stormy night to look for her.

She avoided Storm's gaze, even though she could sense him watching her from time to time.

Matt hadn't joined them for breakfast. Lynette felt compelled to thank him in person. If not for his expertise, she might still be stuck on the edge of a lakeside cow pasture. Or worse.

After thanking the cook again, she made her slow and clumsy way to the front of the lodge and outside, to where Robbie said his stepfather was packing up more gear. Lynette suspected the white, extended-cab pickup was Matt's. A large cooler, a few tackle boxes, and a pile of duffel bags next to it served as clues.

"Matt?" she said, hoping Renee's husband was close by. When there was no reply, she repeated herself, only louder this time.

"Yeah?" Matt's head popped into view from the other side of the truck. "Oh, hey, Lynette. Give me a second, will you?"

She waited. Were her hot cheeks red with embarrassment? A light breeze blew off the lake toward the lodge and she turned into it, hoping to cool her face. There was no one on the sand or dock. It was still early.

"How's the ankle? And the head?" Matt said from behind her.

She turned, careful to maintain her balance on the too-tall crutches. "My ankle will be fine. Unfortunately, despite lots of physical therapy, it goes out on me. My head is surprisingly clear this morning, if that was your subtle way of asking whether I'm painfully hungover after that fiasco."

He grinned at her. "It was, but that probably wasn't a very professional thing for me to say."

She returned his smile with a tentative one of her own. "Lucky for me, you aren't acting in your professional capacity this morning. If you were, you'd probably slap me with a charge for boating under the influence or something. I'd prefer it if you stayed in sassy, best-friend's-husband mode."

His smirk told her the thought might have at least crossed his mind, too.

Lynette broke eye contact with him and studied the sidewalk between them. She noticed the chalk outline of a butterfly. A child at the resort must have drawn it. The butterfly reminded her it was possible to rise again after getting mired down in a mess.

She looked back up. "Listen, Matt . . . I don't know how I can ever repay you for what you did for me last night. I hate that I put you in danger with my stupidity. Please know how sorry I am about all of it."

Matt nodded, then crossed his arms over his chest. "That type of thing is all in a day's work for me, and I had help. But you did scare my wife. For that reason only, I might be open to some kind of payback. Renee tells me you are quite the business tycoon. If the day ever comes when she needs some business advice, we might come to you for guidance. Then we'll be square again. How's that sound?"

Lynette laughed, checked her balance, and held a hand out to Matt, careful not to drop a crutch. "That sounds like you're letting me off too easy, because you know I'd help Renee regardless."

When Matt leaned in to clasp her hand, Lynette glanced over his shoulder at a second, larger pickup she hadn't noticed earlier. The unique color and size of it looked vaguely familiar.

Just as Matt's hand encircled her own, her mind flashed back to the morning Annie and Relic stopped by to help her haul away the pile of pine clippings. An expensive-looking truck much like this one had slowly driven by, not once but twice. She'd thought it odd but chalked it up to residual paranoia from city life.

"You feeling all right, Lynette? You seem a little wobbly on those crutches."

She pulled her hand from Matt's to grasp the crutch handle under her right arm. She steadied herself and forced a laugh. "You'd think I'd be more stable on these things by now. Say, Matt, is this white truck yours?"

"Yep," he said, waving a hand at the piles of gear beside it. "How did you guess?"

"Whose truck is that burgundy-colored one, then?"

Matt looked over his shoulder at the second pickup. "The maroon one? Sadly, that one's *not* mine. Isn't she a beauty?"

"I suppose," Lynette replied, sure now that it *was* the same truck she'd spotted in her neighborhood.

"That one is Taran's. Robbie begged him to let him drive it back to camp this morning. It has all the bells and whistles money can buy."

"Taran?"

Matt chuckled. "Oh. That's right. Renee said Taran went by the name *Storm* when you guys were kids."

The front door of the lodge opened, and the man in question strode out.

"He's always been Storm to me," Lynette said, shifting to fully face the owner of the fancy truck.

"Hey, Lynette," Storm said, after a quick nod to Matt. "Is he going to slip the cuffs on you now for that stunt you pulled last night?"

Lynette ignored the jab. "Have you been stalking me?"

Storm pulled up short. "What?"

"That truck over there," she said, pointing. "Is that yours?"

"Yeah . . . ?" He drew the single word out slowly, as if trying to figure out what Lynette was getting at.

"I've seen that exact truck drive by my house more than once. I know you've been spending time at Owen's, so that puts you in the neighborhood, but whoever kept driving by my house in that truck always went by real slow. Like a stalker."

Storm threw his head back and let out a hearty laugh.

Even after thirty years, this near-stranger still knew exactly how to push her buttons.

"I'm serious, Storm. I saw you. It was creepy."

The lodge door opened again and Owen, Henry, and Robbie all joined the trio on the front sidewalk.

"Who's ready to get back out on the water?" Robbie yelled. He bounced over to the pile of gear and started loading it into the back of Matt's truck.

Storm glanced between Lynette and Robbie, then looked at Matt. "You got room for Owen and Robbie? I need a few minutes with Lynette, and I don't want to hold you guys up. Robbie can drive my truck later."

"Sure," Matt said, walking over to help Robbie finish loading things.

"Actually, I wanted to catch Jackie, too," Owen said. He took a couple of backward steps toward the lodge that he'd just exited. "That all right with you, Taran?"

"Fine," Storm replied, but he didn't look away from Lynette.

"No wonder you two have such terrible luck fishing that lake over by Ruby Shores," Robbie said to Storm and Owen. "You obviously have commitment issues. To fishing, I mean."

The young man laughed as he slammed the back of Matt's truck and climbed into the backseat with a wave. "I'm going to hold you to your promise to let me drive, Taran!"

Henry, who had watched them all with interest, held up his cell phone toward Owen. "Call us when you get back over to camp and we'll meet up again on the water."

Chapter Twenty-Seven

Only Lynette and Storm remained on the walk between the lodge and the parking lot.

"Is there somewhere we can talk?" Storm asked.

The need to know why Storm had repeatedly driven by her house overshadowed Lynette's earlier embarrassment over her rescue. She looked back toward the beach. Two of the red Adirondack chairs sat on the sand not far off the walkway. She could hobble that far.

"Let's grab those chairs over there."

He nodded and walked beside her, keeping his steps measured. When she noticed the way his gaze snagged on Renee's totem pole, Lynette nodded at it. "The woman who carved that promised us it represented her great-great-grandfather. He was a truth seeker, and anyone who gazes upon it will be forced to tell the truth."

Storm pulled up short in front of the pole to stare at the carvings. "Seriously?"

Despite how nervous Storm's presence made her feel, Lynette laughed. "No. We just thought the totem poles were cute when we saw them at a luau on our girls' trip to Maui. Renee had one shipped here."

Storm rolled his eyes, then motioned for her to precede him across the short expanse of sand to the chairs. "Be careful."

"Obviously," Lynette said, frustrated over having to maneuver across sand on crutches.

Once they were both settled in the chairs, Storm took the crutches from Lynette and laid them off to the side. Her eyes found the tiny butterfly tattoo on his inner arm, drawn to it like a magnet. She wondered if the butterfly she'd spotted on the sidewalk by the lodge had been a sign that she needed to clear the air, once and for all, with this man.

She cleared her throat. "Now, I need to know why you were at Owen's the other day, and why you kept driving by my house."

He sighed and faced the water. A pair of sunglasses hung from a strap around his neck. The strap probably kept them from flying off while fishing in a boat. Lynette felt a twinge of disappointment when he put them on against the glare of the morning sun. She wanted to look into his eyes to help gauge the truth of whatever it was he was about to tell her.

"I suppose Owen and I are like you and the rest of your friends here at Whispering Pines. We met when we were kids, and we've stayed in touch ever since. We've even been business partners. I don't get back to Ruby Shores much anymore, but I do still have that lake house I lived in, back when you and I dated."

A shiver ran down Lynette's spine at the mention of Storm's old house. She'd never told Storm, or anyone else, the truth behind what she had been running from on that long-ago night when she'd crashed his truck.

"You cold?" he asked. She couldn't tell through his sunglasses whether he was looking at her.

"No. Go on." She had no intention of bringing up that night, and she hoped he wouldn't either.

"I spend most of my time on Nantucket during the summer months. Bought a place out there about five years ago. It needs some pretty extensive renovations, and I finally got around to lining those up this summer. Since it isn't really livable at the moment, I came back to Ruby Shores and finally got the old lake house cleaned up. I may sell. Owen gave me a hand out there with a project, so I returned the favor by helping him with his fancy deck."

Lynette wasn't sure why she'd assumed no one from Ruby Shores had kept in touch with Storm. He and Owen had gotten along when they'd all worked together at the pizza place, though Storm was two years older.

She would have loved to pepper him with questions about his life and career through the years, but that would make her look too interested. Instead, she'd let him drive the conversation.

He shifted in the chair. "I got sand in my shoes."

She watched as he kicked off a pair of hiking shoes and socks. The man could use a pedicure. Not that Lynette treated herself to them often these days, but still. If he saw her grin, he ignored it.

"That was my truck you saw this summer. The windows are dark, so I hoped you wouldn't see that it was me inside."

"Trust me, you don't look much like the old Storm I used to know. I doubt I'd have recognized you, even with the windows down. But maybe, if you want to stay incognito, you shouldn't drive around in such a flashy truck."

He kicked a little sand. "Touché. I guess you've always had a thing for me and my trucks. You were bound to figure out it was me."

"Don't flatter yourself," Lynette said. It was a valid point, but not one she'd ever own up to.

"I could say the same to you," he replied with a quick tap on the arm of her chair. "Because, believe it or not, I was looking at the *house*, not you."

She batted his hand away. "Ouch. Way to deflate a girl's ego."

He laughed. "Fine. I was looking at you, too. I knew who you were, and I wanted to see if you'd changed much. I'm human. But I'm being honest when I say that I was checking out the house. I'd hoped to buy it if it ever went on the market. But then my old nemesis swept in and bought it right out from under me."

Lynette wasn't sure she'd heard him correctly. "You want to buy my house? But why?"

"No, I wanted to buy Raven Black's house," he said. "The house used to belong to Sybil Wall before she passed. I believe your mother worked with Sybil at the nursing home, right?"

She was having a hard time following. "You knew Sybil?"

"I certainly did. I even spent time in that house when I was a little kid. In *your* house," he clarified. "This will probably come as a surprise, but Sybil was family. And so is Raven, of course, but she and my mom butted heads so badly that I never really developed any kind of relationship with her."

"You're related to Raven?"

Storm nodded. "I doubt she even remembers me. Her brother was my father. Sybil was my great-grandmother."

Lynette sat up straight and leaned her body toward Storm. "Was Gideon Gage your father?"

Storm pushed his glasses up on top of his head. His eyes, still the same piercing blue, held hers. "My father died a long time ago. How do you even know his name? Did Sybil or Raven tell you or your mother about us?"

She could tell the answers to those questions were of vital importance to him, but she doubted her answers were the ones he wanted to hear. She shook her head. "No. I'm sorry. I mean, if either of them told Donna about you, she kept that to herself. But how is it you never told me any of this when we were together?"

He shrugged. "Why would I? My father died when I was a kid. My mother's family never accepted him. My grandfather on Mother's side insisted, right until the day he died, that my father ruined any chances she had to build a family with a good Catholic boy. Truth is, Dad knocked Mom up when she was only nineteen. They married, but the hard feelings ran deep. How well did you know Sybil?"

Lynette could hardly believe the family ties between Sybil, Raven, and her old boyfriend. But she remembered the way her breath had hitched when she saw the headstone in the cemetery back in Ruby Shores. The last name of Gage had seemed like a coincidence. Just because she'd dated a guy named Storm Gage when she was seventeen didn't mean it was the same family. A man named Kenneth was the only person she'd ever heard Storm refer to as Dad. His mom's name was Delaney, and they'd divorced a few years before Lynette met Storm.

None of that matched with what little she knew about Sybil's family.

"I found Sybil's grave. And her husband's. Donna explained to me that Sybil and her husband—I forget his name—only had one daughter. I think her name was Eleanor. There was a headstone marking the grave of Eleanor and her husband, too. The names Raven and Gideon were listed on the bottom. I knew Raven had a twin brother who died of cancer. I can't believe you are Gideon's son."

Storm held up one hand to stop her. "Why would you be spending time in a cemetery looking at headstones?"

"We found some old pictures in a locked box, and Donna was trying to remember who was who in Sybil's life."

"You call your mother Donna?"

"We worked together for years. Habit."

"Were there other things in the box?" he pressed. "Anything interesting?"

The sun was hurting Lynette's eyes, and she wished she'd grabbed her own sunglasses. She held up a hand to block the sun and give her eyes a break. "Well, not money or anything else terribly valuable, if you were wondering why someone locked the box."

"What can I say? I'm a practical man," he said with a laugh.

"There were the two wedding pictures—it would have been your grandparents' wedding then. Two locks of straight black baby hair. They tied one with a pink ribbon and one with blue. We think they had to belong to Raven and her brother. Come to think of it, you used to have straight black hair like that."

He ran one hand over his shiny scalp. "The years haven't been kind to me."

She had to disagree—he still looked very fine to her—but she'd keep that to herself.

"What else did you find?"

"There was a ring," she said. "The setting looked vintage to me. The center stone is probably a diamond. Donna told Raven about it—about everything we found—and she's holding on to it for her. They'll swing by Ruby Shores the next time they're in Minneapolis." She thought back to the other items, then chuckled. "There were a handful of small stones. I think they were probably crystals, because Sybil was a little woo-woo. She studied old religions and told my mom about them. We even found a deck of tarot cards. I actually brought those out here, to Whispering Pines, just for fun. Renee pulled the Death card and got all freaked out. I felt bad. But last night, when I thought I might drown out there after being so stupid, I wondered if that card was actually meant for me."

She let out a nervous giggle, but Storm didn't look amused. "Don't joke about drowning. My dad's parents drowned, leaving him an orphan. Believe me, that fact bounced around inside my head a few times when we were searching the dark water for *you* last night."

She reached for and caught his hand in hers, giving it a reassuring squeeze. He sounded so despondent at that moment. The gesture was automatic, but she dropped his hand the second she realized what she'd done. He pulled his back and crossed his arms, tucking both hands in.

"Sorry," she said. "Reflex."

He shrugged. "Forget about it. Anyway, Sybil's fascination with many religions, including the occult, was the main reason my mother's family refused to acknowledge my dad's family. Then, after my father died, that was it. Mother forbid me from having any contact with my aunt or my great-grandmother."

Lynette considered this. "How old were you when your father died?"

"Ten or so. Mother never was the type of woman to survive long on her own. She married again and had another kid. That's why there's such a big age gap between me and my only brother. I'm fifty-two, he's thirty-six now."

Lynette was more interested in Storm's connection to Sybil than his mother's story. His mother had been horrible to her when they were dating. She still suspected the woman had been home on that terrible night when Lynette's attack left her with no choice but to take Storm's truck without permission.

She turned her attention back to Storm. "You were ten when Gideon died . . . Were you in my house before he passed away? In Sybil's house, I mean?"

He rocked his head from side to side, as if he was trying to remember the details from so long ago. "I think it was after he died. Sybil wasn't exactly someone who liked to follow the rules. She didn't care that my mother didn't want me to see her."

"I guess that runs in the family, too," she said.

He smiled. "I wasn't supposed to go by Sybil's. Ever. Of course, that was all the more reason for me to ride my bike past there when I was a boy. Once in a while, she'd be home and spot me. She'd invite me in and load me up on her famous chocolate chip cookies. In fact, I told Donna that when I was in your kitchen last week."

"Donna knows you were Sybil's great-grandson? And you were in my kitchen *last week*?" Lynette asked, shocked.

Was this yet another secret her mother was keeping from her?

"No, she didn't recognize me. *That* must run in *your* family," Storm laughed. "But seriously, she had no idea. Owen introduced me as Taran, because that's what he always calls me. She was already upset about the water in your basement. I thought it might throw her off too much if I told her who I really was."

Then Lynette had another thought. She pulled her phone out of a side pocket in her capris and opened her photos.

"Are you going to take a picture of me for her and tattle on me now?"

"Maybe I should," she said, but then she shook her head. "No. I have an idea. The only other things in the box I found were pictures of a young boy. We had no idea who he might be. But now I'm wondering if it was you. I snapped pictures of the photos to share with Raven, so hold on a sec . . ."

Once she found them, she handed her phone to Storm.

"Well, I'll be damned."

"So, Taran Gage, are you the young boy in the photos?" she asked, as if he were on the stand in a mock trial.

"It would appear so," he said, holding the phone closer for a better look.

She watched him struggle to see the picture. Maybe it was the bright sunlight, or maybe it was just because he'd, like her, passed the half-century mark.

"If you'd like the original pictures, swing by sometime," she said. "But back to what sent us down this fascinating path. Why did you want to buy the house? You don't live in Ruby Shores. Did you just like it that much as a kid? Or is it to get back at your mother and family for trying to alienate you from your father's family?"

He flipped his sunglasses back down. "I wanted it for my brother. For Shane."

"For Shane? You just said your brother is thirty-six years old. Isn't he old enough to buy himself a house? I can tell from your fancy truck that you've had some financial success, but that seems overly generous."

When he didn't return her smile, she suspected she'd said something wrong.

"Storm?"

"Shane was born with developmental disabilities. He'll never be able to live independently. Our selfish mother washed her hands of both of us years ago. His father, Kenneth, died a little over a year ago. I hated that man for the way he'd treated all three of us, but the one good thing he did was provide for Shane. Now I'm all Shane has left. I want to find a large enough home for him to live comfortably with a caretaker and that I can visit from time to time. Sybil's house would have been perfect. I used to tell Shane about it when he was a toddler. I'd pretend it was a castle and our great-grandmother was a white witch. He'd have loved to live there."

"But I stole it out from under you when I bought it from Raven before it could even go on the market. Believe it or not, sometimes my friends accuse *me* of being a witch. Ironic, isn't it?"

He sat on the edge of his chair and rested his forearms on his knees. His thumb went to the small butterfly tattoo. "You couldn't have known I wanted the house. It's been decades since I last talked to my aunt. She wouldn't have had any reason to think I'd want the house, either. I don't think she would hold my mother's appalling behavior toward her and Sybil against me, but we don't have a relationship."

"I still can't believe we did that," Lynette said.

As if he'd been miles away in his mind, her comment snapped his attention back to her. "Did what?"

"Got matching tattoos," she said, nodding toward his arm. "I wasn't even eighteen yet, but you convinced the tattoo artist to do it anyhow."

"I'd given her plenty of business up to that point," he said with a grin.

"And she thought you were sexy," Lynette added.

He wriggled his eyebrows. "So did you. You asked her to place your tattoo in a much more private spot, I seem to recall. Did you keep it? Or did you regret it and have it removed?"

She expelled an exaggerated sigh. "That, Mr. Taran Gage, is no longer any of your business. By the way—"

Shouts coming from the lodge interrupted their banter. She'd been about to press him on the origin of his nickname, Storm, when Jackie's voice yanked her attention away.

Even from their chairs in the sand, Lynette could see that Jackie was upset, and poor Owen must be on the receiving end of her tirade, since he was the only other person she could see.

Storm let out a low whistle. "Something has *her* panties in a bunch."

Disgusted, Lynette pushed up out of her chair. Unaccustomed to her need for crutches, she started to topple to the side when her ankle couldn't support her. Bracing for a mortifying collision with the hopefully forgiving sand, she slammed her eyes shut, preferring not to see Storm's amusement over her clumsiness.

But she didn't fall. He might be older, but his reflexes were still razor-sharp, and his chest wasn't nearly as forgiving as the sand would have felt. It happened so quickly; she froze. He might have pulled her a hair closer before releasing her, but she couldn't be sure.

He stepped back but grabbed one of her hands to help her balance on one foot while he picked up her crutches. "Careful. We aren't as young as we used to be. A fall could cost you more than an ankle."

His teasing helped break the tension, and she gratefully accepted the crutches.

But the tension between Jackie and Owen sounded like it might be escalating, and she stretched to see around Storm. "Think we should break the two of them up?"

"Or we could watch. It might be entertaining."

She shook her head, then embarked on her trek back to the easier-to-traverse sidewalk. "I hate that saying, by the way."

He followed, kicking sand at her heels. He was still barefoot and carrying his shoes and socks in his hand. "What saying?"

She grunted, frustrated with the physical effort it was taking to stay upright on the uneven sand, but also over her dislike of condescending, sexist comments, like the one he'd made about panties.

It was time for the men to get back to their fish.

She suspected Jackie was feeling the same way.

Chapter Twenty-Eight

Lynette held her tin coffee cup out for Renee to fill again.

"That's the last of it," Renee said, shaking the last drops into Lynette's cup.

"Maybe it's a good thing our girls' trip is almost over," Kit said, setting her cup on the deck. It was Friday, and they were all going home on Sunday. She had her back to the water so she could face Lynette and Renee in the red chairs, as well as Annie and Jackie as they perched on the opposite side of the dock. She reached out to grab hold of the side of the canoe that bobbed beside the dock. "We are out of coffee, and I'd hate for Lynette to ruin anything else out here at the resort."

If Lynette's coffee wasn't so hot, she might have tossed it at Kit. She was tired of all the teasing she'd had to listen to about the damage she'd done to Renee's new canoe. She'd already pulled Renee aside and offered to replace it, but Renee insisted that wasn't necessary. Someone was supposed to swing by the resort later today to take it in for repairs. They'd come by boat, pull it over to the public landing, then take it in for patching and repainting.

"There was already a long scratch down the side of it from an incident one of the resort guests had with it last month," Renee had insisted. "I was going to get it repaired anyhow. A couple more scratches won't make that much difference."

Lynette didn't believe her friend, but she was too tired to argue. Instead of throwing her coffee, she downed it all, ignoring the burn.

"Another rough night, Lynette?" Annie said. She lightly tapped Lynette's foot, which rested beside her on the dock. "Maybe we should have taken you in to get this X-rayed yesterday."

Her ankle wasn't the cause of yet another sleepless night. The nightmare had returned, possibly spurred by Storm's mention of his old lake house. She had no intention of ever telling Storm about that night, but maybe, after so many years, talking to her friends about it might help. If she couldn't start getting some decent sleep at night, she'd start seeing cross-eyed during the day.

"My ankle isn't what's keeping me up," she said as she put her empty cup on the dock next to her chair. "I actually still have lots of nightmares about something that happened to me the night of our graduation."

Kit nodded. "I'd have nightmares, too, if I rolled a pickup truck like that. You're lucky you survived that night."

Kit had no idea how much danger Lynette had actually faced that night, beyond the accident with Storm's truck. But was she really ready to talk about the way she'd put herself at risk and what happened next?

Maybe it was finally time. The man who'd tried to hurt her was long dead.

"Did any of you ever wonder why I was driving too fast on that curvy road that night?"

No one replied immediately.

Then Jackie cleared her throat. "You were going through some things back then, Lynette. We were never sure exactly what your mom's boyfriend did to you, but based on how mad Storm got and how seriously my father took the situation as your high school principal, it was bad. I remember how you insisted we meet up with Storm earlier in the night to drink some beer with him before going to our grad party. I always figured you found more beer after you snuck out of the boring party."

Lynette shook her head. "They didn't charge me with drinking and driving. By the time I rolled Storm's truck, the one beer I drank hours earlier was long gone. Remember how we all ate a bunch of mints and onion rings before going to the graduation party so no one would smell alcohol on us? I don't even remember anyone giving me a breath test after the accident, though things were a little fuzzy. I hit my head and cut my cheek in the crash."

She traced the faint line that ran down her cheek. It wasn't the only scar that night had left her with.

Annie tapped Lynette again, this time on her uninjured ankle. "Why were you driving so fast that night?"

"Do you want the entire story, or just the abbreviated version?"

Renee checked the time on her phone. "It's only eight in the morning. We have all day. Besides, I wasn't with all of you the day you graduated, so I don't even know what party you're talking about."

Lynette remembered how terrible she'd felt when Lavonne had mentioned how often her daughter felt like the oddball in their group, specifically because of situations like this.

She nodded at her old pen pal. "In that case, I'll start at the top."

Lynette closed her eyes and started talking. She told them about the shadows that always seemed to lurk in her mind back then, and her anxiety level as she sat in that boring party. She even admitted to her terror over thinking she might be pregnant.

When Kit tried to interrupt, Lynette raised a finger and said she'd get to all of that with her story.

Lynette had no idea how long she had talked, but by the time she opened her eyes, a young family had set up camp on the beach. "Why didn't you stop me? Could they hear me?"

Jackie reached over and put a comforting hand on Lynette's shoulder. "Of course not. Don't worry. They aren't paying any attention to us. But how can you be so sure that Storm's mother was actually home that night but refused to help you? What kind of person would do that?"

Lynette shrugged. "I never really knew her. Storm brought me home once and introduced me to her, but she was always incredibly cold toward me. I'm not sure why. Yesterday, when I talked to him, he told me some other things about her that make me think she is just an all-around terrible person. Her car was in the garage that night. I thought I saw a light inside the house when I banged on the door and yelled for help, but no one came. She was there. I'm almost sure of it."

Kit nodded. "No one helped, and that's awful. But you were afraid the jackass that attacked you could still find you in the dark? How?"

"Well, remember, I was only seventeen, and he'd just attacked me. I wasn't thinking clearly. He knew me from work, and he also knew I was dating Storm. If he knew Storm lived on the lake, not too far from that picnic shelter where he took me, then he might know to look for me there. Part of me was terrified that I'd killed him with that tool I smacked him across the head with, so I really was just out of my mind with fear."

Annie shook her head. "I hate that he took you to our favorite picnic spot above the lake. You must have felt awful when we went there for my wedding party. And then again when the four of us went there after I left Michael. You know, you'll think this is crazy, but I was worried about you back then."

"Worried about *me*?" Lynette said. "You were the one going through hell."

"But I could tell something was bothering you, too. You drank so many wine coolers, so fast. It seemed out of character."

"It wasn't as out of character as you thought, but I'll get to that later. For now, let me finish telling you what happened that night. Now that I've started talking about it, I feel like I need to purge all of it."

She thought about where she'd left off before spying the other guests on the beach.

"You'd just backed Storm's truck out of the garage," Annie supplied.

"Thanks for the prompt," Lynette said, nudging Annie with a toe. "For a while, I thought I'd made it. I found my emergency twenty-dollar bill in my purse and planned to stop for gas. Then I saw headlights behind me. I was sure it was him, coming for me again. I panicked. That's when I started driving too fast and missed the curve."

"He'd found you?" Renee asked, her eyes wide.

"Truthfully? I never knew if it was him or just some random vehicle."

All four of her friends sat for a moment with her story. The only sound was the call of a loon, out on the lake, and the laughter of the three young kids, farther down the beach.

"But you never reported him for what he tried to do to you," Kit said.

"Why not?" Annie asked, before Lynette could even reply to Kit. "He almost *raped* you. He should have paid for that."

Lynette reached toward Annie and patted her on the top of her head. "I love how faithful you always are to all of us, Annie. Even after all these years, you hate it when life doesn't treat us fairly."

Annie nipped playfully at Lynette's hand, and it helped to break some of the tension.

"You obviously never told Storm the truth of what happened that night, or he would have killed the guy," Jackie said.

"That's exactly *why* I never told Storm why I took his truck. I'd already wrecked it. And it was my own stupidity that landed me in that creep's pickup. If Storm would have gone after him for what he did to me, I could have literally ruined his whole life with my actions. Instead, I let him think I was just this crazy girlfriend, taking his pickup out for a joyride."

"He wouldn't have blamed you, you know," Annie said. She shifted to drop both her feet into the water on the side of the dock. "He'd have tried to protect you."

"Exactly my point."

Annie kicked at the water and it splashed up onto Renee's legs.

"Really?" Renee said. She gave Annie's shoulder a light push.

Annie kicked again. "I just hate that we didn't keep Lynette safe that night."

Lynette snorted. "I'm not as nice as Renee. If you try to take any of the blame for this, I'll push you in."

"What happened to the guy who attacked you?" Kit asked. "And I notice you never say his name. Why is that? Did we know him?"

Lynette shook her head. "I don't think you'd have known him. Honestly, when I was in that hospital bed, after the crash, I almost told a police officer who came in to take my statement. But I chickened out. I felt like such a fool for getting myself into that predicament. So I kept my mouth shut. Two weeks later, I was glad I did."

Annie swung her feet back out of the water and spun to face Lynette again. Water from her feet crawled across the wood to tickle Lynette's toes. "Why? Did someone else make him pay?"

Lynette nodded. "Do you guys remember how, after my accident, Donna packed us up not long after, and moved us away from Ruby Shores?"

Everyone nodded, even Renee.

"Donna was at work, finishing up her last day. At that point, she'd grounded me for life. She wouldn't allow me to leave the house, which I wouldn't have wanted to do anyhow. My face hurt, my ribs ached, and I had terrible cramps."

"You weren't pregnant, after all?" Kit asked.

Lynette bit her bottom lip. "I never knew for sure. Part of me thinks the accident caused more internal damage than the doctors suspected when they examined me. That was the heaviest period I'd ever had. Sometimes, when it's super cold and damp outside, my bones just ache in my pelvic area. And even though I never really tried to get pregnant, there was this one guy I dated in my thirties I never used any kind of protection with. I could have raised a family with someone like him. I took chances, but nothing ever came of it, and I sometimes wonder if that accident left me unable to get pregnant."

She really hadn't intended to get into all of this with the girls. She shook her head and, before they could ask more questions about what she'd just said, searched for the story string in her mind. "Oh, yes. My attacker. Donna left me a stack of newspapers, and I remember this next part like it was yesterday. I was rolling up my favorite A&W mug in newspaper, the one Mom was so mad at me for stealing years earlier, when I saw his face."

Annie shrieked and clapped the deck. "He got busted for something else."

"Nope," Lynette said. "It was his obituary."

"Tell me you didn't hunt him down and finish the job yourself, Lynette," Renee whispered, eyes wide, obviously teasing.

"I did not! I had nothing to do with his demise. The obituary was brief, but it mentioned him dying at home. He was thirty-two—older than I thought—and unemployed. I'd thought he was a college student or something. Through the years, I've built up this profile of him that probably has zero truth to it, but his death meant I no longer had to worry about him finding me."

Renee dumped a little coffee out of her cup into the lake. "The guilt probably did him in."

"But you still have nightmares about it?" Jackie said. "Do you think maybe it's time for you to talk to a specialist about this?"

Lynette took a deep breath and closed her eyes again. No one pushed her for an immediate answer.

Is it time?

"You might be right, Jackie. I thought maybe talking to all of you about it would help me move past it. If that isn't the case, I promise to make an appointment to see someone. Fair?"

"Fair," Jackie agreed.

"In fact . . ." Lynette continued, bracing herself. "In case you haven't noticed, I may also need some help with my drinking. I've struggled with it, on and off, through the years. Annie, you said you noticed my drinking when we'd gotten you home after you left Michael. Well, it wasn't long after that when I realized I needed some help to get sober. I spent a month in rehab, and it was one of the toughest things I've ever done."

Annie's eyes welled with tears. "Why would you go through something like that and not reach out to any of us for help?"

Lynette shrugged. "I wrote Renee about it. So she knew. But it was something I didn't want to talk about."

Kit smiled. "See, Renee, sometimes you know things that the rest of us don't!"

"I guess that's true," Renee said. "Lynette, don't be ashamed to ask for help. There are excellent programs out there, and you've had some traumatic experiences in your life to work through."

Renee's comment made Lynette think about the trauma Donna had also endured. She considered telling her friends what she'd overheard Donna tell Lavonne about her abusive father and dead sister, but decided that was something she needed to discuss with her mother first. But the part about Donna not being happy in Ruby Shores wasn't as dramatic of a story, even though it was still upsetting.

"Annie, are there folks I could see in Ruby Shores for my drinking? If not, I could fly back to New York for some sessions."

Annie crossed her feet under her. "Sure. I can give you some names."

"Thanks, I appreciate it. Speaking of New York City, a little bird told me Donna isn't sure our move to Ruby Shores was the right one. I'm thinking maybe she's right," Lynette admitted.

She told them bits and pieces of what she and Kit had overheard, leaving out the parts that might hurt any of her friends' feelings.

"The mothers of the Kaleidoscope Girls might travel together?" Annie asked when Lynette got to that part of the story. "Well, we can't have them getting a jump on us! Where are *we* going next year? Who is up for planning?"

Renee waved a hand. "It's my turn!"

Jackie looked skeptical. "You've done so much for us here at Whispering Pines, Renee. Let's see . . . Kit planned Maui, Annie got us to Arizona, and Lynette got creative since she was planning during the worst of the pandemic and brought us here. I haven't planned a full-blown girls' trip yet, either. Maybe it's *my* turn."

"I know," Renee said. "But I have an idea. I'm not ready to talk about it yet, but I'll do some investigating. Jackie, if it doesn't pan out, I'll call you and we can put our heads together on it. Does that work?"

Jackie nodded. "Let's just make sure that wherever we go, we'll be too far away for any men or mothers to crash our party!"

Lynette raised both her arms. "To be fair, both groups showed up because of me. My mother because we are painfully codependent and she didn't want to miss my birthday, then the guys because I was stupid enough to get drunk and think it was a brilliant idea to take a boat to a bar."

Everyone but Jackie laughed. "I am still so mad at Owen for keeping Storm a secret!" she said.

"Is that what you two were fighting about yesterday?" Lynette asked. "Well, maybe not *fighting*, because I actually didn't see Owen yelling back at you. But you were certainly in his face."

Jackie wilted a little in her chair. "It felt unfaithful. You know? I lived through enough of that with my ex, and it just felt . . . I don't know . . . *sneaky* for him not to say anything."

Lynette felt a twinge of guilt. "I actually knew Storm was hanging out with Owen some before I came to Whispering Pines."

This admission was met with stunned silence.

Kit was the first to recover. "You knew Storm was back, but you didn't tell us?"

"What was there to tell? My cat escaped the house. I chased after her and got caught in a lilac bush. This huge bald guy had to untangle my hair so I could get out."

Jackie's frown turned into a hiccup, then giggles. "Did you know it was him right away?"

"No. As you may have noticed, he's changed."

Annie wiped at a tear. She was finding Lynette's story quite entertaining. "But he's still *very* sexy."

"I didn't notice," Lynette lied.

No one looked like they believed her.

"How did you figure out it was him?" Kit asked.

Lynette thought back to the scene that played out next. "My cat ended up on this little platform at Owen's house, high above the deck the guys were working on. This big dude went up front to get a ladder, came back, then wouldn't let me climb up to get Ebony. He insisted I wouldn't be able to reach her. But my poor kitty got so scared, she jumped. I freaked. He fell off the ladder trying to catch her and landed flat on his back. When I rushed over to make sure he wasn't dead, I saw it. Then I knew."

"Saw what?" Annie asked, still wiping at her face.

"His little butterfly tattoo. The one that matches mine."

Everyone froze. She hadn't meant to mention the tattoos. The only other people on Earth who knew Lynette had a tiny butterfly tattoo on her inner upper thigh were her various lovers through the years. But of course none of them would have known the history behind it.

"Forget I said that," Lynette said, knowing full well that it was too late for that.

"Well, obviously Storm survived his fall," Kit said with a wink. "But what about poor Ebony?"

"I'm sure the cat was fine," Jackie said, waving Kit's question off.

It was Lynette's turn to laugh. Jackie loved dogs, but she'd never be a cat lover.

"I want to hear more about these matching tattoos," Jackie said.

Lynette's cell phone rang. "Saved by the bell!"

It was Donna calling. She took the call, and all the amusement she'd been feeling from talking with her girlfriends fled the moment she heard the quiver in her mother's voice. Donna wasn't prone to hysterics. Something was seriously wrong. Donna's words confirmed it.

"Mom, I'll be home just as soon as I can," she said, hanging up and pushing out of the chair. She'd made it down to the dock without her crutches.

"What happened?" Renee asked. She stood as well.

"That was Donna. Bad news. One of my basement walls is collapsing. I'm so sorry, you guys! I know we'd planned to stay until Sunday. But I need to get back. Mom already called the general contractor that oversaw the renovations I've done on the house. I should be there, too."

Everyone else got to their feet.

"I brought you, Lynette, and I'll take you home," Annie said, gathering up all of their coffee cups.

Renee opened her arms, and Lynette stepped into them. They rocked back and forth for a moment.

Once they pulled away, Lynette caught Renee's hand. "Thank you, Renee. I know you might not believe this, but I feel better after coming here. There is something very special about Whispering Pines. You know I'm only a phone call away, if you ever want to talk business. This place is too special to give up on."

Renee brushed a quick kiss across the back of Lynette's knuckles. "I won't give up. I promise. But it's nice to know I have someone who reminds me so much of my Aunt Celia in my corner."

Annie caught both Renee and Lynette up in another hug, then motioned Kit and Jackie in, too. Kit rolled her eyes, but reluctantly joined them.

"I don't know what I'd do without all of you," Lynette said. "How did I ever get so lucky to find four fabulous friends like you?"

Annie tugged at one of Lynette's silver curls. "I have no idea. But I guess we should all just say 'thank you,' because we are all gifts to each other."

back home

RUBY SHORES

2021

Chapter Twenty-Nine

LYNETTE MADE SEVERAL KEY decisions during the drive home from Whispering Pines.

First, she would never drink again, period. No more treating herself to a cocktail here and there. If her own will wasn't strong enough, she would get back into a program. She knew she'd come too close to hurting herself with that crazy stunt she'd pulled on the lake. Even worse than her own safety, she had put others' lives at risk in the process. Her anger had opened the door for the alcohol to sneak back in and overcome her defenses after she'd worked hard for years to loosen its grip.

Second, she would let her anger at Donna go. While she'd certainly overheard some disturbing revelations while her mother visited with her new friends around the fire, Lynette shouldn't have been listening in the first place. She would feel a tremendous sense of betrayal if Donna ever eavesdropped on her private conversations with her girlfriends. What if her mother had heard the things she'd told Annie and the others out on the dock that morning?

She'd been wrong to listen, but that didn't mean she could forget what she'd heard.

Having Donna in her life was as much of a gift as her other lifelong friendships. Not all daughters considered their mothers to be friends, too. Lynette didn't want to taint their relationship with anger or resentment. Instead of confronting Donna about the truth behind her estrangement from her parents, as well as her discontent in Ruby Shores, she'd allow those conversations to occur organically, in their own time.

Annie pulled into the driveway. "Are you ready to show me the progress you've made on your shed?"

Lynette looked between the commercial vehicle already parked in the drive and her old friend. "Would you mind if we waited until I make some genuine progress? My contractor is here. That's his truck, and I should probably get inside and talk to him. I'm not excited to see the shape of that basement wall, but ignoring it won't make it go away."

Annie snapped off her seatbelt. "I understand. Let me help you with your bags. I know your ankle is still sore, and these last couple of hours in the car were probably enough time for it to stiffen up again."

Lynette appreciated the help. Ten minutes later, she thanked Annie for both her understanding around her need to head home two days early and the ride.

"Donna?" she called out in the empty kitchen. "Ebony?"

Where was everyone?

A banging sound from the basement caught her attention. Ebony was likely hiding in the house somewhere, avoiding the commotion, and Donna might be downstairs with the contractor.

Bracing herself for the mess she'd undoubtedly find, she headed for the basement stairs, grateful for the support of the thick wooden handrail on the way down.

"Hey, guys," she said, taking in the piles of rubble and what looked like some type of wooden frame set at an angle against the failing wall. "This looks scary."

The man who'd competently directed earlier renovations and repairs on her house glanced her way. "Hi, Lynette. Sorry to interrupt your vacation. You maybe didn't need to rush home. I think this temporary structure will hold things until we can get some heavy equipment in to do the excavation in a week or two."

Lynette stepped off the lowest step, teetering slightly on her ankle.

"Don't tell me you hurt that ankle of yours again, Lynette," Donna said.

Lynette smiled at her mother. A smudge of something marred her left cheek. "It'll be fine. You have a little something here, Mom," she said, brushing away the dirt when Donna reached her side.

"This could have been much worse, if you didn't get us in here right away to shore this baby up," the contractor said. "Good thing your mother called me right away."

Lynette took a deep breath of relief, then coughed when she inhaled some of the dust in the air.

"Relic caught this, actually," Donna interjected. "I should have thought to check the basement when I got home from Whispering Pines after the water that seeped in earlier."

Looking around, Lynette realized Relic's dedication to monitoring her house was yet another gift related to her lifelong friendship with the Kaleidoscope Girls. Relic had to miss out on the guys' fishing trip because he'd stuck with the commitment he'd made to Lynette. She'd have to remember to flip him some extra cash. The mess in front of her would be expensive to correct, but it would be nothing compared to the cost if half the house had collapsed.

"You ladies should probably go up. My guys need to jackhammer now, so the dust is going to get lots worse. Be sure to close the door at the top of the stairs, too, so we can contain the mess."

Lynette didn't have to be told twice. The mess made her anxious, and she could only imagine what the cleanup would cost her.

Once they reached the kitchen, she caught Donna up in a hug. When she loosened her arms, her mother pulled back, looking at her with surprise.

"You've never been much of a hugger. What was that for?"

"Thank you for calling me about the basement this morning. I know you felt guilty reporting yet another house emergency, but I suppose that's what we get for buying an old money pit like this. You took care of the water problem on your own, but this is a bigger deal."

Donna pulled out a chair and sat. "I had some help with the water, too."

Lynette thought of Storm. "Tell me more about how you got that cleaned up."

Donna ran a finger across the kitchen tabletop. "I did the same thing as I did this morning. I asked for help."

"Nothing wrong with that," Lynette said. "Sometimes it takes many hands. You mentioned Owen came over and helped Annie's husband and son. Someone was with Owen, too, right?"

Donna nodded. "Big guy. He drove an even bigger truck. We got lucky because he had an industrial-sized Shop-Vac in the back end of his pickup, bigger than the one we borrowed from Owen before. I could tell he and Owen were close, the way they joked around with each other. Now that you mention it, the man had actually been in this house before. When he was a kid. He said he knew Sybil. I suppose that's what happens in a small town. Everybody knows everyone. I'm still not used to that."

Lynette found it interesting that Donna hadn't recognized Storm.

Sure, he looked different from the twenty-year-old boy who'd dated her daughter, but it hadn't taken Lynette long to recognize him. "Did he look at all familiar to you?"

Donna tilted her head, as if trying to picture him again. "Owen's friend? I don't know. It was hot that day, and I'd bribed them with beer, so we all sat around the table up here for a few minutes. I wondered if maybe Owen and the guy with him were related. Maybe brothers? But Owen said no, they'd just worked together through the years."

At the mention of beer, Lynette pulled a waste basket out from under the sink, remembering her earlier decision about alcohol. The first step in total abstinence had to be getting all booze out of the house.

"Was there any beer left after that?"

"Maybe one, in the fridge," Donna said, watching her. "Thirsty?"

Lynette sighed. She didn't plan to tell Donna the truth about getting drunk and going out in the canoe, but her mother knew of her lifelong struggles with alcohol. She never really approved of Lynette having an occasional cocktail here and there. "No, I don't want to drink it. I want to get rid of it. All of it."

Donna's eyes widened, then she nodded. "Good idea. There are a couple of bottles up in that cupboard, too."

Lynette could feel Donna's gaze on her as she cleared out the fridge and cupboards. Glass bottles clinked together in the garbage.

"Why all these questions about the guy with Owen? He had a strange name. It started with a T, I think . . ."

"Do you remember the boy I went to prom with?"

Donna harrumphed. "He was hardly a boy. He was a young man, and he was way too much for you to handle in a first boyfriend."

At seventeen, Lynette would have vehemently argued over that. At fifty-one, she could concede that Donna made a valid point.

"*He* had a weird name, too," Donna continued. "Storm, right?"

Then her mother sat up straighter in her chair, as if she'd just made the connection.

"Wait. Weren't Owen and your date friends back then?"

"More like coworkers, but yeah, Owen and Storm got along. They fished together sometimes, outside of work. Owen and Renee even rode with us on prom night. That wasn't the original plan, but something was wrong with Owen's vehicle."

Ebony finally appeared. Perhaps their voices had drawn her out. She brushed against Lynette's legs, then headed for Donna. Much to Lynette's amazement, Donna scooped the cat up and settled her in her lap.

"What? We bonded while you were away," Donna said. "Are you trying to tell me that was *Storm* here with Owen that day? The main thing I remember about your date was his long dark hair and tattoos. And he always seemed to wear all black. I worried you'd end up with tattoos, too, if you stayed with him, or something worse."

Lynette had always wondered if Donna ever noticed her small tattoo. It was in a private spot on her body, but Donna was her mother, and she'd taken care of Lynette through the years. It was possible. But based on her comment about Storm's tattoos, it didn't sound like she'd ever noticed it.

Lynette set the full garbage can by the back door, then took a seat across from Donna again. "Believe it or not, that *was* Storm. I guess his real name is Taran. Taran Gage. But I only ever knew him as Storm Gage. I doubt I'll ever think of him as a *Taran*."

Donna nodded. "Yes, Taran, that was the name Owen used when he made introductions."

"Mom, does the last name Gage mean anything to you?"

"No. Should it?"

Lynette shrugged. "Maybe. Do you remember what Raven's maiden name was?"

Donna drummed her fingers on the table. "I guess I only knew her after she was married. She's always been Raven Black to me. Which seemed poetic."

Lynette smiled as her mother petted the ink-black cat she'd gifted to her daughter. "Sybil would have approved of a black cat living in her house."

"Probably." Donna sighed and set Ebony down on the floor. "Why are you curious whether your old boyfriend's last name meant anything to me?"

The cat walked out of the room with her head held high.

"Looks like I need to make it up to her for being gone," Lynette said, watching her new pet snub her. It gave her a minute to consider how best to explain about Storm and Sybil to Donna. "Mom, do you remember how Raven's mom drowned? Her last name was Gage."

Based on the confused look on Donna's face, this was news to her.

"But how would you know that? When we found the wedding pictures in the box, we were still trying to figure out who was who."

Lynette shifted in her chair and grimaced when she bumped her ankle against the chair leg. "Not that I'll be heading out on my morning walks again right away, now that I'm back, but do you remember that morning when I walked all the way to the cemetery on the edge of town? After we saw the names on the backs of those pictures?"

"I do. It was hot, and you were gone a long time."

Lynette laughed. "You can stop worrying about me now, Mom. I'm all grown up."

"It's a mother's job to worry about her daughter. Not the other way around. Remember that."

Lynette suppressed a sigh. Conversations with Donna often got derailed.

"Do you want to hear this about Storm or not?"

"Honestly, I'm not sure. That boy was always trouble. Though I admit I admired the way he stood up for you when we had that unfortunate incident with the man I was seeing."

Heavy footsteps on the basement stairs cut into their conversation. The contractor stuck his head in to say that he and his team were going to call it a day, but they'd be back in the morning. It surprised Lynette that it was already five.

Once the house was quiet, Donna met Lynette's gaze again. "I still feel guilty that I brought an awful man like that into our lives."

Donna had apologized many times over the years for her poor judgment, and Lynette had forgiven her long ago. "I know, Mom. But can you focus for a minute? I thought it would fascinate you to learn that Storm is actually Sybil's great-grandson."

Her mother's shocked expression was exactly what Lynette had expected.

"You're probably wondering how I found that out," she continued. "Apparently, Storm and Owen and Henry started talking about taking a fishing trip when they were here cleaning up the water in the basement."

Donna nodded. "There was talk of fishing."

"Someone remembered Matt talking about the good fishing near Whispering Pines," Lynette continued. "So, long story short, the guys lined up a fishing trip out there. They'd promised Renee and Annie to steer clear of the resort, since we'd already had one group of family members crash our girls' trip."

The wink she gave Donna might have softened the point she was making, but her mother still had the grace to blush.

"But then something came up at the resort that required Matt's attention," Lynette said, glossing over the messier details. "The guys swung by, and I had a few minutes to catch up with Storm. He admitted to being over here, in our house, but he knew you didn't recognize him."

Donna raised both palms, halting Lynette's monologue. "Wait. Back up. Storm claims to be Sybil's great-grandson? But that isn't possible. Raven had no kids. And Eleanor was an only child."

"But *Raven* wasn't," Lynette said, leaning toward her mother. "Remember? She was a twin. She had a brother named Gideon. He died young, too. But not before he got a woman named Delaney pregnant and married her."

Donna sat back in her chair with her mouth open. "Neither Sybil nor Raven ever mentioned any other family, aside from a comment or two about Raven's twin."

"They were estranged," Lynette said. "According to Storm, his mother's family never accepted Gideon or any of his relatives. There was an unplanned pregnancy and shotgun wedding. Plus, Delaney's parents raised her in a strict Catholic family. Her father in particular hated the things Sybil loved to study and teach. I guess Raven and Delaney, even though they were sisters-in-law, hated each other."

Donna nodded. "I've met Storm's mother. She is *not* a pleasant person."

"So you believe me?"

"I suppose it's possible, but I want to confirm it with Raven."

Lynette hadn't thought of that. It was a good idea. "When you called her about the box, she'd said she would come by sometime for it, right? I showed Storm the pictures I'd taken of the things we found in the box. He claims to be the little boy in the pictures."

Ebony came back into the kitchen and meowed beside her empty food bowl. Lynette pushed back from the table, but Donna stood.

"Stay off that ankle. I'll feed her."

Lynette watched Donna pull a can of cat food from a lower cupboard. Her mother seemed to enjoy having a pet around.

As Donna scraped the food into Ebony's bowl, she said, "Maybe it's him in the pictures. Maybe it's not. But I want to talk to Raven."

"Fair enough." Lynette wasn't sure whether it mattered in the end, but she was curious, too. "Say, speaking of Raven, there's something else I wanted to ask you about. I know you'd said that years ago, when we left Ruby Shores, Raven promised you that if she ever sold this house, she'd call you first. But why? Did you dream of moving back here someday? I know this old house is beautiful, and you loved Sybil, but I've never really understood that part."

Donna took the empty cat food can over to the door and untied the garbage bag to add it to the trash. "Lynette, I always felt bad for how often we moved around, especially in those years before we moved here, to Ruby Shores."

"Mom, I was only in third grade when we came here."

"I know, honey, but those first eight to ten years of a child's life are important. I wish I could have given you a better sense of stability when you were young. Then, when I started coming here with Sybil and Raven, you came along a time or two. I could see how much you loved it. When we left Ruby Shores like we did, and you were so upset to leave, I thought maybe I could make it up to you someday. Raven and I were friends. It was hard for me to leave, too, but she was always quick to remind me that no matter where you and I lived, as long as we had each other, that was most important. I think losing her own mother left her with some deep scars. I doubt she believed that I'd ever want to come back here, but she kept her promise and called me when they were preparing to list the house. With the pandemic sweeping through New York, and your recent sale of the company, it seemed like the perfect solution."

Donna's explanation wasn't new. She'd said all this before, but given recent developments, Lynette was understanding her mother in a new light. Based on what she'd overheard Donna tell her friends' mothers, the older woman wanted more than a quiet life in Ruby Shores.

Maybe Lynette did, too.

"Mom, if I tell you something, do you promise you won't be mad or disappointed in me?"

Instead of taking her seat again, Donna crossed over to stand behind Lynette. She dropped a kiss on the top of her head. "Honey, you could never disappoint me."

Lynette knew that wasn't true, but she let it go. It was something family often said to each other. "I'm not sure moving here was the right move. And I feel terrible admitting that, because you gave up everything to come here with me."

Donna snorted. "Oh, Lynette. Sometimes I think you and I are too much alike. I could say the same thing to you. After all, I came to you with Raven's message about the house."

"But you aren't happy here, are you, Mom?"

Donna wrapped her arms around Lynette's neck from behind and rested her chin on the top of her head. "I'm not unhappy, dear. Don't worry. We'll figure things out just like we always do. We just need to stick together."

Lynette patted her mother's arms. Donna was correct that they always seemed to make their way through things together. But maybe the time had finally come that they'd each be happier if they stopped compromising, thinking they were making the other happy, and found their own paths for once.

Chapter Thirty

THE CONSTANT *BEEP-BEEP-BEEP* OF the backhoe was getting annoying. Lynette wished she'd remembered to bring her earbuds to the shed to try to drown out the noise.

Her forearm ached from the up-and-down and back-and-forth brush strokes, but her little potting shed was undergoing its last big transformation, right before her eyes. Her original plan was to paint the shed to match the house, but her trip to Whispering Pines, where the wood siding of the resort's cabins blended seamlessly with the surrounding trees, gave her new inspiration. The combination stain-and-sealer she'd gone with was allowing the natural grain to shine. Upon closer inspection, she didn't think anyone had ever used paint on anything except the trim and doors. She still hadn't decided on a trim color. The old red paint had faded to a pinkish hue around the windows. The blue on the door had held up better, but it was tired, too.

As she bent down to reload her brush, she peeked through a window. While she was still finishing up on the outside of her little backyard getaway, the inside was almost done, and she'd exceeded her own expectations.

A layer of insulation behind the drywall on all the inner walls and ceiling would make her she-shed more comfortable, regardless of the season and extreme Minnesota temperatures. She'd hired help to install a small heating and cooling system. Most of the mechanics sat on the outside of the building, masked by a short fence. A tiny sink in one corner—made possible by someone's foresight to lay plumbing all the way to the shed to facilitate planting—would give her most of the comforts of the main house.

The only things lacking were a toilet and shower or bath.

She'd picked out the shed's new windows for both their promised durability and their aesthetics. Lynette could picture herself curled up inside on a snowy winter day with a book and a cup of tea, relaxing on the deep plum-colored velvet sofa. She'd selected the tile flooring for practical reasons, but the thick, colorful rug over the tiles would keep her toes toasty.

"I swear, you're more excited about that tiny shed out there than you've ever been about any of the rooms you poured so much money into in the main house," Donna had said to her that morning over breakfast.

Lynette had reminded her she still felt most comfortable in smaller spaces after all their years in New York.

This afternoon, after she finished with the stain, she planned to walk downtown and visit the used bookstore. A new bookshelf—closely resembling those in Renee's library at Whispering Pines—covered most of one wall. It was exciting for Lynette to start filling the shelves. She'd likely have to call Donna for a ride home, given the boxes of books she hoped to purchase.

A van door sliding open or closed caught her attention during a lull in the noise from the heavy equipment working on the far side of the house. She set her paintbrush down, shook out her sore arm, and walked around to the driveway on the other side of the detached garage.

"Yes!" she said with a clap of her hands. "Do you have a delivery for me?"

The delivery driver, his legs bowed as if he'd been a cowboy in another life, turned to her with a flat, square package in his hands. "I do if you are Lynette Howe."

"That's me!" she assured him, hurrying forward to accept the package. Her ankle was almost back to normal. She'd been careful with it for most of the month after returning from Whispering Pines, though she was now trying to walk each day again.

"You seem excited about whatever is in this package," the older man said, smiling at her enthusiasm.

She waved the box at him. "A girl can never have too many projects!"

"And that's the truth," he said. The twinkle in his eye made her wonder what he liked to do in his spare time. At least, she hoped he had some time for the finer things in life. He looked to be older than Donna, and she had to wonder if he worked because he had to. "Enjoy!" he added, before climbing back into the cab and driving off.

Lynette gave the package in her hand a little shake. It was tempting to rip it open and make sure the photo album inside was what she thought she'd ordered, but her fingers were sticky in places with splattered sealant.

In keeping with the theme of mirroring some elements found in Renee's library while still adding her own unique twists, Lynette had decided to compile a book that could capture favorite memories from their girls' trips.

She hoped this would be the first scrapbook of many, documenting their travels, and she wouldn't tell her friends she was putting it together until the first one was full. They all took lots of pictures with their phones, but between Renee's scrapbook of extra pictures and the box of letters Lavonne kept for her, Lynette had gained a new appreciation for the value of documenting some of life's high points.

But that project would have to wait until she'd put the finishing touches on her she-shed. She'd put it inside on the bookshelf for now. Maybe tonight she'd sit down and order prints of some of her favorite photos on her phone.

A light breeze tangled in the ringlets that had escaped the messy knot on the top of her head, and the hair tickled her face. She paused on the old cobblestones between the house and shed, stuck her package between her thighs to free her hands, and redid the topknot.

"I'll never understand how you can do that without a mirror and look like you just stepped out of a salon."

Lynette jumped at the unexpected sound of her mother's voice. "Don't scare me like that!"

Donna laughed. "I'm sorry. I didn't mean to. Women pay hundreds to get curls like that, you know, but they're never as pretty as when they're natural."

One stray curl still bounced in front of Lynette's eyes. She tugged it straight so she could see it better. "You don't think the gray makes me look old?"

When Lynette looked to Donna for the validation she was hoping to hear, she noticed the woman was carrying a large bucket full of gardening tools. "I prefer the term *silver* to 'gray.' And no, you are a gorgeous woman, no matter the color of your hair. I like this more natural look you've taken on since we've been in Ruby Shores."

"You do?"

Donna moved to her rose garden and set the bucket down with a grunt. "I do."

Lynette remained unconvinced. "You have to say that. You're my mother."

"Actually, I don't *have* to say anything. But I would like to be honest with you. And I'm being truthful when I tell you how pretty you look. Are you about done with the stain? What do you have there?"

Lynette glanced down at the package, still clenched between her thighs. "I decided it would be fun to make a scrapbook of our girls' trips."

"That's a lovely idea. Do it now, while this latest trip is still fresh in your mind. Time goes by so quickly, and if you don't do it now, you might put it off." Donna pulled a wicked-looking trimmer out of her bucket. "If you ever need evidence of how quickly the seasons change, just watch Mother Nature. Look at how my roses have faded and the petals are falling. I need to get these bushes trimmed up while it's still nice outside."

Lynette hated to even think about the reality of the upcoming Minnesota winter. She'd be comfortable inside her shed, but the harsh reality of cold, bleak surroundings held less appeal.

Had Donna made any actual travel plans with Patsy and the other mothers to escape for a girls' trip of their own?

Donna clipped a spindly branch as Lynette passed by. "Do you smell that? It's my favorite smell of autumn. A sure sign that September has arrived."

"All I can smell is this stain I've been using all morning," Lynette said, sniffing at a dark spot on her hand. "But now that you mention it, the air smells like burning leaves. I suppose I'll need to add raking to my list, too. At this rate, I may not get to this photo album until Christmas."

As she tapped the lid to the stain closed, Lynette caught a whiff of herself. She needed to shower before walking down to the bookstore. The heat of summer was behind them, so she wouldn't get too hot on her stroll.

The stain on her hands proved as difficult to remove as the pine sap had been when she'd trimmed the evergreen away from her she-shed. By the time she turned off the water, her fingertips looked like raisins.

She toweled off and slipped into a loose-fitting athletic outfit she'd ordered from her old company last week. She still wanted to monitor the quality and variety of their products. It was a hard habit to break.

The top felt too snug around her hips, though it was her usual size. Now what? Call and complain? She hated it when customers did that. Her first thought always used to be that the customer had ordered too small of a size, because their company sizing was accurate. If that was still the case, maybe she needed to size up.

The bathroom scale mocked her from the corner of the room.

Val had spoiled them with lots of amazing food at Whispering Pines, and Lynette had fallen off her exercise wagon, thanks to her bum ankle. This was the first week she was back to daily walks.

Fine, maybe it's me.

She considered changing but then left the too-small top on. It would remind her not to eat too much at dinner.

Bending at the waist, she wrapped a towel around her wet hair. Her phone rang from where she'd set it on the back of the toilet. She straightened, taking time to adjust the towel before checking to see who was calling.

The name on her screen was a complete surprise.

"Well, hello, stranger," she said after picking up the phone and moving the towel away from her ear. "Aren't we technically still in that uncomfortable stretch of time when we're only supposed to communicate through our lawyers?"

A heavy sigh came through the phone. "Technically, yes," the woman on the other end said. "But you were the one who taught me that sometimes it's better to go straight to the source."

Lynette laughed. She really didn't mind Frankie calling her direct. Keeping lawyers in between their communications had proved to be quite difficult. "I suppose I did. Believe it or not, I was just thinking about calling you. I ordered one of those new cotton athletic sets you released last month."

"And let me guess," Frankie said. "It's too small."

"So it isn't me, coming home from an almost-two-week vacation, all fat and sassy?" The towel slipped, so Lynette pulled it off and finger-combed her curls as she held the phone to her ear with her right shoulder.

"I suspect you'll always be sassy, but I couldn't speak to the *fat* part," Frankie said. "God, it's good to hear your voice. Things aren't the same around here without you."

Lynette switched ears, then swiped on her deodorant. "Life is pretty different for me, too. In fact, today I stained a shed."

Frankie made a noise of surprise. "I never took you for a manual-labor kind of girl. Isn't that hard on your nails?"

The question had Lynette studying her naked, slightly jagged fingernails. She wondered if her salon back home—in New York, that was—had survived the pandemic shutdowns and reopened. Frankie lived in a different section of the city than Lynette had, so she wouldn't know.

"Honestly, you might not even recognize me if I walked through your doors today," she admitted.

"Why don't you come for a visit and we could test that theory? When you left, you promised to come back and see us, but you haven't yet."

Her lawyer had strongly cautioned Lynette and Donna about maintaining any kind of ongoing relationships with their prior staff, at least until she'd received all the payments and they were well and truly beyond the sale transaction. Given his advice, Lynette hadn't really considered a trip back to their old headquarters.

"Lynette, did I lose you?"

"No, no, I'm still here. You just got me thinking. Maybe a quick trip would be fun. But I'm sure that wasn't the reason for your call. Did you have a question you couldn't find an answer to? I'll help if I can, but I'm sure lots has changed since I left."

She checked her reflection in the bathroom one last time, then flipped the light off. If she didn't get started on her walk soon, she might not have as much time to shop at the used bookstore as she'd hoped. There was always tomorrow. Even after more than a year away from her old company, Lynette still struggled to appreciate and remember the true freedom with which she now lived her days. It was a wonderful perk that she tried to remind herself of when she was feeling blue and missing her old life.

"Actually," Frankie said, "that's why I called. We were wondering if there would be any way we could convince you to come back and work in a consulting capacity. There are still so many things that we're struggling with, some of which you might have even caught wind of in the media."

Lynette wandered into her bedroom for socks, but Frankie's surprising offer had her taking a seat on the end of her bed instead. "A consultant? The board hated the idea of consultants. Have you gotten their approval?"

"I mentioned it in passing. They gave their tentative approval, pending guidance by the lawyers on both sides of the sale. What do you think? Are you already so entrenched in retirement life that I don't have any hope of getting you back here, or do you sometimes miss us as much as we miss you?"

"For how long?" Lynette asked, trying to process the notion.

"Well, that would depend on you. We'd take you for two weeks, two months, even up to a year."

Donna stopped in the hallway outside of Lynette's bedroom. "Who are you talking to?" she whispered.

Lynette held up a hand to silence her. "In a minute," she whispered back. To Frankie she said, "I'm going to need to think about it. And call Kevin. My lawyer, I mean. When would you like an answer?"

Frankie sighed. "Whenever you're comfortable giving us one. But please, Lynette, we are serious. We'd pay you, of course, and maybe we could even work out some kind of living stipend, since you don't have a place in the city anymore."

Lynette rubbed the back of her neck. "Give me a few days, all right? You're really catching me off guard here. I promise to call you back soon, by the end of next week at the latest."

She hung up, then fell onto her back to stare up at the ceiling.

"Is everything all right, Lynette?"

"I'm not sure," she admitted.

Donna came into her room and sat on the bed next to her. "Who called?"

Lynette turned her head to look at her mother. "Frankie. Can you believe it? I haven't talked to her for at least six months, and that was just for one quick question."

"From the way you're acting, this was more than just a question."

Lynette sat back up, then sidled closer to Donna. She dropped her head to her mother's shoulder. "Mom . . . Frankie asked me to come back in a consultant role."

Donna patted Lynette's hand. "And you didn't know how to tell her no."

She laughed. "You're usually pretty good at finishing my sentences, but not this time. I'm actually considering it. Of course, I'll need to call Kevin first and ask all kinds of lawyerly questions. He'll hate the idea, but unless there are legitimate reasons not to, then maybe I will. Is it bad that I'm excited? Would you want to come to New York, too?"

She felt her mother's shoulder rise, as if she was taking in a deep breath. "What if you did it by yourself?"

"By myself? Why?" The questions were automatic, but hadn't Lynette also been thinking about finally forging a path that didn't necessarily include her mother?

Donna let out a little giggle. "Lynette, you are fifty-one years old. Don't you think it's about time you took on a project all by yourself?"

Lynette couldn't quite believe how scary that actually sounded. "Mother, you don't even like it here! You *loved* New York."

"And now I might be ready to try visiting Switzerland for a while. Or Aruba, depending on the season."

The elation she'd felt over the idea of a temporary work assignment back in New York City ebbed away, replaced by the hurt she'd felt while eavesdropping on Donna's conversation with Lavonne at Whispering Pines.

"You don't want to live with me anymore?"

"I didn't say that."

Lynette shook her head. "Actually, you did. I heard you. Out at Whispering Pines, when you were sitting around the fire."

Donna's eyes widened and she fiddled with her silver ring. Lynette gave her a moment.

Her mother cleared her throat, then rubbed her forehead, as if a headache might be forming there. "Lynette, the only time I even hinted at the topic of our current living situation was during a private conversation I was having with friends. Did one of them discuss it with you afterward?"

"No . . ." Lynette closed her eyes as shame washed through her.

"You were listening, then. What, were you lurking in Annie's cabin with the windows open? And how much did you hear? I can't believe you would disrespect my privacy like that."

Lynette chanced a glance at her mother's face, hating the tears shimmering in the older woman's eyes. She wished she hadn't admitted to Donna about the eavesdropping. But not as much as she regretted listening in the first place. Maybe she should let her mother think she could keep some of her secrets.

"I wasn't at Annie's. I was reading on the screened-in porch at Kit and Jackie's. My cabin was miserably hot. I swear I wasn't trying to listen, but when I heard you say something about dreams, I admit it piqued my interest. I shouldn't have listened and I'm not proud of myself. I'm sorry. But why didn't you tell me you weren't happy living here with me in Ruby Shores?"

Donna stood and paced over to the window overlooking their back-yard.

Lynette watched her and wondered if she was trying to remember the exact timing of the different topics discussed around the fire that night. Should she admit to hearing Donna's heartbreaking tale about her long-passed sister?

Perhaps someday she would discuss that with Donna, too. But her mother's apparent upset, coupled with Frankie's surprise offer, was already weighing heavily on her heart.

"Honestly, I've always placed your happiness above my own," Donna said, turning back to face her. "But maybe we'd both benefit from some time apart. What we have, Lynette, is special. I don't want to ruin that. Let's just think about it. Moving here might have been a little rash. I don't want to make that mistake again."

She turned toward the bedroom door, but paused. "By the way, Raven is swinging by tomorrow afternoon. I thought you might want to say hello to her. Did you know that after Raven and her husband moved to Salt Lake, they rented this place out for a while, before deciding to sell? Would you ever consider something like that?"

Had her mother already forgiven her for eavesdropping on her conversation? She seemed more resigned than mad. But Donna's question did strike her. Rent out this house? The thought had never occurred to Lynette, but then again, Donna was sometimes the more forward-thinking woman in their partnership.

Lynette's phone buzzed with an incoming text.

Donna walked out, stopping at the doorway. She didn't look at her again. "You have lots to think about, so I'll leave you to it. We can talk more about this later."

Even if she wasn't mad at Lynette, she was disappointed. Not that Lynette blamed her.

They'd both hurt each other.

Her phone buzzed again. Welcoming the distraction, Lynette glanced at the text. It was from Storm. He was leaving town in a few days, but he thought they still had a few things to discuss, so would she like to grab a quick drink? Then he sent a follow-up text with a laughing emoji and a suggestion of coffee instead. He didn't think he had another boat rescue in him.

She dashed off a quick response, to which he came right back.

The lighthearted banter was a relief after the scene with Donna. Now her walk to the bookstore really was going to have to wait. She'd rather go sit on her new couch in the shed and think through things.

Something told her she and Storm had plenty of unfinished business, too.

Chapter Thirty-One

DONNA SAT AT THEIR kitchen table with her morning coffee. The house was quiet.

Too quiet.

Lynette was out walking. Her daughter had said little since their brief discussion in Lynette's bedroom yesterday.

Did Lynette overhear anything else?

Talking with Lynette about their future—*futures*—was scary, but part of her also thought it was long overdue. Their impromptu move back to Ruby Shores more than a year ago really had made sense at the time. But now . . .

Why does change have to be so hard?

Donna liked to think she knew her daughter better than anyone else, and that phone call from Frankie yesterday had put a sparkle in Lynette's eye that had faded in recent months. Maybe spending time in New York again was the right thing for her daughter, even if it could just provide her with the closure she didn't get because of the circumstances of the pandemic.

Lynette might need to go back, but Donna didn't. She'd always dreamed of seeing more of the world, and at seventy-two, there wasn't any more time to waste. Before they'd left New York, she had already made tentative plans with Chester to tour Europe, but then the world shut down and put things on hold. She'd never mentioned her plans with Chester to Lynette.

Chester, her old neighbor back in the city, was the one potential draw for Donna to tag along with her daughter. But, deep down, Donna knew both she and her daughter would benefit from following different paths. It would be a first for them, but a necessary first.

She cradled her coffee mug between both hands. The silver ring on her left middle finger *tap-tap-tapped* against the stoneware cup. Her nervous habit irritated Lynette, who had often accused her of never being able to sit still.

Was she just naturally twitchy, or had she felt confined for too long?

She unwound her fingers from her mug and slipped the ring off. The skin below was pasty-white and indented after eight years of never taking it off.

Lynette had lost the matching ring in the lake at Whispering Pines. At first, a rush of panic had filled Donna when she heard the other ring was gone. The blessed rings had served as important touchstones during her struggle with breast cancer. She'd expected to never take hers off again, attributing much of her healing and recovery to the special matching rings.

But sometimes when she noticed it on her finger now, it transported her back to that terrible time instead of giving her a feeling of appreciation for surviving. Was the ring making her feel fragile? Had Lynette's ring made her daughter think of Donna as frail, too?

She set the ring next to her coffee and rubbed her finger.

It felt . . . freeing.

The sound of footsteps on the back stairs brought a smile to her face.

Lynette wouldn't be back from her walk yet, so it must be her old friend, Raven.

"You two really have done some amazing things with this place," Raven said, accepting a cup of coffee. "I know the house was looking tired, but when faced with using a hefty chunk of our hard-earned savings to give her a much-needed facelift, or letting someone else with a fresher vision bring her back to life, it was an easy decision. Our low-maintenance condo in Salt Lake is the better option for us at this stage."

Donna sat across from her old friend. "Are you still working full-time? I would think you'd want to retire before long."

They continued to catch up, as old friends do, on each other's lives.

Raven noticed the silver ring, still on the table, and picked it up. "This is pretty."

"It is. Lynette had a matching one, but she lost it."

"I gave up on wearing rings years ago. The skin on my hands is so dry, I'm constantly putting on lotion." She handed the ring back to Donna.

Donna examined it and laughed when she noticed the gunk stuck in its crevices. "I think I'll clean this up and tuck it away in my jewelry box. It is pretty, but it represents a different time in my life. Now, when I look at it, it reminds me of when I was sick. I'd rather focus on how good I feel most of the time nowadays. But speaking of rings, I should go grab that box I called you about, so we don't forget why you actually swung by."

Raven checked the time. "My husband will probably be back to pick me up in a half hour. I wish I could stay longer, but this was just a quick trip."

Donna hurried up to the spare room where Lynette had stored the box. It was a shame that her daughter was going to miss Raven today.

Raven was at the kitchen sink when Donna got back downstairs. "The improvements you did to the kitchen look amazing. But I noticed the cracked cupboard door is still here. I was so mad at Sybil and those tarot cards of hers that day when I slammed it too hard and broke it."

Donna set the box on the table. "Speaking of tarot cards, here you go."

Her visitor left both of their empty mugs in the sink and returned to the table. She opened the box. The wedding photographs were on the top. Raven removed them and sat down.

"These are very similar to the ruined ones from Sybil's room at the home," she said, running a light fingertip across the faces of her long-lost family members. "I hate that my grandfather wasn't there to watch my mom grow up, or to attend her wedding. I only ever knew my grandmother as a widow."

Donna knew Raven had suffered a similar loss. Neither of her parents, the bridal couple in the picture Raven held, had been alive for her own wedding. "The names on the back of that made Lynette so curious that she visited the cemetery where you'd told me they'd buried Sybil. She did a little detective work of her own there, and that's how we figured out those were your parents."

"She did?" Raven glanced up from the picture. "Boy, I haven't been to their graves in years. I should probably swing by there on our way out of town today. I only wish we could have buried my brother there, too. Then I could show my respects to all of them."

Raven's mention of her brother reminded Donna of the strange twist Lynette had revealed regarding her old high school friend. She motioned toward the box. "There are some newer pictures in there, too. Have a look at those."

"There are?" Raven set the two bridal pictures on the table and pulled the box closer to look inside again. "I'm glad those tarot cards aren't in here. Did you take my advice and burn them?"

"Really? They aren't?" Donna said, surprised. "Lynette had to have taken them out, then. I wonder if she took them with her to Whispering Pines. It would be just her style to want to play around with the cards with her friends."

"That's fine. I have no desire to see them again. Oh, here are those other pictures you mentioned."

Donna watched her old friend's expression as the other woman studied the image of the young boy, but it was impossible to guess what Raven was thinking. Then she noticed the way Raven's hands shook when she dropped them on top of the older photographs.

"Do you have any idea who that boy is in the pictures?"

"I have a pretty good idea, but I don't understand," Raven said, meeting Donna's gaze.

"Is it a relative?" A twinge of guilt followed her question, given she might already know the answer.

"He looks just like Gideon, my brother. But it can't be him. The photograph is too new, so it has to be his son."

Donna hated the pale, pinched look on Raven's face. Maybe she should have tossed those pictures to prevent the pain her old friend was so obviously feeling. But that would have felt wrong, too. She waited, giving Raven time to process what she was seeing.

Raven finally shook her head and pointed at the boy in the picture. "This is crazy. Sybil must have kept in touch with him, even after Gideon died."

"So you do still have family, beyond your husband?" Donna asked, careful to keep her tone low and unemotional. She didn't want to further upset Raven.

"Technically, yes, but I haven't thought about him in years. I know that must sound awful. But my foolish brother got involved with this shrew of a woman. She got pregnant, and he ended up marrying her, but it caused a huge rift. Her father was against the very notion of his precious daughter having any kind of relationship with a boy who wasn't Catholic, let alone marrying him. To compensate, Gideon disassociated from us. It almost broke Sybil's heart. She'd already suffered so much heartache. It was like we lost Gideon, even before he got sick and died. I only saw their baby one time, at his christening, but Sybil said something inappropriate about the ceremony to Gideon's in-laws, and that was that," Raven explained. "Or so I thought. This tells a slightly different story, though. See this car in the background of the one photograph? That was Sybil's. Which means the boy must have been here, or with Sybil somewhere, when he was much older than an infant."

Donna reached across the table and picked up a picture. "What was the boy's name, Raven?"

"Taran," she said. "Why would Sybil keep something like this from me?"

"You called your brother's wife a shrew a minute ago. Did the two of you ever get along?"

Raven's bitter laugh provided the answer even before her words. "Never. I hated the changes I saw in Gideon from the moment he met her. It was like he turned into a different person. Why couldn't she see that, aside from Sybil, Gideon was the only family I had in the world?"

"Whatever happened to them after he died? Your brother's wife and child, I mean."

Raven shrugged. "I heard things over the years, but I never actively tried to keep tabs on them. I think she remarried a few years later, maybe even had another kid. But from the looks of this, Sybil kept closer tabs on them than I did."

Donna squirmed in her chair, considering whether to share what she knew of Taran and his mother. "All of that happened a very long time ago," she said, deciding to test the waters a little. "That boy in the pictures would be a grown man now. About Lynette's age. Would you ever want to look him up?"

Raven grimaced. "I don't know. Maybe? Of course, none of what happened was his fault. He was a child. But I suspect his mother poisoned our name. I doubt he'd want any kind of relationship with his dead father's sister after all this time."

Donna wasn't so sure about that. She decided her friend deserved to know what little Donna had learned about Raven's adult nephew. "Raven, the boy looks happy in the pictures Sybil kept. I, of all people, know how unfair it is to judge someone by the type of parents they had."

This earned her a curious look from Raven.

Donna waved a hand. "But this isn't about me. Raven, a month ago, we had some water in the basement, and Lynette was out of town. I needed help, so I reached out to Owen down the street. He's helped us out a few times around here. An old friend was visiting him, and he came along to help clean up the basement. When they finished, I invited them up here, to the kitchen, and offered them a beer."

Raven narrowed her eyes at Donna. "Okay. I'm sorry about all your basement problems. We honestly didn't know those issues were cropping up, but I don't see how—"

"Raven, the name of Owen's old friend was Taran," Donna said, cutting Raven off. "He said he'd been here, in the house, as a kid. He said Sybil even fed him chocolate chip cookies. But he never said he was a relative."

Raven drew in a shaky breath. "It has to be him! 'Taran' isn't a common name."

Donna reached into the box and pulled out a tuft of hair. "There is more. Do you remember, years ago, when we left town so suddenly? I quit at the nursing home and moved away from here with Lynette?"

Raven stood and retrieved both their cups from the sink. "I think I need more coffee for all of this," she said, splitting the last of the coffee in the pot between the two. "Sure, I remember when you left. It was shortly after Lynette had that terrible car accident. I hated to see you go, and not just because of how much you helped Grandma Sybil at the home. I considered you a friend. But I could tell something serious was going on, so I accepted your decision."

Donna sipped the coffee Raven handed her. The now bitter brew fit the distressing story she was about to share.

"Lynette was dating a boy named Storm. It was his pickup she was driving when she had the accident. She took it without his permission, the night of her high school graduation. Earlier that day, some things related to a man I was dating had bubbled to a head, and I felt awful. My gut told me to call in sick to work and keep Lynette home with me. Not only was she upset about how the man I'd been dating treated her—of which I knew nothing about until then—but something else was going on. I suspected she might be pregnant, though she never let on that she was. A mother just knows sometimes, you know?"

Raven's expression reminded Donna that her friend knew little about a mother's intuition, given her own had died while Raven was young and she wasn't one herself.

"I'm botching this," Donna said.

"No, go on. I'm dying to hear how this all ties together. Because I'm assuming it must."

Donna felt something brush against her leg and looked down to see Ebony there. She hadn't even noticed the cat wander into the kitchen, but it felt like Ebony was giving her encouragement to continue.

"I'm sorry. This is complicated," she said. "Anyway, you knew Lynette back then. She had the uncanny ability to get what she wanted, and what she wanted the night of her graduation was to go out with her friends. The entire group of them ganged up on me, convincing me they'd stick together. But Lynette snuck out of the grad party without her friends and wound up wrecking Storm's truck. When I got to the hospital, the doctors gave me a rundown of her injuries. There was the possibility of a concussion, a terrible cut down one cheek, and other bumps and bruises. No one mentioned a pregnancy test. When I got her home, I saw wrappings from her sanitary products in the garbage, so I figured I'd been wrong about the possibility that she'd been stupid enough to get pregnant. It was the one blessing from that awful time."

"That had to have been a relief," Raven said.

Donna nodded. "It was. But I was still worried. I knew she was head over heels for this kid, and he was a couple years older. I had mixed feelings about him. He obviously cared about Lynette, and he stood up for her. But he projected an image of sorts that made me nervous. Also, they never seemed to be able to keep their hands off each other, even around me. I was wrong about Lynette being pregnant, but I worried it could still happen. Plus, her friends were all heading off to college, but there was no money for Lynette to do the same. She could have tried for scholarships, of course, but she was reluctant to make any specific plans after graduation. I knew that had to do with the boy. I started wondering if it might be best to get her away from Ruby Shores. To move. Moving would be expensive, but I found a way."

Raven reached across the table to grasp Donna's hand. "What an awful predicament to find yourself in! You should have come to me for help."

Donna snorted. "I didn't know you that well and I've never been good at asking for help. Lynette was furious with me, but I hoped she'd get over it with time. And she did, eventually. I still think leaving was best for her, but it was hard to drive away from Ruby Shores. We'd both built a life."

"Did she ever hear from him again? Her boyfriend, I mean. And what kind of name is *Storm*?"

"As far as I know, she didn't talk to him again until decades later. In fact, it was only about a month ago when she ran into him. He was with Owen."

Donna watched to see if Raven was piecing things together yet.

"Owen? Wait . . . Owen seems to be the common denominator in your stories today."

"Raven, Storm and Taran are one and the same. I didn't recognize him in this kitchen that day. When he dated Lynette in high school, he had long black hair. Like this," she said, holding up the tuft of baby hair from the box. "He's bald now, and much broader. He goes by Taran as an adult. It shocked Lynette when she ran into him. When they talked, he admitted to being in this house before because it used to belong to his great-grandmother."

A silence descended in the kitchen again, much like the one Donna noted earlier, before Raven's arrival.

Finally, Raven cleared her throat and glanced at the time. "Oh heavens, I have to leave soon. I am so shocked by all of this, I don't even know what to say."

Donna got up from the table. "I'm so sorry to dump all of this on you."

Raven picked up her purse from the kitchen floor and stood. "Don't apologize. That Sybil might have maintained some kind of secret friendship with her great-grandson shouldn't even surprise us. That woman did what she pleased, but I always try to remember how good she was to me. If I were to decide I wanted to meet this nephew of mine, do you think he'd be willing?"

The sound of a car pulling into the drive by the garage and the toot of a horn reached them.

"I have no idea," Donna said. She took a step toward the back door to walk Raven out, then remembered the box. "You should take this."

Raven looked from Donna to the open box on the table.

"There are a few more things inside that we didn't talk about," Donna said when she saw Raven's hesitation.

"Actually, would you mind if I just took the wedding pictures?"

"But what about your mother's ring?"

Raven reached inside and pulled out the ring. She held it between her fingers and studied it closely, then held it out to Donna. "You should have it."

Donna took the pretty vintage piece from Raven with a shake of her head. "Why would you give it to *me*?"

"I never wear rings. I have no one else to pass it on to. It's a beautiful piece that meant a lot to Sybil. She'd hate for it to be hidden away. Wear it. Or give it to Lynette. Sybil considered you family, too."

Donna felt torn but knew Raven's husband was waiting for her. "Why would I want a cursed ring?"

Raven laughed and some of the tension in her expression eased. "Maybe it's time we quit assigning blessings, or curses, or any kind of meaning at all, to *things*. It's just a ring, and it would look good on you. You seem to have an open finger, now that you are going to stop wearing your cancer ring."

Not wanting to argue, Donna dropped the ring back into the box and motioned for Raven to follow her outside. "Who knows? Maybe it was a young Taran, or *Storm*, who hid the box in the shed for Sybil. Maybe I should have Lynette give *him* the ring."

"I hadn't thought of that," Raven said, pulling the kitchen door shut behind them as they headed for the garage. "If he really is family, Sybil would probably like that idea, too."

Donna headed for the driveway, but Raven veered toward the old statue of her mother as a young girl. Once she reached the tired rose garden, she reached out a hand to touch the girl's leg.

"I love how carefree they made her look."

Donna expected Raven's husband to give his horn another quick tap, but he didn't. She moved over to stand beside her old friend in front of the fountain.

"Thank you for telling me about Taran, Donna. All signs point to him telling the truth about who he is. Secrets can be so damaging, can't they? If Sybil would have been honest with me about staying in touch with my brother's son, maybe I could have had some kind of relationship with him over the years, too. Not that it's her fault that I let Gideon's wife ruin things for us. I want to discuss all of this with my husband. If I decide to reach out to my nephew, could you get me his contact information?"

"I'm sure I could," Donna said, putting her arm around Raven's shoulder. "You know where to find me, should you need anything."

Donna watched as Raven and her husband pulled away. Should she have admitted the whole truth to her old friend about the events surrounding their departure from Ruby Shores more than thirty years ago?

It wasn't until an hour later, when Lynette called to ask for a ride home from a used bookstore downtown, that Donna realized the importance of one of Raven's parting comments. Lavonne had said something similar to her around the firepit a month ago.

Secrets really were damaging to a family.

Lynette deserved to hear the truth about theirs.

Chapter Thirty-Two

L YNETTE RAN UPSTAIRS TO change clothes after depositing her two new boxes of used books in her shed. She would shelve them later; right now she needed to change. Storm was swinging by to pick her up and take her out for ice cream. It was too late in the day for coffee, but neither of them thought a drink was a good idea, and Storm had to leave in the morning.

She smiled. Even though the man was leaving town the next day, this was feeling a little like a date.

"Lynette," Donna yelled up the stairs, "can you come out to the porch when you're finished up there? I have something I want to talk to you about."

Her phone pinged with an incoming text. Storm was running late. He could pick her up at three o'clock, if that still worked. She checked the time, then let him know that would be fine.

What does a woman wear on an ice cream date with an old boyfriend? Or was she reading too much into this? For all she knew, Storm might want to clear the air about ancient history, then blow out of town for another thirty years.

Deciding she needed a little armor against the uncertainties that lay ahead, she selected one of her older yet favorite flowing tunics to wear over a comfortable pair of slacks. Both were from one of her store's special curated lines. If she felt her confidence flagging, all she'd have to do was look down at her outfit to remind herself that she really had built a successful business from scratch. If she could handle that, she could handle anything.

Once downstairs, she found Donna on the porch with a book. "Is that from Sybil's library? Or did you nab something from one of my boxes?"

"Sybil's," she said, closing the reddish-hued hardcover. She tossed it onto the wicker coffee table and motioned for Lynette to take a seat next to her. "You look nice. Are you going out?"

Lynette had purposefully avoided telling her mother that Storm was picking her up. "I am. But not until three. Was there something you wanted to talk about?"

"Oh, are you doing something with Annie?"

That rankled a little. "No . . . I kind of have a date. For ice cream."

Donna's eyebrows shot up. "A date? Really?"

"You don't have to act so surprised, Mother. Besides, it might not be a date."

"With that lead-in, you're going to have to tell me who this date slash not-a-date is with," Donna teased.

Lynette decided she was much too old to be sneaking around with Storm again. "It's Storm. He's leaving tomorrow, but he reached out to talk."

"Hmm," Donna said, looking thoughtful.

Lynette moved to stand, but Donna put a hand on her knee to hold her in place.

"There was something I wanted to discuss with you. It's a topic I maybe should have talked to you about years ago, but part of me thought that if I didn't give voice to it, it wasn't real."

Lynette had an inkling about what Donna meant. "That sounds ominous."

"I suppose it is. You see, dear, I haven't been completely honest with you about my home life when I was a girl. Or the real reason I left."

She watched Donna rub her hands together. It seemed her mother should have worn some armor today, too.

"Wasn't *I* the reason you left? You getting pregnant with me?"

"No," Donna admitted. "I know I let you think that, but I actually left home a bit earlier, at eighteen. I didn't get pregnant with you until I was twenty. But things at home were always bad. My father was a mean man, and he abused my mother, both physically and emotionally. She was almost as bad as he was, so I had a tough childhood."

Even though Lynette had overheard Donna telling Lavonne this same thing, it hurt so much more to see the pain in her mother's eyes as she spoke. She couldn't make Donna relive it all yet again by pretending not to know. "I'm so sorry, Mom. I wasn't completely honest about how much I heard that night. I did hear you tell Lavonne about your sister and your folks," she whispered.

Donna's eyes sparkled with unshed tears. "I should have told you the truth a long time ago. I hate that you learned about it that way."

Lynette clasped her mother's hands. "And I hate that you've lived with this for so long. You lost a sister? I could have had an aunt?"

"You would have had an aunt, if she'd lived," Donna said, pulling one hand free to wipe a tear off Lynette's cheek. Her thumb skimmed the scar there.

"Don't smear my makeup," Lynette hiccupped.

The levity seemed to help Donna. She smiled. "Irene was a beautiful person, with a heart of gold, and you'd have loved her. Sometimes you remind me of her."

"I wish I'd met her. Do you want to talk about how she died?"

Donna placed her hand over her heart. "I'd rather not go into too much detail. As I guess you heard me say, there was an accident on the stairs during a fight. Irene fell and hit her head. I heard her scream, but it was too late. After that, I cut off all ties with my parents. Because, you see, even if her fall was truly an accident, which is what they told everyone, they were still awful people, especially Father. Please never think I robbed you of the possibility of a relationship with your grandparents. Trust me when I say you wouldn't have wanted to get to know them."

Lynette absorbed her mother's words. The ceiling fan whirring above them was the only sound.

"My father, then?" she eventually asked.

"I'm sorry, baby," Donna said. Her cheeks turned crimson at the question. "Life wasn't easy after I ran away. Or after I left, I suppose I should say, since I was technically an adult. But it wasn't until I was lucky enough to give birth to you that I truly grew up. Those years in-between were almost as difficult as my years at home. But you . . . you are my greatest gift in life. Even though I can't be sure of your biological father, and you were unexpected, you were the best thing that ever happened to me."

Lynette took her hands from Donna's grasp and fanned her face. "That's a lot to take in, Mom. Do I look a mess? Should I go fix my face? I appreciate you telling me, though. I always wondered why you would never talk about your life before I was born, or who my father was."

"Your face is fine, dear," Donna said. She sat farther back on the sofa and crossed her legs. "I still can't quite believe you are going out with Storm this afternoon. By the way, I talked to Raven about him when she was here earlier today. She confirmed she had a nephew named Taran Gage. He was her brother Gideon's son, but bad blood left them estranged. Raven hated her sister-in-law and had no idea that Sybil remained in contact with Taran until I showed her the pictures we found in the box. I told her what you'd found out."

It was a relief to learn Storm had told her the truth about his ties to Raven and this house. "Raven's sister-in-law was Storm's mom, right? I hated that woman, too."

"You hated his mother? Why? Did she say something to you after you wrecked his truck?" Donna asked, uncrossing her legs and leaning forward.

Lynette snorted before she could stop herself. Maybe if Storm's mother hadn't been so cruel and ignored her cry for help, the accident never would have happened in the first place.

Donna looked like she was waiting for an answer to her questions about Storm's mom. But how could Lynette tell Donna about how the woman had ignored her cry for help without sharing the whole sordid tale?

She couldn't.

Then the irony of it all revealed itself to her. She and Donna were so much alike. They'd both held tight to stories of deep trauma they'd each suffered, keeping their secrets for decades. When they finally found the courage to open up about the tragedies, it was to their girlfriends instead of to each other. But until mother and daughter both found a way to be honest with the other, neither could truly heal.

She'd learned her mother's secrets, but only because she'd cheated.

It was time to truly come clean.

"Mom . . . the reason I crashed Storm's pickup that night was because I was running from a man who attacked me."

Donna's hands shot out and grabbed both of Lynette's in a tight grip. "He came after you after we looped in the authorities? Oh my God, Lynette, you should have told me! How were you able to forgive me for letting that man into our lives?"

Lynette glanced down at her fingers. The tips were turning red because Donna was squeezing so hard. It took her a second to realize where her mother's imagination had jumped. She yanked her hands free, then clasped her mother's more gently.

"Mom. Stop. It wasn't that prick of a guy you were dating. It was someone who used to hang around the pizza place where I worked."

"What?"

She took a deep breath, then proceeded to tell her mother everything. For once, Donna didn't interrupt. When she got to the part about stumbling across her attacker's obituary while packing to leave town, Donna collapsed against the back of the wicker sofa. Her eyes were closed, but tears leaked down her cheeks.

"Oh, Lynette . . . I hate that you've carried that awful story inside for thirty years."

Lynette rubbed Donna's knee. "It never would have happened if I hadn't been so stupid and climbed blindly into a stranger's vehicle."

Donna dashed a rough hand over her cheeks. "Don't we make quite the pair?"

"I've always said that," Lynette agreed. "But what do you mean, exactly?"

Donna let out a bone-weary sigh. "We both blamed ourselves for the actions of horrible, selfish men. Neither of us reached out for help from anyone."

"Well, *technically* I begged for Storm's mother to help me while banging on the door of their lake house, but the bitch ignored me."

Donna smacked the sofa cushion with both hands in frustration, then squeezed the edges of it so tightly that her knuckles turned white. "She *ignored* you?! And to think I let that awful woman run us out of town."

Lynette tilted her head, convinced she couldn't have heard her mother correctly. "Mom . . . why did we really leave Ruby Shores like that? After my accident, you had us out of town within two weeks. It all felt very rushed, and I was heartbroken to leave my friends. And Storm, even though he wasn't speaking to me after the accident. I always felt like there was more to the story that you didn't share with me. Did that awful woman have something to do with it?"

Donna gave her a small smile, and Lynette could sense the melancholy behind it. "I'm a little ashamed to talk about it."

"I promise I won't judge," Lynette said. She just wanted answers.

"Well, you might, but why not just get all of our secrets out in the open as long as we've started? As Renee's mother, Lavonne, told me that night while we visited around the firepit at Whispering Pines, secrets are poison. Did you hear her say *that* while you eavesdropped? Raven said something very similar, earlier today. Fine. Here it goes. Storm's mother, Delaney Erickson, wanted us out of town, and she offered me ten thousand dollars, cash, if we'd go quietly."

"No, she didn't," Lynette whispered, shocked. "Why would she do that?"

Donna squirmed.

"Mom?"

"She thought you were a bad influence on Storm."

Lynette paused at this, then burst out laughing.

"You don't feel bad about her thinking that?" Donna asked.

"*Bad?* If anyone was a bad influence, it was Storm. Donna, I'd never had sex or even alcohol before I met him."

Donna slammed her hands over her ears. "La-la-la, I don't want to hear this," she said in a singsong voice.

Lynette pulled her mother's hands down. "Oh, stop. You already knew that. I tried to be sneaky, but you weren't dumb."

Donna shuddered. "I still don't want to hear those things about my seventeen-year-old daughter."

"I was almost eighteen!" Lynette laughed. "Storm's mother was an awful woman. I knew she didn't like me. And taking her son's pickup without permission, then totaling it, probably did nothing to endear me to her. But I wouldn't have guessed she'd pay money to get rid of me. I wonder if Storm knows . . ."

"I have no idea," Donna said. "Honestly, honey, I was also feeling terribly guilty about the other situation, too. I worried that if Storm got his hands on my ex, he might do something we'd all regret. There seemed to be so many valid reasons for me to take you away. I was ashamed to take her money, but it gave me the ability to set us up nicely somewhere new."

The two women sat quietly for a few minutes, both thinking through the heavy things they'd just discussed.

"I don't know about you, but I feel better now that our secrets are out in the open," Donna said.

Ebony appeared in the doorway and looked between the two of them. It reminded Lynette of yet another secret.

"I have one more confession to make, Mom, and then I promise there's nothing left to tell," Lynette said, watching the cat saunter into the room. "But first, I have a question. Why was that teddy bear I always played with as a kid so important to you?"

Donna sighed. "It was one of the few things I took when I left home. It was Irene's."

"Damn," Lynette whispered.

"Why? Do you know where it disappeared to?"

Lynette pointed at Ebony. "She did it."

"Did what? Now you sound like me and Irene, blaming each other for things as kids."

"Brace yourself," Lynette said. "Ebony ripped the bear's head off. I'm sure she thought it was a toy for her."

But Donna didn't react the way Lynette had expected, either. "I wondered when you'd get around to telling me the truth. I found what was left of him, shoved in a bag."

Lynette burst out laughing. Would the two of them ever stop hiding things from each other?

The doorbell rang.

Lynette popped to her feet. "Do you want me to bring you home a cone?"

Donna stood, too. "Actually, I want you to invite Storm in. I'd like to have a word with him."

Lynette felt her smile slip away. "Why? What are you going to say to him?"

"Don't worry, Lynette, I don't intend to embarrass you. Now answer the door before he gives up on you."

The bell rang again. Ebony followed on Lynette's heels. "No sneaking outside," she said to the cat as she swung the door open.

Ebony tried to slither around Storm's legs, but he was too quick for her. He scooped her up and handed her to Lynette. "She's still trying to put the sneak on you, huh?"

"Come in."

The cat wasn't in the mood to be held, and it took everything Lynette had to hold on to her while Storm closed the door.

"I'd offer to bring her along, but I don't allow cats in my truck," Storm said, a teasing note in his voice.

"And I don't think they allow cats in an ice cream parlor. Dogs maybe, if one claims it as an emotional support animal, but not her. Besides, she's bonded with my mother more than me." Lynette stopped, realized she was rambling. She focused on the sleeve of her tunic for a second, gathered her composure, then met Storm's inquisitive gaze. "Donna would like a chance to say hello before we leave. Do you mind?"

She studied his face, being careful not to look him up and down. This new Storm fascinated her. He was the old Storm, but not.

"Should I be nervous?" he asked.

Lynette chuckled. "I doubt much makes *you* nervous. Come on. She's in here."

"It might surprise you," she thought she heard him say as she turned away, but she couldn't be sure.

They found Donna in the kitchen instead of the screened-in porch.

"I know the two of you met again, earlier this summer, but Donna, this is Storm. Storm, this is Donna. Or should I call you Taran?"

"Either is fine," Storm replied.

Lynette thought he looked nervous, which surprised her.

"It's good to see you again, Taran. I'm sorry I didn't recognize you when you and Owen helped me dry the basement."

Donna's easy comment seemed to put their visitor at ease. He extended a hand to her and said, "And I'm sorry I didn't tell you who I really was."

Lynette wasn't sure if he was apologizing for not clarifying that he was an old boyfriend of her daughter or Sybil's long-lost great-grandson. He'd probably assumed Lynette had told Donna about his ties to this house.

"How about a fresh start?" Donna said, motioning for them both to take a seat at the kitchen table.

"Oh boy, Mom," Lynette said, looking between the chairs and Storm. "We probably should get going. Storm might still need to pack, since he's leaving tomorrow."

Storm pulled out a chair and motioned for Donna to sit. Then he did the same for Lynette. "I travel light" was all he said.

"What was it you wanted to discuss, Donna?"

"Excuse her," Donna said, tapping on the tabletop. "She isn't overly patient."

Storm wagged his head and shot Lynette a smile.

"Lynette told me you claim that Sybil Wall was your great-grandmother and Gideon Gage was your father."

"Mother," Lynette said, hoping her mother would catch the warning. What was she up to?

"That's correct," Storm said. He didn't look fazed. "Raven Gage-Black is also my aunt."

Donna pushed her chair back and stood. "I spoke to Raven earlier today."

Lynette could see the surprise on Storm's face the second before he schooled his emotions.

"Today?" he repeated.

Donna walked over to the kitchen counter and picked up the wooden box Lynette had found in her shed. Lynette hadn't noticed it sitting there when they'd walked in.

"Yes. She swung by. I wanted to give her this, but it turned out that she didn't want it. Do you recognize the box?"

Storm extended a hand, and Donna brought it to him.

"It looks familiar. I think this is the box I put out in the old garden shed at Sybil's request."

Lynette racked her brain, trying to remember if she'd told him she had found it in the shed.

"I thought it might have been you," Donna said.

Storm set it on the table in front of him. "Do you mind if I open it?"

"Be my guest," Donna said with a flourish of her hand, before sitting down again. "Raven was interested in the wedding pictures that were in there. They were of her parents and Sybil."

He nodded as he browsed through the contents. "What, no tarot cards?" He winked at Lynette.

She shot a glance at her mother. Storm was still getting her into trouble with Donna.

"We wondered about those, too," Donna said, meeting Lynette's eyes.

"They're in my bedroom. I took them to Whispering Pines with me. I thought it would be fun to show them to my friends, but it didn't exactly go as I'd expected."

Donna smirked. "Imagine that."

Storm laughed suddenly as he gazed at the pictures. "I assume Lynette told you this is me?"

"She did," Donna said. "Raven confirmed it as well."

At the mention of his aunt's name, Storm grew serious. "Does she know I'm in town?"

Donna shrugged. "She knows you were here helping me in the basement. I honestly didn't know if you were still around until Lynette mentioned your date."

Lynette tried to kick her mother under the table but banged her weak ankle against a table leg instead.

Storm ignored her groan. "What did she say about me?"

Donna's expression softened. She must have heard the longing behind his question, too. "It shocked her to learn that you'd been here as a boy and had some type of relationship with Sybil. It didn't sound like she got along with your mother, and she'd only ever seen you once, as an infant."

Storm sighed, then looked in the box again. He pulled out the vintage ring, studied it, then put it on the tip of his pinkie finger. "Was this Sybil's? Why didn't Raven take it?"

"When I first told her about it over the phone after Lynette found the box, the ring and wedding pictures were the two things she was most excited about. I forgot to mention the pictures of you then, since we didn't even know who the boy was," Donna admitted. "Raven said Sybil wore it, as did her mother-in-law before her. So it is quite old. When Eleanor, your grandmother, married, it passed to her. Sadly, they found it on her body after she'd drowned."

Lynette gasped. "That's awful."

"Water can be very dangerous if you aren't careful," Storm said, pinning Lynette with a warning look.

Donna ignored them both. "But today, Raven decided she didn't want it after all. She doesn't wear rings and has no kids to pass it on to. She suggested I take it. Or give it to Lynette. Sybil liked us both. She even joked that *you* could have it, if you had any interest. You are the only family she has left."

Lynette could see his Adam's apple jump.

"She said I could have it? But would you rather keep it, Ms. Howe?"

"Call me Donna," she said with a shake of her head. "No. That wouldn't be right. You should have it."

Storm slipped it off the tip of his finger. "I'd like that. Thank you."

Lynette watched as he carefully placed it in his shirt pocket, then fastened the button to secure it.

"Raven will reach out if she's interested in seeing you. Of course, you get to decide whether that is something you want, too, Taran."

Storm looked around them, his eyes taking in the kitchen. "I've always liked this place. It would be nice to meet Raven if she decides that's what she wants. The only family I'm close with these days is my brother, Shane. And my son."

Lynette's eyes were resting on Sybil's wooden box when he mentioned a son, and everything went wavy for a beat.

"You have a son?" Donna said. "Lynette didn't mention that."

Storm surprised Lynette again by reaching for her hand. "We have lots to talk about. I suspect we've both done lots of living since we last saw each other. That's why I suggested ice cream."

Uncomfortable with the physical contact, Lynette eased her hand out of his and stood. "If there isn't anything else, Donna, Storm and I should go."

Donna pointed toward the box. "Is there anything else in there that you'd like, Taran? Do you want to take it all?"

Storm got to his feet and tapped his shirt pocket. "No. This will be plenty. I appreciate what you did for me today, Donna."

Donna looked up at the man. "Do you mean the ring?"

"Not exactly. I appreciate the ring, don't get me wrong, but I was referring to the bridge you built for me to find my way back to my father's family."

"You are welcome," Donna said with a smile. "Lynette and I were just discussing how families and secrets aren't a good mix. Now, you two kids should get going. I hate to keep you from your ice cream any longer."

Lynette shoved her chair back against the table and headed for the back door. "Let's go out this way, Storm."

She didn't even look back for fear Donna would fabricate yet another delay.

Once outside and down the stairs, Lynette waited for Storm to reach her side.

"I really am sorry about that. I hope you didn't feel like a teenager getting the third degree in there."

Storm shook his head. "I meant what I said. I appreciate Donna talking to Raven for me. Besides, I always enjoyed hanging out in Sybil's kitchen."

Lynette smiled up at him. He sounded sincere. She turned to walk around the front to his truck, but he caught her arm.

"Hold up a second, will you?"

She watched him turn in the other direction and wander over to the water fountain. He reached a hand out and let the water rain down around his fingers. "You'll want to winterize this before long."

"I will," she said. "We didn't have it out here last winter. Annie and her son helped me pull it out of the shed." Then she remembered that was the same day that she'd spied him driving by so slowly, though she hadn't yet known it was him. "Or maybe you saw us wrestle it out here if you drove by here a third time that day."

He laughed, and she suspected he knew exactly what she meant.

"Did you know the sculptor modeled this after your Grandma Eleanor when she was young?"

"Actually, I did. Sybil told me that when I snuck over here on my bicycle one day," Storm said. He dried his hand on his pant leg, then extended it to her. "Should we go get that ice cream now? At this rate, it'll have to count as dinner."

Lynette let her fingers entwine with his, but she kept them loose. She didn't want to rush anything. Together they walked to his pickup, and he opened the passenger door for her. He surprised her by dropping his hands to her waist and brushing a light kiss over the tip of her nose before lifting her up and onto the seat.

It all happened so fast, she wondered if she'd imagined it. "What did you do that for? I can get in and out of a pickup, even if it's as big as this one."

He laughed and slammed her door. Once he was behind the wheel, he rested his hand across the back of her seat's headrest. "The one time I gave Donna a ride in this, I had to give her a boost. So I thought, like mother like daughter. Besides, the last time you got out of one of my trucks, they had to cut you out with the jaws of life, so we should be extra careful."

She took a playful swing at his midsection and he cringed away, but his arm stayed where it was. He had to use his left hand to shift it into gear. Her mind flashed back to an earlier time when he always threw his arm across the back of the bench seat and played with her hair as he drove. He'd had to use his left hand to shift back then, too.

If this fancy new truck had a bench seat, it would have been easy to slide over next to him like she used to, but bucket seats and a center console made that impossible.

She expected him to pull into the street, but when he didn't, she looked over to find his gaze on her. "Is something wrong?"

He sighed. "Lynette, I shouldn't have teased you about the accident. That was a terrible time. I know my mother never liked us dating, and when you wrecked the truck her ex-husband had given me as a graduation gift, she lost it. Her ex was furious, too—not that the two of them were really on speaking terms anymore. But I know Mom went and talked to Donna. Or at least she told me she was going to. Then you just left. Without so much as a word. I should have come to you, despite their warnings to me to stay away. I'm sorry I didn't fight for us. I'm sorry for all of it."

She played Donna's rendition of what happened after the accident beside what Storm was saying. "You knew about the money, then?"

"What money?" He looked confused. She believed that he really didn't know his mother had paid Donna to skip town with her juvenile delinquent daughter.

"Never mind," she said, breaking eye contact with him. "Wait? Did you hear that?"

He leaned forward, as if listening to his truck's motor. "Hear what?"

Lynette laughed. "My stomach. I'm starving, and unless I get ice cream soon, I don't know what I'll do."

Storm relaxed back into his seat and eased the truck away from the curb. "We can't have that now, can we?"

She felt his fingers at the base of her neck as he played with her curls. He didn't seem to mind that her hair was silver now instead of the rich color of her youth.

"So . . . you have a kid? How about a wife?"

He gave her hair a playful tug. "No wife. Like I said, we have some things to talk about. We better order double scoops. This could take a while."

Lynette reached up and captured his hand, bringing it around to rest in both of hers. "Storm, where are we going?"

He bent his arm up, bringing her hands with, and kissed her closest knuckle. "Right now? We're going for ice cream. After that? I'm not sure. But I'm open to suggestions."

He relaxed his arm again, and as their conjoined hands came to rest on top of the console, she spied his tiny butterfly tattoo.

This time she didn't comment on it, but the memories of what this man meant to her as a girl, regardless of how young she was, flitted through her mind as he drove them through the streets of Ruby Shores.

Epilogue

Lynette snuggled under the cozy afghan Annie's mother had given her at her Whispering Pines birthday party. As she sipped her iced cider out of a wineglass, her gaze swept over the blazing lights of New York City's skyline. Her apartment was barely larger than an efficiency, but the views were expansive. She approved of the combination, knowing she was lucky not to be staring at the brick wall of a neighboring building. The temporary living arrangement would serve her needs just fine until June. Sure, a few essentials were lacking, such as glassware, but she'd already started a list of things to bring back from Ruby Shores after the holidays.

Her timely arrival on the afternoon of November 30th had allowed her to settle in at the apartment and then catch a cab downtown in time to watch the lighting of the Rockefeller Christmas tree. She'd considered calling a friend from her days in New York to meet for a late dinner, but ultimately decided the ease of a solo adventure held more appeal. There would be time to catch up with a few of her favorite people in the city later.

Her lawyer, Kevin, hadn't loved the idea of Lynette returning to New York to act as a consultant for her old company, but after many debates, they agreed on the details. She was using these first three weeks of December to reacclimate herself to things, learn what changes the new owners had made, and prepare to start off strong in early January.

Despite the relaxed ambiance she'd created with glowing candles and soft music, she felt an inner excitement that had been missing from her life lately. Maybe it was the energy of the city itself. Or the mental stimulation she was already feeling back in the office.

She heard the *ding!* of the elevator in the outer hallway and a soft knock on her door. Jumping to her feet, she tossed the blanket aside and set her glass on the low coffee table.

No, while the city and her work were stimulating, the main reason for her excitement was standing on the other side of her apartment door.

It only took a few skipped steps to move from the couch, across the living room, to the apartment door. She flung it open, then caught her visitor up in a rocking hug.

Renee's laughter filled the surrounding space, and Lynette's heart swelled with cheer.

"I can't believe I'm really here," Renee said, following Lynette into the apartment. "Did you know that I've never been to New York before?"

Lynette shook her head. "Yes, you mentioned that this summer and again when you called, but I can hardly believe it. December is the perfect time to visit. I'll take you to see all the holiday sights."

Renee pulled off her stylish jacket and hat, tossing them over the back of the only side chair in the living room. "I only have Saturday and Sunday. My flight leaves late morning on Monday. I doubt that will be enough time."

"Love those," Lynette said, pointing to the warm-weather clothing. "You dressed appropriately for strolling around downtown."

Renee walked over to the large windows, cooing over the view. "I am a true Minnesota girl. Winter has nothing over on me. This view is incredible! I think I'd sleep right out here every night, on the couch, if I was you."

Lynette shrugged. "Lucky for you, this place is small. I was going to give you the one bed, and I'd take the couch, but if you like, you can sleep out here in the living room."

"I do like," Renee said, dropping onto the couch.

"Would you like a drink?" Lynette offered.

Renee seemed to notice the wineglass for the first time. Her head swiveled immediately in Lynette's direction, concern etched in her expression.

"Relax, it's apple cider," Lynette said. "This apartment is cute, but our only options to drink out of are plastic cups from a pizzeria, three mugs, or wineglasses."

"I'm sorry. I shouldn't have jumped to conclusions. Apple cider actually sounds perfect. But maybe hot instead of cold. My jacket is warm, but it is damp out there!"

Lynette smiled as Renee pulled the afghan over her shoulders. "I thought you said you could handle whatever weather winter threw at you."

"I love this afghan," Renee said, pulling it snug around herself.

"Don't you recognize it? It's the one Patsy gave me at my birthday party," Lynette said. She moved to the tiny galley kitchen to heat some cider for Renee.

"That's why it looked familiar. I wish my mother could crochet like this, but she's too busy baking and experimenting with new recipes with my sister, Val."

Lynette filled one of the mismatched mugs with cider and popped it into the microwave. "Don't interfere with the magic those two create when they combine their talents in the kitchen. I'm sure Patsy would make one of these blankets for you, too. Annie said she has a closet full of yarn. I think she donates lots of afghans."

Renee nodded. "My mom helped some of my nephews make tie blankets a few years back, and they donated them to local nursing homes."

The microwave beeped, and Lynette dipped a finger in to test the cider's temperature.

"I saw that," Renee said from right behind her.

"Holy—" Lynette yelped. "Don't sneak up on me like that!"

"Sorry. I'm starving. Got any chips? Or popcorn?"

Lynette opened the one cupboard where she kept a few snacks. Since she'd been back in the city, she did most of her eating at the many restaurants she had missed during her time away. "I don't have much in the way of groceries, since I'm only here for three weeks. I'm going back to the house in Ruby Shores for Christmas and New Year's. When I come back, I'll stock up." She spied a tube of Pringles and handed them to her friend. "Here. We loved these at camp. Those should take the edge off, then we can either go out for dinner or order in."

When she pulled open a drawer, countless takeout menus threatened to spill onto the floor.

Renee laughed. "While I am dying to see some of the city sites, I'm exhausted. Plus, it's nearly impossible to order in like this at Whispering Pines." She pulled a handful of menus from the drawer. "What if we stay in tonight, catch up, then get an early start in the morning?"

"That sounds perfect," Lynette said. She took the cider jug out to the living room and topped off her glass. "I know this adorable little breakfast place close to here. I hope you brought comfortable shoes for walking, because we'll put on some miles tomorrow."

"I take it your ankle is better?"

"It is, and I'll wear my snow boots that provide good traction and support."

Based on Lynette's recommendations, they placed their food order, then settled next to each other on the couch with the afghan stretched between them.

"I can't tell you how excited I was when you called to see about a weekend visit," Lynette said, swishing the cider in her glass. "We've barely talked since I had to rush away from Whispering Pines to attend to my collapsing basement wall."

Renee popped a potato chip into her mouth. "I take it your house is still standing?"

A bit of chip landed on Lynette's hand. "Eww," she laughed, shaking it off. "And you still eat your Pringles like that twelve-year-old I met at summer camp."

"You'd think I'd know better than to eat with my mouth full," Renee said, grinning. "Sorry. But seriously, why do we do such a crummy job of keeping in touch between trips?"

Her comment reminded Lynette of the gift she'd picked up with that very question in mind. She twisted and stretched for her Vuitton bag that she'd brought back to New York. The movement pulled the afghan off Renee, and she tugged it back.

"Speaking of doing a better job of keeping in touch, I picked you up an early Christmas present," Lynette said, digging through her scuffed leather bag.

Renee set the tube of chips on the coffee table with a grunt of protest. "I didn't bring anything for you!"

Lynette found the box in the bottom of her bag, pulled it out, and handed it to Renee. "And I didn't take the time to wrap it. I just happened across this in a booth at a Christmas market I wandered through after watching them light the tree on my first day here."

"Oh, this paper is so pretty! I love the tiny butterflies up in the corner. It reminds me of when we were kids, chasing butterflies at camp."

Lynette nodded. "Me, too! The woman selling this stationery said they are her own hand-drawn designs. It made me think of how fun it used to be when I'd received one of your letters in the mail. And you know how I love to support woman-owned businesses. Do you think we could get back to being real pen pals again? Emails and texts aren't quite the same."

"Aww," Renee said, holding up her gift. "I'd love that!"

"Perfect, because I bought myself a box, too. That one has a watercolor design that kind of reminded me of a kaleidoscope. So neither of us have an excuse now. Our first New Year's resolution can be to get back in the habit of writing each other letters."

"You're on," Renee agreed. "Speaking of kaleidoscopes, Jess mentioned Seth is working on that stained-glass window for your house. I can't wait to see if the pattern will be like looking through a kaleidoscope. Seth is so talented. I bet he pulls it off."

"I can't wait either, but he said it will be spring before he can put it in. Which works, since I'll be here until June."

Renee pulled her portion of the afghan up to her neck. "I'm so glad I'm here."

"I'm glad you are, too. Now, tell me what's new in your life."

She was sorry to see her friend's shoulders slump at the question.

"I guess I just felt like I needed a break from the worries back home,"

Renee admitted. She kept her eyes on the skyline instead of looking toward Lynette as she spoke. "Matt has had some close calls at work lately. As you know, law enforcement isn't currently experiencing nearly the level of respect they used to have out in the communities. He doesn't talk about it, but I know it wears on him."

Lynette felt for Renee. "I'm sure you can never really prepare yourself for the stress of marrying someone with a job like his. I sure like Matt, though. Do you realize how lucky you are to have found not just one, but two amazing men in your lifetime? I never met your first husband, but you always seemed happy in the letters you sent to me back then."

Renee sighed. "You're right. I am lucky. I just need to keep reminding myself of that, and have faith that nothing terrible will happen to Matt. He does his job because he truly feels he can make a positive difference, even though that vision can be tough to hold on to some days."

Lynette could sense that, even though her friend's worries over her husband's safety were valid and real, there was more. "And how are things going at Whispering Pines? Do you feel like things are solid in your business?"

Renee grabbed the chips again. "Not as solid as I'd like. In fact, I was hoping I might bounce some ideas off of you as to ways I might shore up my reserves again. When Celia first left the resort to me, she had set money aside in escrow to help with things like taxes and ongoing maintenance. She was an astute woman, and the piece for the taxes will be there for me to draw from for years to come. But the hit we took in 2020 because of the pandemic will be hard to come back from. I applied for and received an emergency PPP loan, but it wasn't enough to make up for the lost revenue. The buildings out there are old, aside from our new house, and it costs money to keep them structurally sound and all the mechanical systems working."

"I can only imagine," Lynette said. If she thought her home in Ruby Shores was costly to maintain, the resort had to be that much more expensive. "I'd love to talk through your ideas, both this weekend and anytime. After spending nearly two weeks out there this summer, I have an even better appreciation for how special your place is. I'm fully committed to helping you keep it viable."

There was another knock on the apartment door.

"There's our food!" Lynette said, kicking off the blanket.

"The doorman let me in downstairs," Renee said, looking toward the door in surprise. "But I saw my name was on a list. They'll let food delivery people come up?"

Lynette laughed. "Only from certain restaurants, and I wasn't kidding when I said we were ordering from a local landmark. You are going to love their food."

"That was delicious," Renee said, hanging up a dishtowel. "And easy cleanup."

"I told you," Lynette said, tossing the last of the takeout containers into the trash. "We ordered the perfect amount. What would you like to do now?"

Renee stretched. "Point me to your bathroom. Then, I'd love to settle back on the couch and hear all about what's been happening in your life since August."

Since the two of them were spending the weekend in New York City instead of Ruby Shores or Whispering Pines, Lynette supposed she had plenty to share with Renee. "Pass through the bedroom to get to the bathroom. It isn't ideal, but this is New York."

Lynette settled on the couch again while she waited for Renee. So much had happened. She wasn't even sure where to start.

"Since when did you take up scrapbooking?" Renee asked as she flopped back onto the couch minutes later.

Shoot!

She'd meant to put that stuff away instead of leaving it out on the small table in the corner of her bedroom. "I wasn't going to show you that yet. But *you* inspired that project, actually."

"Me? I don't do much scrapbooking. I have boxes of photos from when the kids were young, so I should do more of it, but I don't make the time."

Lynette figured she might as well fess up. "I loved the scrapbook you put together of the extra pictures that didn't fit on your gallery wall in the lodge. You know, the one you keep in the library? Between that and the fun we had looking through the old letters your mom kept, I thought it would be fun to put together a scrapbook of our girls' trips. I'm just doing a few pages per trip, since I hope there will be many in our future. Speaking of which, have you decided what we should do next year? I know you were pretty adamant about being the one to set things up, though Jackie offered to help."

Renee nodded. "I love the album idea, by the way. As far as next year's trip, nothing is definitive yet, but I'll figure out whether my idea will work by January. I know we'll need to book flights and that kind of thing."

Lynette had left herself some flexibility in her consulting gig in case any personal travel came up. "Are you thinking before or after June for our trip in 2022?"

"Before I knew you would be here in the city until June, that was the month I was thinking, but if that wouldn't work for you, we could push it."

"Don't worry about my schedule. I'll make whatever you come up with work. But won't you give me at least a hint?"

Renee tilted her head, as if considering her request. Then she grinned and got off the couch. "Where did you put my backpack?"

"Over there, behind the chair." Lynette hoped she'd come back with some travel brochures, but when all she had was a half-full bottle of water, she sighed. "You aren't going to tell me, are you?"

"You need to work on your observation skills, Lynette." Renee took a sip of the water, then set the square bottle on the table.

Lynette looked at both her friend and the bottle again before she realized. It was the Fiji brand, the same kind Lynette usually picked up while flying.

"Are we going to Matt's house on Fiji?"

Renee laughed. "I don't know yet. Maybe. I keep asking him, and he keeps telling me he's working on his rental calendar. The only way he could justify keeping it when he moved from the island to live with me was to rent it out. We were supposed to go there the summer of 2020, but for obvious reasons, that wasn't possible. He's also still talking about the possibility of selling it, because it is kind of a headache, owning property so far away. It might not work out, so promise me you won't tell the other girls."

"I promise. Fiji would be *amazing*. I haven't been anywhere tropical since we went to Hawaii, and after a winter in Ruby Shores, then New York, I'll be ready. Donna is actually on a beach down in Mexico right now."

"Good for her! I was going to ask what your mother was up to. Who is she traveling with?"

Lynette grinned. "Chester."

"*Chester*, huh? Is this a travel buddy only, or a romantic interest?"

Lynette had been wondering the same thing. "All I know for sure is Chester lived in the same apartment complex as us when we were here in the city. His unit was on the opposite side of Donna's from mine. Apparently, they kept in touch after we moved to Ruby Shores, and he'd been on her to take a trip. I'm so glad Mom is doing some of the travel she's always dreamed of. I never appreciated how much she wanted to see more of the world."

Renee tucked her feet under the afghan. "Speaking of mothers and travel, do you think our moms will ever pull a trip together? I know they all talked about it at Whispering Pines."

"I think we should encourage that," Lynette said. She knew Donna would love it.

"Say, if Donna is in Mexico and you are here, who's watching your cat? What was her name?"

"Ebony. She's actually spending a few weeks at Kit's condo, since she's my only other cat-lover friend. I'll pick her up when I fly back into Minneapolis for Christmas, then she'll come here with me in January."

Renee nodded, then yawned.

"Maybe we should call it a night," Lynette said. "I have extra sheets and blankets for you."

Renee grabbed her hand. "Not so fast. We have one other important thing I've been dying to ask you about, but we haven't gotten around to it yet."

Lynette had a pretty good idea what, or who, Renee was so curious about. "Can't it wait until breakfast?"

"No, it cannot. So. Storm. Have you talked to him since he rescued you from imminent death at Whispering Pines?"

Lynette snorted. "You are so overly dramatic."

"Since I'm on husband number two, I obviously believe in romance. And romance is always more fun with a little drama thrown in. Now, come on. Spill it."

Lynette turned her gaze back out to the skyline, and a crescent moon caught her eye. There were many things she loved about New York, but the way all the other lights seemed to mute the moon's magic wasn't one of them. She preferred the bright moonlight of Ruby Shores. Or Whispering Pines. Maybe she was a romantic at heart, too.

"Lynette?"

"Fine, but I might disappoint you. I've only seen Storm once since Whispering Pines. He reached out and wanted to talk about things," Lynette said, keeping her eyes on the moon sliver.

"Talk?" Renee said. She sounded disappointed.

"We went out for ice cream. It was nice. He told me about the son he shares with his ex-wife. It sounds like they have an amicable relationship, but she has the boy most of the time. I think Storm said he's twelve."

Renee finished her water, then sighed. "This isn't sounding like there was any kissing involved. I remember how you guys couldn't keep your hands off each other at prom. Has the spark fizzled?"

From Lynette's perspective, there was still plenty of zing between her and her first boyfriend, but there hadn't yet been an opportunity to explore things further with Storm. She shrugged. "The only kissing involved the tip of my nose and one knuckle, but he does still intrigue me. I don't know. He was leaving town the very next day, and I got so caught up in arranging all of this that our only communication since our ice cream date has been over the phone."

They both sat quietly for the next few minutes. Lynette tried to imagine what Storm might be up to at this very moment.

"Well, I guess we'll just have to wait to see what happens," Renee said around another yawn.

Lynette slapped the couch and stood. "I'll get those blankets."

She went to her room to grab the bedding for the couch and checked her phone on the charger. A new email had come in from Storm. She clicked it and smiled when she saw he'd sent back a signed PDF of their rental agreement. Things were progressing on schedule, and she hoped his brother would enjoy living in Sybil's old house.

Renee was pulling a set of pajamas from her roller bag when Lynette got back to the living room.

"This is a hide-a-bed, so I'll make it up for you if you want to use the bathroom to change quick. These gigantic windows are amazing, but they offer little privacy."

After zipping her bag shut, Renee stood and faced her. "So when will you see him again?"

"Who?" Lynette said, but she knew exactly who her friend meant.

"Storm! Because you *are* seeing him again. Even from across the room, over breakfast in the lodge the morning after Storm and Matt rescued you from, well, *you*, we could all still feel the attraction between you two."

"You talked about us behind my back?" Lynette asked, trying to sound surprised.

It was like they were right back to being teenagers again.

Renee smirked. "Talked about you? Heck, we took bets on how long it would take Storm to thaw you out again."

With a mortified shriek that could have won her an Emmy Award, Lynette pretended to be appalled at the notion. She even whipped a pillow at Renee, knocking her friend onto the chair.

Both women dissolved into laughter, and Lynette thought how wrong Renee was when she said she hadn't brought her a gift for Christmas.

Renee's weekend visit to help Lynette reacquaint herself with this city, and maybe even say a proper goodbye—to this kind of life instead of the rushed one she'd experienced—was the only gift she needed.

Author's Notes

I hope you enjoyed this fourth book in *The Kaleidoscope Girls* series! I loved traveling back to the Whispering Pines resort with these women. It has become such a special place in my heart. My first series revolved around Whispering Pines and revisiting some of those storylines, along with Renee's extended family, made this book especially fun for me. I hope you enjoyed reading it as much as I did writing it!

Ever since the characters of Kit, Annie, Jackie, and Lynette first came to life in **Better with Friends**, I've felt particularly drawn to Lynette. Maybe it was her glamorous lifestyle. Her relationship with her mother was also something I wanted to explore further. Finally, having the chance to pull her long-ago bad-boy first love back into the picture left me with plenty of ideas as I sat down to write.

My initial outlines for each of the books in this series always have an annual girls' trip that will make up about one-third of the timeline. I drew on personal travel experiences when trips took the girls to Hawaii and Arizona. But writing about vacationing on a lake in the Midwest feels like home to me. Up until about ten years ago, we'd take our family on summer vacations to various resorts in Minnesota lake country. Then we purchased a cabin back in our hometown in North Dakota. Now I spend as much of my summers there as possible, working and playing, with the water only steps away. I can easily "see" full scenes at Whispering Pines playing out in my mind and imagination as I write.

The next book, **Life with Friends**, will take the girls to a place with plenty of walks beside the ocean, lots of sunshine, and happy memories for Renee. Any guesses as to where they'll go? It's somewhere I've never visited, so I'm immersed in lots of videos and books about their destination. If only I could have managed a research trip there in advance of my writing! It wasn't to be, but maybe someday!

Not only will the fifth book include a trip to an exotic locale, but the girls still need to help Owen figure out what to do with their old summer camp land. Maybe Lynette won't be the only one who gets to reconnect with someone from her past. Most importantly, I can't wait to reveal more ways these amazing women will continue to support each other through the unending changes that seem inevitable during midlife.

There's nothing quite like the love and support of old friends.

The Kaleidoscope Girls is my second fiction series. If you also read my first series, did the title of this fourth book resonate with you? Did you remember how each chapter in the books in that series was titled "Gift of . . . ", a nod to the idea that life is full of gifts? Even the most challenging chapters almost always include important lessons. That fun naming convention was the inspiration behind this book's title.

At the same time I was writing **Gift of Friends**, I was also doing a refresh of that first series. I learn new things with each book I write, and I realized I wanted to give my first novels the *gift* of brand-new covers. New artwork also allowed me to tweak a few other things, too. I renamed the series from *Celia's Gifts* to *Gift of Whispering Pines*. I made minor updates and reformatted the interiors, and wrote new sales blurbs for all seven books. I even tweaked the reading order because too many people were missing my **Capturing Wishes** title since it wasn't always included on the series page for some of the online vendors. With these updates, I can now produce large print versions, box sets, and more. Stay tuned!

Diving back into so many different aspects of my earlier books has reminded me of how fun it is to spend time with Renee's extended family at Whispering Pines. Maybe I'll have to do more of it in the future. What do you think?

You'll find more information on all my books and links to them on my website. While you're there, be sure to sign up for my newsletter so you'll never miss the latest news including release dates, glimpses into what goes into creating my books, and more.

Thank you for coming on this writing journey with me. I love reading and writing alongside you!

THANK YOU!

Dear Reader,

I would like to thank you for taking the time to read **Gift of Friends**. I am so grateful you selected it and I hope you enjoyed this fourth book in my *Kaleidoscope Girls* series.

If you don't mind taking a few more minutes with this book, I'd appreciate it if you would leave a review. Reviews are extremely helpful and much appreciated.

Next up in this fun series is **Life with Friends (Book 5)**. A girls' trip to balmy Fiji will give Renee and the rest of the Kaleidoscope Girls a chance to escape their troubles back home, if only for a little while. Pack your bags and come join the party!

For links to all of my books and to sign up for my newsletter, please visit my website at www.kimberlydiedeauthor.com.

Wishing you my very best,
Kimberly

The power of enduring friendships continues in Life with Friends. Together, five forever friends are learning to embrace life in their fifties, courageously redefining

themselves.

Jackie, Kit, Annie, Renee, and Lynette have all faced a kaleidoscope of challenges in their lives. They've emerged stronger, thanks to their unwavering support of each other. Now, as they gather on the pristine beaches of Fiji, they'll realize their journeys of self-discovery are far from over.

These women have all faced personal traumas, mended shattered hearts, and walked away from unrewarding careers or relationships. They've healed. But despite the peaceful beauty of the islands, doubts and fears will resurface. Can their friendship provide the strength they'll need to overcome new hurdles?

Life with Friends, the captivating fifth novel in *The Kaleidoscope Girls* series by Kimberly Diede, weaves a tale of resilience and companionship, taking readers from the earthy sands of summer camp to the exotic beaches of Fiji. Whether you're a long-time fan or new to *The Kaleidoscope Girls* series, join these inspiring women as they prove that life's richest moments are better when shared with friends.

You'll find information about where to purchase this and other books by Kimberly Diede at www.kimberlydiedeauthor.com.

About the Author

Kimberly Diede writes contemporary novels that weave together family, friends, hope, and romance. She writes family sagas, suspense, and women's fiction that you'll find hard to put down. She truly believes we are never too old for second chances in life.

Kimberly enjoys spending the short months of her Midwest summers on the lakeshores of Minnesota and North Dakota. Nothing beats writing and hanging out with family and friends at their cabin. Her love of tradition and all things vintage comes through in her decorating and her stories.

Be sure to follow Kimberly on social media to catch glimpses of the junk she drags home to repurpose and to get updates on her latest books.

Website: https://www.kimberlydiedeauthor.com/
Facebook: https://www.facebook.com/KimberlyDiedeAuthor/
Instagram: https://www.instagram.com/kimberlydiedeauthor/
BookBub: https://www.bookbub.com/authors/kimberly-diede